Praise for Jimmy Whit

'An entertaining read' *Su*

'A racy pot-boiler of an autobiography' *Night & Day Magazine*

'One of the most entertaining biographies of the year' *Independent on Sunday*

'The twisted hand that fate has dealt White in recent years – testicular cancer, the deaths of his mother and a brother, a very public bankruptcy – has only made snooker's vast armchair army of fans draw him closer to their collective bosom' *Daily Mail*

'A breathless romp' *Daily Telegraph*

'Yehudi Menuhin loves to watch Jimmy White. One maestro recognises the other' Clive Everton, *Evening Standard Magazine*

'A glorious picaresque' *The Times*

'Jimmy's the ultimate player's player. He thrills the public . . . but the players get even more enjoyment out of watching him because he strikes the ball so well' Terry Griffiths, *Daily Express*

'Jimmy White has been an icon to two generations of men; the George Best of baize' *Esquire*

'Jimmy's harum-scarum attitude to life has never altered, even though he is now a household name. One of the loveliest things about him is his naturalness. Stardom has come and touched him and left him exactly the way he was' *Sunday Mirror*

'He may play a spellbinding game, full of invention and dash. He may even be the best snooker player in the world – but he is loved because he is naughty . . . and therein lies his abiding appeal' Sue Mott, *Sunday Telegraph*

'Mercurial, enigmatic, exciting' Alex Higgins

'If in all of us there is a cavalier spirit, free or longing to be free of society's more blatantly preposterous conformist illusions, then we see in Jimmy a glimpse of our better selves, a hero fearless and alive and, of course, at risk, perennially at risk' Eamon Dunphy, *Independent on Sunday*

'The transformation of Jimmy White from snooker's loveable rogue to devoted father and husband may have surprised his legions of fans but not his wife, Maureen. She believes that after years of hard drinking and fast living, Jimmy has at last found the right balance. He is just beginning to enjoy the good things in life and he's never been happier' John Hennessey, *Daily Express*

JIMMY WHITE
with Rosemary Kingsland

BEHIND THE
WHITE BALL

My Autobiography

arrow books

Published in the United Kingdom in 1999 by
Arrow Books

12

First published in the United Kingdom in 1998 by Hutchinson

Arrow Books
The Random House Group Limited
20 Vauxhall Bridge Road, London SW1V 2SA

www.randomhouse.co.uk

Addresses for companies within The Random House Group
Limited can be found at: www.randomhouse.co.uk/offices.htm

The Random House Group Limited Reg. No. 954009

A CIP catalogue record for this book
is available from the British Library

ISBN 9780099271840

The Random House Group Limited supports The Forest Stewardship
Council (FSC®), the leading international forest certification
organisation. Our books carrying the FSC label are printed on FSC®
certified paper. FSC is the only forest certification scheme endorsed
by the leading environmental organisations, including Greenpeace.
Our paper procurement policy can be found at
www.randomhouse.co.uk/environment

Typeset by SX Composing DTP, Rayleigh, Essex
Printed and bound by CPI Group (UK) Ltd, Croydon, CR0 4YY

For my biggest fan, Shane Halls.

CONTENTS

LIST OF ILLUSTRATIONS

1: My first ranking tournament. The party went on for seven days. (Lancashire Picture Agency.)

2: *top:* My mum, Lil, showing off the trophies.

bottom: My dad, Tom, is as proud as punch.

3: *right:* Me and Maureen in love. (Phil Spencer, courtesy of Mirror Group.)

4: *top:* Me in the world Matchplay with my old rival, The Nugget. (Photography by *Derby Evening Telegraph*.)

bottom: Me, Tony Meo and Steve Bailey outside the Pot Black Snooker Hall one day, laughing because we got all the money.

5: Me at work.

6: *top:* One of my better times with Higgins. The only time you have a good time with Higgins is when it's flying for him!

bottom: Me and Barry Hearn. He's obviously talking about money – that's why we're smiling.

7: *right:* This is me happy. I have to practise because I have a match that evening and I've been on a bender for two days and I've just realised where I am.

8: Me having a holiday with the family in Majorca.

9: *top:* Dad, Peewee, me, Dionne my niece and Con Dunne, one of my best friends from New York. I've just got beat in the Benson & Hedges in London, but I still manage to smile.

bottom: My princesses.

10: *top left:* 1984. Me and Lauren when she won the picture of the month in the *Mirror*. She got £1000 that we put in a trust fund in William Hill's. (Courtesy of Mirror Group.)

top right: John Nielsen and a friend, Ron, at the wrestler Steve Viedor's birthday party. (Courtesy of John Nielsen.)

bottom: Me with a fellow genius.

11: *top:* 1998. First round of the World Title at Sheffield. Me and Hendry during a break. (PA News.)

bottom: Steve congratulates me. I knew it was genuine because he's a good lad. (PA News.)

12: Me, looking 'different league'. (Chris Smith.)

ONE

THE HOLY GRAIL

In the late summer of 1982 Alex Higgins and I did a small tour of Northern Ireland. For Alex, who had recently won the world snooker championship for the second time, it was a coming home, a soldier of fortune's triumphant return to his Belfast roots. The semi-final of that same world championship I had played against Alex a few months earlier in the Crucible at Sheffield was to go down in history as being one of the 'great' matches, with fifteen million viewers glued to their television screens. It had not been all that long since I had taken the world amateur crown in Tasmania and turned professional, so the Irish tour was a sell-out even before the two of us set foot in Ireland.

The promoter, whose name was George Armstrong, had some kind of caravan business, where he rented out mobile holiday homes, so this tour was something of a sideline for him. He hired one of those big motor-homes – a Winnebago, I think – complete with driver, to save money on hotels. One thing he stressed was that he wanted Alex to bring his world cup with him to display at all the venues.

'It'll set the evening off, see,' Armstrong said, 'give them all something to remember. Two world champions, like, and that bloomin' marvellous cup up there for them to admire.'

Alex, outspoken as ever, retorted, 'When I play snooker, people remember it!' However, he did bring his enormous cup in a presentation case, and we drove to the first venue where we were to give an exhibition. The cup was carried out of the van and into the local social club like the Holy Grail, to be given pride of place at the end of the table where all the little boys clustered around it, wide-eyed with awe to think that this was the real thing amongst them in their little town or village.

For the first couple of days everything went as planned with the driver – who also happened to be the owner of the van – taking care of us. After two or three nights of the tour, we arrived in Derry and passed the most charming little country hotel, right on the banks of the river. By now, Alex had had enough of slumming it and declared we would have a nice dinner and spend the night in proper beds, not breathing each other's air in the confines of the van; so Alex, Armstrong and I checked into the hotel and the driver slept in the van with all our clothes, snooker cues – and, of course, the famous cup.

In the morning, there was no sign of Armstrong and a few inquiries revealed that he had absconded with the takings for the entire tour. Alex's first thoughts were for his cup. He went out to the van to make sure it was still there. What he hadn't bargained for was the fact that by some system of bush telegraph, the driver was ahead of us – he knew that Armstrong had done a bunk, and he wanted to be paid for his services and the hire of his van. He refused to even open the door of the Winnebago in case Alex – who was quick on his feet – nipped in a bit sharpish and got his mitts on his own trophy.

Alex stood in the car park and hammered on the door.

'Open up, I want my cup,' he said, speaking quite calmly to start with.

The man's head popped through the window. 'You can't have it,' he declared, 'come back when you have my money.'

'Be sensible, I didn't hire you,' Alex said quite reasonably. 'It's my cup and I want it.'

'You'll have it when I've been paid,' said the driver, slamming the window shut and drawing the curtains across.

Alex banged on the door again. 'I demand to be let in,' he said, slightly louder this time.

'Go away!' yelled the driver. 'I've told you – you'll get your cup back when I get me money and not before.' Obviously, the driver had a point. He wanted to be paid too, and didn't have many cards to play in order to get his money. He wasn't interested in points of law and who owned what.

I was standing idly by, watching while Alex stalked past me and marched in to the hotel manager. 'Sort this out,' he told him. 'It's your car park – and I'm beginning to get a little annoyed.'

With Alex, the word *annoyed* could – and often did – mean that anything bizarre and out of the ordinary could happen, so the manager was right to wring his hands, stutter and allow a look of terror to flicker back and forth across his features. He did his best. He scuttled out and had a word with the driver, or at least attempted to, but the curtains remained obstinately closed.

'Right,' said Alex, his short stock of patience expended, 'that's it. I'm calling the police. Time is marching on and we have an exhibition tonight, people to please.'

Soon, a lone bobby on a bicycle pedalled up, indignant that he had been called away from his Sunday morning lie-in and a nice big fry-up. He parked his bicycle, took off his trouser clips and got out his notebook – straight out of a forties movie.

'Christ! We'll be here all day,' Alex snapped.

'Right, let's get the facts,' the constable said. 'Name . . . Hurricane Higgins.' He carefully wrote down our names and a wide grin spread across his face. This was the time of the Troubles, as the Irish problem was called – but that had been going on for a very long time, and was nothing compared with the matter of the Snooker World Cup being held to ransom.

The constable strolled across to the van and rapped smartly on the door. 'Open up in the name of the law!'

It was not the first time Alex had heard that phrase and he grinned briefly. There was no response, so the constable tried all the doors, rattled the handles and attempted to peer in through the firmly curtained windows.

'The bugger's gone to ground,' he laughed.

'I'll shoot him,' Alex snarled. 'No. I'm a guest here. I'll *have* him shot! In '66 a dog nicked the world cup for football – and a dog's just nicked mine for snooker.'

'No need for dramatics, Mr Hurricane,' the constable said. 'We can sort this little matter out peacefully, don't you be worrying yourself now.'

Alex and I retired to the bar for a long cold one, while the constable went indoors to telephone his sergeant for advice. This ransom business was thirsty work. Soon the constable joined us.

'I reckon I have time for a small pint,' he said, rubbing his hands. 'We'll have this cleared up for you in no time, gentlemen, and you can be going on your way.'

The next time I glanced out of the window, I noticed that the car park was beginning to fill up. I nudged the constable, who was starting on his third small pint, 'It looks like your sergeant's arrived with reinforcements,' I said as a police car drew up, closely followed by several other vehicles with no distinguishing marks, of the kind known as 'ambulance chasers'.

The constable sank his pint, gently set his helmet on his carrot-coloured thatch and made his way outside, where he stood chatting to his sergeant before the pair of them attempted a pincer assault on the wagon. The driver merely turned the radio up louder and hurled insults from behind closed doors. The two policemen soon had to admit defeat and strolled back to their HQ in the bar to consider their options.

Twenty minutes and a phone call later, the chief inspector turned up with blue lights flashing and siren blaring. He leapt from his car with all the determination and authority that befitted his rank, eager to restore the famous cup to its rightful owner. The van remained firmly shut. The hotel staff and a couple of American tourists, who said they were staying there to savour the charm and quiet of the old country first-hand, drifted out to watch.

Eventually, the American woman asked her husband what 'snooker' was. He said that it was an early, primitive version of pool.

'Primitive?' snorted Alex. 'I'll have to put them straight. I have never been primitive in my life.'

I headed him off at the pass with the suggestion of another Guinness, but by now it was impossible to get any service so Alex and I decided to help ourselves. We went back outside with beers in hand as the priest, still dressed in his cassock, arrived from the church opposite after mass, along with most of his flock, who stood around in their Sunday best, enjoying the sunshine and a good gossip.

The priest gave us a friendly nod. 'Ah, 'tis a lovely morning. Now a nice drop of Guinness would go down a treat, one's throat gets so dry you know, giving a sermon to the sinners.'

'Help yourself,' I offered generously, on behalf of all sinners.

'Ah yes,' the priest sighed, as he came back outside, burying his nose in the black and white of an overflowing mug, 'I'll just wet my whistle and then I'll sort this out in no time at all. People listen to a man of the cloth. Tact is required in a situation like this – tact!'

Suddenly a huge television van arrived and a camera crew skirmished for parking space with a couple of local radio reporters.

'It's like market day at Connemara Fair in the old days,' chuckled the priest, as a couple more cars drew up, along with another television crew.

Soon, battle lines were drawn as the two crews jostled for the best position. Push came to shove, and the sergeant threatened to arrest everybody.

During the Troubles there was a big army presence. Over the years, Alex informed me, he had got used to it – but it was all new to me and when the troops arrived in their armoured cars, I thought we were in deep trouble. Any moment now, and they'd be parachuting in. A light armoured vehicle blocked the car park exit, with enough ammunition to blow us all to kingdom come – hotel, van and Alex's world cup.

A soldier, in full camouflage dress and bullet-proof vest, sprinted across from his armoured car and hurled himself beneath the van. He appeared to be planting something small and round on the underside.

'Things are getting interesting – they're going to blow him to smithereens with that limpet mine,' observed the hotel chef, ignoring an order to go back to his kitchen from the hotel manager, who was busy counting heads, having realised that he could make a quick fortune with more passing trade than he normally saw in six months.

'They're not blowing my cup to smithereens,' Alex bawled, 'I worked hard to earn that thing.'

'Now oi don't tink it's a limpet mine, now oi tink it's just a microphone,' said the priest.

'It's Hurricane Higgins!' cried a member of the press corps and there was a surge towards him. 'Jimmy White!' screeched someone else, and we were surrounded. From the van, we could smell bacon frying.

'B'Jesus,' said the priest, who was being pushed and shoved along with us. 'The bloody man is cookin' himself some lunch. It's like the Easter Rising itself out there, and he's having a fry-up!'

It occurred to us that the driver had got food, a tankful of water that had been filled only the night before and a chemical toilet. He could hold us off for a month.

Leaving a few of their compadres on picket duty, the press gradually drifted to the bar, where a full-scale party was now in progress. Yarns were being spun, glasses were chinking, sausage rolls and sandwiches were being passed over the heads of the crush. Some people were singing. But Alex and I couldn't relax. This ridiculous business had been going on since ten in the morning – and, even though Armstrong had absconded with the takings, we had an exhibition booked for that evening a hundred miles away for the fans who had paid in good faith to see us. We couldn't let them down.

'I know I'm stupid, but he's won,' Alex said, and got out his cheque book. Waving it like a flag of truce, he banged on the van door. 'Okay,' he shouted, 'I'll pay up. How much are you owed?'

The curtain was flung back, the window shot down and the driver's head emerged. 'I knew you would come round to my way of thinking,' he laughed. 'It's two hundred and fifty quid, sir. And I do take cheques.'

That little caper cost Alex more than we ended up being paid – which was zero – and to this day he still doesn't know why he didn't stop the cheque. The rest of the tour was rescued, thanks to all the ensuing publicity, by Conway Tables, a company that made snooker tables – God bless 'em.

The entire scene in that car park in Derry was like the Keystone Cops – and it will stay with me for ever – just as long as Alex doesn't. I love him to death, but . . . Now, did I tell you about the time he moved into my bathroom in the Liz Taylor and Richard Burton suite at the Gresham Hotel in Dublin? A white suit he was wearing, and he wouldn't move out. He said the gaff was too good for a South London urchin – while *he*, Alex Higgins, was an aesthete. But I might have misheard.

TWO

SOUTH LONDON

My father's constant companion is an old daft dog, with the unlikely name of Mercantile. Whenever visitors knock on Dad's front door Merc, who turned out to be mostly collie when she grew up, makes one hell of a racket. This gives Dad the excuse to explain how she was named after the Mercantile Credit Snooker Classic that I won against Canadian Cliff Thorburn in 1986.

It was a sensational match that went the distance to 12-12, with me needing a snooker to stay alive and only a pink and black left. Now, as anyone knows, you can't have a snooker with only the black ball left and pulling off a snooker with only one ball to hide behind under pressure with big money at stake is far from a piece of cake. But I made it – and potted the black to win. However, although it's exhilarating, a match like that completely drains you whether you win or lose, so when I got back to my own manor I got together with a few friends to unwind.

Coming out of the umpteenth pub I saw this little puppy tied to a lamppost with a bit of old string. The weather was terrible and the poor little thing was shivering violently. If ever a dog was an orphan of the storm, this was it. I walked towards her and she started jumping around and whimpering so I undid the string, and stuffed her inside my coat to warm up. Then she licked my face and that was it, there was no going back.

Except of course, back into the pub, to ask if she was anybody's and to have a quick one while I called home. 'Mum,' I said, 'I've found this puppy, freezing cold it was—' I started.

'And I suppose you want us to give it a nice home, Jimmy?' Mum said.

'Oh, go on, Mum,' I wheedled.

'Well, you better bring it home,' Mum said. 'No promises, mind.'

Mum's gone now, but twelve years later, old Merc keeps Dad company, surrounded by photographs of the family and doing her best to guard the snooker trophies I won when I was a lad from Tooting in 'Sarf London'.

They call it South of the Water. There's something about South London that is entirely different from any other part of the city. South London is in my bones and I'm part of its fabric, which makes me feel good. Even though I no longer live there, it's still home and I like it.

On the other side of the Thames there's the West End (I might occasionally go to the outskirts to support Chelsea); then there's North London – which used to contain Ron Gross's Snooker Centre, a big part of my life – and the East End. The Krays came from the East End and that's where they used to operate from before they got some serious bird. They used to have their own snooker hall, appropriately enough within the sound of the Bow Bells – The Regal in Eric Street, just round the corner from the notorious pub The Blind Beggar, where they shot Jack 'The Hat' McVitie. The Regal was well-known as a den of thieves, where villains kept their tools in the lockers under the seat, their swag out the back and where they picked up useful gossip.

A day out to the seaside from the East End meant Southend; whereas from South London it usually meant Brighton or Margate. The Old Kent Road – 'yer actual Old Kent Road' – begins in South London. All our history and all our yesterdays passed this way, as did our victorious armies and the blokes coming back from Dunkirk – salt of the earth like my dad, Tom White. Our equivalent of the Kray gang were the Richardsons, who referred politely to the other side of the water as 'Indian Country' before they and their henchmen, including 'Mad' Frankie Fraser, also went down in the line of duty.

You have to be from South London to understand it. Every borough really feels like the village it once was, with its own nature and traditions and its own kind of people. Like anywhere else, there's folklore and folk memories that go back a long way and there's still some old people around to remind us of our history and of who we are.

My mother, Lilian, was a Tooting girl, but even though my parents more or less spent their entire lives together in Tooting, my dad, Tom, came from Merton and, as far as he is concerned, Merton is the one and only place. 'My lovely Wandle,' he says fondly, going back in time to when the River Wandle flowed through green fields the colour of a brand-new snooker table. 'There's shopping centres and car parks all over the gaff now, it's a disgrace,' he says. But in parts, like Abbey Mills, you can still see the stream and even a water mill alongside a busy road.

Dad was born right by the Wandle in 1919. It was a friendly and vibrant neighbourhood, with gypsy wagons pulled up on the green banks and a community of black people, who all seemed to be musicians, living down one end of the street. On high days and holidays a black band with banjos and horns and washboards and tambourines hammered away at the top end, just like it was New Orleans; the gypsies in the middle produced a squeeze box, a mandolin, and a fiddle or two and everyone danced in the street, enjoying themselves in a community way which is probably gone for good – at least, I never saw it in my time.

Rats, which had been trapped and kept in cages, were let out for the boys to have a bit of fun, catching them in their caps to win a tanner a time (that's two-and-a-half pence in today's money). At the end of the day everybody crowded into kitchens with tables piled high with delicacies like pigs' heads and trotters, jellied eels and winkles and big fruit cakes, all washed down with Hamilton beer. The last third of the beer left in a bottle, by now a bit flat and warm, was always passed to the kids under the table, where they sat out of the way, getting quietly sloshed. This strong locally brewed beer was named after Lady Hamilton because she and Admiral Lord Nelson once lived it up in a mansion with landscaped grounds where today a large supermarket stands. So much for tradition.

Dad's mother was married at the time to his father's best friend, who was killed right beside him in the trenches in 1914, just after they arrived at the front. My granddad went to see her, to tell her how it had happened, they got together and Dad came along. Dad was in the second lot, as they called World War Two. He was actually exempt because he was doing dangerous work at the Arsenal at Bridgend, in Wales, but three of his mates had joined and he didn't want to be left out. It wasn't easy for him because he had a skin disease that made him allergic to the prickly khaki issue. If he hadn't worn his pyjamas under his uniform he would have scratched his way through the war. Two years later, he was one of the remnants of the British army, pulled off a

French beach by a trawler. Most of the boys, including Dad, were so traumatised by the shelling they had taken, they were sent off to a madhouse in Northumberland to recuperate. After a few days, Dad slipped off home for a little unauthorised leave. He returned to the army but they didn't even notice he'd been away.

Dad met my mother, Lil, in a coffee shop in 1943 while repairing military lorries and waiting for his medical discharge from the army. If she had been sitting in a teashop he would never have met her because he was probably the only man in the entire British army who didn't like tea. They got talking, realised they had friends in common and hit it off. When Nan – Dad's mother – asked them when they were going to get married, he replied, 'I'll think about it, Mum', but no, they never did get around to marrying and were happy for fifty-three years.

My name, James Warren White, comes from both my grandfathers. I was the youngest, the baby of the family, born 2 May 1962. About the time when I was on the way, Dad's father died. Apparently, the old man had saved up a tanner a week towards his funeral expenses in a loan club, so the money was there to bury him and pay for a good send-off from Knox's tin chapel, a kind of shed-like funeral parlour in Merton High Street. My nan and her friend had gone round there to pay their last respects, which included laying him out in a kind of wicker basket chair and washing him so he'd go clean to Heaven.

This was all new to Nan; she had never seen a corpse before, let alone a naked one, but, by the time my dad arrived, the two women had entered into the spirit of the thing and were cracking such jokes as, 'My, you're dirty, Whitey!' – 'Used to 'ave a barf every Saturday, old Whitey, you know, whether he needed it or not!' as they soaped away, giving him a good scrub down.

Dad looked at the brass plate on the open lid of the

waiting coffin alongside and read – *Thomas James White*.
Thomas had been used up on my brother, Tommy, so
that left James going spare. My other grandfather's
surname was Warren. Over the soapsuds it was settled
that, if I were a girl, Mum could call me what she liked,
but if I were a boy I would get both my grandfathers'
names. Then, with my granddad dressed in his Sunday
best and laid out in his coffin, they all retired to the little
pub next door to the famous tin chapel for the wake and
to reminisce over the merits of Merton versus Tooting.

A couple of months later I was born in a prefab in
Balham. Now the government is listing prefabs as Grade
II historical buildings; but back then they were just
temporary dwellings erected in the aftermath of masses
of war damage when bombs flattened half of London.
The war did some people good; for a few years Dad got
plenty of work building new schools so when my three
older brothers, Martin, Tommy, Tony and my sister,
Jackie, came along, Mum was able to stay at home and
take care of them. When I was a few months old, my
parents moved to a proper council house in Topsham
Road, Tooting, with three bedrooms and a boxroom
which was mine. It was perfect for me, a cosy little den
that I could make into anything I wanted it to be. Now
the one place I *didn't* want to be was in school. People
think that it was snooker that took me away from my
lessons; but, to be honest, I was truanting long before
then. I was Huckleberry Finn, a boy who couldn't sit still
at a desk and stare at the blackboard. I wanted to be out
there, having fun, learning a more interesting kind of
stuff, looking for the next adventure that lay around
every corner.

THREE

THE WALKING STICK

Victor Yo was, quite literally, the boy next door. He was twelve months and I was a toddler of two years, when we were introduced in our prams on the pavement outside our adjoining homes. If Mum knew what Victor and I and the gang were to get up to as soon as we were let out on our own, I'm sure she would have badgered Dad to move at once. To be fair to Victor, it was mostly scampish fun that I introduced him to. I was the leader and he was the follower. According to him, I was not so much Huck Finn as an Artful Dodger and he was a wide-eyed, gullible little Oliver Twist following along, but keeping a low profile while I instigated the mischief.

To start with, Victor and I went to Hillbrook Primary, delivered there by our respective guardians – in his case his nan, with whom he lived – until they saw that we could handle ourselves, after which we took ourselves to school. Wilder than any of the other whippersnappers, by about the age of eight or nine I was well-versed in the art of truanting and egged the others on to join me. As soon as we signed the register we used to bunk off and roam the streets.

When I was eight or nine I was having a bit of a scrap with a good friend, Colin Prisk, and a couple of kids from another school outside Zan's Snooker Hall. We were rolling about on the ground, all arms and legs and pounding fists, bloody noses and scraped shins, with people side-stepping us as they walked by, muttering, 'I'm going to call the police if you don't pack it in,' which, as usual, we totally ignored. Adults were always threatening to sort us out and hardly ever did. Colin and I were losing the fight, so I glanced round to see if we could make a break for it, when I heard the pounding of feet and spotted reinforcements coming – but for the other side.

By now, the fight had taken us into the porch of Zan's and just at that moment, someone stepped over us and went inside. As the swing doors opened wide I caught a glimpse of a world I never knew existed. It looked warm and inviting, dark and mysterious as a cave. Without thinking I shot in, closely followed by Colin, and we hurled ourselves beneath a snooker table.

The floor was awash with cigarette ash and stubs and there was a kind of dusty, musty, beery, smoky, almost soot-like smell. Men's voices were low, trousered legs and scuffed shoes shuffled by. I heard the click of balls and then a clunk and a faint rumble like thunder as a ball dropped into the pocket and ran along the channel just inches away from my face. If, like Alice, I had fallen down a rabbit hole and dropped into Wonderland, it would have been like this.

Years later, people have said it was Zan's that stopped me going to school. The fact is, I rarely went to school. When it was raining we knew we could hide in there until it stopped, slinking in underneath someone's coat or behind someone built like a house. It was nine months to a year before I even played a shot but I used to watch. The place fascinated me long before the game did. Some summer nights I used to climb out of the front-room window at home and go to Zan's because it was somewhere to go – and far better than trying to sleep. Someone would take pity on me and buy me a cup of tea and I'd sit on the sidelines and watch, just taking it all in. It was better than telly! This was real cowboy territory – full of villains and good gossip.

Like a frontier town or the Klondike, all kinds hung out in the billiard and snooker halls. I've seen some sad cases where starving men who once used to be great players have begged for food and people turned their faces away. There was one guy named Flash Bob, ex-public-school boy, who'd been a male model in his gilded youth. Everything about him was a mystery. He'd sleep in his car, an old banger parked outside, and come in with his toothbrush in his mouth, ready to wash in the squalid toilet.

Very posh, he'd drawl, 'I say, has anyone enough for the price of a cheese roll in this pisshole?'

A couple of people would laugh, but mostly he was ignored. After making himself presentable, looking lean and hungry he would saunter out. No one asked questions in that twilight world. The next week he'd have a brand-new suit on and a flash car outside. In his newly manicured hands he'd wave a wad two inches thick and if someone slunk up to him asking for a few bob, he'd sneer, 'You two-faced bastard, you wouldn't even give me the price of a cup of tea the other day.'

The owner of the hall was Ted Zanicelli, an elderly man with a heart of gold, who developed a soft spot for me. Zan's son had a shop which sold girlie magazines. Everyone was into something. Mad Ronnie Fryer was a complete nutter. You only had to look at him and it would scare you. Jack Nicholson played a gangster in a film called *Prizzi's Honor*, where his father had taught him how to stand in front of a mirror and practise 'hosing fear' on people with his eyes. In the end, he got so good at it, even his father was scared shitless. Well, Ronnie Fryer was like that. If he spotted a kid sitting on a table he'd come over and slap him. Zan used to give him money to keep him happy so he'd go away and leave us all alone. One day, there was a bit of trouble and the police came bustling in with a big Alsatian dog. A burly sergeant gave me the evil eye. 'I know you, boy,' he said. 'You should be at school.'

'Nah, I've got the day off,' I lied.

He looked around and clocked us all. 'You're wanted!' he barked at a couple of men, who made like they weren't really there at all. 'Okay,' he said, 'we better get the bastard out of the cellar.'

The minder released the dog and it shot down the stairs. There was a horrible howl that broke off into a whimpering, and then silence. It was Mad Ronnie down there, and he had killed the dog. I was learning, the hard way, that things like that happened in this shadowy underworld I preferred to school.

Mad Ronnie came to a sticky end. One day, Big John Nielsen and Terry Monday, two players who regularly used Zan's, bumped into Ronnie in the street and they arranged to meet in the club the next day for a money game or two. Big John was waiting there the following afternoon, knocking a few balls about, when the doors burst open and Ronnie roared in like Hagar the Horrible. His eyes were rolling, his face was red and he was frothing at the mouth. I shot under the table as usual when Ronnie was around and that day he looked as if he could gnaw my legs right off.

'I've fucking killed him!' he bawled.

John had heard all this before. He casually potted another practice red and asked, 'Who've you killed, then?'

'Terry!' Ronnie shouted, 'I done him!'

'What, you mean *really* done him in?' It was dawning on John that this could be serious business.

'Yeh, he annoyed me, didn't he?' Ronnie said, beginning to come down. 'Poor old Terry, he was a good mate. He shouldn't have got on me nerves, though, should he?'

It appeared that on his way to Zan's, Mad Ronnie had met Terry and within moments a row had flared up and he'd killed him with his bare hands, just like the poor police dog. Of course he was arrested and banged up. Later, I heard that he had committed suicide with cyanide in jail.

A few things I had heard Dad talk about started to slot into place. Some of his building work took him into Soho, where he met quite a few gangsters, men like Billy Hill, who wanted work done on their clubs. I heard him tell Mum once, when he was working in Old Compton Street as a subcontractor on a delicatessen, that Billy's wife, Aggie, had popped along and shouted through the builder's rubble where Dad was sawing away that she had a nice little job for him in Billy's club, which for some reason was called The Modernaires. Billy and Aggie were separated, but Billy used to see her every Saturday and give her a big bunch of roses.

'Drop in and we'll discuss it over a drink, eh, love?' said Aggie with a wink.

'Blimey,' Dad said to Mum, 'she only wants the ceiling done strawberry pink!'

Mum laughed as she peeled the spuds. 'That's a funny colour for a ceiling.'

'It's a funny colour for a night-club,' Dad said, 'more like a whore's bedroom – not that I would know, would I? But you know what I mean,' Dad added. 'I'll do anything to suit people. And there's a couple of white fivers in it for me.'

Now that, I understood. White fivers – the big old-fashioned ones that don't exist any more – were something that at the age of nine I had never actually had in my hands, but I had seen plenty being passed around from my den underneath a snooker table where I slid unobtrusively when dodgy deals were going down.

Mostly, we were just kids, kicking our heels. Although our exploits seemed very daring to us, they weren't malicious. We'd go on excursions to the West End, without a single penny, bunking all the way on bus or tube. We'd find amusement arcades, stroll into museums like we owned the place ('What a joke,' I bragged, not seeing the irony, 'what if we was to run into our class on a museum visit?') We'd prank about round the city centre, looking for thrills. I'm not sure what we hoped to find. We were always being chased out of arcades and shops and we would helter-skelter away, screaming with laughter. When we were hungry – which was all the time, given that we'd spent our dinner money on cigarettes – we'd find a sympathetic shopkeeper, usually a woman since they were a soft touch, and tell her we were orphans who had run away from some cruel institution, and hadn't had anything to eat for two days – or was it three?

'Ah, poor little loves,' we'd hear, and grin at each other horribly as she turned to pop a few chocolate bars or pasties into a bag. 'Go to the police station,' she would urge, 'and tell them what's been happening. Perhaps they'll send you to another home. It isn't safe for nice kids like you to be out on the street. Shame, it is, a crying shame.'

Sad-eyed, we'd give the assurances she wanted to hear before running round the corner, to collapse laughing against a wall and share the spoils.

Getting on and off the tube without paying was an achievement we prided ourselves on. We'd devise as many daring ways as we could to get through the barrier and, if a new kid was with us, we'd invent the most dire stories of what would happen if he got nicked. In fact, it was dead easy to shoot over the low barriers. We'd make a long run from the top of the escalators and by the time we had built up speed it was a quick leapfrog, off and out. But we were into danger and excitement, and *easy* became boring, so we were always looking for ways to make our exit more challenging. One time, I decided to do it fancy, leaping over with no hands. As I went over, I saw a navy-blue uniform approach and then I hit the barrier with my foot and heard a sickening crack. I shrieked with pain – Victor said he would never forget that yell, it echoed all around the station and along the tunnels and had people turning in their tracks with shock. I have never experienced pain so fierce, but I got to my feet and half-hopped, half-ran for it. I wasn't scared of being nabbed by the authorities – it was the thought of being caught and Mum finding out that I wasn't at school, which was a hundred times worse.

We belted out of the underground station and didn't stop until we got to the end of the road, where I couldn't hold the pain in any more and collapsed on the pavement. My sock looked as if a cricket ball had been stuffed down the side.

'Crikey, look at his foot!' I heard Victor say with pride before I passed out. Victor called an ambulance and I was carted off to hospital. My foot was badly broken – and has never been strong since – but even then I wouldn't own up to how – or where – it had happened. My parents came to the hospital and I made up one of my usual cock-and-bull stories.

'A pick-up game of football, it was, against those other lads. Just bearing down on the goal, clean through I was, with only the goalie to beat, when I was scythed down as I pulled back my foot to shoot. Next thing I knew I was in an ambulance and . . .'

'You shouldn't play with boys who can't play fair,' said Mum, all thoughts of telling me off for not being in school forgotten. 'It's a disgrace.'

Of course, when I got home amongst my pals, I was a local hero, hobbling about with my leg in plaster and using a walking stick, hamming it up for all it was worth.

By then I had left the primary school and moved on up to the Ernest Bevin Comprehensive School. During the day I didn't see Victor, who, a year younger than me, was still at the primary school, although we still met up in the evenings and at weekends. One of the things that had altered our relationship was my growing passion for snooker. I couldn't keep skiving off into Zan's without being changed by it in some way.

I remember the first time I ever played on a snooker table. It was table nine. My brother, Martin, who was older than me and at work, occasionally used to play in Zan's and one day he asked if I'd like a go with his cue. I couldn't wait! The lure of the green baize drew me like a magnet. It's a funny thing because, although most snooker halls are squalid dives, so that when you go in with clean shoes you leave looking as if you have been shuffling along in downtown Pompeii, the tables are always kept beautifully. The nap of the baize is carefully brushed and under the lights looks almost radiant, like the emerald green of an Irish bog. It is a people's theatre in the round, where in the wings everyone waits their turn or watches, fascinated. While you are at the table, bathed in that pool of golden light, you are touched by magic. It is an exhilarating feeling, one that captivated me from the very first moment I actually held a cue in my hands and focused on the coloured balls. It has gripped me ever since.

That first week, I think I played snooker for about a hundred hours. I just went home to sleep. I hardly ate. Mum kept putting food in front of me, but I was on such a high I just wasn't hungry. I was in love – with snooker. Today I get more of a buzz because I'm more experienced and I know where I am. But, then again, it's more terrifying because the game is so high-powered, the players are better than they have ever been, and the stakes are huge – which is a great kick to me. I like risk and challenge.

But, back then, despite my new-found passion, I was still a schoolkid, at least at heart and, with my twelfth birthday coming up, when Martin asked me what I wanted – a snooker cue or a racing bike – I went for the bike. I should have opted for the cue: because naturally, I had the bike for only two days before it was stolen from outside the snooker club – where I was inside borrowing someone else's cue. It was shortly after this that I broke my foot and used a walking stick to hobble around. Had I gone to school a bit more I might have learned that the cue was developed from the mace – a kind of high-class walking stick that showed how important you were – in about 1730. It wasn't long before I started using my stick instead of a cue when nobody would lend me theirs and got quite proficient with it. For some reason, whatever I used, I could always pot those balls!

It was also round about then that I met Dodgy Bob, who drove a black cab. He was to have an enormous, if dubious, influence on my life. One day Bob took me over to Neasden, to Ron Gross's famous snooker club, and Steve Davis, who, at the age of seventeen was starting to make quite a name for himself, dropped in. In an idle moment I started to pot balls with my walking stick, shooting them in fast and accurately.

Steve watched in amazement when I scored a ton. He came on over and actually laughed, which for Steve is quite something. 'Hey, kid,' he said, 'you're as good with that stick as most people are with a cue. You'll go far.'

FOUR

DODGY BOB AND ALL THAT

One of the faces I had noticed around Zan's was Tony Meo, a fifth-former from Ernest Bevin Comprehensive, which he had entered at the age of fourteen after his Sicilian father had died and the family had moved from Central London to Tooting. Tony's mother brought him up in the family restaurant – she also kept a clothing store – so, as I always good-naturedly teased him, he was okay for grub and threads, and it's a fact that he was a plump, well-nourished boy who was a bit of a fashion plate. He also loved to go disco dancing, something that didn't interest me at all until later, when I realised that they all danced as badly as me and that John Travolta was one in a million.

At school, Tony was a champion table tennis player, but very few people knew how good he was at snooker, probably because when he used to bunk off to play, he was caned, so he stopped bunking off or mentioning his interest. We had always chatted a bit at Zan's but it wasn't until I started at the same school that we got really friendly. Tony was a very good player, accurate and fast, and when he was playing a crowd always gathered to watch. From the moment I started to play, we gravitated towards each other and sort of teamed up. Our relationship probably wouldn't have gone any further than that – nor gone into the realms of snooker legend – if it hadn't been for Dodgy Bob.

His real name was Bob Davis, but there were some lurid rumours surrounding him. Bob is dead now, so I won't speak ill of him – and in fact I don't think ill of him. I was streetwise enough to watch out for myself.

They called him Dodgy Bob because he used to have a lot of really young kids around him. When I got to be fifteen or so I could see what was happening. He was into all the seedy parts of our world. Tall and skinny, he always seemed old (he was about eighty when he died), still going around the clubs with young boys, still driving a black taxi.

We met him when I was thirteen and Tony Meo was fifteen or sixteen. By then a new housemaster, Arthur Beatty, had taken over at our school. He played a bit of snooker himself, so we thought he would be more understanding. We tested the water a bit and didn't get into trouble – at least, not immediately, so we waded in a bit deeper.

Tony and I were practising in Zan's one afternoon, when this man, about sixty or sixty-five, came in. He stood around, a lager in his hand, watching us, not saying a thing until we had wrapped up a few frames. He approached and introduced himself, telling us that he owned a black cab and was semi-retired, so he could take time off to suit himself.

'You're good, very good,' he said. 'I think we could all make a little dough if we team up.'

At the word dough our ears pricked up. Tony and I were usually too broke to pay for the tables, though if the club wasn't too busy Zan would let us play for nothing, so that it looked a bit busier. No one likes an empty club.

'So what's the deal?' Tony asked.

'We'll start off slow, like, see how you get on,' Bob said. 'I'll take you over to this club I know in Neasden and I'll back you and Jimmy against some snooker players who are into money matches. I'll give you—' at this a crafty look came into his face that I learnt to recognise '—I'll give you ten per cent each of whatever we earn.'

'Ten per cent? That ain't much,' I said.

'But see, I'm taking all the risk,' Bob said. 'Suppose you lose, I'm out of pocket, aren't I? You're just kids – you'll be up against some sharp geezers. And if you think about it – that's twenty per cent I'm forking out when all you'll be doing is what you like to do anyway. You could earn yourselves a lot of money instead of hanging around here picking your noses.'

Tony looked at me and I shrugged. 'Well, Tone, we ain't earning very much right now,' I said. 'Anyway, it'll be good practice – at someone else's expense,' I added, giving Bob a cheeky look.

'Well, let's go for a ride then, shall we?' said Bob, wiping a dewdrop from his sharp nose and heading for the door. He was so long and thin he looked like a question mark. That should have given me a hint, told me to think about the whole set-up. Dodgy Bob was to take us for a ride in more ways than one, but there was a trade-off of sorts that suited us at the time.

We didn't tell our parents where we were going. Off somewhere – who knows where – in a taxi with a total stranger would not have gone down well with my mum. She'd have had a fit, so I didn't bother. Bob drove us across London and introduced us to the Neasden Snooker Centre. The owner, Ron Gross, was to become a good friend over the years and still is. In fact, many a time I ended up staying over, sleeping on the sofa in Ron's front room and in the mornings, when one or other of his daughters, Janette or Tina, came in to blow-dry their hair before going to school, they would try not to wake me. They needn't have worried. Usually I had only just got to bed and a bomb going off under the sofa wouldn't have disturbed me.

For about six months we went regularly to Neasden in the back of Bob's old-style sit-up-and-beg black taxi. We nearly always won our matches but, as I've said, we were bound to be taken for a ride because while Bob did give us our measly ten per cent, we didn't know how much he had put on the game in the first place – so it was ten per cent of whatever he said it was – and that was usually next to nothing.

All of a sudden, Bob decided that we'd put enough practice in and were a sure-fire bet for some bigger games he'd heard about on the outskirts of London. As soon as we'd signed the register we'd bunk off down to Zan's where Bob would meet us and we'd decide where to go. We did very well, as a matter of fact. We won a lot of matches. We were very eager. When we had cleaned up all around London, Dodgy Bob started to look further afield, choosing places we'd seen advertised as 'a nice day out' pasted up on the underground or train stations. We didn't go too far away, perhaps to Herne Bay or Bedford, Brighton or Aylesbury – anywhere we hadn't already been or that we liked the sound of, we'd be off, one scruff and one Little Lord Fauntleroy sitting in the back of the limo, our chauffeur, the Question Mark, who looked like an undertaker, hunched over the wheel upfront. When you think about it, these were remarkable days out for two boys who really should have been in school. But school was not where we wanted to be.

We'd roll up at our destination round about midday and find the local working man's club. We'd stroll in, normal-like, not wanting to look too much like the young guns from out of town arriving for a shoot-out, and Bob would find out who the best player was, and if they liked to play for money. While Bob was doing this, taking care of business, Tony and I would knock a few balls around the table – taking it easy, not showing our ability too much. The word would soon spread around town and come night-time all the best players would emerge from the warrens and rat-runs and the serious business would start. It wasn't really a hustle because we were still just kids, throwing down a challenge. It was fun and we were playing grown, experienced men. The thing was, we very rarely lost!

When we got back to London, we'd go to the Golden Egg, a touristy arcade and gaming kind of joint in Oxford Street, where you could have a hamburger, to divvy up the money. I would see that cunning look come into Dodgy's eyes and he would slip his long, gnarled fingers into his pocket and draw out a slim sheaf of notes. I always knew that he had split the winnings earlier and the real wad was tucked away, probably under the seat of his taxi in case he was done over. We always got well and truly rumped.

But we got our own back on him – though funnily enough, not on purpose. Bob worked us so hard, sometimes we could barely stand, let alone play. In the small hours of one morning, Tony and I were so dog-tired after sixteen straight hours of playing that we could hardly stay awake. We had yawned our way, blurry-eyed, through half a dozen games, losing spectacularly. Bob had obviously gone down for a lot of money and he was livid. From the back of the taxi we could see his long thin nose quivering with rage. Something about it struck us as wildly funny. We were so exhausted we were almost stoned and we couldn't stop laughing. Bob got grouchier and grouchier, snapping at us through the window and still we laughed, rolling all over the slippy back seat and on to the floor. We laughed for about two hours, and in the end Bob just slung us out in the middle of the West End and drove off. We were lucky he didn't get nasty that time because I knew what he could be like. Sometimes, when I was late, he used to give me one across the face, pretending he was half-larking; but I knew he never was.

I met some remarkable characters during my time with Dodgy Bob, not least a geezer known as John the Arab. His real name was John Taylor and he wasn't an Arab. To this day no one knows what he did for a living, though some said he was a chauffeur and that the fancy car he drove wasn't his. There was always a crowd of people watching when the Arab played. All the other tables would stop. They'd be like a swarm of rats, waving their money, making bets. He'd go, 'Right, you're on for twenty – you're on – and you're on – and you're on,' and then suddenly it was a case of 'no more bets, please, gentlemen' – though that's not what he said.

John was a strange cup of tea and very picky about who he played as well as who he bet with. There was a kind of aura that followed him about. People treated him as if he was some kind of Godfather figure. Of course, when the game finished, if you didn't come up and pay, you never got to bet with him again. He didn't come to you, he just stayed by the table, as aloof as a sphinx, seeming to take in nothing, but taking in everything.

The rats would swirl about and shuffle from one table to another. One or other would try to fool him by changing their hats, say from a baseball cap to a trilby with a feather in the side and, with a leering kind of grin, say, 'I'm on for twenty.' The Arab would just ignore them. He had a brilliant grasp of who was betting on a game and who paid, or never paid their debts. Eventually, all the rats dwindled away until there were just a few he'd gamble with.

The first time I met the Arab was at Ron Gross's when

I was fourteen or so. To my surprise he offered to play me, which was remarkable since he was very picky. The game was hot and the Arab was betting big money. I was winning to the tune of £400, when Geoff Foulds came in. He was the London champion at the time.

He came across and gave me a muddy look, 'I've booked this table,' he said.

In those days you never booked, but I was naive and he ended up bullying me off the table. The Arab stood by waiting until we had sorted it out and said sod all. I had to sit back and watch Foulds win about six grand. Now, I was playing well and that could have been me walking away with the Arab's money – and I always have that at the back of my mind when I speak to Geoff. I still like him – and I like his son, Neil, a lot more.

The Arab let me play him on and off for about six months and I got to like and respect him. Tony Meo and I didn't like taking his money – but we were so hot it seemed we couldn't lose – and we worked for Dodgy Bob who was more like that wily old Fagin than anything. I don't know why we allowed him to have that power over us, unless it was because he was willing to put up the kind of money we didn't possess and he had opened our eyes to our own potential as well as to the wide, dirty, exciting world beyond Tooting and Zan's. But no. When I think about it, what did we really know? Nothing. We were raw, like snooker-squaddies. Chancers. Eager, but dumb.

The Arab had a strange and regular habit. As the game progressed towards its end, if he had a pink and black ball game left on the table, he used to stop and say: 'Now I'm going to pray to Allah, so don't no one bother me,' and he'd go to the toilets.

No one wanted to upset him or interfere with him because he used to feed a lot of people at the time, all the little rats and their hangers-on depended on him for a living. He was allowed to disappear out the back for ten minutes or longer and people would say to a newcomer heading that way – 'Don't go out there for a minute or two 'cos the Arab's praying to Allah,' – although they would be thinking that he was probably counting his money. That he might be doing a bit of the old Mohammed's marching powder never occurred to me back then.

Meanwhile on the table a pink and black would be twinkling away under the lights, like baubles at Bethlehem – with everyone waiting for the Wise Man to return. Sometimes, when there was just a black left you could hear a pin drop because a lot of money always rode on those games.

I found out later that what the Arab was actually doing was jacking up heroin. He'd come back with a massive smile on his face and play his shot and he'd be as smooth and mellow as a jar of honey.

Once we met him at the tournaments they held at Pontins at Prestatyn. He was a very different man away from his customary environment, a live-wire who won the talent contest for singing, a twinkle-toed smoothie who twirled around the dance floor to win the ballroom championship. When they had the old men and women doing aerobics, the Arab was there, going through the moves on the sidelines, cheering them on, a greatly changed and dynamic man. I could hardly believe what I was seeing.

Then nothing was heard of him for ages. His neighbours in his flat in Kensington were alerted by that peculiar smell the police know so well. When they broke in, they found him dead. He had been there for four months, having overdosed on heroin.

Even at the end, he showed how straight he was. He had prepared and left lists of his debts, all his gambling debts as well as more normal things like credit card and utilities, and had left the money to pay them. It was all done properly, which was why people said he must have committed suicide; the hotshot who literally took the hot shot. You never know unless you read the note.

Life on the road with Dodgy Bob was hard work. It was only a laugh in retrospect, when Tony and I would swap yarns with our mates over beers – something I got into as a way of releasing the tension. People might raise their eyebrows at a kid drinking so young, but not many thirteen-year-olds are chased out of snooker halls at three o'clock in the morning. In one place in Liverpool, we started playing two guys, the best in the area. Halfway through the game their manager stomped across and said to Bob, 'You're nothing but a cheapskate hustler! We want all our money back.'

'Leave off,' Bob said nastily, standing up to him. 'You know my boys, they've been around a while and you're just bent out of shape because they're too good for your boys. So don't give me any grief, okay?'

Next thing, the locals were doing the Millwall shuffle towards us. Someone showed Tony a lump in his pocket that looked like a gun and we just split. Dodgy Bob Davis didn't bother to wait for us; he was in his taxi and off. Meo went out the door and to the left and I went out the door and to the right, diving down back alleys, ducking around corners, convinced I could hear running feet following me. Somehow I ended up in Lime Street Station. Meo caught the coach home – but that was the end of Dodgy Bob as far as we were concerned. He should have waited.

I was in a pub once with a few mates, having a laugh when a guy approached me.

'I'll give you a game of pool for a fiver,' he said.

I didn't like the look of him and said, 'I don't want to play, mate.'

'Come on, mate,' he urged, 'one game for a fiver.'

If I didn't play he would be miffed – and if I played and won he would be *really* miffed. So I played. I broke the balls up, potted one and then potted the other seven and the black. Without a word he passed over a crumpled fiver and left. I carried on having a few drinks and thought nothing more of it. My mates and I left the pub and went to a night-club. What we didn't know was that he had been waiting and watching and followed us there. However, the doorman didn't like the look of him either and wouldn't let him in – probably because he had this axe. So he started chopping down the door.

'Oy, Jimmy!' the doorman said, 'there's a nutcase out there, looking for you.'

'Oh, really? Tell him to piss off,' I said.

By now, the door was in splinters. The doorman and a couple of bouncers, armed with baseball bats, moved into position then rushed out and flattened him. Later I heard he had been sent to jail for some other grievous bodily offence and was in the medical block. He had pictures of me pasted up all round the room, and would stare at them muttering dire threats.

Generally, I have a talent for being able to spot trouble brewing early and often I'd lose money on purpose. Say I was winning £500, I'd see that the guy is gone. He has that glazed look and wants to gamble his car, his kid's piggy bank, his wife's jewellery – *her* – anything just so he can keep going and eventually prove himself a winner. A true sportsman. You know he's in too deep, and the next stage is usually hysterics, panic, and then anger – so you let him win some back, because if you didn't you'd probably not leave that night in one piece. I used to spot these situations and, touch wood, made it home safely. I saw a man once shot in the legs in a snooker club in Wimbledon, so you know anything can happen.

One shocking event that happened in a snooker club in

Windmill Street in London's Soho, involved a certain snooker player, who must remain nameless. He was told to arrange a rendezvous in the club with a particular character who had been accused of being a grass; and to ask no questions. Just do it. The customers who asked him were hard cases and he knew if he didn't, he'd be in trouble. The meeting was arranged, the grass arrived. Someone called out softly, 'He's here!' and everyone who knew they had no business there scattered, the doors were locked and the real game of the evening started. It was a deadly game, involving all the trays of snooker balls from behind the counter. The grass was literally stoned to death. The police pulled the guy who was the bait in for questioning, with no result. He kept his mouth shut of course – no choice. The police banned him from setting foot in the West End again, an illegal curfew he was forced to obey because he knew he'd be picked up and hassled by all the cops at West End Central, who were mightily pissed off, to say the least. Soho was smaller in those days, faces were more recognisable, you could walk along and see half a dozen people you knew. The Bill could warn you to keep away back then, stay off their manor. Today, it's full of tourists and people you don't know.

Sometimes when I arrived back home with the milkman, I would sneak in and Mum thought I'd been there all night. I'd throw on my school uniform, give myself a lick and a promise and be waved off on my way to school. I'd get as far as next door then nip up the front path over the sill in through the window, into bed with Victor – his nan wasn't as alert as my mum – and we would doss half the day away, preparing for another night of fun. If I had gone to school I would have been useless anyway.

My love affair with snooker had come as a complete shock to Victor. He had heard that I was hanging around

Zan's with Tony Meo and someone had said I was good; then with Dodgy Bob acting as my so-called 'manager', earning a few pounds. In my spare time from hustling, I joined Ron Gross's snooker team and started to win a few amateur championships.

Now it all began for me in earnest because these matches were reported in the press. News was filtering out that I was more than just a wild young kid. Victor said to me recently, 'Jimmy, I never realised you was a genius.' I was tempted to reply, 'Me neither,' but I don't like to tempt the Fates. Compliments from old friends are compliments indeed. As soon as Victor started to take on board what was happening, he was in it up to the neck with me, just as he had always been from about the age of six or seven. He started to come out with me, not to play, but to watch. And now, it wasn't just me coming home with the milkman, but Victor as well. Some nights when we got to his house, it was all lit up like a Christmas tree. A relative of his, a waitress at the Playboy Club, was living there and she'd come home with some real-life Bunny Girls. Other friends would drop by to socialise, so there always seemed to be a party going on. The girls were still wired to the ceiling after their job, wanting to chat and come down. A game of poker would start up, drinks would be poured and the carnival rolled again. I was fascinated by these giggly girls running around in their negligees, taking off make-up, relaxing and drinking cocoa. It was a bizarre scene for a thirteen-year-old boy, almost like a dream. At times, I felt I was in the pages of an erotic magazine – and probably was. Thirteen is a very impressionable age.

FIVE

THE CUE

I don't know how long it was before my school cottoned on to the fact that my attendance was erratic, to say the least. The housemaster, Mr Beatty, must have realised something was up when he opened his daily paper at breakfast one morning and read an article about me making my first century at Zan's at the record-breaking age of thirteen. It was such a startling event that it was widely reported. (Kids do it today at twelve and it's not even mentioned – in fact, snooker is going to be an Olympic sport in 2004. All this, of course, shows how snooker is now regarded as a proper sport and children are encouraged early on to practise. My practising was all done in the dark, snatched illegally when I should have been at school.) Ted Zan even had a cup specially made and presented it to me – although it was kept behind the bar so everyone could see it.

The newspaper report that Mr Beatty read said:

Jimmy White is the London and Home Counties Boys snooker champion and he registered his first ton at Zan's Club, Tooting. A substantial crowd watched the break

and the applause which greeted his even hundred when
he took the blue put him off the pink which rattled in the
jaws. His clubmate, Tony Meo, a 16-year-old from
Tooting, rattled in breaks of 105 and 117 in the same
week.

There was an exchange of telephone calls between my
mother and the school authorities, a flurry of letters and
no end of house calls from the truant officers. I ignored
all the lectures and threats until Mum was at her wit's
end. It was no good telling me that if I didn't go to school
I would never get a proper job – it wasn't a problem as
far as I was concerned, I *had* a proper job, one that, for
all its risks, was fun and at times paid very well. The
trouble was, when we had the dosh, Tony Meo and I
would squander it, betting like there was no tomorrow.
Once, we won £1500 at snooker in the morning – an
enormous sum then – and had blown the lot by 4.30 that
afternoon at the bookies. Far from feeling depressed, we
were wildly elated as we made our penniless way back
home on the train, dodging the inspector when he came
round to check the tickets. We told ourselves there was
always plenty more where that came from; and often
there was.

There was a lot of money to be made, but for us it was
just an everyday something to win and lose. When your
luck runs out you're still only as broke as if you had
blown it anyway. At times I can remember being really
skint without enough to bet to get a game going, or
having to scrounge around for a few coins to feed the
table meter so I could practise.

I couldn't reveal any of this casual black economy
world I now inhabited to Mum and Dad, because they
would have been furious – not just for going into a
bookies or for squandering such vast amounts of money
but also because they knew that, as an amateur, only very

small sums of money were allowed to be won.

On one occasion, when I was playing a properly regulated match at the local British Legion, bets suddenly started to be laid and I didn't want to miss out. I didn't have a bean on me, and ran all the way home to try to cadge a fiver from Dad. All he had was a screwed-up ten-bob note (50p today). Getting the ironing board out, with Mum watching in amazement since I'd never ironed anything in my life, I smoothed out the note and raced back to the hall. Hours later, I came home and poured over a grand in crumpled notes on the living room carpet. My whole family was stunned that so much could grow from so little.

In fact, Mum and Dad were often hard up. With such a large family to keep, at times life was a struggle. I remember once, when a debt collector came round, Mum sent me to answer the door while she hid in the coal cellar. 'She ain't in,' I said, when I opened the door. 'When will she be back?' asked the man. 'Hang on,' I said, 'I'll go and ask her.'

But even though Mum was proud of my improving amateur status, carefully clipping out a growing pile of newspaper cuttings which reported the league matches I played in, she was worried about me being dragged to court for truanting so blatantly and perhaps being sent away to a home (I'm serious) where I wouldn't be able to play snooker at all.

She would escort me to school, almost dragging me there by the ear like a cartoon character. As soon as I could, I did a bunk. Short of chaining me to the desk, there was nothing they could do. I remember once being pulled out of Zan's by Mr Beatty himself and frog-marched back to school. It was no good – I was off again the next day. The police used to come in to Zan's to check things out. Ridiculously, Tony and I wore our school blazers inside out to try to look inconspicuous –

with the stripy lining and the label showing. The police used to clip us around the head, with, 'Go on, scram!' and we'd disappear for a few minutes until the coast was clear and be back in there like a shot.

Mum started to come in regularly, give me a little slap around the side of head (if I didn't see her coming), drag me outside . . . then give me two quid and let me go back in – she was a wonderful woman like that. I knew she was thinking – 'Well, what's the point of punishing him? He'll nip off soon as my back is turned' – and she was right.

Some Friday nights my despairing parents and my older brothers would be roaming the streets looking for me. At midnight, my brothers would knock on the doors of Zan's. I'd dive under table nine, which was in the darkest corner, while Ted opened up – 'No, Jimmy's not here – haven't seen him all evening.'

And at three o'clock in the morning, I would walk the few hundred yards home with my winnings. Often I had cleaned someone out of their entire week's wages. I'd give them at least twenty-five per cent back – not because I felt sorry for them (I did, a little) but because I wanted them to play me the next week.

Mr Beatty even came to the snooker hall to watch me play, so he could get a handle on how to deal with me. He said he was impressed. 'You're very good, Jimmy. But, and this is important, you can't earn a living from playing snooker. School's important.'

I didn't tell him I had been earning hundreds of pounds – and squandering it. I promised to go to school and I might have gone once after that little chat. Mr Beatty despaired, especially when tests revealed that I couldn't read. I didn't care – I could tot up almost any sum in my head. I could understand a betting slip and I could count money. Barry Hearn, who became my manager for a while, was to later say in gambling parlance: 'Jimmy could work out a Yankee at the age of

twelve, but he couldn't tell you the capital of France –
which, of course, is Monte Carlo.'

In the end, putting his job on the line, Mr Beatty
dropped by Zan's and had a serious talk with me. I think
that the newspaper articles had convinced him that
snooker was very important to me and that I was taking
it just as seriously as another kid would take soccer or
chemistry lessons at school. Snooker *was* my education.

'Look, Jimmy, this can't go on. There's a problem.'

'Yes, sir,' I said. 'You're right. I've got to work on my
safety shots.'

'It's not that I personally have a problem with your
obvious love for this sport, I play a bit myself,' Mr Beatty
went on, 'but you have to be educated.'

'Yes, sir. I study the pros – I'm getting better all the
time.'

'Well, what shall we do about this, Jimmy?'

'Can't you change my birth certificate, sir, say I'm
older than I am?' I suggested, all wide-eyed innocence.

Mr Beatty hid a grin. 'Look, Jimmy, if you promise to
come to school in the mornings and put some effort into
your lessons, you can slip off in the afternoons. If you
repeat that, of course I shall deny it. I can't say fairer than
that. Is it a deal?'

'Oh yes, sir!' I assured him, amazed by this display of
common sense from a schoolteacher. It *was* a fair deal –
unfortunately, I was a hopeless case and soon slipped
very rapidly down the primrose path that they say leads
to hell. In my case – the very next day; but it led to a way
of life that has given me great enjoyment and a good
living. I think I was very lucky. Without my gift, and
having the opportunity to work at it, who knows how
things might have turned out?

One thing I still didn't have was my own cue, even
though I was winning so many amateur matches. It's no

good asking myself why I didn't just buy one when I was flush – a thirteen-year-old doesn't think of logical things like that.

Ken and Len were the managers of the snooker hall at the time. They worked shifts and I knew I could get round them to borrow someone's cue when the owner wasn't around. The cue I actually wanted to borrow was almost like a magic wand. It had a very long ferrule that seemed to do wonderful things. It belonged to Big John Nielsen, who was about twenty years older than me. John had an nice easy manner and was kind to kids like me and Tony. He knew that we usually didn't have a dime and would pay for the tables and give us a game, letting us share the magic cue.

I knew John's habits. He'd come in, play and then be gone. He wouldn't be back until the next day or whenever, so I would badger either Ken or Len to let me have the cue, although John had told them explicitly that no one was allowed to touch it when he wasn't there. It wasn't until fifteen years later that I owned up. I was sitting on my own outside the King's Head one day when I saw John walking by. I hailed him and we had a drink together, talking about old times.

I said, 'John, I'm going to tell you something I never dared tell you at the time. Remember that cue with the big long ferrule?'

John nodded. 'Best cue I ever had. There was something about it – I could do things with that that I couldn't do with anything else. I used to lock it in the office at Zan's – no one was allowed to touch it.'

I said, 'Well, whenever you wasn't about I used to borrow it – and that's what I learnt the game on – your cue.'

John started to laugh. 'I said it was magic! As it happens, my game's never been the same since I broke it.'

It was a sad story. John was playing for high stakes and nothing was going right. He kept on losing and in a split second of anger and frustration (I've mentioned before he's a big lad, very strong) he just whacked the cue across the edge of the table and it snapped in half. The half that snapped off circled up and away almost in slow motion and went spinning off somewhere in the dark. It was a tragic moment and he was sorry as soon as he had done it – so was I!

Stories like that remind me of why there is no point in being too protective. If you depend obsessively on your cue and something goes wrong, you can be devastated. I look after my cues but I have learned to accept it philosophically if something happens to them. (More of this later.) The following are examples of a near-miss and two obituaries: once, during a tournament, I lost my cue and retraced my footsteps to the twelve pubs I'd fallen in and out of the previous night. Fortunately I found it at the first one I tried. Joe O'Boye had his cue stolen. Alex Higgins had his favourite, the one with which he won his first world title in 1972, trodden on by a hotel porter and smashed. (Alex gave me one of his favourite cues when we were spending a lot of time together in the early 1980s. I can't remember if it was the one with which he won his second world cup, in 1982.)

The cue I used to win my World Amateur title in November 1980, I gave to a good friend Peewee, with whom I shared many adventures. He lost it when his car was stolen by joyriders. Just like the World Cup for football, the cue was tossed over a garden hedge as being of no value and later recovered – although it was never reported if a dog named Pickles (as with the World Cup) had snuffled it out. But my name was on the cue and eventually it found its way home to me. Now Peewee hadn't told me he had lost it and when it came back into my hands I thought he had been careless – so I gave it to a physically disabled young boy I'd befriended. Eventually Peewee got to hear about it – and was miffed. I offered him another cue with which I had won another title, but he wanted the World Amateurs cue. We fell out for a couple of months, but, very generously I must say, he forgave me, and when he discovered how much that cue means to the kid, he was as pleased as punch.

Steve Davis forbids anyone outside his immediate circle to touch his cue and rarely lets it out of his sight. If he is interrupted during an exhibition he immediately breaks the cue and slips it back into its case, almost ritualistically tamping it into place with a neatly folded green Matchroom towel. Steve's like that; organised, tidy, careful with his stuff.

Ideally, one would keep a cue in a shockproof, waterproof, flameproof metal box – sending it to a specialist for repair every six months or so, because the force with which the ball is struck warps and splits the wood. The action and feel is like the neck of a guitar. No wonder the old bluesmen gave names to their guitars, like Lucille – though I have never yet heard of a player naming their cue.

I can't even put a tip on a cue. Alex, on the other hand, prides himself on the fact that he can do everything himself. When he was at school as a boy he did woodwork (I was never there to do woodwork) although Alex says he was terrified of the lathe. However, he is very good at drilling inside and is able to improvise with equipment and materials when push comes to shove.

Alex would be a good person to have around if you were playing snooker in the middle of a desert, for example. There are people who, when they take a shot at the edge, damage the cue, breaking off the tip. Alex can take it all down and add another piece at the end. Because the strength must run all the way through the cue it has to be done properly. I can't say I have ever seen

Alex put this unusual ability into practice though – along with the rest of us, when needs must he buys a new cue or sends away for service.

People like Alex and Steve Davis have had only two or three cues in their lives. I can't remember how many cues I have had – dozens probably. Sometimes I'm lucky and get a good one that works for a while until it can't be repaired any more; at other times, I just can't get on with it. At the 1998 Welsh Open I felt very frustrated because the ferrule was loose and in the end I had to retire to wad a bit of paper and jam it in the end – this was during a world ranking event! The days when I could play a game with a walking stick are long gone – possibly because the tables are so fast now – or maybe it's to do with attitude and state of mind. The television cameras and the almost temple-like atmosphere during tournaments is a far cry from the rough and tumble of the scruffy old snooker halls where I prefer to play.

It would be ideal to be able to use several cues during a match, although of course it's impossible – you wouldn't get the flow or the continuity; you have to be fluid and keep moving around the table, clearing it; not prancing back and forth to your corner to change cues. Another consideration is that in the televised games there is no time to keep walking back to your corner to pull out the right cue, as if you're playing golf and have your bag standing there to choose from.

Every cue has a role, even the new big Berthas. Some cues – like John Nielsen's magic wand – will do anything – but most will do no more than seventy-five per cent of what is expected of them because there is no such thing as a multipurpose cue. It's a power tool and it's a caressing instrument as well. You need a cue to give you all these things to complement your skill. It's your inner self – your inner knowledge – that gives you the ability to play all shots with the same cue. You can have an eagle eye, but you need to have something else too, and it's called discipline. The cue is a discipline – the table is a discipline – the balls are a discipline. You have to know instinctively how they all work together. You have to love them all, like a chef loves food before he cooks it and while he cooks it.

Every table is different. To start with, not only have they made the pockets smaller and the balls more uniform and lighter, but they've changed the cloth on tournament tables. The cloth, or baize, used to be specially made felt, with a short pile, like velvet or like a carpet. Now it's woven flat, like furniture or curtain fabric. There is no pile to act as a drag on the ball for purchase and spin – which is why it is faster. You needed a heavier cue to drive a ball through the pile, so now they are lighter because weight is not needed as much. A lot of the shots have been taken out of the game by people who don't know anything about it. New people coming into the game will never know, and that's a shame.

I tell people, when they ask, that I am a purist. A strange kind of purist, because by that I mean when I have to choose between a tactical shot or one from the heart I will usually go for the heart. To me, that is stretching the limits and is pure. Letting go is a pure discipline, in thought; in sex; in invention; in spirit. In a way, you could say I have a great curiosity to see what will happen. Safety is an option I use more and more – but safety is boring. I think the audience, too, thrill to the unexpected, the dangerous play. It's what made players like Alex and me household names and so exciting to watch. Alex and I have debated this and, according to Alex, I can't be a snooker purist because I have never played billiards, as he has. Also, to be a purist you have to play to win – and shots from the heart don't always cut it. Now he tells me!

I met a legendary player once, someone acknowledged as the greatest billiard player in the world – Joe Davis. Tony Meo and I went to meet him when we were with Dodgy Bob. We were playing an exhibition in a private house, a gaming party really, where there were about thirty people betting thousands. Dodgy had told us to do our best, which was a bit silly because I always did my best. We played five frames of snooker, me and Meo. I made a 133 – Meo made a 118 – then Meo made a 90-odd – and I made a 70-odd. I finished off with another century. Now that's fantastic snooker anywhere, and for kids it was heroic.

Afterwards, when the great Joe Davis came across to talk to us, he was charming. But according to Dodgy, when he took him aside and said, 'Well, what do you think of my boys?' Joe Davis retorted, 'I'd send them back to school, they're a pair of wankers!'

Tony Meo was livid. It could be that this was Bob's way of getting us to practise more – but I don't think so. More likely, Joe Davis had lost a bundle.

When I was fourteen Dad arranged a charity exhibition match at his local working man's club, the United Services at Balham. Through Ron Gross, he booked star names like Alex Higgins, Terry Whitthread, Geoff Foulds and Patsy Houlihan. Alex had a habit of not showing up, and with the insurance for a no-show costing £40, Dad decided to book Willie Thorne for that amount which would ensure the show could go on if Alex didn't turn up. The others played for nothing, but this is no reflection on Willie – he had to come a long way. Tony Meo and I were also booked to play, and there was a full-blown referee and scorer. It was all very professional and we made £2000.

I was on tenterhooks, wondering if Alex Higgins would show up because he was such a brilliant player. I couldn't wait to watch him in action. He turned up and I beat him. As Forrest Gump once said, 'And that's all I have to say about that.' In fact, I was struck dumb.

Alex might have a baroque reputation, but he is extraordinarily polite. After the exhibition, when my dad was thanking him for coming, Alex said, 'It was my pleasure, Tom. You get loads of promising kids and some are more promising than others. Some burn out. But one like Jimmy shines.'

From that day Alex used to get in touch with Dad and say, 'Tom, I'm playing in Southend – could you get Jimmy down here? He can take over when I have a rest.'

To be invited to play with Alex Higgins on a regular basis was like a dream come true.

Dad bustled off to have a word with Mum, and she shook her head doubtfully, 'Well, Tommy, I don't know – Southend? You might break down. The van's playing up.'

'Oh Mum—!' I'd hop up and down (embarrassing), 'I'll go on the train!' (blackmail).

Dad would say, 'Don't you worry about that, Lil, I'll get the old van out, we'll get there. It's what the lad wants. He needs this kind of practice to make him good – to make him great.'

When we arrived at the exhibition, Alex would take me to one side and explain the terms in his high, light, Belfast brogue. He'd tell me that I could play five or six people during the interval, while he had a rest. It cost six or eight bob to play a frame. If I lost, they got their money back. If I won, I could keep it. Since I won nearly every frame, I usually ended up with about ten or twelve pounds, which I would always hand over to Mum. That was me, trying to be a good boy.

Most importantly, Alex played with me and one or two of the other promising kids, using us as sparring partners. Once when Dad was thanking Alex for the experience, I overheard Alex reply, 'This is someone out of the ordinary. Young Jimmy shows promise – and I like the person as well as the player. He's a nice kid.'

Over the years, Alex and I have often talked of the old days, and how important his encouragement was to youngsters like me. Alex was always willing to be kind to promising young players, because when he was a kid he was sickened slightly when he watched a couple of notable players who came over to Belfast and instructed the young players to smash the balls so they could show off their own prowess.

Alex said when he played as a young kid he always played a very open game – whereas these guys went over the top and ruined them. Alex thought people like me should be encouraged by a good example.

I learned technique from Alex, who was a great innovator at playing shots that people had never seen before, making the white balls do things that other people couldn't do. I have seen him standing with his cue almost vertical, looking for all the world like a matador. The pose, the dance, the spin and the recoil as he took his cue away fast and elegantly after playing a shot. Now *that* is art.

I wouldn't go as far as to say that I copied Alex's particular and inventive style because obviously I have my own way of doing things, although Alex has said that I have the perception to read the game the way he does and to make the white ball do pleasing things not only to my eye but to the spectator's eye. The reason you play any sport or game is because you get enjoyment and excitement out of it and it's the same for the spectators. It's the speed aspect as well. We are both fast thinkers and quick players and all these attributes and co-ordination and vision combine well.

*

Exhibitions and ordinary snooker hall matches can be far more exciting than competitive tournaments because there's no formality, and the standard of snooker is often better: Alex reckons that he's left a lot of his best play on the practice table. There are a few matches that I rate as my personal best. One was the semi-final against Alex that I lost in 1982. The UK Championship was the best professional match that I ever won, against John Parrott in 1992. But the best match of all – one I will never forget, and nor will the spectators – was against Charlie Poole in Earlsfield.

Charlie wrote my first snooker book (a how-to manual) and he is one of the most fantastic players you have ever seen in your life. I rate Charlie Poole, Patsy Houlihan and Alex Higgins as the three greatest snooker players I've ever seen – and two of them didn't even play professionally. (Hoolihan did for a short while but even he doesn't really count that.) The reason I rate them so highly is because they were potters and entertainers. They didn't care about timing a game – safety shots were too boring for them. Play to win – that is to say, beat the opposition.

Anyway, in my most memorable game, someone took me from Zan's to play Charlie for a fiver a frame. We finished up eight frames each and we stopped. Apparently, the people who watched it said it was the greatest match they'd ever seen in their lives. There were balls going everywhere, in the lampshades, off the cushions.

I've had great times in front of thousands of people; but those three – Charlie Poole '77; Alex '82; Parrott '92 – are the games that stick in my mind.

SIX

LENNY AND THE FRUIT MACHINES

I've known Lenny – Leonard Alfred Cain; to give him his full name – since I was about twelve. Older than me, he was a Wandsworth chap who came to my neck of the woods for the snooker. In fact, most players do roam about a bit from club to club, looking for a bit of action. It's a bit like the Wild West on a Saturday night when a hired gun rides into town.

What appealed to me first was Lenny's sense of humour. He could talk fast, in rhyming slang, still does, and keep the jokes and yarns spinning out for hours. What besotted me was his talent at fiddling fruit machines, taught to him by an Irishman known as Moby Dick. I didn't look on it as stealing because the machines were all rigged anyway. Money for old rope, we used to say when we watched the men come round to empty them.

I was fast at working out odds and very quickly calculated what the odds were on winning the jackpot, let alone anything else, so by helping myself, I felt I was redressing the balance. It wasn't even like conning the establishment where the fruit machines were kept, because they didn't make anything like the owners. That is no excuse – but, as a kid, I looked on it as a great prank, not a lot different from scrumping a farmer's apples. This was fun I wanted in on, and I badgered Lenny to teach me the tricks of the trade – he was the sorcerer and I was his more than willing apprentice.

I didn't do it all the time; mostly I did it to get a few quid to hustle on the snooker table. I was proud of the fact that I could get maybe five or ten pounds out of the fruit machines and end up with a couple of hundred crisp notes in my waistcoat pocket to take home – so it was like seed money to me. Lenny and I worked as a team. He'd been doing it for seven years, but with me egging him on, we both perfected the technique and kicked the ante up a few rungs.

The method was a coin on a piece of cotton, wrapped around your finger just once – three times around and if anyone approached, you couldn't let go and were caught red-handed, your fingers swollen where the thread had cut in. So once around the joint, and you lowered the coin until it clicked, pulled the coin back up and bingo!

As soon as anyone approached and asked, 'Hey, what's happening here, mate?' you'd let go – the coin and string would drop into the innards of the machine – and you'd be out the door.

The fruit machine designers were always trying to keep ahead of us, trying to make the things foolproof. With the newer machines you had to go in through the side, actually drilling a tiny little hole and inserting a piece of metal coat hanger that you'd heated up with a gas lighter. You'd slide in the hot rod and feel the gates open, one by one – and bingo, again. I wasn't into that. Too risky. You could be standing there, drilling away – and a drill, a hole and a length of red-hot coathanger are a bit hard to explain away.

Some things bring the memories flooding back. This geezer we know, he is the absolute business – he drives you nuts because he is so unreliable, but never mind. Anyway, it was at the Rose and Crown, down Wandsworth High Street. He's phoned Lenny up, 'Get in there, sharpish,' he says. 'There's a good fruit machine, lovely position,' and so on. I'm not saying he set us up, but he was a suspect because it did turn to be a set-up.

Still, we went along and sussed out the place. All I had to do was make out I was putting records on the jukebox and at the same time block Lenny in so no one could see what was going on. But the management were wise to us. They snuck up on Lenny from the rear and in his ear someone bellowed, 'Got you!'

Quick as a flash, Lenny lets the thread go, straight in the machine – whoosh – and there's nothing to see. Just at that moment 'Money Honey' by the Bay City Rollers dropped on to the turntable and blasted out all over the place while I collapsed in giggles.

Often, we went further afield, and combined the fruit machines for a laugh and a snooker exhibition for the business. On one occasion, I went to Herne Bay with Lenny, Tony Meo and another chum, name of Joe le Boc. After playing the exhibition that night, we wound up in a squalid little bed and breakfast with grubby sheets and fleas. In the morning we went out to get a few quid, checking out the pubs and a café, where we spotted a fruit machine in a good position.

Joe and Tony were going to do this first one for practice because it was almost foolproof, while Lenny and I kept a lookout. From the back we heard a strangled squawk from Joe, like something had gone wrong. I think he got the thread wrapped around everything in sight.

'I can't do it,' Tony hollered as he rushed past us, white about the gills and acting as if he was about to be nicked and banged up for ten years.

In the end we agreed that we would split up. I would maintain my winning partnership with Lenny, while the novices, Tone and Joe le Boc would stick together to sink or swim. We'd do as many or as few fruit machines as we wanted, no recriminations. By lunch time, Lenny and I had taken about £40, a nice day's money back then and the duo of Tony and Joe a woeful tenner.

When we met up for a drink and to compare notes, Tony said, 'It's no good, I can't work it.'

'Never mind, mate,' Lenny said kindly, 'It's all just a laugh, innit? It's no big deal.'

I can't believe the laugh we had down in Yarmouth, when we went to an exhibition at the police ball. Lenny and I were both off our heads, on the town all day, doing the fruit machines, then jiving away at the ball, surrounded by about five hundred policemen that night.

We went right over the top, doping the fruit machines, which was handy because we were getting a few quid (about £90 each before 3 in the afternoon); then it was time for a spot of gambling from 3–5.30. From 5.30 to 11 at night we carried on the assault. We made about £320 a night, proper money. The only thing that really screwed us up was that we didn't stop.

We were arrested once not far from Tooting, of all places. It started off with us acting out the Artful Dodger and Fagin roles, teaching a few rats to do the fruit machines. Whenever we needed dosh, we'd send them out and, good as gold, they'd come back with the loot – just like Fagin's gang.

We were sitting in the pub, counting up our two-bob bits, when someone reported us – no surprise, really, blatant we were. Coins were rolling everywhere as we stuffed the money in our pockets and made a run for it. We got caught. If we had fallen in the river we would have drowned with the sheer weight of the metal. Instead, we were stuffed inside a police van that was so old it barely made it back to the nick without falling to bits.

The police were convinced we had done a gas meter – which was a charge of breaking and entering. Without telling our parents, they kept us inside for ages while they hunted around the district looking for a burglary that had never happened, trying to find a crime that fitted that mountain of two-bob bits. Eventually, the next day, Mum heard the news on that mysterious South London grapevine and shot over to the police station, screaming, 'Have you got my son?'

As soon as I heard her, I started to moan and groan, 'Ooh, don't hit me! Ooh, me head!'

'I'll bleedin' kill you,' Mum raged at the station sergeant.

Since no burglaries were reported in the neighbourhood, they had to let us go.

There was always something happening. We had a mate, Charlie, who, like Lenny and Victor, lived with his nan. One of her lodgers, a strange old geezer we called Night Gallery, had a smelly horrible old parrot, worth a fortune. When we were round there visiting Charlie, we used to look at the mangy thing and discuss selling it. Honest, that's the way we thought. That's what went on in our minds. Buy, sell, thieve, spend, drink, gamble, lie, hide . . . we were proper little toerags. Many a time we were inches away from stuffing that parrot in a pillowcase and nipping round to the local pet shop, but decency and a sentimental love of all living creatures prevailed.

Lenny's nan was an absolute diamond, who'd fetch us cups of tea, sandwiches, anything when I dropped by. I remember a time when I had stopped off on my way to an exhibition and I left my togs behind on Lenny's nan's sofa. At home they were frantic because they imagined – rightly as it turned out – that I had forgotten the date.

Mum went looking for me in every place she could think of, and somehow she got hold of Lenny's address and arrived on the doorstep, asking if I was there.

'No, love,' said Lenny's nan nervously, feeling guilty. She felt she ought to be saying we *were* in because my mother looked so anxious – but we weren't. I was such a scallywag, not stealing from cars like some of my mates, but into all kinds of mischief. I was far worse than Lenny.

By now, Mum was ensconced in an armchair, drinking a cup of tea. 'And by the way, I've been meaning to say, but that Lenny of yours, he's a terrible influence on my Jimmy,' said Mum. The fact that she had never actually met Lenny was neither here nor there.

'Oh, is that right?' said Lenny's nan, not sure where this conversation was leading. Actually, she loved me and always tried to protect me – but choosing which side to take, mine, or her grandson's, was perplexing.

'Jimmy's got to go to an exhibition and we're all out combing the streets for him,' continued Mum. 'Are you sure he didn't say where he was going?'

'No, he's not here – but his clothes are, will that do?' said Lenny's nan, not realising she was falling into a trap.

As soon as Mum heard that, she was even more convinced that I was around, lying low. I'm sure she didn't believe a word the poor woman was telling her. In the end she took all the clothes and stormed off to catch the bus to the snooker hall in Wandsworth High Street where Lenny usually hung out. She walked into the snooker hall and confronted Jock, the owner, demanding to know if he had seen me.

Now Jock had a kind of Scots accent, although he hadn't ever been to Scotland to the best of my knowledge. 'Och, no, I haven't seen Jimmy for days,' said Jock.

'What about Lenny Cain? Is he here?' demanded Mum.

Jock nodded across the room, 'Yon's Lenny Cain.'

Mum marched over to him and, hands on hips, she was into him – *you've took my son! You've done this and you've done that!* concluding with the usual speech that all mums have learnt by heart, about their boy being led astray.

The man she was wading into was about fifty-five years old, which in her eyes, made matters far, far worse. She wasn't to know that this was Lenny Cain's dad, same name, and he – not knowing that he was the subject of mistaken identity – wasn't about to take that from any-body, not even from a tiny little woman he'd never met before in his life. All of a sudden here he was, getting accused of all that Lenny was supposed to have done – but hadn't – because no one ever led me on.

Very peeved, chin out, he snarled, 'Just who do you think you are talking to?'

Mum continued with her verbal assault, most of it quite insulting. Well, how was she to know?

Raising his voice to a bellow, Lenny Cain Senior barked, 'You've got the wrong feller, woman!'

'What?' said Mum, refusing to back down. 'Are you or are you not Lenny Cain?'

He raised his voice, 'Jock! tell her! Mark her card!'

Across the room, Jock was laughing fit to bust. 'Och, yon's Lenny Cain, right enough,' he hooted.

Now Lenny Cain Senior had just divorced his wife and he didn't want a earful of this. He yelled, 'I've just got rid of petticoat junction. I don't stand bollocks from women!'

Fortunately, some kind soul took pity on Mum and explained that this was Lenny Cain Senior and that the whereabouts of Lenny the Younger was a complete mystery, as it usually was. That completely took the wind out of my poor mum's sails, and she returned home in the vain hope that I would turn up in time for the exhibition.

The following night, having lost Lenny along the way, but not having returned home, I went to the Pot Black Snooker Hall in Clapham Junction. Steve Davis was at one table along with Tony Meo and a few of the others. I started playing Meo on number two table and later I spotted Lenny come in and go behind the ramp. Apparently, he was out to con a Greek he had fallen out with. Not a bad con – just a practical joke involving a Swan Vestas matchbox, and three matches.

Lenny was setting the Greek up nicely when my frame finished. I wandered across to see what Lenny was up to. 'What's that?' I asked, nosy as ever, watching Lenny arranging the matches. (Don't ask me to explain exactly how this is done, but it's all clever stuff!)

He said, 'Nothing. Don't bother about it – go on back to your table.'

But I was into everything and continued to interfere. 'How does it work?' I persisted, convinced I was missing out on something.

In the end, Lenny just sighed and gave up. 'All right – don't blame me,' he said. 'Here—' and he pushed the matchbox over to me. 'But you're only allowed to use one finger.'

I karate-chopped the horizontal match as directed and there was a whoosh! as all the matches ignited. Burning sulphur scorched my hand. I hopped up and down with the pain.

'See – it's your own fault,' Lenny said, aggrieved. 'You wouldn't leave well alone. I was out to get this geezer here—' and he glared at the Greek.

The next day I was back at the snooker hall, playing the Ginger Nut – as we affectionately call Steve Davis –

a massive bandage wrapped around my thumb, like
something from a *Carry On* film – and did they all laugh!

Jock's dead now. He was a strange man, always starting
his sentences off with, 'I've got something tae say to ye,
mate.' Once, when I needed a lot of money in a hurry, I
asked him to lend me fifty quid. He said, 'Och nae, I
couldna do that, mate,' so I forgot it. Moments later he
sidled up to me and muttered, 'I've got something tae
say to ye, mate. Come round to my house and I'll see
what I can do.'

I went round his house, and he pushed five grand into
my hand. I was astonished. I didn't need that much, but
I kept it anyway – never look a gift horse in the mouth. I
paid back every penny, as he knew I would.

Jock owned about forty houses and a soap factory.
He'd go there all week, and every weekend come to the
Wandsworth club. He was a great snooker player and
liked to drink large amounts of scotch while he played.
Sometimes when he approached you and opened his
mouth to mutter, 'I've got something tae say to ye, mate,'
the fumes would make you reel. He also smoked
untipped fags, which has some relevance to this story.

One night during a big match, Lenny said, 'Jock's
going to explode in a minute.'

I said, 'And why is that?'

Lenny grinned conspiratorially and touched his finger
to his nose. He had put a small firework, a banger, in a
tipped cigarette he had just offered to Jock. Lenny had
really taken his time with the booby-trapped cigarette. It
was a work of art, one that looked completely normal.
But Jock didn't like tipped cigarettes – so he snapped the
tip off (that end that doesn't have the banger in it) and
put the fag in his mouth – the end with the banger –
walked about, with it dangling as usual. Jock always
played with a fag dangling and he would never take it out

of his mouth until it was burnt right down, tight as a duck's arse. He was on the pink in this competition – and just as he lined up his cue, the fag exploded in his mouth.

He dropped the cue and chased Lenny around the table, yelling, 'I'll have you, Lenny Cain!', black stuff all over his lips and up his nose.

As soon as he could stop laughing, Lenny said, 'It ain't all that bad!'

Jock replied, 'I've got something tae say to ye, mate—'

I'm also a great one for practical jokes, the more infantile, the better. Lenny and I had a favourite one that nearly always worked and regularly had us in stitches. We were on the train, the Intercity 125, straight through to Sheffield, and standing in the bar, drinking vodka.

People kept on walking through and the doors kept opening and closing, going swish, swish, swish, driving us nuts. One waiter was the worst culprit. Each time he came by with his trolley, he kept warbling in a prissy little voice, 'Do you mind not standing there—' when it was obviously the only place to stand.

'We're just having a drink,' I said.

'You're not supposed to drink standing in the gang-way,' he replied, snidely.

As soon as the waiter was out of earshot I produced a nice crisp tenner and grinned at Lenny. 'Have you got a piece of string?'

Like a boy scout, Lenny always travels with a pocketful of junk. As he says, you never know what you might need. We fastened the tenner to the string, and when the waiter was on his reverse sweep, Lenny casually dropped the note in the gangway right behind his legs. Sure enough, the waiter copped it as he walked by with the trolley.

Lenny whispered to me, 'I don't know how he's going to go for it, Jimmy, but he's going to make his move.'

The waiter walked past, then he doubled back and swooped like a rusty ballerina. Lenny quickly whisked the tenner away.

Then he's on the floor, the waiter – he's chasing it – he's banged into the door, he's lost the plot completely. The door has opened up ahead of him and he's fallen through the gangway. I was doubled up laughing as Lenny called out, 'What's happening down there?'

We tricked another pal, Lofty, in the snooker hall with the same tenner – when a tenner was a tenner and worth something – which I dropped half sticking out behind the cue-rest in front of my seat, between my feet. Lenny put the note on a very long piece of cotton and waited at a distance. Lofty was at the table when he spotted it. His game went to pieces as he was torn between winning the frame or diving on the tenner before someone else grabbed it. Greed won. Soon, as we knew he would, Lofty made his move, casually indicating that he needed a cue rest – the very one that was under my seat, ignoring the one hanging under the table.

Just like the waiter, but with less camp grace, Lofty dived – and Lenny jerked the string. The note went floating up in the air and off – and Lofty was gone chasing it as if it was a kite-tail. He didn't stop to wonder why it was on the move, they don't; they never do – nor why I was practically on the floor, howling with laughter.

A group of us, Kenny Harvey, Knockin' Norman, Lenny and I all drove up to Manchester to do an exhibition in Bernard Manning's snooker hall which is actually run by his son – yes, there is a Bernie Junior. Bernard – who has his own comedy clubs elsewhere – set the tone of the evening by telling a couple of right blinding jokes, which he made up about my exploits, but it was all in good fun. At the end of the night, we were all having a steady drink in the bar when I decided it was time to leave. At the time

I was managed by Barry Hearn, and, as usual for events like this, he put his white limousine and driver, Robbo, at my disposal. While the car had a lot of useful gadgets one can't possibly live without, the one thing it did not possess was a bar with an ice bucket.

'Hang about, Jimmy,' Knockin' Norman said, 'we can't drive all that way back to the Smoke without ice for the vodka, now be fair, mate.'

'I ain't gonna chore the ice bucket,' I said, which in Queen's English means I don't take things to which I'm not entitled.

But someone filled it with ice and took it off the counter of the bar anyway, a nice stainless-steel ice bucket worth a bob or two but certainly not rare nor valuable. As we piled into the limo and the motor was fired, Bernard Manning came running out of the snooker hall – though, to be fair, it could have been his son. It was late at night, you understand, and I wasn't directly involved with the removal of the ice bucket. Anyway, whoever it was, Senior or Junior, they stood in front of the limo, arms outstretched, almost being mowed down beneath the wheels. As soon as the car stopped, they dived head first through the window and snatched the ice bucket, complete with ice. It would have been embarrassing if we could have stopped laughing.

SEVEN

MAUREEN

When a reporter asked me how it felt to break records, to do a ton at the snooker table at the age of thirteen, I made some kind of polite response. But when she asked me about girlfriends, I looked at her, confused, and mumbled, 'Eh? What?' – because I was baffled by the question. Girls didn't figure in my life at all, except as giggly little things who sat clumped together in the classroom that I rarely honoured with my presence.

I must have been a fast developer, because barely six months later and certainly before I had attained the grand old age of fourteen, I met Maureen Mockler. Maureen wasn't the girl next door – she was the girl who lived in the next street. She was a good friend of Tony and his childhood sweetheart, Denise, who he was to marry quite soon – but for some reason I had never met Maureen.

I was sitting in the local burger bar with Tony and Denise when Denise began to make faces and wave to somebody outside. I turned my head and saw a girl with shining blonde hair looking in through the window signalling back.

'Who's that?' I said.

'My mate, Maureen,' Denise informed me. 'You'd like her, Jimmy, she's as daft as you are.'

'Yeah, Jimmy – ask her in,' Tony grinned, one arm draped along the bench seat where Denise was sitting. 'Go on, she's all right.'

With the others egging me on, I slouched nonchalantly over to the door and stepped outside. I saw that she was even prettier close up, with a light dusting of freckles, a smile that lit up her face and cornflower blue eyes.

'Hello, you're Jimmy, aren't you?' she said. 'I've seen you on telly.'

'Yeah, they interviewed me on *Nationwide*,' I said. 'Did you like it?'

'Oh yes, I thought you looked very nice. Lovely.'

We stood there a moment longer, while I hunted around for something to say. Although I was streetwise I had never really talked to a girl before – at least not a girl I fancied the look of – and I wanted to appear cool. Then I remembered what I had been sent outside to do. 'Denise said, are you coming in?'

'Well, all right then. Just for a minute,' she said.

A day or two later I bumped into her again at the end of the street and marvelled to myself that I had never seen her around – and now, here she was again, twice in a couple of days. I asked, 'What are you doing?' – which, down our way, really meant, 'Will you go out with me?'

We stood and chatted. I told her I was off down to Zan's to practise. At that time I was leading a schizophrenic existence, hustling all over and getting into no end of scams – then dressing up in the dinner jacket and bow tie that Mum had bought for me at Burton's and playing dead straight in various amateur tournaments where the prize money was often as little as £10 for coming top of the league. It never even covered expenses.

Always the gentleman, I gave Maureen my phone number. 'Ring me at the weekend,' I said casually. 'Maybe we could go out to the pictures or something.'

'All right, Jimmy. That'll be nice,' Maureen said.

'I'll see you, then,' and I sauntered off like Joe Cool.

She telephoned on the Friday night and Mum picked up the receiver. The conversation went something like this:

'Hello?'

'Can I talk to Jimmy?'

'And who might you be, then?'

'Maureen.'

'Maureen who?'

'I'm a friend of Jimmy's.'

'My Jimmy doesn't know any girls. What do you want him for?'

That was enough – Maureen wasn't going to talk to a combative mother who wanted to know the ins and out of everything and she hung up.

Bristling all over, Mum slammed the receiver down and shouted upstairs to me that some rude little cow had hung up on her. 'Maureen she said her name was. I'll give her what for if she ever calls again!'

I bumped into Maureen again next afternoon and I didn't let on that I knew about the phone call. But Maureen told me. 'I telephoned you and your mum gave me a very hard time,' she said indignantly. 'All I did was ask for you and instead I got the third degree.'

'Yeah, it's all my fans,' I lied. 'Ever since being on the telly, they've been calling. Mum's been trying to keep them away from me, know what I mean?'

'Well, just you tell your mum that I'm not a fan,' Maureen said, with that fiery Irish spirit I was to get to know so well. 'And if I want to talk to you, I will.'

I grinned. 'You'll like my mum when you get to know her better. She just thinks she's looking out for me.'

Changing the subject, I asked if she wanted to go to the pictures.

'Okay, if you like,' said Maureen.

'How about tonight?' I asked.

When we met outside the cinema, she was wearing a T-shirt and jeans and looked just right, nice and casual. I was glad she hadn't dressed up, even though I had made a sort of effort and had my least creased jacket and a clean shirt on. It was cold when we came to walk home and Maureen shivered. I took my coat off and gave it to her. I think that was when she decided about me.

I was not yet fourteen – she was a year older, and yet, in many ways, I was quite worldly. But wise? Probably not. There was something about Maureen that made me feel just right being with her. For her part, she said that I handled myself like Tony Meo, and, by that, she meant I acted like someone older than my years. Well, I'd been around, I told her, I'd seen a lot of stuff. I don't think she realised exactly what I meant – nor what she was letting herself in for; and when she found out the half of it, she entered into the spirit of the thing and went with me everywhere.

Tony, of course, always looked dapper and stylish – while I was a scruff. Seriously, I was a scruff. Having asked Maureen to go with me to the church disco one night, I thought I should wear something better than a pair of dirty old sneakers. I'd left it a bit late to go shopping, but the matter of a decent pair of shoes somehow became of paramount importance and I decided to borrow a pair from Tony. Locally, he was Mr *Saturday Night Fever* personified, king of the disco. He had all the right gear, too.

I went round to his house and knocked on the door. Mrs Meo, a volatile Italian lady, asked me in and I explained my mission.

'Hey, Tone, lend me a pair of your shoes, mate. I'm going to a disco with Maureen.'

Tony looked pained as his eyes fell on the disgusting objects I wore on my feet. 'I can't lend you my shoes – you'll ruin them!'

'No, I won't. I'll bring 'em back, immaculate, I promise,' I wheedled.

'No, I can't do it,' Tony said.

'Hell, Tony, they're only shoes and you've got millions,' I persisted, affronted that he was turning me, his best mate, down.

But Tony was adamant. He loved his forty-four pairs of shoes, all polished in neat rows in his cupboards, with his rows of immaculate jackets and nearly-new shirts hanging above. Then his mother, who was a demon knitter who turned out wonderful sweaters, joined in excitedly, saying her boy looked after his clothes and why should he lend them out to a street urchin like me? She had a point and made it a joke, but by then I was upset.

'Well, stuff your shoes – who needs them?' I said belligerently and shoved at the door. There was a slightly broken pane of glass in the frame and my hand shot through, cutting my finger to the bone and spraying blood everywhere. Poor Mrs Meo. She felt really bad, even though I admitted it was my fault, as it was.

So with stitches in my hand and blood all over my sneakers, I took Maureen out dancing. She didn't seem bothered by the footwear and taught me the right steps. I was having a great time, thinking that this dancing lark was a bit of all right and maybe I'd try it again next week when, to my absolute total mortification, Mum came to fetch me home.

'It's past your bedtime, Jimmy,' she said, glaring at Maureen. 'Don't you have a home to go to, miss?' she added for good measure. I could have died.

When I saw Maureen again, she asked if my mum had thought I was in bad company, going out with her. Our parents didn't know each other even though we were only in the next street. Perhaps if they had been friends, Mum would have been kinder to Maureen. She took to her eventually, but it took Mum a while to realise that my regard for Maureen was a two-way street and that, young as we both were, I wanted to be with Maureen as much as she wanted to be with me.

At least, I did whenever I wasn't with my friends. I have to be honest – in those days my mates nearly always came first. It was more than peer pressure. It was *Men Behaving Badly*; it was the Knights of the Round Table; it was the *Three Musketeers* (or more), one for all and all for one. Except for Tony, because he wouldn't lend me his dancin' boots. No, seriously, pick any combination – and none of them included girls. I didn't really understand what this laddish thing was – and most women never do get to understand it at all. It's just always been like that. It's nothing like the friendship women have for each other. The relationship men have with their best mates has its own code, its own rules. Mostly it's about keeping face. This has brought Maureen and me to the brink many many times.

Maureen soon became a permanent part of my life though it was to be some time before we lived together. After I stopped working with Dodgy Bob, Maureen would come with me on the train, all over the country. It was different going with her, more like seeing all the places through a soft-tinted lens. We'd go to far-flung places like Manchester or Grimsby and stay the night in some inexpensive little bed and breakfast, where we'd snuggle up and watch the television until dawn.

'This is lovely, it's really nice, Jimmy,' Maureen used to say as we walked around, taking in the sights and sounds, as I checked out the location of the snooker hall. Maureen went into hundreds of seedy dives with me, although, as a rule, they weren't a place for women in those days. I'd grown up in the dark and thought nothing of the squalor. The halls were grubby, the toilets were grim and the language and drinking strong. But she'd sit, quiet as a mouse to one side, and people got used to seeing her with me. I'd give her my money to hold, and my coat, and tell her to be ready to run if I gave the signal. She looked after my cue case and she looked after me. We were like Bonnie and Clyde, only we weren't robbing banks. We were just having fun together.

EIGHT

ROWING TO TASMANIA

Henry West was my first real manager. I know that Dodgy Bob described himself as that when my career started to take off – and, to be fair, it was Bob who took me over to Ron Gross's club, which in turn got me on the amateur circuit and legitimised me; but he was not what I call a manager. To start with, I think he took ninety per cent of what I made.

Henry West, on the other hand, was a loud, jovial pikey, who wore more gold than Cleopatra. When Tony Meo and I first met him he used to go into the pubs that had pool tables, take out the existing tables and dump them on the pavement or the back yard and replace them with his own. When the publicans confronted him, he would face them down. 'I've just taken over,' he'd say. 'Get on the blower and tell them to come and take their tables away – you won't be needing them, will you?'

To understand the business side of this, it is necessary to say that pool tables and fruit machines all had meters you had to feed and were usually supplied to pubs by an outside company. In a way, it was nothing to the publican who actually supplied the table or machine – he kept them in there as a service to his customers and made what he made – as simple as that. Usually, they wanted as little trouble as possible, and let the sharks who swam in those seas fight it out with each other. It was a dirty and competitive business and you had to be tough to survive in it.

Henry had been a boxing promoter. An ex-boxer, he understood the angles and could look after himself, and, I reckoned, he could look after me. Tony Meo signed with him and he had John Virgo and Patsy Fagan, too. Over a drink, Ron Gross once told me, 'When Patsy first came over from Dublin, he was only sixteen years old and broke. Once or twice, for a fiver, he was a decoy for the three card trick merchants in Oxford Street that caught all the tourists. He was the one behind them that burnt their ear with the cigarette in his mouth. When they jumped and turned to see what was happening, his partner had the cards swapped.'

I much admired Patsy, who was UK Champion in 1978, Champion of Champions at Wembley and rated as one of the top players in the country. I was sad when, after a car accident, his nerves were shattered. He got what he described as 'the yips' and quite literally froze when he went to hit a ball. It's been over twelve years since he last played.

'Jimmy wanted me to manage him,' Henry said at the time. 'He was just fourteen, but he was gambling and drinking like a fish. I said, "Sorry son, you're not on." He begged and begged me to change my mind. "I'll be good, honest gov'nor," he said.' Henry also used to enjoy telling reporters about how he was home once and there was a knock at the door. It was three heavy-looking blokes demanding £200 that I was supposed to have owed them from a card game. 'I pointed to my nose,' said Henry, 'and said, "You can take it out of there if you think you're hard enough. Either that, or I'll have you nicked for allowing a boy his age to gamble." I never heard from them again.'

All this kind of stuff was good copy for the sports-writers. Henry, one of the most colourful people in the business, didn't care if it wasn't always exactly the truth; he was doing what he knew best – promoting. He and his wife, Jackie, ran the business from home and called us 'The Family'. They impressed on me that I *was* family, so it was up to me to support the others and show a united front, just like me and my mates, type of thing. All for one and one for all. This, I understood. John Virgo, in fact, lived with Henry and Jackie for some years. Later The Family grew into the 'Magnificent Seven' as more players signed up.

Before joining Henry I used to go to the Pontins Summer Festivals, which were put on partly as enter-tainment for the holiday-makers, and also to fill the chalets, because thousands of players from all over Britain turned up, pushing and jostling for position. It was a very smart move on Pontins' part, soon copied by Warners and Butlins. Pontins used to pay a handful of top pros as a lure, and all the unseeded ones paid to have a go at playing them. When you registered, your name was put on a list so you had a rough idea of the day you were supposed to show up – but no time was set down, since there were only about twenty numbered tables and you never knew how long a match would last. You were called twice and if you weren't there, you were scratched, so you had to turn up. It was worse than rush hour at Waterloo Station. Everyone would be milling about on a kind of gallery or cakewalk, where the officials sat, that had wide stairs leading down to the actual playing area. As soon as a table was free the registrar would call out, 'Tony Meo!' – 'Yes!' – 'Jimmy White!' – 'Yep!' – 'Table 3!' – and off we'd go. You could only get sixty or seventy people round a table – and everybody wanted to be round ours. It was like a rugby scrum, and often we would have to stop until the officials made the crowd stand back so we could actually use the cue. I always felt embarrassed for the players who only had two or three people watching them.

Nobody wanted the infamous table seven, because when it rained, the roof leaked on it. When the balls were hit fast, they planed through the baize sending up a spray of water. Rumour had it that if a window were left open, passing ducks would spot the emerald green bog and land for a swim, or sometimes a couple of robins and a blackbird were spotted having an early morning splash and looking for worms down the pockets before the players arrived.

We were in a very vulnerable position on the tables down below, and were lucky that none of the mob up on the cakewalk got so drunk or disgusted that they would chuck empty bottles down on us. I remember playing Kirk Stevens once in an exhibition in Scotland, when some wee Jock threw a pint glass from the balcony. It landed on the blue spot and exploded like a bomb. Broken glass flew everywhere, ripping the cloth. That was the end of that exhibition. The place erupted and we made one of the fastest exits ever, barely escaping being torn limb from limb. There is nothing like a drunken Gorbels mob, baying for blood. It's like *Braveheart* on Tennents.

But Prestatyn was always a lot of fun. Alex Higgins was there one year, livid because he hadn't been invited. He turned up as a non-invitee professional – and he won, beating Terry Griffiths in the final. Everyone was in the bar, having a sing-song and leaning on a splendid grand piano played by Con Dunne's twin brother, Richie, who is a good pub-type pianist. There was Alex, Alex's sisters were over from Belfast, everyone singing away, having a right old time. Then Ron Gross got up and started to sing

– and believe me, Ron can't sing. All of a sudden, as if in protest, the piano collapsed, all four legs splaying out like a dead elephant. Everyone was still singing, Richie was still playing. The next night, the piano was upright – with chains all around it protecting it from the barbarian hordes.

Another time, Ron was there, due to play in the fourth or fifth round of the tournament and dying for a drink – but it was ten a.m. and the bar didn't open until eleven. Ron needed a drink because he got the shakes. Another snooker player, 'Lager' Bill Werbinuik, needed about eighteen pints of lager a day to keep his hands steady. Ask those Harley Street specialists. Even the WPBSA conceded that this is a medical condition. Ron knew it was hopeless even attempting to play like that, so he tried to delay things while his enormously understanding wife, Betty, actually walked all the way into Prestatyn to the off-licence there, just to buy him a flat pint of whisky.

Then she walked all the way back because she didn't drive and there were no buses. Ron hadn't been able to delay matters and the game was in progress. As she walked through the door clutching the bottle in a brown paper bag, he succeeded in potting the last black – and the bar opened. Ron was astonished that she had walked six miles just for him.

After winning the UK Amateur, Henry entered me for the World Amateur title, which that year was being held at Launceston in Tasmania. We had to qualify at the Home International Amateur Series in Prestatyn, in which I was playing for England; so once again I headed for Rhyl and the North Welsh coast that by now I was very familiar with.

Henry gave me one word of advice before I left London. 'Don't drink too much,' he said. 'They don't like it and they'll be watching you.' He particularly singled out the head of the Amateur body, Bill Cottier, as being the man I should be aware of. 'He can make you or break you,' Henry warned, 'so watch it, maintain a low profile, keep your head down – and keep out of the bar.'

Winning the World Amateur title was very important to me. I had promised myself that I would capture all the amateur titles I could before turning professional. I felt so hot and shining at the time, I really felt that I could have won the world professional if I had gone for it right that minute. I was invincible. It seemed I could do no wrong on the table. But I thought I had plenty of time ahead of me and wanted the hat-trick.

'Henry, I won't touch a drop,' I solemnly promised him before catching the train to North Wales, leaving Maureen in London so I could concentrate on the job in hand.

So, we were at the bar, Joe O'Boye and I, having just a half of lager, with our dress suits on, waiting to be called for our first match. Now Joe O'Boye, who was the current holder of the world amateur title, was a famous drinker in the snooker world, and I wasn't far behind, despite my youth; but I had remembered my promise to Henry and was being good. I was lifting the glass to my lips when behind me I heard Bill Cottier's booming voice, 'That's it! – you should be ashamed of yourself, Jimmy White! You won't be playing today.'

I turned around and tried to explain that we had only just got there, and it was only lager, but Bill, a high-ranking Liverpool policeman, was adamant.

'Oh well, if we're not playing we might as well relax and enjoy ourselves,' said Joe, and ordered two quadruple vodkas and orange.

'Cheers!' I said, knocking mine back and ordering two more.

Three hours later, at about nine o'clock that night, long after most games are well on the way to conclusion,

Bill came and found me. 'Jimmy, you're on. Table number 9.'

Too stunned to talk, almost too drunk to move, I gazed at him through bleary eyes and seized hold of the bar so I wouldn't fall down.

'Well, get a move on with it, you're playing against Wales. They're waiting for you,' said Bill and stalked off.

'Wales? Do I know him?' I said. I took a hesitant step or two, discovered that the floor didn't sway too much, and made my way to the right table, by the grace of God and tried and tested pub skills. The balls were set up and winking at me. Shakily, I took hold of my cue and made a 59 break. 'Not doing too bad, Jimmy me lad,' I told myself, before collapsing to the floor like a sack of potatoes. I hauled myself up by grabbing at a pocket, where I remained despite requests to move. For the next three frames, I scrabbled for corners and pockets as I made my erratic way around the table, everything spinning. A shambling wreck, I managed to get through most of the match, like all drunks, convinced I was fooling everyone. Then all of a sudden I missed a red and collapsed on the floor, where I remained in a catatonic state beneath the feet of my opponent, Steve Newberry.

Wales won 3-0. Their team, stepping over and around me and singing like a celestial choir, was delirious, which was more than my team was.

Bill Cottier came storming up and told me I was a disgrace. From my position on the floor, among the cigarette stubs and beer bottle tops, I gave him a bit of the verbals. 'That's it, you're definitely not going to Tasmania now! You're out!' he snapped, leaving me to stagger to my chalet, where I fell across my bed and passed out, still fully clothed.

When I woke, I was still very drunk, with Bill Cottier's last words still ringing in my head. 'You're not going to Tasmania now!' To the few mates who were sitting around playing cards and waiting for me to be the life and soul of the party again, I sat up and announced, 'I'm going! I'm absolutely, definitely going to Tasmania! and I'm going now!' And made my way to the bathroom to run a bath.

Meanwhile, late as it was, still smarting from my abuse, Bill Cottier had telephoned Henry and told him I was out of the team. Henry jumped into his car, to see if he could talk Cottier and the committee round. He arrived at my chalet around one-thirty a.m. to find me in an overflowing bathtub, fully dressed in my dinner suit, using my cue like a paddle.

'What the hell's going on?' Henry stormed.

'I'm rowing to Tasmania,' I said. 'I'll get there myself if they won't take me.' And I dipped my cue back in the water.

Henry threw most of the others out of the chalet, all except Joe O'Boye, who was sharing with me. Henry couldn't very well dispose of him, since it was his chalet too. He dragged me out of the tub and sat me on the bed, water puddling all around. 'Right, now, we've got to sort this out. Do you want to go to Tasmania or not?'

'Yes, I'll row there,' I said.

'Jimmy, don't be such a xxxx all your life!' Henry glared at me and threw a couple of towels in my direction. 'Now get undressed, dry yourself and get some sleep. I have to talk to the committee. I'll see you later.' With a final glare, he went out, and I heard the key turn in the door. He'd locked us in.

I dried myself but didn't climb into bed. I pulled on jeans and a T-shirt and Joe O'Boye and I went out through the window to have another drink at the bar. The band was still playing and there were Henry and Bill Cottier, twirling away in the crush in the middle of the dance floor with their partners. They never even noticed us.

★

I was fined £200 for being drunk in the bar before a match and, after a long dressing-down, I was allowed to go to Tasmania after all. Henry had persuaded the amateur board that there would be a public outcry if I was banned from being allowed to compete in what was, up to then, the most important match of my life. Also, as English Amateur champion, I was automatically entitled to compete. Henry continued to lecture me about my behaviour, insisting that if I didn't straighten up I would lose. This was a marvellous reprieve I'd been given, so I should respect it as such.

'Well, I do, Henry,' I assured him. 'I never mean to let people down, honest. It just sort of happens, if you know what I mean? And that Bill Cottier, he hates me. He always arrives when—'

'No, I don't know what you mean,' interrupted Henry. 'You just have to grow up, Jimmy, and be a bit more mature.'

Mature was a word that definitely was not in my vocabulary. But to make sure I wouldn't go off the rails too much, Henry, who was travelling to Tasmania with us, wouldn't give me any money at all. He sat with his arms folded across his wallet, ignoring my pleadings. Officially, we were permitted £1500 expenses each, which Bill Cottier had indicated he would dole out to us at the rate of £40 a day on arrival. Joe O'Boye and I weren't having any of that. On the plane we pestered Bill for our entire allowance until he finally gave in and agreed that we could have it as soon as he changed some traveller's cheques.

As soon as we arrived, we practically frogmarched Bill to the American Express counter. 'I don't know why I'm giving in to you,' he complained as he counted out our money. 'I know it's wrong, I know it's a bad move, I know you will let us down. This is a disaster actually happening while I'm doing this.'

As soon as we had the readies in our hands, we grabbed our cases and went to the races. We took off without waiting for the official coach, which was transporting the others to the hotel so they could rest up and get over jet-lag. We had never been to Australia before, but I had a truffle-hound's nose for racetracks and casinos. We didn't sleep, we just kept going, betting on everything that moved. If there had been a race for dead donkeys, I would have bet on that. Not surprisingly, after two days, our pockets were empty. If you turned us upside down and shook us, not even a bent Australian cent would have fallen out.

We hitched to the hotel, where the team, refreshed and well-fed, was making ready to fly out to Tasmania when we shuffled in, unshaven, unkempt and starving. We scrounged a bit of food and this time got on the team coach. Somehow, we had to get through ten days in Tasmania, eating and sleeping somewhere other than a ditch, because we had to shower and dress properly for the tournament, and you can't keep sleeping in other people's rooms. We found a hotel that would take us and feed us without money upfront because the manager knew why we were there – the tournament was one of the biggest things happening in Tasmania that year – and he couldn't imagine that any member of the UK team would not settle up sooner or later. Unfortunately for him, he had just met a couple of past masters at that game. He would come to our room every day and ask when was our money going to come through, and every day we would make up some cock-and-bull story that wore thinner and thinner as time progressed.

And *we* would have worn thinner and thinner ourselves, if it had not been for the breakfast that came with the room and the food that Larry Rooney, a player from Belfast, supplied us with. Experts at foraging, we also helped ourselves to the buffet for the tournament big-

wigs. Our hotel room was unbelievable. It would knock
the wrecked rooms that rock stars are supposed to leave
in their wake into a cocked hoop. In the desperate search
for something to eat in the early hours, I remember
coming across an abandoned tomato that had been there
so long it was petrified, and plates of mouldy sandwiches
buried beneath piles of dirty clothes. Because we came in
at three or four in the morning we had requested that no
one went in our room; so subsequently it was never
cleaned or tidied. But it was so disgusting that no
self-respecting maid would have trodden beyond the
threshold without a flit-spray and a rat-catcher.

Henry West was there with Rufus, his minder, having
a good time and ignoring my pleas of poverty. He
thought if I were kept short of money I would stay sober,
but there are always ways and means. Now Henry was a
huge man, tall and bulky with the boxer's build gone to
seed; while Joe O'Boye, slender and fair-haired, was one
of those people who, when they've had too much to
drink, has lots too much mouth. The combination of a
big sober man and a seven-stone drunk can be fatal. On
this occasion, as Joe got drunker, he became more
abusive, until he went too far and Henry went for him. I
rushed between them, which, given that I was quite
skinny myself, was pretty stupid.

'Henry, you can't hit Joe,' I shouted, 'he's seven stone
and you're about twenty. Stop it! You'll kill him!'

Henry calmed down and I dragged Joe away. As we
walked out of the door, Joe couldn't resist one last
riposte, thinking he was far enough away to make a run
for it.

That was it. Bellowing like a bull, Henry charged with
his head down. Joe and I literally ran for our lives.

Despite the chaos, I won the tournament. Of course I
did. In fact, I could have done it just by potting, because
in those days I was so good. It was fantastic to win – but

I knew I would. It was a round-robin competition, and the organiser, who was also a competitor, put all the weaker players, like the Fijians and the Indians and the Papuan New Guineans, on his side for the draw, so he was bound to win all his rounds. It seemed like he'd put all the good players on my side, but I beat them all – including Steve Newberry, who'd thrashed me that drunken night in Prestatyn. I knew when I got to the final that I was playing somebody who didn't deserve to win, who I could give a 50 start to. It was so predictable that we had my winning party the night before I played – and I still beat the guy 10-1 with a hangover. Such are the sweet joys of youth and confidence.

The next day we were due to fly out to India. The hotel manager knew we were leaving and lay in wait for us because we had definitely promised he'd get his money. Funnily enough, he had refused our offer of a cheque, insisting on cash. 'What's the world coming to?' I told him. We kept dodging him and, at the eleventh hour, sneaked back into the hotel, stuffed all our clothes into our suitcases – suits and shoes in Joe's case, the dirty washing in mine, then slunk out of the back door and ran to the coach. Halfway across the concourse, my bag broke and I left an incriminating trail of dirty socks and underwear in my wake. The coach doubled back, giving everyone on board the opportunity of having a good look. Roaring with laughter, they all made crude comments about the disgusting state of our laundry, while Joe O'Boye and I, adrenaline evaporated, cringed in our seats.

The first thing we had to do in India was buy new socks, shirts and underwear. It was a mad place. I've been back a few times since, but it never seems any less of a shambles. The standard of snooker is fantastic, though billiards is the preferred game there, with a long history and tradition.

There are beggars everywhere. It's hard to get used to their clutching persistence and terrible deformities. At first, we gave what we could, but the more we gave, the more they came back and followed us in droves. Finally, for the sake of peace, we learnt to walk about with our eyes averted, as our forebears must have done. It gives the wrong impression, but it keeps you sane. However, there was one small group that we found behind our hotel who Joe and I took to our hearts. There was something about them, and about their den mother, as we came to call her, that was a bit special.

She was only about eleven years old and astonishingly beautiful. There was a serenity and an inner glow about her that I'll never forget. She looked after these kids so fiercely, gathering them up at night and herding them back to pool the pitiful quantity of coins they'd been given during the day. She used the money to feed and clothe them. One of the boys, who had stumps on his hands and knees, used to scrabble along like a spider. Without her to care for him, to wash and feed him, he surely would have died. In India, you die a little bit inside every day.

At night, after we'd played, Joe and I would go round the back of the hotel to where the children slept by the boilers and find them cooking rice and scraps. We'd sit round their fire with them for hours, not even sharing a common language, but somehow communicating. When the others in the tour were invited to grand receptions at the British Embassy, we would duck out and escape to our boiler-room children, preferring to hang out with these real people than all the braying fakes in their air-conditioned cars. It still makes me angry to think about it.

After we met the children, we gave them as much as we could – on condition that they gave up begging for that week. They continued to beg, of course. They didn't know how else to live. When our little Madonna of the Boilers saw us she used to tell all the local kids to leave us alone. One night we took them all out to a restaurant for the first time in their lives. As Joe and I went to walk in the door like a couple of Pied Pipers, all these little beggar children following behind, wide-eyed and nervous, the big Indian doorman went as if to smack them. 'Don't,' I said, 'they're with us,' and ushered them in. We looked around for a considered moment, then Joe said, 'No, it's not good enough for our guests,' and we walked out.

I've been slung out of enough gaffs, good and bad, to know what it feels like and, for once, I was seeing it from a much sharper perspective – knowing how it must be to live your entire life like that, unwanted. All the kids loved us for that, but I didn't do it to be loved. I felt revolted by the way some children have to live. We took them to dinner in a more sympathetic establishment and had a wonderful time. These children became our friends for too short a while. The one with the stumps looked after our cues at the matches. It made me feel very humble to watch him sit on the floor below the table, beaming with pleasure that he had a proper job for once.

That time, I won the Indian Championship against Arvind Savur, the Indian champion, 9-7 in Calcutta. I have been back several times. Somehow, the romantic movie and North-West Frontier vision I'd had of the country as a careless youth of seventeen never returned. I remember when I arrived at a venue I would throw my cue case into a swarm of people. One of them would catch it and they'd be given about £10 for the day. That was about six months' wages to them. To me it was nothing. It didn't seem right – and that's why I tossed my cue case like a bride's bouquet because you can't be choosy with fate and survival. The last time I went, the poverty and utter squalor was so depressing that Ronnie

O'Sullivan and I paid £600 extra each to fly home two days early. We can't all be Mother Teresa.

A month after we got back from the tour Bill Cottier died. I hope we didn't do his head in. Poor old Bill. Joe O'Boye and I were incorrigible – but I like to think we made him laugh just a little.

The last time I went to Australia, out of a group of about twenty snooker players, Steve Davis was the only one who didn't get dishmopped – while Alex Higgins was so stoned that he ended up in Bangkok, lost in the monsoon.

One of the first things you drive past after you leave the airport at Sydney is Ranwick Racetrack, scene of the beginning of my financial debacle during the World Amateur tournament. Known as the Legal Eagles, a motley crew of lawyers have hung out there for years, making more money out of gambling than they do from law. So that must be a lot of dosh. Alex won 24,000 (Australian dollars) here once; while all Joe O'Boye and I ever did was lose our shirts.

I would go to Ranwick every day. One person I saw frequently there was a promoter who had been given carte blanche to organise the Rothmans tournament. The prize money was advertised as $400,000, a sum that everybody knew was a joke. That was about the total Channel 9, the TV company, reputedly put on the table so he had to announce that was what was available. In fact, the amount that trickled down to the players was a lot less, the winner getting only about $30,000 Australian. We saw for ourselves how well this man was doing when at the racetrack he would throw $50,000 bets around. The system has been changed since then and over-advertising the prize money, shall we say, doesn't happen any more. Well, not often.

We always used to stay in the King's Cross district at the unfortunately named area known as Pox Point. It was a terrible place, far worse than King's Cross in London. You could drive past a whole mile of girls in leotards, plying their trade on every street corner in every doorway. I've been to some bad gaffs in my time, but that was bad. In one basement dive a senior policeman always sat at a table as drunk as a sack, with the girls queuing up, all the way down the stairs and round the corner of the street, cash at the ready to pay for their special spot which he noted down in a ledger. The wrong arm of the law.

On our last day in Sydney we were all invited to a barbecue. What we didn't know was that the innocent-looking chocolate cake handed around by our genial host was well-laced with hash, or skunk as the locals call it. After sampling this, Alex Higgins, who weighs eight stone wet and never finishes a leg of chicken before saying he's had enough, was like Oliver Twist, asking for more. He attacked four plates of dinner with relish, then tucked into another load of that beguiling chocolate cake. Bill Werbeniuk, who always had a fistful of lager, walked around with nothing but a pack of cards in his hand and a great stupid smile on his face; and Tony Meo threw up.

During the course of the party, Tony Knowles announced that he was going home via Thailand. 'You could go home that way, as well,' he told Alex. 'Why not meet me there? I've been heaps of times and it's great.'

Alex declined. He put in an early morning call at the hotel to catch his flight home, but fuelled with those mind-wobbling hash brownies and more food than I'd normally seen him eat in a week, he slept on. By the time he woke up, he'd missed his flight, as we all had – except Steve Davis, of course.

Now, the hash did strange things to Alex's state of

mind and he decided to join Tony Knowles after all, even though he didn't know exactly where he'd be. A fourteen or fifteen hour journey is a long spur-of-the-moment detour to take when you only have two hundred bucks on you and you're not even sure where in Thailand you're going, or why. All Alex could remember Tony mentioning was some beach that he had promised was like Torremolinos, the Spanish resort, just outside Bangkok. When Alex eventually arrived, he hopped into a taxi to drive him what he erroneously believed was a mile or two down the road. Six hours later, he was still in the taxi, watching the meter tick his money away.

Sure enough, the hotel Tony had vaguely mentioned was closed for the season. 'What season is that?' Higgins asked the caretaker. 'The hurricane season,' he was told. Alex just nodded his head at the wisdom and inevitability of it all.

Next, he spent two days roaming around that out-of-season holiday resort looking for Tony. His cashflow was helped considerably when he fell in with a bunch of Americans who wanted a few games of pool. Finally, sickening of bad pool and the place itself, Alex caught the bus back to Bangkok, starting off at the front of the bus and very rapidly moving to the relative safety of the rear as the octogenarian driver hurtled over potholes at 100 mph and shot past ravines and precipices with the engine sounding like it would fall out with every jolt. However, determined to check out of the country, Alex bumped into a man who said he was a local agent for EMI records. Apparently, as a side-line, he owned a roller-skating arena and a nightclub among other enterprises. Convincing Alex that he could show him some dazzling sights he persuaded him to stay on and arranged to pick him up from his hotel that evening,

As Alex stepped into the car, the heavens opened and the monsoon started. Three hours later they had travelled just one mile. 'Hell, I've had enough of this,' said Alex. 'Take me to the airport.' (Yes, there was an adjective before the word 'airport'.)

That took another four hours of driving through a solid wall of water. Indeed, Alex thought they must have missed the road altogether and were now driving along the bottom of the river. By the time they arrived, the water was up to the middle of the car doors and up to his knees inside.

His new-found friend, the driver, was unperturbed. 'Jolly nice weather, ho ho ho,' he chortled. 'The monsoon's come a little early.'

'I wish I'd never come at all,' sighed Wet Alex.

At the airport Alex insisted he wanted a seat on a plane out of there – any seat, any plane, would do. He was manic. Instead, he found himself the lone passenger on a parked, deserted plane, looking out upon an invisible airfield, lashed with more water than Niagara Falls – still getting wet.

He could have been on a ghost ship in the middle of the ocean. He could even have been me, rowing to Tasmania through shark-infested waters. In fact, he could have been dreaming. Maybe he'd wake up at the barbie back in Sydney and discover that the elusive Tony Knowles was there all the time, on an accidental high after that dangerously seductive skunk cake. Then he would kill him.

NINE

THE CRACK

The word 'crack' comes from the Gaelic word 'craic', which means, I believe, a story. This, then, is an Irish story that follows its own meandering pace and maybe there is no end to it because, like all good cracks, there was no real beginning that anyone could remember. Me? I just sort of drifted into it and floated along on it, like one of Huckleberry Finn's summertime escapades downriver. People shake their heads and say that a lot of things do tend to sort of happen to me and it's true, they do, because I don't have a nine-to-five and the only discipline I have is the discipline of the game and the competition season. For the rest, there's always an adventure just around the corner.

Until Maureen became pregnant we didn't live together, in a place of our own. But as a single mother-to-be, she got a tiny little flat in Battersea. The flat was a bit crowded. Not only was Maureen expecting our first child, but a good friend, Paul Ennis, had come over from Ireland and was sleeping on our settee. When another buddy, 'Peewee' John Malloy, dropped in for a drink and a chat one afternoon, I decided to give Maureen some space and the three of us went round to Ron Gross's house in Neasden for a drink.

Round at Ron's, we got out the pack of cards, bought a bottle of whisky and a case of lager and sat there all afternoon. As midnight approached, Paul suddenly had a brainstorm. We thought he was about to keel over, but he had just remembered that it was his twenty-first birthday the next day and his family were laying on a nice little bash for him – the problem was, the cake, the vol-au-vents and the champagne were all waiting for him at a Dublin hotel; and here he was in London, flat broke and the worse for wear, as we all were by then.

'I've got to get home,' he announced. 'I can't let my mum down.' Before I knew what was happening, he had talked Peewee and me into going along with him.

'You come with us as well, Ron,' I said, 'You'll enjoy it. You could do with a break.'

'Don't be daft,' Ron said. 'I can't go to Ireland, I've got a club to run.'

I said, 'All right then, but if you can't go you'd better lend me three hundred quid, 'cos we've got to go and we're skint.'

Ron laughed and produced a wad of money, so we rushed off in a cab to catch the last train to Liverpool and Holyhead. Before we got to the station, we stopped off at one of those open 'til all hours ethnic off-licences around King's Cross; but we must have been completely out of it because, for some bizarre reason, we bought three bottles of Drambuie, one each. I don't know why we bought Drambuie – perhaps that's all they had. I can't stand the stuff – I'd rather have had a bottle of vodka. Anyway, in that Aladdin's cave, we also bought a carton of cigarettes, a couple of packs of cards and pen and paper to play kaluki – and we were all set.

'Are you gonna call Maureen and let her know where you're going?' one of the others suggested as we steamed down the ramp to the platform.

'Too late, we'll miss the train,' I said. 'Anyway, she'll be asleep now. I don't want to wake her up, do I? I'll call her from Dublin, no problem.'

The train was almost empty, like it had been waiting for us in some eerie time-warp. Just the three of us sat in a carriage in what seemed like our own little pool of light, playing cards for a few bob a game and swigging – God knows why – Drambuie from the bottle. We were about half an hour out of London when we started arguing. The cards went up in the air, the money flew all over the carriage and Peewee said, 'Sod this! What the hell are we doing here?' and threw his bottle of Drambuie out of the window.

I said, 'I can't drink this stuff either,' and slung mine out.

Naturally, Paul threw his bottle out, then the cigarettes. Then everything else was chucked out and we were sitting on the train, another three hours to go, with no cigarettes, no cards, not talking, nothing to drink, the buffet closed and a headache each. There was nothing to do but go to sleep. I leaned back and closed my eyes and felt the train rocking along. Suddenly the motion and the booze hit me. I felt my stomach lurch and rushed to the lavatory just in time to spew up in the sink. The train was reeling, and my head was rocking. I sat there while, in the words of a writer from North London, I was 'refreshed by a brief blackout'. When I could see properly again, I turned the taps on full-blast and made a half-hearted attempt to clean up the mess. But, in my sorry state, it was all too much so I headed to the adjoining loo, where I washed my hands and face, took a few deep breaths and tried to sober up.

I stumbled back to my seat and nodded off again. Later, when I woke, I looked to see what time it was, but there was nothing on my wrist. My poncy diamond dress watch was not there. With the usual paranoia of the drunk, I shook Peewee awake and demanded to know where my watch was.

'What are you on about?' Peewee mumbled.

'Me watch!' I said, 'the one with diamonds at three, six, nine and twelve. That watch! Some bugger's nicked it!'

'Well, I ain't got it,' Peewee said in an aggrieved tone. 'And I don't need to know the time. Now piss off! I'm dying.'

I shook him awake again. 'I didn't throw it out of the window with the Drambuie, did I?' I asked. 'Tell me I didn't.'

'You probably did,' Peewee said. He yawned and I caught a blast of his boozy breath. 'You're daft enough to do anything. It was a fairy's watch, anyway.'

By now I'd woken Paul as well so he could help us all remember what had happened. Then suddenly I became aware of a very unpleasant smell. It wasn't Peewee, it was a flood of water coming down the train from the toilet, with little bits of stuff bobbing and floating about like a nightmare vegetable Henley regatta. The horrible stench of bile, beer, and sickly-sweet Drambuie, hit the nozzies. In a flash I remembered what had happened. I had taken off my watch to wash my hands and face and had left it on the basin. By the looks of it I had left the taps on in the first washroom.

I sloshed back not looking down, and, incredibly, there was my watch, sparkling up at me from behind the taps. Fortunately, it was two o'clock in the morning, and the train was deserted. Any other time, I suppose I would have lost it.

Naturally, we moved down a few more carriages and settled back to sleep. By the time we arrived at Holyhead and clambered up the gangplank on to the boat we were still drunk. Our idea to try and liven up was to sit on the

deck in the fresh air. I say fresh. In fact there was a brisk
storm blowing, spray lashing across our faces and it was
absolutely freezing. But I have to say that, even if you're
dying, there is something magical about sailing across the
Irish Sea at dawn, hearing the seagulls cry and watching
the sun come up through the night clouds.

By now we were all starving, but the restaurant was
closed. Isn't it always? 'Okay, leave it to me,' I said, full
of myself, and disappeared down the stairs. I found my
way into the kitchens and bared my two blue lips in what
I hoped was a grin at the chef, who was having a rest.
'Oy, mate, couldn't do us a couple of breakfasts could
you?' I wheedled, like Oliver begging for just a teeny
bowl of gruel. People do recognise me. I don't think it
was charm, more the fact that I looked like a pathetic
orphan blown in from the storm that worked the trick,
because the chef – very nice of him – fired up the stove
and cooked us three lovely breakfasts, which I carried off
on a big tray. I do remember there wasn't much tea left
in the steaming mugs by the time I hit the heavy doors to
the upper deck and stumbled into a gale, but the meal
went down a treat. When we anchored at Dun Laoghaire
at six in the morning, we could walk off the boat like
men.

Paul's family were still in bed when we breezed in
through the front door of their little house, Paul first,
with Peewee and me in tow. His mum got up and rushed
around to get us some tea and offered to cook us a good
Irish breakfast. We would have eaten it too, if we hadn't
been so knackered. It was a matter of hello, I used to be
Jimmy White and this used to be Peewee, a cup of tea
and has anyone got a spare bed? There weren't too many
rooms to choose from, but we didn't care. We hopped
into whatever had just been vacated and as soon as our
heads hit the still-warm pillows, dented with someone

else's heads, we were out for the count.

Paul had played snooker for Ireland, so his family were well up on who was who in the world of the cue. They had thought he was coming back on his own for the birthday party, but, when they were introduced to me and Peewee, they were over the moon. I was the youngest player to win the English Amateur title *and* the youngest to win the World Amateur championship, and that meant a lot to them, as it did me in those days. Since my return from Tasmania, I had turned professional and was starting to play some high-profile televised games.

At the birthday party later that night they introduced me to Conleth Dunne, a Dublin promoter, and we discussed doing a couple of exhibitions while I was over there. Con's twin brother, Richard, was the Irish National coach. He also had a snooker club and of course, a little pub. These days Con doesn't drink, but back then he was your Dublin roaring boy, living above the pub and helping out at the bar. He'd wake up each morning and get outside of a bottle of gin. That used to set him up and he would glide down painlessly for the rest of the day and on into the wee hours. In the end, Richie banned his twin from having a drink, even a quick nip, on pain of excommunication. But Con was getting up early in the morning, and on the pretext of cleaning up, he'd empty some of the tonic bottles, fill them up with vodka and put the tops back on and put them back on one end of the shelf where he knew they would be.

When the punters come in lunchtime, they'd say, 'Do you want a drink, Con?' Richie would look round to show he was keeping an eye on him, wag his finger, and Con would say, all demure, 'Oi tink Oi'll just have a tonic water,' and he'd pour himself a nice little glass of neat vodka from the bottles at the correct end of the tonic shelf.

This went on for months, with Con drinking his little

clear soldiers and Richie puzzled and watching him like a hawk as he careened all over the gaff. But in the end the books – rather like Con – couldn't be balanced at all and Richie jacked it in. Con joined his other brother, Terry, in New York and they opened a club called Tramps on West 21st Street. He's not had a drink since!

Obviously we couldn't time-share beds at Paul's home for long and had to look around for somewhere else to stay. Fortunately, Peewee knew Phil Lynott from Thin Lizzie, who had always said, 'If you ever come across the sea to Ireland, come and stay with us.' The band owned a beautiful mansion right on the beach at Sutton, a few miles north of Dublin on the Howth Peninsular. It was a magnificent spot. None of the band was there since they were touring Japan, but Phil's mum was in residence and immediately she said, 'Come on in, boys, make yourselves at home.' There was no bed-sharing here, the house was so big we were given a spacious room each and there was even a maid to tidy up. Not that we made a mess, but the band had a big Alsatian dog called Gnasher – like the dog in the *Beano* comic. Whoever got up early enough walked him along the shore, which wasn't that often. One morning Gnasher had an accident all over the lovely 'used to be' white carpet in the hall and we banished him to the beach. We were out in snooker clubs and pubs most of the time, and, when we were in, we stayed in the lounge watching Phil's tapes and listening to music. At the time Thin Lizzie's *Breakout* album was big – and on reflection, that was what I had done – broken out.

By now the few days I had intended staying in Ireland had stretched to a week. Maureen was used to me popping out for a packet of cigarettes and disappearing for two or three days at a time but by now she would be wondering just exactly where I was. I kept telling myself

I should telephone her and my new manager, Geoff Lomas, but I knew they would tell me to come home. I think there was a cut-off date when I switched off and I knew I wasn't going home unassisted. However, if I had come to terms with that thought, which is debatable, I kept it to myself.

Moral coward that I am, after three weeks I called my mum at home in Tooting. 'Where are you, Jimmy?' she asked. Everyone was looking for me.

'I know, Mum,' I said, 'but I'm doing lots of exhibitions and everything's fine. Tell Maureen I'm okay, will you?' Before she could tell me to call her myself, or drag my whereabouts from me, I said I had to go – and did. We were having such a laugh. The crack was indeed good.

It's absolutely amazing what we convince ourselves of, and how quickly we can change gear. A concerned frown can turn to a smile as we hang up the phone. We're full of it. It must be in the DNA.

Duty done, I sauntered off along O'Connell Street looking for a bit of fun. It found me, in the shape of a certain Walter Lusher, a young promoter about my age – twenty or twenty-one. Lusher and his brother owned a large department store in the heart of Dublin, and he also ran a leisure centre in Dublin. He asked if I was interested in doing an exhibition with Alex Higgins. 'It would be great if I could put on an evening of the Whirlwind and the Hurricane,' he enthused. 'You'd go down a storm!' he winced. 'Sorry, I couldn't resist it, Jimmy.'

It was very short notice, but, several glasses later, we seemed extremely confident that he could set the thing up and get the crowds in. We discussed money, which seemed no object, but the mansion at Bray was by now a little far out of town for 'exhibitions', and I asked if he could put us up closer to where the action was.

'No problem,' he assured me. 'Leave it to me.'

He drove us to the Gresham Hotel in the heart of Dublin on O'Connell Street. I'd wanted to be where the action was, and here I got it. A stone's throw from the Liffey. Streets lined with historic bars and pubs. Historical note: the Gresham was built by Thomas Gresham in 1817, a handsome town house with sphinxes jutting out of the wall on the first floor. It exuded luxury, with oil paintings, massive chandeliers and tons of marble. I was amazed when we were ushered into the magnificent Elizabeth Taylor and Richard Burton suite on the sixth floor. This is the luxury suite with magnificent views of the Wicklow Hills from its own bar, that only movie stars and other celebrities visiting Ireland can afford.

'Will it do?' said Lusher, grinning.

'Are you sure this isn't a mistake?' I asked, gazing at the acres of blue carpet that were the same colour as Liz Taylor's eyes.

'It's all yours,' Lusher said.

There were two bedrooms at opposite ends of the suite, the size of aircraft hangars with ensuite bathrooms tiled in pale grey. I turned on a gold dolphin tap and at once a geyser of boiling water rushed out, steaming up the gilded antique mirrors. Peewee said, 'It's like a Turkish harem.'

The lounge was in the centre, stuffed with antique furniture. There was a kitchen and the bar was filled to the brim with unopened bottles and crystal glasses. Lusher told me to order anything else I wanted on room service. 'Champagne, oysters, lobster, whatever you like, it's yours,' he said generously.

Pandora's Box, once opened, was hard to close. Events went roller-coasting along and, once news got out on the network that we were installed very largely with whatever we wanted and deep, soft sofas and a thick-pile carpet to crash out on, the party started. As it does.

UB40 dropped in – how does that song of theirs go – oh yeah, 'Red red w-i-n-e, gone to my h-e-a-d' – and things did go to my head. Days flowed seamlessly into each other. Somewhere in there I called Alex Higgins. He looked in his diary and agreed he could fit in a quick exhibition or two. Lusher booked a suite for Alex on the floor below us, and was there to meet him at the airport when he flew in.

Alex took one look at his own suite and, with that pained expression that I was getting to know so well, said, 'This can't be right. I always stay in the Elizabeth Taylor suite when I come to Dublin.'

'Well, I've put Jimmy in there,' Lusher said, tactlessly.

'No problem, we can swap,' said Alex with complete assurance that I would move out for him. If I had been alone, I might have done just that. But there were dozens of people camped all over my suite and I couldn't expect them to pack up their stuff and trek to the floor below. When I wouldn't give way, Alex took himself and his valise up to my suite and, dressed like Noel Coward in a marvellous white suit, ensconced himself at the bar. That night, he moved into the bathroom of the Richard Burton bedroom where he spent the night sleeping in the capacious bathtub, still wearing his white suit. I got him, though. A couple of nights of discomfort was enough – the day after, he was in back in the suite below, although he never stopped sniping, trying to make me feel guilty. After all, in his eyes, hadn't I been the little twelve-year-old he had practically taught how to play all those years ago?

Now, here we were, seated on high stools at the permanently stocked bar, *in my suite*, as equals, working our way through all the bottles on the shelf. We put on a straight face long enough to do a couple of exhibitions in the leisure centre. Maybe we weren't sober, but, as someone said seriously back then, 'How can you tell?'

Alex liked the old world aspect of the Gresham – 'It was an Irish gentleman's house,' he told me perfectly seriously, 'which is why I fit in, Jimmy, and you don't.' The Gresham was also where he had long been in the habit of buying Irish Sweep tickets off the porter. He would resell them at a profit to Terry Rogers, the booker. Con was in his brother's pub one day when Alex came rushing in. 'Quickly, I must have two hundred pounds!' he cried. Con didn't have any cash about, and ended up by borrowing some. Alex immediately took it across the street into the bookies and put the lot on a horse. He lost, and Con saw him tearing up the ticket as he sauntered off down the street.

'I thought it was a matter of life or death,' said Con, 'and now I have to pay the money back, so I'm the loser.'

'He could have won,' I said.

'And if he had, do you think he would have paid me back? No, he'd have put the lot on the next race,' Con said piously.

Through Con and Richie I did a few more exhibitions here and there. I think they called them 'debaters' – like how to stand, how to hold the cue, 'this is a snooker table' and 'this is a white ball'; 'this is a pint of Guinness' and so on. We would drive into the middle of absolutely nowhere, remote little villages, where the hotel had pigs, soda bread, stout, ruddy complexions and two beds stuck together for a bridal suite and, of course, a pub. Blink, and you were drunk, married and out of town. In the morning we turned around and headed back to the bright lights of Dublin.

One night, Con asked me if I would do something very special for an uncle of his, a great fiddle player, seventy-five years of age, who was having a presentation for his music in a country village in the middle of nowhere. 'His name is Willie Burn,' said Con, trying to paint a picture to persuade me. 'He has never married and lives in a little thatched house, in the heart of the Bog of Allan. He's a wonderful old guy, Jimmy, you'd just love him.'

'The Bog of Allan, eh? Sounds like my kind of place,' I said.

Con's face lit up. 'So you'll make the presentation, then? Oh, I know how much it'll mean to me dear old Uncle Willie! He's the only man in the village to have a TV, so he's seen you play.'

It was all agreed. Willie Burn was flabbergasted that I was coming out there, and ran off to tell the entire Bog to get themselves down to the pub for 9.30 that night.

Con had a 280 SE Mercedes, a great beast of a car with a sunroof. The night of the presentation, eight of us crammed inside and roared off. We were all steaming, including Con, who was driving. Halfway there, going through the little town of Lucan, I hear we went through two red lights and over the double white line in the centre of the road, several times, so it was hardly surprising when a motorcycle cop pulled us over. We could see he was irate as he walked towards us, slapping his gloves on the car and peering inside like it was a cage full of monkeys.

'Oi tink I'll just get out of the car, so he won't be smelling the fumes,' said Con.

The policeman asked Con how many people were in the car.

'Er – eight,' said Con. 'Do you want to see the insurance?' No one ever insured their cars in that part of Ireland and Con was thinking the policeman was about to make a *faux pas*.

'No, we won't bother with the insurance,' said the policeman, 'just show me your licence.'

As Con fished around for the licence, the fumes of alcohol, more potent than petrol, hit the policeman's nostrils just about the same time as Peewee struck up a

match to light a cigarette. The long arm of the law shot
through the window to grab the box of matches. 'Jesus!
You'll blow us all to kingdom come,' cried the policeman. 'Are you all damned fools, or what?'

By now, Con had found his licence. He had lived in
London for fifteen years, so the licence happened to be
an English one, which riled the policeman further. 'And
I'm leaving Ireland in the morning,' Con added for good
measure, knowing this meant the policeman wouldn't
bother to issue a ticket.

Thwarted, the policeman asked where we were going.
Con told him about his uncle in the country and that I
was going to do the presentation and was, in fact, right
there in the front seat next to him. Sourly, the policeman
said, 'I don't give a damn if you've got the President of
the United States in there, you turn this thing around
and go back to where you've come from. I'll be watching
out for you so you needn't think you can wait ten
minutes and then continue. If you come through Lucan
with your car in this dangerously overcrowded state, I'll
impound it, and lock you all up for the night for being
drunk and disorderly.'

Con couldn't turn there, so he drove on for a bit with
the cop in front. When we reached a spot where we could
turn, the cop watched us in his rear-view mirror, and,
satisfied we were turning, took off.

I said, 'We can't let your dear old uncle and the Bog of
Allan down, Con. They're all waiting there for the
presentation.'

'Well, we can't go through Lucan,' said Con. 'What's
to do?'

I said there must be back roads, we'd trust to luck and
steer by the Pole Star. 'Right,' said Con, staring up at the
dark sky overhead and wondering which one of all the
myriad of stars up there was the Pole Star. We turned off
the main road and drove through tiny little country lanes

so narrow that fronds of green vegetation lashed at us through the open windows of the car on both sides and a curious cow, leaning over a gate, mooed right in Con's ear when he slowed to check a signpost. Swaying round the bends, I felt moved to stand up on the car seat, stick my head out through the open sunroof and bark at the moon. I could smell meadowsweet and horses as we flew along. Somehow, we made it, arriving more or less on time. It was a grand evening, the crack was good amongst kind and warm-hearted people who knew how to tell a tale, sing energetically to Willie Burns's world-class fiddle playing and dance the Irish jigs.

After a few more drinks for the road, we were back outside the Gresham Hotel at 4 o'clock in the morning with two police cars right behind us, sirens blaring. One car pulled up in front, the other beside us so we couldn't make a quick dash for it.

Two cops approached and compared Con's number plate with a notebook in his hand. 'That bloody police-man, he's put my number out all over the country,' Con moaned. 'They'll be impounding my car for sure.'

One of the policemen looked inside the car. 'Is Jimmy White in there?' he asked.

Con admitted I was, and the next thing, they'd whipped out their kids' autograph books and when I'd finished signing, it was, 'Lovely to meet you, Jimmy, look after yourself now,' before they got back into the police cars and disappeared into the night.

With our baby due soon, it was panic stations in London. They found out I was in Ireland and I guessed a SWAT team would soon be arriving, so I said to Peewee, 'I've got to go home. I'm going to get murdered, but I've got to go.' He nodded.

The next day we went to the airport and I bought two tickets, but just before we were called to board, I said to

Peewee 'No, I ain't going. I'll go tomorrow. I'm not ready to die. I'm a young man. In my prime. In Dublin. In trouble. With a very bad hangover.'

All the way back to the city I kept chewing my knuckles and mumbling, 'I've got to go home, got to go home.'

'Of course we've got to go home,' Peewee agreed.

When we got back to the Gresham, I looked at him. 'I thought you got on the plane,' I said.

'No, I'm still here, helping you because you're in trouble,' and Peewee began to laugh.

I phoned Mum up to tell her I wasn't coming yet. 'Jimmy—' she started, with that tone of voice all mums have for clean underwear, grub, homework, a proper job and Christmas with the family.

'I know, Mum, I know,' I said. 'I'll talk to you later—' and moving swiftly into 'Got to go right now' mode, I went.

For days after, bells seemed to ring a lot. They weren't in my head. It was the telephone. Everyone back home calling to see when I would condescend to return. They now knew where I was. All would be forgiven. But I wouldn't answer. I got someone else to say I was out. I was! But my time was up. My new manager, Geoff Lomas, turned up and I hid. Alex Higgins's manager came over and we both hid. Deeper and deeper into the walls I went. I became smaller and smaller, able to sink into the thick pile carpet. I could put a hand over my eyes like a child and nobody could see me. You know judgement day will be due, and when it comes, it'll be a real shit-rain – but you've got to avoid it until all options have run out. Are we not men?

We were men at the bar in that enormous suite. I imagined Richard Burton seated there on a high stool, glass in hand, smoke wreathing round his head, a wry smile on his face. Richard Burton, where are you? I need advice!

At least three times I went to the airport and three times I turned back. I didn't want the party to stop.

Con Dunne had illegal poker machines all around the pubs in Dublin; he even had them at little hardware stores in all the little country villages, where the bored wives of farm-workers could play the day away and dream they were in Las Vegas instead of at home cooking their husband's tea. When we were skint – which was regularly, given the number of betting shops we honoured with our custom and the all-night card sessions – Con would say, 'We'll just pop down the pub and get you a little cash.'

He'd walk in, raid his own machines, change it up behind the bar into fifty notes or so, give it to us and we'd be out again. Back on the razzle.

About this time, John Parrott arrived to do an exhibition. We also bumped into some London boys who had come over in a shoal to dump some 'moody' money in the pubs and clubs. I'd never met them before, but in that musical sea of Irish voices their clipped London accents were music to me, so I got chatting, bought them a drink and they offered to buy me one. They looked a bit hard up so I used to say, 'No, I'll do it—' and they would say firmly, 'No, it's our turn. Here, Jimmy, you get it for us and we'll pay.' They pulled out a wad of money and peeled off a twenty. So here's Mr Simple going up to the bar and unknowingly handing over piece after piece of moody. The change went back into a separate 'bin' and new drinks were paid for with a new note. Very new.

The police came to my hotel and captured me, craftily getting the manager to phone up to the suite, telling me that Maureen was on the phone, it was a real emergency and I was wanted at once. I imagined the worst and belted downstairs, to fall straight into the arms of the law.

The sharp London boys had left town, so the cops had

only me. I asked them what the problem was and they said my dabs were all over a dodgy twenty. Now, when you're smashed it doesn't occur to you to ask just how they knew they were your dabs; or what they had compared them to and where they came from. So they took me away and I was banged up for about eighteen hours. I protested I didn't know it was dodgy money. All I'd done was buy a couple of drinks with it and gave the lads their change.

Con came along and protested my innocence, and the next thing was, he was arrested as an accomplice because he had been seen in the bar with me where the moody money was found. 'No, I was out with Jimmy the night before the night of the alleged offence,' said Con.

Con said when I had been with him the night before, a local night-club owner had approached me and offered me £1500 just to pose in his club for a photograph that he could use for publicity purposes, but I had declined.

'And you're trying to tell me,' said Con, 'that Jimmy White needed to pass counterfeit money when he's turned down £1500 for a photograph? Don't be silly!' Oh, Con lectured them all right.

'The bartender swears it's true,' said the police. In Ireland, a bartender is considered a professional man, like lawyers, teachers, clergy and such.

'All he wants is his picture in the paper,' Con replied indignantly, indicating the press buzzing about the front steps of the police station like flies.

The next day, some top brass breezed into my cell and said, 'You do have a problem, Jimmy me boy.' He gave me what looked like a cunning grin and said, 'But I think we can sort it out.'

'I told your lads, I don't know who they were, I never clapped eyes on them before, straight up,' I said.

He waved away my protests with a casual hand, 'Now, don't you worry about it, Jimmy, 'cos I was thinking to myself, if you jist see your way clear to play this nice little exhibition that I want to arrange, you could beat the rap. They've got nothing on you, of course, and it's all circumstantial evidence – but then again, when the hell did that matter? So, how about it, Jimmy, you don't want to be in the newspapers, now do you?'

'No, I'm innocent,' I said, 'but I'll go along with it only if you help out my friend, Con Dunne.'

Con had got a drink-driving ban for five years, which was of considerable inconvenience to him. We'd had a good laugh, he had kept us liberally supplied with cash from his poker machines and I wanted to do him a favour in return. This was the golden opportunity. I told the big man that I would do the exhibition match so long as he straightened out Con Dunne's sheet.

'Done!' he cried happily. 'Yes, Con Dunne,' I said, 'that's his name,' but he was shaking my hand vigorously. 'Pleasure to do business with you, Jimmy me boy.'

To his delight and astonishment, Con Dunne got his driving ban lifted. It was 'a miracle' he said. I agreed.

As it happens, I did go back to Ireland within a few months, to play in an exhibition match, but under slightly different circumstances, for Detective Sergeant Pat Clelland, whose daughter was seriously ill. We found it hard to get hold of another professional who was free. The combination of the Whirlwind and the Hurricane was what everybody wanted, but Alex was booked. In the meantime, because I had promised, I cancelled all my engagements for a month, never knowing what date would be available. I didn't mind that – to me, a little girl with leukaemia was more important than anything else. John Parrott, who was the up-and-coming new player, agreed to play opposite me in DS Pat Clelland's exhibition at McGriggan's Stadium, which was more often used for boxing. I must say, the police did us proud, making sure that all the tickets were sold, giving us outriders for the drive from the airport into Dublin, and holding a big party afterwards. I beat Parrott 9-1, and was presented with a beautiful crystal bowl.

But, back to my original Irish adventure. It had to stop. We had been living high on the hog in the Gresham for six weeks, the bill must have been in the thousands. I was a tired lad, ready to go home and face the music. On the last day I decided to go and find our benefactor, Walter Lusher, who had kindly paid the vast bill for six weeks' partying. I don't know the full circumstances of his breakdown, but I discovered that he had been carted off to the local loony bin. The staff there unlocked door after door and eventually led me into the big recreation room, where Lusher was playing snooker. When he saw me, he cried, 'Jimmy! Jimmy! Look, this is how you pot balls!' He leaped on to the table and started tap-dancing, kicking the balls into the pockets with his feet.

Peewee went with me to the airport again, but, at the last minute, he got cold feet. 'Now I remember why I ain't going home,' he said. Apparently, when we had jumped on the midnight train and disappeared all those weeks ago, he had been in the middle of a painting job for a friend, John Nielsen. Now, we know John is a big fellow and Peewee knew he wouldn't be happy about having been left with pots of paint and ladders all over the place and work – unfinished, shall we say? So I flew home alone, to about thirty thousand messages and a lot of stick from Maureen; while Peewee stayed a few days more before leaving on the boat with Paul for Holyhead and the annual Pro-Am tournament at Pontins holiday camp in Prestatyn.

They bought a litre bottle of Blue Label vodka for the

journey and were having a jolly-up with a few of the lads, when someone suggested a game of dice. By the time the boat docked they'd been flayed to death and didn't have a bean. Too broke to buy a railway ticket, they caught the train to Crewe and then on to Rhyl and Prestatyn, ducking into the loo whenever they saw a uniform coming along the corridor. They reached the holiday camp at six o'clock in the morning, but the gates were locked, so they sat waiting for someone to come along who they recognised so they could crash out in the chalet they would no doubt have.

'We were done in again,' Peewee told me later. 'All we wanted was a kip. Not too much to ask, is it?'

At nine-thirty or ten o'clock on the Saturday morning, all the faces started showing up. When Steve Ventnor came through the gates they were on him like wolverines. 'Steve, can we just have a wash?' they begged. But they ended up staying in his room for two days, so flat broke they had to tap everybody. 'Sort us out, lend us a tenner,' they pleaded, just so they could eat.

By Wednesday, the bar was buzzing. Friends like Alex Higgins and Bill Werbeniuk and all the usual suspects were there. It was a different feeling in those days, we had more fun. All the players would meet up from all over Britain and elsewhere. Everyone knew everyone from the snooker circuit and all the clubs. It's not the same now. The game is so serious, the people a bit too pompous, officials too officious. Maybe it's all down to TV and everyone taking themselves and their image too seriously?

Eventually, Peewee managed to find a vacated chalet. At about nine o'clock at night he was wandering about the holiday camp when I arrived in a cab from the station. The two back doors opened and I fell out of one door and my mate, Lenny Cain, fell out of the other door. We were absolutely stonkers.

'So, Peewee,' I mumbled, 'you can't get rid of me that easily!'

We crawled to the bar and continued. I told them that on the way up there I had met a trainer who had given me a racing tip. A horse called Far Too Much was 10-1 in a big race and was definitely going to win.

'So lend us a tenner and I'll put something on it,' Peewee said.

'I'm skint,' I said. 'I thought you might lend *me* some dough.'

So off we went around the holiday camp borrowing money and telling all our pals that the horse, Far Too Much, was a cert, we had inside information. I managed to raise a hundred, Peewee got thirty quid, John Virgo had fifty, Terry Whitthread – everybody – we all put what we could on the nag at the tiny little betting shop in the holiday camp. Now the shop was nothing but a big cupboard with a light-bulb and a counter, but on the day of the race there must have been about fifty of us crammed in there, smoking, drinking and watching the race on the television. It's about three or four furlongs to go and the horse is lying at about fifth or sixth. Three furlongs out, it's fourth. Two furlongs, and it's moved to third place. One furlong – it's second. We were yelling and shouting, and chanting 'Far Too Much! Far Too Much! Far Too Much!' urging it on, jam-packed in that little shop. The bookie thought we were mad. Briefly – because it won by four lengths.

The roar went up and we all rushed the window. 'Pay up! Pay up! Pay up! Pay up!' We'd won far too much, and there were too many of us for the betting shop to pay up in cash. Peewee won £330. People wanted hundreds each. I had about a grand to come when the cash ran out, the poor bastard had to get the tear-stained cheque book out. A new joke was invented: in a holiday camp, they have a blackboard where they scrawl in chalk during one

of the variety shows, or bingo, *'Baby crying'* – giving the
chalet number – now, it was a case of *'Bookie crying'*!

That night the camp came alive. Everyone was up for
it, feeding the jukebox, telling stories, relating their own
best racing anecdote. By five a.m. there was no booze left
and they closed the bar. A Scottish bloke ran back to his
chalet and returned with a kind of square briefcase.
Inside were little bottles of brandy and scotch, little
mixers and little silver cups and we toasted dear old Far
Too Much one more time for luck.

TEN

TELL LAUREN I LOVE HER

We might have been too young, but we loved each other and had been going out together for nearly five years. Lauren was not an accident; and when Maureen and I had announced to our respective families that she was pregnant, it had been almost a case of a Tooting version of the Hatfields and the McCoys.

My mum and dad went round to Maureen's house and the parents met for the first time. Things were tense as they skirmished around the picket lines with some introductory chit-chat. Maureen's dad sat in the corner like a neutral observer and didn't say a lot, but our two respective mothers soon got down to brass tacks, determined to apportion blame where they were convinced it was due.

'My Jimmy's never got a girl in trouble in his life before he met your Maureen,' stated my mum, firing the first salvo.

'And my girl would never have got into trouble without your boy. He's got a dreadful reputation,' Maureen's mum responded with a heavy shot amidships.

'Not where girls are concerned! You don't think your

girl didn't egg my Jimmy on?' Mum fired back.

'Mum, it's not Maureen's fault,' I said, trying to get a word in edgeways, 'these things happen.'

'Yes, and we all know *how* they happen,' said Maureen's mum.

'The thing is, what are we going to do about it?' my dad said, acting the peacemaker. 'There's somebody else to consider now, you know.'

Maureen's mum was in no doubt. 'They've got to get married.'

'There's no need for that,' said my mum. 'He's got his career to think of.'

'He should have thought of his career before getting my girl into trouble,' stated Maureen's mum. 'And what about my girl's career? She's got her whole future ahead of her.'

'I'm not in trouble!' Maureen insisted. 'I'm only having a baby – and we want it, don't we, Jimmy?'

I nodded and shifted in my seat; young men are never any good at this sort of family thing. Maureen's mum persisted with her wedding plans until Maureen's response took us all by surprise.

'Well, I don't want to get married,' she said. 'I don't want people to think, oh, she's just doing it because she's pregnant. I'm quite happy the way things are. I'll get a council flat. We'll be okay.'

There wasn't a lot to say after that and summit negotiations petered out.

In due course, as a single mother-to-be, Maureen applied for and was given a tiny flat in a high-rise block in Battersea. Although we shared it from time to time, Maureen never really moved out of her parents' house. She said I was never there and we had such an erratic relationship, there was no point in trying to make a proper home before our baby was born.

'I'm tired of spending night after night on my own,

Jimmy,' she said. 'The flats are noisy and I'm nervous about who might come through that door.'

Maureen had a point; I *was* hardly ever there. I was still acting like Jack the Lad with no responsibilities and, after my extended stay in Dublin, she was so fed up with me, we broke up, not for the first time. I think it was driven home to me just how angry Maureen was when she wrecked my cue. Now, as any snooker player will tell you, this is pretty dramatic stuff, but Maureen has never sat quietly in the background, the little hard-done-by woman.

I'd been out with Lenny Cain for one night or maybe two nights too many, when we dropped into Wandsworth snooker hall. I ordered a couple of large vodkas before noticing that Jock looked as sick as a dog. He shuffled up to me and mumbled, 'Jim, I've got something tae say to ye, mate. I've got a bi' o' bad news for ye.'

'You've got what?' I said.

Jock looked haunted. He glanced all round him and over his shoulder, and whispered, 'Nay, come behind the ramp, Jim, I've got something tae say tae ye, mate, in private.'

'It's okay, Jock, we're all friends,' I said. 'What's up?'

'Well, laddie, you know you told me never tae gi' your cue to anyone?'

I nodded. 'You've lent it to someone, is that it, Jock? Because I don't give two buttons, really. I don't need it for a day or two.'

'Nay, Jim, it's worse than that' – and Jock told me that Maureen had rushed in, all sweetness and light and said, 'Oh, Jock, Jimmy's sent me in for his cue,' and imperiously held out her hand. Taking his life into his hands, Jock had refused. 'Jimmy's in a taxi, stuck outside in the traffic,' Maureen insisted. 'Now, quick, Jock—' – and he's still refused. 'Nay, nay, I cannae do it, lassie.'

In the end, she stamped her foot and said, 'Jock! Will you just give it to me! Come on, I want it now!'

Jock took my precious cue, still in its case, and handed it over, keeping his fingers crossed behind his back that it was all right – because in his heart of hearts he knew the heavens were about to open up and dump on him, big-time. He was breaking his promise to me and he knew that if I really wanted the cue I would have gone in there myself and not sent in Maureen. All his instincts were twanging like over-stretched wire – 'And, Jim, I still gave in to her, I never can resist the women, ye ken that,' Jock said.

As soon as she had the cue, Maureen rushed out of the door, took it out of the case, leant it up against the wall and jumped up and down on it with both feet, breaking it into bits. Immediately, she felt a lot better. She went inside and said, 'Jock, you'd better go and pick Jimmy's cue up. It's all over the pavement outside.'

I looked at Jock and said, 'Yer jokin, ain't yer, mate?'

Miserably he shook his head. 'But I picked it up, Jimmy, what was left of it, and I put it in there,' he said, pointing at the case on the bar.

I opened the case. Off somewhere in my head, I could hear Maureen laughing and I started to laugh too. My cue was shredded like bamboo but all I felt was admiration that Maureen had had the nerve to storm heaven's gate and smite me where it hurt most. She should have been in the marines.

I ordered another large vodka, and toasted, 'Maureen, God bless 'er,' while Jock and Lenny looked at me open-mouthed.

'So yer no' annoyed, Jimmy?' said Jock.

'No, mate, it ain't your fault. Maureen's got the better of us all. She got even. Good for her. Cheers!'

After a few drinks, it dawned on me that I had some matches coming up, no cue, and no money left after the races to buy a new one. 'Hang on,' I said, 'I've got to think about this. I've got to get a new cue.'

'We'll have to do a few fruit machines?' Lenny suggested, only half in jest.

We'd had a couple by then, and it seemed like a solid idea. We staggered off into the night to the nearest likely pub, where the fruit machine obligingly coughed up about sixty quid, enough for a decent cue. It took me about six weeks to get used to it, a lot less time than most players take – many players take months, if not years, to get to grips with a new cue.

When I went round to see Maureen, she slammed the door in my face and said we were through. So I got on with developing my professional career all over the country and this, somehow, always included having a laugh.

My first professional match was at the Goitre, Stoke on Trent, against Patsy Fagan, which I won, 2-1. Usually Peewee drove me to the fixtures in his Cougar, a dangerously fast American car, often all the way up north, to the working men's clubs, where I'd be paid about £250 a time. Sometimes, Peewee got fed up with drinking halves of lager throughout the night, while I was on large vodkas, so, especially when we were up in Scotland or Newcastle, I would book a hotel room. But, when the card games lasted until 5 a.m. there didn't seem much point in checking in. Bleary-eyed in so many anonymous dawns, we would get in the car and drive somewhere else. I'd get in the back with an eight-pack of lager in case I woke up and was thirsty, stretch out my legs and have a kip. 'Lord of leisure,' Peewee would mutter morosely, glaring at me in the rear-view mirror as he fought to keep awake in the driver's seat. 'Shut up, muppet, stop complaining,' I would joke, to Peewee's fury. In later years, when I had a limo, I'd pull up the glass between driver and passenger so I couldn't hear Peewee muttering away and I'd get on the mobile, which for some reason riled him even more.

According to him, things weren't any better when I flew. There was this time when I asked him to take me to Heathrow, where I was due to depart from Terminal 1. It was so early I hadn't bothered to go to bed, knowing I could snatch a few hours' sleep on the plane. When Peewee drove up to the entrance of the terminal I got out my bag and leaned my head inside the car window. 'Leave the car here, mate, come on inside, we'll have a bit of breakfast,' I urged.

'No, I can't, Jimmy, I'm parked on a double yellow,' Peewee pointed out. 'Anyoldways, I've got to get back to Crystal Palace to see this bird who's buying me car off of me.'

'Nah, it'll be all right for half an hour, c'mon, let's go,' I said. 'It's too early for the traffic wardens to bother.'

Naturally, when Peewee came out an hour or so later the car had been towed away. He turned out his pockets and came up with £3. He had to take a train to Crystal Palace, to get the money on trust from the girl who was buying his car, to catch a cab that cost £45 all the way back to the Heathrow car pound, to pay a fine of £120 – out of the £250 he should have got. Breakfast at Terminal 1: one hundred and sixty-eight notes. You won't do that again in a hurry, will you, Peewee?

One of the places I used to hide when I didn't want to go home was at the Vauxhall flat of a black cab driver, Michael Conetta. Mick used to keep strange hours, so it seemed as if his flat was open house to half the night-birds of London. It overlooked Covent Garden market, which came awake at three a.m., so there was always a lot of activity. When you ask Mick about those days now, he can't remember them too clearly, because life was one

long party. As one group left, another crowd would drop
in. Just before I crashed out on some settee or another, I
always seemed to remember that I missed Maureen, but
I wasn't going to let her know. And, on reflection, that
was pretty stupid. It's nearly as stupid as spending £168
on breakfast.

I made it up with Maureen after the cue incident and
promised that I would keep in touch more, make more of
an effort to be around. 'I understand that you have to
work,' Maureen said, 'but I don't want a part-time
relationship.' One day I called, keeping in touch as I had
promised, and Maureen asked, 'Where are you, Jimmy?'

'At the races,' I said.

'Well, you'd better get home,' said Maureen, 'because
after I've watched *Dallas*, I'm going to have the baby.'

'Yeah, very funny,' I said.

'I'm not joking, Jimmy,' Maureen said. She obviously
knew these things because, sure enough, as soon as the
credits rolled round on JR & Co, she called her friend,
Sharon, and they went off to the hospital. Suddenly
jolted into a different gear, I raced to the hospital,
bursting through the doors, demanding to be let in.
Lauren was born by then and I was ashamed that I
hadn't been there. I promised Maureen and my new
baby daughter the sun, moon and the stars, and I meant
it. I vowed I would be a wonderful father and always be
there for her. I told Maureen she was wonderful too and
I'd do whatever she wanted.

'Yeah, yeah, yeah,' said Maureen, having heard it all
before. 'I know you'll do your best, Jimmy.' She was so
much wiser than me. She knew that I did mean well – but
she also knew that I hadn't really had much of a normal
teenage life and needed time to grow up, to spread my
wings before coming back down to earth. I wasn't ready
to settle down. She accepted that. What she didn't accept

were what I called me mates and she called the hangers-on, and never knowing where I was.

'But they're my friends!' I protested. 'Me mates.'

'Some of them are, Jimmy,' Maureen said. 'You've got to learn the difference.'

I kissed her and my new little girl and went off to wet the baby's head, happy that we had reached a new understanding. I felt a new age was indeed dawning. To tell the truth, I was in a state of utter shock. Maureen lying there with a real live baby girl that I was responsible for seemed so unreal I needed time to think. A lot of time. One thing led to another, as things do, and, five days later, it occurred to me that this wasn't the way to start on our new understanding, and that Maureen might be just a teeny bit miffed. I rushed around to the hospital at three o'clock in the morning with such a ridiculous cock and bull story about having been at one end of the earth and about to leave for the other, for the Kiev Classic in Russia or the Congo Invitational, that they let me in.

I threw myself across Maureen's bed, waking her up in order to beg forgiveness. I think she must have been half-asleep, because she did forgive me. I wanted to see the baby, but she wouldn't allow that. 'She's asleep, I'm asleep, all the babies are asleep,' she said. 'Go and get some sleep yourself, Jimmy, you look awful. They're letting me leave today and I want you here to collect me and the baby and take us home. That's *today*, Jimmy, okay?'

I tip-toed to go out of the room. 'Tell Lauren I love her,' I whispered into the darkness and walked smack into the wall.

ELEVEN

A RIOTOUS TIME

Lauren was about sixteen months old when Maureen and I decided to get married. We'd split up yet again and Maureen had started going out a lot. I knew that it was my fault and I thought it would make things better if I asked her to marry me. Being Maureen, she refused, so I said, 'If we don't get married now, then it's definitely over between us.'

Maureen saw that I was serious and agreed. We didn't have enough money for a licence and had to borrow some without saying what it was for. Then we booked the registry office in Wandsworth Bridge Road for the following Monday – it was already Wednesday or Thursday, so it was only four or five days away. We didn't tell a soul because, the way things were, we weren't sure if we would make it to the registry office without falling out again.

'If we're still together on Sunday night, we'll tell our parents,' Maureen decided. I think she might also have told her best friend, Sharon.

The date we had set was 28 March. Maureen said it was so close to April Fool's Day, that all things considered we should get married – if at all – on that day. 'Our relationship's like an April Fool, Jimmy,' she said. 'A big joke.' But we had fixed it up with the registrar for the 28th and neither one of us could be bothered to change it.

On Sundays Mum usually had Lauren for the day, so that morning Maureen told me to tell Mum when I took our daughter around. 'Did you tell her?' she asked when I returned. 'Yeah, sure. She was fine, no problem,' I lied. That was when Maureen told her own mum but not her two sisters nor her schoolboy brother. She said she didn't want to in case we had changed our mind by the next day.

That evening, when Maureen went to get Lauren, she said to my mum, 'Well, what do you think?'

Mum looked at her blankly and said, 'What do I think about what?' which was when Maureen realised I had not mentioned it.

'About Jimmy and me, we're getting married in the morning,' said Maureen – just like the song. 'What do you think?' she asked again.

Well, Mum went ballistic – that's what she thought. She was absolutely furious that there was no time to do any of the traditional things that marked a South London wedding. There was no time to invite family and friends, no time to arrange a wedding breakfast, no time to buy a new outfit and, most important of all, a hat. But under-lying everything, was the biggest problem of all – that even after six years together and a lovely granddaughter whom she adored, Mum was still convinced that Maureen was taking her baby away from her. Eventually, in the fullness of time, as they say, they got on very well and came to love each other very much, but in the early years, it was not easy.

Nor was it easy when Maureen returned home with Lauren. Now she was furious. 'Your mum didn't know!

You coward, you never told her,' she raged.

'I forgot,' was all I could think of to say. 'I was about to tell her when something else happened.' Then, cautiously, I asked, 'Anyway, how did she take it?'

'How do you expect she took it?' Maureen said. 'She was just a bit upset, of course. Sort of pissed off, in fact. But she'll come round when we've been married another six years or so.'

The next morning, before her sister, Helen, went to work, she asked Maureen if it was on or off for the afternoon. 'I don't really know to be honest,' Maureen said. 'Why?'

'Well, how will it look if I say to my boss, Oh I might need the afternoon off – my sister might be getting married and I might be a bridesmaid?'

'Well, take the afternoon off, anyway,' Maureen suggested. Later that afternoon, Maureen was dressed in a black outfit, horrifying her friends when they came over to help out. 'Maureen! You can't get married in black!' Sharon exclaimed. Maureen said she had nothing else. Sharon was wearing a pretty grey outfit, so she took it off and she and Maureen dressed in each other's clothes. Girls are quick, I'm not being patronising – they really are. You have to admire them.

We went for a quick pre-wedding drink at Maxie's, a kind of illegal drinking club at Tooting market, along to the registry office, did the deed and went back to Maureen's mum for a drink with the family. Maureen's girlfriends ran along to the market to get some things to eat and we had a small jolly-up and I think someone gave us a wedding present. Halfway through it, Maureen's little brother, Michael, came in from school, and was choked that we hadn't told him anything. But that was of minor consequence because by night-time, Maureen was talking about having the marriage annulled ASAP and I went home to sleep at Mum's.

The following day it was all over the newspapers. The front page of the *Star* read, '*And Baby Comes Too*' and the phone was ringing off the hook. Maureen and I decided to escape and hide out at Flickers, a club in Tooting, in the afternoon to make up our wedding day tiff and have a private celebration on our own. We had no inkling at all that outside, in the streets, half South London had erupted into flames. The riots had started in the steamy heat of a Brixton summer. In a matter of hours the explosion reached Tooting, where we and a few other people were dancing to the disco music. When it was time to go, the manager said, 'Sorry, you can't leave, there's a bit of trouble outside,' – which was something of an understatement.

Suddenly, the sound system was turned off. We all clustered around in the sudden hush, straining our ears to hear what was happening on the streets. It was like being in a bomb shelter where the muffled silence is almost worse than knowing if your house has been blown up or not. We couldn't stand the silence and in the end some people in the club started throwing things. It started with ice-cubes and escalated to chairs, so we left. Turning right at the crossroads on to the main Broadway – we saw the scene the rioters had left in their wake. Every shop window was broken. There was glass and loot everywhere. Crowds of people roamed aimlessly around. When we walked past a handbag and shoe shop on the corner, Maureen said, 'Oh, that's nice,' pointing to a handbag in a display. I climbed into the big window and started clowning around with the bag over my shoulder, until Maureen told me not to be a prat and to get out of there before the cops came. I stepped down on to the pavement but carried on mucking about, across the road, with the bag over my shoulder.

Then a police car came skidding by. They must have clocked something and I promptly dropped the bag. The police roared back, picked up the bag and said, 'Right, where did you get that?'

It was like Berlin in 1945. The Russians have just arrived and they spot Corporal White, not raping, looting, burning and pillaging; but with a handbag.

I said we had found it, but they didn't believe us, insisting we'd broken a window to get it. We were arrested and taken down to the nick, where it was, 'Hi, Jimmy, how you doing!' from half of Tooting – because half of Tooting had been arrested. They couldn't accommodate us all, so the police had desks in the middle of the street in the sun. It was an incredible scene. We sat on the pavement with our friends, until our names were called. Maureen and I had had a few drinks in Flickers so I probably wasn't at my most tactful. Noting down my details, the copper asked (incredibly), 'How much do you earn a year?'

'I don't know, it depends if I win or lose,' I said. 'Lots, or sod all. It depends.'

That wasn't precise enough for him. 'Look, how much do earn a year?' He banged the table and all my friends lining up behind me or at adjacent tables laughed, which set me off too. I said, 'About a hundred times as much as you do.' The copper looked as though he was going to grab hold of me, but he charged us both instead with looting, and banged us up in the police cells. I couldn't believe they had actually locked us up. We got sober very quickly.

In the morning, our dads came to bail us out, with the usual lectures, until we said we hadn't done anything really, we were only fooling around and then it was, 'Bloody police, always getting it wrong!'

Maureen and I had to go to the magistrates the next day. After being on the front pages for our secret wedding, we were suddenly back all over the papers for being arrested. Where was Max Clifford, king of the PR spin doctors, when I needed him most? He only lived up the road in Wimbledon. There were so many journalists that the courts had to smuggle us in and out of the back way for the hearing, which was adjourned to Crown Court.

It didn't dawn on me that being arrested for looting could cause problems; but this happened at the same time that I signed up with Sportsworld. They had big plans for promoting me with a brand-new image, as if I were a pop star. The idea was that this would lead to some heavy sponsorship and merchandising deals – as against bail, disgrace, a court case and newspapers digging out pictures of look-alikes who had been transported to – yes, Tasmania – on the prison ships. Lord Lichfield was on hold to take some snazzy photographs, after extensive dental work and a new hairdo that was to scare Maureen half to death one night. When I crept into the bedroom at my usual dawn hour, she thought I was a burglar and screamed, pulling the covers over her head.

'It's me, Maureen!' I whispered softly, not wanting to wake the baby.

Maureen sat up in bed, cackling hysterically. 'They've *permed* your hair,' she said, 'and you let them!'

'I don't mind it,' I said, which was true. The new clothes, the photographs, I didn't mind any of them if it helped my career. And with a new family, I was getting quite business-minded. But the court case hanging over my head was like the sword of Damocles – if it fell, my brand-new image (and new hairdo) would be destroyed at a stroke – at least, according to Geoff Lomas, who wanted me to be whiter than white. He even attached a full-time spokesman to me like a limpet mine as a reminder, so I wouldn't open my big mouth and blow it, as I often did.

'It's no good being natural, Jimmy,' the PR man

lectured me, 'if *natural* lets the image down. You can't talk about Zan's and scams and the shady people you know when you're interviewed. We've got to reinvent you.'

That was easier said than done. I would let them dress me up in an expensive suit, then I'd change into jeans and dump the suit under some snooker table or in a corner of my dressing room – or worse, get wrecked and sleep in it. I forgot, or overslept through, interviews, like Keith Richards.

All this work was in preparation for my first big tournament, the Langs Supreme Scottish Masters, at Kelvin Hall, Glasgow, which coincided with my appearance in court. My solicitor wrote to say I couldn't make it since I was playing snooker and the judge was not amused. She issued a warrant for my arrest. I ignored these urgent demands to appear in court and played on, beating Ray Reardon 5–4; Steve Davis 6–5; and Cliff Thorburn 9–4 in the final. I think it even added a bit of an edge to my game. In fact, the semi-final against Steve Davis aroused the most comment because I was the only player to have beaten him in the past year. The *Star* said: 'People were complaining that Steve was too good; the odds uneven; the game boring.' It wasn't much of a compliment to praise me for winning only because it knocked Davis off his pedestal for a while. However, another journalist wrote up a piece declaiming that at the age of twenty I was the youngest English Amateur champion, the youngest World Amateur champion and now – the youngest winner of a major pro tournament. I was more interested in the prize – a magnificent £8000.

Of the Sportsworld new image treatment, I was reported as saying, 'None of this is going to make me bigheaded. Even if I had ten grand in my pocket, when I walk down the street in Tooting everything is still the same.'

There was still the matter of the South-Western Crown Court hearing which was postponed for some six months. My barrister had told me that the WPBSA might ban me from playing, for bringing the game into disrepute if I were found guilty – something that I hadn't taken into consideration. This was getting far more serious than I had realised. When we went into court, we were very subdued because we were convinced that we wouldn't get off. I was told that by ignoring the summons to appear in court I hadn't done my case any good.

'We need a miracle to win,' my barrister moaned.

Straight out of *Rumpole of the Bailey*, the miracle turned up in the shape of an entry in a policeman's notebook. When the policeman was reading from his notes a record of how he had seen us from a certain angle, our barrister looked at the diagram he had in front of him and as quick as a flash he realised that we could not have been seen from that particular angle.

Brilliant. Case dismissed.

TWELVE

I DON'T DO TRICK SHOTS

I had first met Manchester snooker-hall owner, Geoff Lomas, in 1979, when I appeared in one of his pro-am tournaments. I knew he managed Alex Higgins and that was as good a reference in my eyes as anyone could have. To me, it proved he must have the patience of six saints and the energy of an Olympic sprinter to keep up with Alex, who was a hurricane in private life as well as on the table. When I wanted different management, I bumped into Geoff again at a Benson and Hedges tournament at Wembley.

I didn't want to approach him directly in case I got the brush-off, so I asked a mutual friend to make the approach. Geoff said he hadn't got the time to handle anyone else. Alex was as much as he could cope with, which I understood only too well. However, a few weeks later, Geoff was talking to Harvey Lisberg, owner of Kennedy Street Enterprises, a famous Manchester-based company that represented such pop luminaries as 10CC.

Geoff said to Harvey, 'Look, I've got a lad who needs representation. We might be able to do something, but I can't devote all my time to him.'

Harvey was always interested in sport. Colour TV had made snooker an overnight sensation. There was something seductive about all those coloured balls and the green of the table – it was both relaxing and exciting; and people, it seemed, couldn't get enough. Harvey said he had watched me at the table a few times and thought I was an exciting player, one of the hottest young hopefuls around. He thought it would be great to represent somebody like me who seemed to have the world at his fingertips.

It was agreed that Harvey would handle the more artistic side – that is, my image, the media, the sponsorship deals and so on; while Geoff, as an owner of a snooker hall, would have a more 'hands on' approach to my schedule and organise my matches. In fact, while Harvey kept at a distance from technique, Geoff was very much into the whole coaching aspect, something I wasn't keen on. To this day I have never had what could be termed a coach, although in my early days I absorbed things just from being around some brilliant players.

Harvey and Geoff went to see Henry West, who agreed he would sell on my contract for £10,000, which came out of Sportsworld (the new company set up initially to manage me), with Harvey and Geoff acting jointly. It wasn't to be very long before Alex was also signed up to Sportsworld.

It was decided that my career would be handled scientifically. Now 'scientific' is a word that I personally wouldn't associate with myself, but I'm amenable to most things and, if they wanted scientific, then who was I to spoil their fun?

The approach was three-pronged.

First, they would change my image – tidy me up, fix my teeth (I had an overbite), curl my hair and persuade me to dress flash – in other words, make me look more like one of the pop stars that Harvey managed.

Then they would look for endorsements, merchandising deals and model assignments. When I heard the last bit, to say I was taken aback would be an understatement. Me, a model? Already I could hear my mates in fits and wincing every time they met me. Harvey brought me back a beautiful dress suit from the South of France and they curled my hair. When I stared in the mirror I was amazed at how different I looked.

Problems they hadn't thought of quickly surfaced. For example, when West End tailor, Tommy Nutter, offered me the kind of sponsorship deal which Harvey thought could ultimately earn me around half a million pounds a year (with other similar deals coming in on the back of it), I was ordered to put sticky tape over the logo on my waistcoat because no advertising deal existed between BBC TV, the WPBSA and the Jameson Whiskey International at Newcastle. It didn't help playing the tournament with my chest crackling every time I moved.

Secondly, Sportsworld wanted me to take the game more seriously, like Steve Davis. In fact, this is where the scientific bit came in. I was to approach the game like a chess match, with caution, planning and cunning. Comments from me like, 'I can't predict how I'm going to play. When everything's right, a funny feeling comes over me, my whole body is affected. I get all warm and my head starts to buzz. I know then that I can't miss. I'm unbeatable, but it doesn't last,' used to bother Geoff.

'You have to be able to predict how you're going to play,' he said, trying to make me see sense as he saw it. 'Your game has to be more scientific – you've got to practise, practise, practise. You can't tumble out of a card game and into a major snooker tournament with minutes to spare, everybody biting their nails.'

That bit was true; but, 'I get there, don't I?' I said. 'Anyway, nobody can predict how they're going to play, it's all down to the way the balls go,' I pointed out quite reasonably.

'I'll never criticise or interfere with your play, Jimmy,' Harvey said. 'A manager's got a job and it's not playing on the table. He should keep out of that because the player knows best. When it comes to the snooker table, the manager is in a different light-year. But the manager can look after everything to do with a player's life, the bookings, the sponsorship deals, the business side.'

'Okay,' I said, casually, 'whatever you want, Harvey.'

I think Harvey was bothered by my casual acceptance of their big plans. The reality would be far different. My lackadaisical ways inevitably would drive him potty because Harvey is very organised, very tidy and efficient, as you have to be to run such a big organisation successfully. Me, I was only running myself, playing the best game I could at any particular time. All this scientific talk just gave me a headache.

I read in the paper the other day that, statistically, the most popular answer when a doctor asked a patient, 'What's the matter?' – or 'What seems to be the problem?' was 'It's doin' my head in, Doc.' Apparently most people find it very hard to articulate how they feel about very much, especially about things they don't want to think about, and the generic term for this is indeed, 'It's doin' my head in.' I knew what it felt like.

I remember once I played Harvey at pool in a bar on a teeny table, all crooks and curves. In one frame, Harvey potted every ball and left the black dead in the middle of the bottom cushion – about seven inches from the hole; and about four inches in front of it was the white. Absolutely safe, as he thought.

'I see you've left it for me,' I said, and going up, I doubled it at a hundred miles an hour, straight into a pocket.

Harvey laughed, and turning to a friend who was

watching us, he said ruefully, 'You can't play with people like that, they're in a world of their own.'

Harvey was always amazed at the way Stephen Hendry's manager, Ian Doyle, used to watch and criticise Stephen's play. 'I can't believe he has the nerve to say that about somebody who is so talented,' Harvey said. 'It's like me telling Elton John he was no good on stage one night and to sing a little better.' (Harvey actually promoted some of Elton John's concerts, so this comparison was quite valid.)

Thirdly, I was to learn a few trick shots so I could give good exhibition, as the snooker groupie said to the player. I tried a few shots, like rolling the white ball slowly and hitting a complete line-up of reds into a corner pocket before the white ball got there; bouncing balls over cups, and that kind of thing but after a while I found I had no patience. I would leave all that to brilliant trick shot champions like Mike Massey.

'Come on, just set the balls up and we'll play a few games. I'm sure I can entertain 'em in that way,' I said, and I was doing well, having just won the Scottish Masters against Cliff Thorburn. The *Guardian* said: 'Jimmy "Whirlwind" White took three world champions by storm, to win the Langs Supreme Scottish Masters . . . he started his rout of snooker's big guns when he defeated seven times world champion, Ray Reardon. He then met south-east Londoner Steve Davis in the semi-final and beat him 6-5. Things were looking glum for the youngster early in his final match though. He was 3-0 down against Canadian, Cliff Thorburn, also a former champion . . . then the Whirlwind started playing more like a tornado . . .'

Ray Reardon said he was so disgusted with his snooker after our match that he was thinking of retiring. 'I don't mind being beaten,' he said, 'but I feel disgraced by losing as I have today.' He blamed his cue. 'It's all in my mind but I have spent 18 months looking for a new cue since the one I had for 30 years cracked up. I'm so desperate that I'm thinking of getting out of snooker. The turmoil is breaking me up inside.' I was sad for Ray, but at that age I was bewildered at the idea of retiring over a cue.

Harvey and Geoff were delighted by my first major win and I think that was when they decided to pull out all stops to help build my image and career. We discovered that if you added to the mix the very newsworthy fact that Harvey was a celebrity in his own right through his association with so many pop stars – like Brian Epstein was through being connected with the Beatles – my new launch took off like a rocket.

Whatever snooker players did, the papers wanted to know. Harvey was amazed. Instead of having to 'sell' me, trying to persuade some editor or another to commission a kind of soft-focus feature, he was actually fighting off the press assault. I was used to having my picture taken. I was even used to nice little features, like the one the *Observer* ran when I was just sixteen, when they named me Mumm's 'Sports Personality of the Week' – 'Little big shot on cue', the headline read, going on to say (referring to the champagne that came with the write-up) 'our only misgiving was whether he'd be permitted to get wired in to the bubbly stuff.' Little did they know I'd been into the bubbly and the G & T and the lager – into anything I could lay my hands on – for years. I could have run a pub.

Harvey asked me if I could cope with what he thought could be screaming fans and mass hysteria. 'Can you handle it, Jimmy?' he asked anxiously. 'There could be people trying to break into your home, camping on your doorstep. Believe me, I've seen it.'

'I don't mind signing a few autographs,' I said, crossing my fingers behind my back. I had missed so much schooling that my reading and writing were almost non-existent. Maureen actually taught me more in a few months than I'd learned at school – not the fault of my teachers, I hasten to add. You can't teach a boy who's never there. I was thinking of the day when a fan had asked me to write 'All my love, Jimmy White', and Peewee at my shoulder had whispered in my ear what to write, letter by letter. Obediently, methodically, I had carefully printed 'You are a fat pig signed Jimmy White'.

The hit song at this time was 'Jimmy Mack'. I was stunned the day I arrived at the Crucible, the theatre in Sheffield where the World Cup is held, to be besieged by fans, who had changed the words to fit, chanting *Jimmy White – You're all right!* and *Jimmy, Jimmy White – you're going to win tonight.* At first I thought it was set up, that one of my mates was playing a practical joke or Harvey had hired a group of cheerleaders, but when they rushed at me screaming this anthem, and I felt the power of their genuine emotion, I knew what the Beatles felt like. Well, almost. There's a marked difference between a hundred fans and a hundred thousand.

Afterwards, I asked Harvey how I'd done. 'Wonderful, Jimmy,' he said approvingly. 'You waved, gave them a big cheery grin, you're a natural. It was very sweet of them all.' Nowadays it's called 'meet and greet'.

'Well, they're nice kids,' I said, and I mean that. I won't leave until I've signed every autograph book, let them take snaps, had a little chat, especially with the ones in a wheelchair. I am very moved by those less able than us – they always have to make the most tremendous effort in life and anything I can do to help them, I will.

There are a few who I will always make special arrangements for because I feel they deserve it, kids like Shane Halls. Shane was two and a half years old when I first met him in 1984 at an exhibition match between me and Steve Davis at the Derby assembly rooms. Shane was born with a rare condition which in layman's terms means 'fixed joints' – he can't bend his arms or straighten his legs. As a young child he couldn't do what normal children can do, which is sit on the carpet and play with toys, so basically, he spent his first few years in front of a television set, watching the sport. Over the years, Shane's condition has got worse. His mother, Pat, told me recently that my interest in him has given Shane the courage to go on in the most severest of pain, which is quite a lot for me to live up to.

If I am in their area, often I will ring up out of the blue to arrange for the family to watch me play, pleased that I can lay everything on to make life just a little easier for them for perhaps twenty-four hours. It does so much to boost Shane's interest in life. I don't see the wheelchair he is trapped in – I see the boy sitting there who some day wants to be a sport journalist, even though he is almost immobile and can't write.

Liz Metcalfe is someone else who won't let her disability hold back her zest for life. She told me that she had wanted to meet me for ages, but, because the MS she suffers from has confined her to a wheelchair, it didn't seem very likely. Then she met John Nielsen, who arranged for her to meet me at Wembley for the Benson & Hedges Masters. We hit it off right away, as if we had been old friends from way back. I arranged for her to come back the next day when I was playing James Wattana. I even got Ronnie Wood to spend the evening pushing her wheelchair around, helping her up and down stairs and lifts – and escorting her to the door of the loo! Ronnie and I have even taken Liz to a disco.

I have an extra soft spot for nurses and will always help them if possible. Sue Doyle had nursed John Nielsen when he had cancer of the throat some years ago and when I was playing Tony Knowles at Sheffield in the World Championships, I arranged for Sue and her husband, Chris, to come up. Rooms were in short supply that fortnight but I was glad to give up my hotel room to them, moving in with another player. 'It was like a second honeymoon,' Sue told me.

Some months after I signed to Sportsworld, Alex Higgins also came aboard (moving sideways from being represented solely by Geoff), thus starting to fulfil a major plan that Harvey was formulating, which was to form another league in competition with the WPBSA, whom many people were unhappy with. Barry Hearn and Steve Davis had done this with Matchplay, using the powerbase of Steve's Number One position in the world rankings. Harvey thought that as soon as Alex or I won the title, then he could move fast on the sponsorship side, build up our profile to an even greater degree and strike deep into the heart of WPBSA territory. In Harvey's opinion, Alex had been the greatest draw of all time, but it had been eleven years since he had last won the world title, in 1971, and the wide press coverage of the dramas of his private life had frightened off all sponsorship deals. 'If we'd had Alex when he was twenty-five or so, maybe we could have done it,' was Harvey's opinion.

In their eyes, that left me to carry the flame – but, although I was to win the Scottish Masters and the Northern Irish Classic (beating Steve Davis 11-9), I still had not landed the big one.

The relationship between Alex Higgins and Sportsworld was to be short and not very sweet. In a tide of alcohol and acrimony, Alex walked out, much to Harvey's secret relief. Three weeks later, Alex won the 1982 World Championship at Sheffield, with tears all round. But Harvey didn't cry because, as he said, even if they had still had Alex signed to them, there was no guaranteeing his good behaviour; in fact, he said, only tears were guaranteed. They could also confidently predict that Alex Higgins would be the only title holder with no sponsorship deals to his name. Geoff Lomas, on the other hand, was inconsolable. He had managed Alex for some years, struggled through tantrums and bad publicity, and felt he deserved a share of the glory.

Alex had beaten me 16-15 in the semi-final in 1982. It would have been easier for our managers if we had taken different routes and come together in the final. But it wasn't to be. The other semi-final was Reardon v Charlton and Reardon went through.

In that semi-final, though, I was ahead 15-13 and 41 points to nothing up when I missed the black off its spot. They said I was cracking under the pressure – even today, people say privately that a sucked thumb softened my resolve and that I was moved to sentiment by the sight of Alex's toddler, Lauren, upfront, after all Alex's domestic troubles. That's nonsense – my own little tot (also called Lauren and older by a few months) was also there – in fact both little girls and both wives were watching together. I just missed the shot, that's all. Alex took his time, cleared up and went on to take the match.

Millions watched this semi-final on TV. The headlines read: 'Tear Jerker'; 'Higgins taunts the Whirlwind'; 'Higgins in Final after a Thriller'; and 'Higgins Weeps for White'. There was even a picture of me drinking a glass of milk. (I couldn't show my face for weeks!) Seriously, as I've said, Alex won the final and I was happy for him. Delirious for the bastard, if the truth be known.

One down, one to go. After Alex walked, Harvey and Geoff left me in no doubt that I was to wear his mantle for Sportsworld by winning the title next year. It was a big burden, and if there is one thing I don't enjoy, it's having the heavy weight of responsibility placed on my shoulders. For the public, snooker is an entertainment. For me it's a profession – but it's also great fun. A lot of it is in the laps of the Gods. When I play, it's always because I enjoy it. When it stops being fun, then maybe I'll stop playing. And of course I want to win, we all do. But to be told you *have* to go out and win – that you are *expected* to go out and win – well, that can do anyone's head in.

Since my agency was in Manchester, it made sense for me to get a place there to live. Harvey told me I had enough money to buy a flat and, with Geoff to help house hunt, we bought one about a hundred yards from his own home. Maureen and I went up a couple of weekends to organise the move; but somehow, we never got around to it. Geoff and his wife, Helen, were such warm, friendly people that we felt more comfortable just staying with them. One occasion that will always stick in my mind was a late night after a long day. Maureen and Helen elected to go to bed early, but as far as I was concerned, the day was still young. I suggested to Geoff that we popped along to his club for a quick game and a nightcap.

By the time we returned at three o'clock in the morning, we were both very merry – particularly me. Geoff stayed downstairs to lock up and I felt my way to bed. Now, it was a strange house, so the fact that I crawled into bed with Helen mustn't be misconstrued. It was the stuff of French farces. Geoff came up a few minutes later to find his wife and me both in the same bed, both soundly asleep.

Drunk and infuriated, Geoff wasn't having any. (Neither was I, come to that.) He dragged me out of bed and out of the door in the general direction of my own room. I made my way unsteadily along the hall and tumbled down the stairs. It was just as well that I was relaxed, or I could have broken my neck. They found me in the morning lying on the carpet at the bottom, cuddling the stairpost.

Soon, after a series of similar lapses, Geoff started

taking his job very seriously, even to the extent of giving me a public warning about my late nights, my drinking and my gambling in an open letter to a newspaper. So I had the bizarre situation of Harvey paying good money to kill stories while Geoff was busy dishing the dirt to the same editors – and no doubt earning a buck or two into the bargain.

My gambling did bother Geoff because I treated money so casually. On one occasion, during a six-man challenge match between England and Canada, that was held in Newcastle, I borrowed £100 from Geoff for a quick flutter, which I lost. The next day, I was so sure that Tony Knowles was going to beat 'Lager' Bill Werbeniuk that I borrowed another £100. Tony won, so now I had £200 – which I promptly lost that night at cards. Then I thought I had a winning hand, and rushed off to find Geoff to borrow another £100 – which he peeled off resignedly with a lecture. I won that game, and had £600 in a fat bundle of tenners to prove it.

The next day, as we were leaving Newcastle, the car broke down. We went to a café while Geoff called the AA. When Geoff joined us I slowly counted out the tenners, just to wind him up. I could see he was expecting me to pay him back his £300 – but I'd just seen a bookie's, and with a good tip on a dog, I nipped across the street to put the lot on. By the time the AA van came, I was skint.

'What about the three hundred you owe me?' Geoff asked, amazed by my cheek.

I grinned at him, 'Look, Geoff, if I'd paid you back I would only be bumming it off you now, wouldn't I? So I've saved you a lot of hassle.'

Geoff was speechless and immediately noted it down in his little notebook so he could hit me over the head with it later. 'How do you think it feels, Jimmy,' he used to say, 'when you're supposed to get on a plane to Dublin and you phone me up ten minutes after the plane has left and say, "Hi, Geoff, what am I going to do?" And I've got to hire a private plane to take you. How do you think I feel?'

He really was serious about trying to fathom me out – not realising that I can't even fathom myself out. People are always saying I should do this – or I should do that – or starting sentences with, 'The trouble with you, Jimmy,' as if they are gurus. In the end, although I didn't know it, Geoff actually produced a guru to get into my brain. He thought a doctor of psychology would help them all get a handle on what made me tick from their new, scientific point of view so they could get me to be on time, to stop leading them such a merry dance – and to win every match I played, no doubt, which as any player can tell you is almost impossible because nobody is a machine – except maybe the 'Alien' Hendry!

I was staying at Geoff's home on my own without Maureen, when Geoff came into the living room with this chap, who he introduced to me as a friend. Suddenly Geoff looked at his watch and said, 'Oh, is that the time? I've got to fly. I'll be back in an hour.' And he was gone.

The man laughed as he settled in his chair and started to chat to me about this that and the other. After about two hours Geoff returned, the man stood up, shook hands and disappeared. What I didn't learn, until years later, was that he was a doctor and he had come to the conclusion that nothing motivated me.

'Nothing!' he'd written in his report. 'Money doesn't motivate him because he's had money since he was twelve years of age. Not glory, because he'd won everything by the time he was sixteen or seventeen.'

I presume that money didn't motivate the doctor of psychology and that, as he'd failed completely with my consultation, he did not present a bill.

After reading this report, Geoff thought, 'Well, I'll bloody well motivate him because I'll shame him!' And that was when he wrote the open letter to the paper. What he was really looking for was to change me in every way – to change my image, to make me glossy and slick, someone else altogether. In fact, he didn't really want to manage me, or even Alex Higgins – he wanted to manage Steve Davis. Unfortunately, you can have all the scientific approaches in the world, but you can't make human clones. At least, not yet.

Even Harvey got on my case, lecturing me about the stories he kept reading in the papers, despite his best efforts to kill them. I would be thrown out of one hotel because the manager objected to me ordering eight breakfasts one morning when the room was supposed to be occupied by one person. Instead of knocking politely on the door and discussing it with me, he wrote a formal letter, which somehow got leaked to the papers. I didn't think it was a crime to put your friends up, especially when you've been up all night playing cards and not sleeping in bed anyway – which reminds me of when the Kenyan team came over for a tournament. They cooked all their meals on a little primus stove in their room. It was the smell of bacon wafting on the morning air that drew the hotel manager's attention to this illegal soup kitchen going on under her nose.

Harvey called me in and complained that he would never get endorsements for me when all he read in the papers were stories about me being drunk and disorderly in hotel rooms.

'I don't get drunk and disorderly,' I protested.

'No, *you're* a very quiet person, Jimmy,' Harvey agreed. 'It's your friends. You surround yourself with the most peculiar people and it reflects on you. "Disorderly" is not a word Brylcreem want to hear in connection with someone they're sponsoring.'

'But they're me mates,' I said. 'We're just having a laugh.'

Harvey also used to nag me about the unsociable hours I kept. As an example of how he wished I would be, he used to refer to a tournament in Glasgow, when I was playing Steve Davis in the final. The morning of the final, Harvey came down to the hotel dining room at eight o'clock, to find Steve sitting at the table. When he'd eaten his egg, Steve carefully folded his napkin and nodded politely to Harvey. 'Excuse me, I hope you don't mind,' Steve said, 'I have to go down to the local club to put in some practice.'

By then, with me nowhere in sight, Harvey was thinking 'That bloody Jimmy's probably just gone to bed – and that is who he is competing with.'

Harvey did have to drag me out of bed with about ten minutes to go to make the bell; and, as predicted, I got thrashed. Afterwards, he said to me, more in sorrow than in anger, 'You really had no chance, Jimmy. You don't allow yourself a level playing field.'

Harvey's personal favourite story, that to him sums up our relationship, relates to the time I played in a tournament in the Midlands. In those days, Harvey was quite a gambler himself, and when I got to the final against Ray Reardon, he decided to have a flutter, putting £400 on me to win at odds of 7-1 against. This was quite a substantial sum back then and these were long odds.

'You could have beaten Reardon at that time blindfolded with one hand tied behind your back,' Harvey told me, 'but at the eleventh hour, I suddenly decided to lay the bet off.'

Harvey had told his wife, Carole, his intention. Indignantly she had said, 'You can't! You can't bet against your own man, it's not right.'

Harvey had said to her, 'But I haven't seen Jimmy all day. He's been out all night, God knows what might happen in the match.'

But Carole was determined that Harvey should do the

gentlemanly thing, and he let the bet ride. The next day, after Reardon had beaten me, Harvey came charging up to me and said, 'You cost me £3000!'

I was amazed and asked him what he meant. 'I backed you 7-1 and you lost,' Harvey said. 'You should have won – but all that drinking and cavorting last night ruined your chances.'

'Well, you're bang out of order, you are, betting on me, when you knew I could've lost,' I told him. Harvey's mouth dropped open with amazement at being told off by me when in his eyes I was the one who was out of order.

The kindest thing Harvey did for me was after Kirk Stevens's magical 147 in the 1984 Benson & Hedges Masters at Wembley. Kirk looked like a Californian rock star that day in his all-white outfit, including shoes, quite a shock for the stuffy rules that said we had to wear black. Actually, he was wearing some black – the border to his white waistcoat. I don't know how I kept a straight face when I found out he'd pinched a pair of trousers out of my wardrobe for the quarter-final against Steve Davis – and when they turned out lucky for him, he refused to give them back.

But, my pants aside, the flair and elegance with which Kirk potted those balls was mesmerising. I have seen video replays and I'm sitting there watching with a great goofy smile on my face. However, Harvey felt that the psychological aspects of that dragonfly dance of Kirk's would knock me for six and drain my confidence. During the interval, when the cheers had died down, Harvey came to my corner very much like a manager does to a boxer between bouts and gave me a fatherly pep talk.

'Forget the 147 – it was wonderful; but it was one of those flukes that happen once in a blue moon. You have to focus on winning,' he said.

Well, I don't know if it was Harvey's kind advice or not – but I went on to win that game; and, eventually, the tournament against Terry Griffiths, 8-3. The prize money was £35,000 and that was when it hit home – that you could make a living, and a very nice one too, from this game.

At the party afterwards, Geoff told my mum that the reason he thought I had won was because of the 'open letter' he'd written in the newspaper. 'It made him see sense,' Geoff said.

'Oh, really?' Mum said, daintily sipping her Scotch.

None of my little peccadilloes have really affected my career. But one affair did cause me grief. It was suggested that I had been taking bribes. Now, I might do many things, but for me, bribery in the game is and always will be, absolutely out of the question. Again, it was another set-up, but one that I had to take very seriously and couldn't ignore.

It was the first day of the 1984 Benson & Hedges at Wembley Stadium. Although I wasn't due to play Willie Thorne in the first round for another four days, I had gone in early to get a little practice. A man I had never seen before in my life approached me. 'Jimmy,' he said, his eyes darting about like balls on stalks, 'can I have a word with you?'

'Do I know you, mate?' I said.

He produced a card and again repeated that he wanted to have a word with me in private. He refused to say what it was about, although I noticed that he was carrying a small case. I took him into my dressing room and said I had about five minutes. Before I had finished talking, he flipped open the lid of the case. It was full to the brim with cash.

'Thirty-five grand,' he said, proffering it to me. 'You can count it.'

Now, you can't help it, you have to take a little look, your hand reaches out and you're flicking the corners of the bundles.

'It's a lot of money,' I said. 'So what's it got to do with me?'

'It's yours if you let Willie beat you, 5-2.'

£35,000 was what the overall winner of the tournament would get after a lot of effort, not to mention luck, because you never know how the balls are going to run – and here he was offering it to me to bow out.

I didn't hesitate for a moment. 'Clear off, mate,' I said. 'Willie Who?' – no, seriously what I actually said was, 'You know I can't do that.' And I couldn't have done. You can't live with being bent, not if you love the game.

The man muttered a couple of threats and slunk off. Now I was totally paranoid, wondering why he had picked on me. Nobody is fooled. The only people I have known pull a stunt like that were the Franciscos and they got caught out. I have known amateurs do it and we ostracised them. My dad, who goes to nearly all my big matches, especially the ones in the south, was in the bar when I went and told him what had just happened. He was furious. 'We'll have the bugger arrested! Let's have a look at that card!' he bawled. 'Who does he think he is!'

I calmed him down because I didn't want a drama. 'It's okay, Dad, I sent him on his way with a flea in his ear. I don't want this blown up in all the papers or people will say there's no smoke without a fire. You know what they're like.'

Dad sank back into his seat. 'Yeah, you're right, son,' he said. 'But he should be stopped. It's right out of order, picking on a youngster like you.'

By an astonishing coincidence, I did beat Willie Thorne 5-2 – going on to win the tournament and capturing the £35,000 prize, so I won the money straight.

However, the following year, at another Benson & Hedges Masters at Wembley, I got a death threat down the phone. At first, I took no notice; until a nastier threat was made in an anonymous phone call to a newspaper about what would happen when I met Cliff Thorburn in the semi-finals. Extra police were drafted in at the arena and I was also given two armed guards for the week of the tournament, great guys, who spent every minute of the day with me, including sleeping at my home.

Eight years later, during the 1995 Embassy World Cup tournament in Sheffield another so-called betting scandal reared up when Peter Francisco and I were suspected of being involved in what was referred to as a £60,000 betting coup. I was tipped off by bookies when I was beating Peter 7-2 overnight. The following morning I went on to win 10-2, the exact score that apparently everyone had bet thousands on, particularly in London's West End, where there seemed to be a betting syndicate putting on £500 at a time. Dozens more, at £50 a time, were placed all around the country. I was 12-1 on, to beat Peter; while the odds on winning 10-2 stood at 5-1, according to *Mail* sportswriter Peter Ferguson. In the opening session the score went to 2-2, then it was an easy canter and I won the next eight frames, but, after the doubt crept in, bets were suspended. I didn't know what else to do other than play my normal game. The WPBSA launched an immediate inquiry. Their chairman, John Spencer (who was himself a three-times world champion), gave key evidence after watching every shot of the twelve-frame match, before I was called in to spend six hours closeted with the board at the Grosvenor Hotel. After looking at all the evidence, they cleared me of any suggestion of wrong-doing. Afterwards, I commented, 'The game is too big and too clean for anything crooked to be involved.' Sadly, it wasn't true where Peter was concerned. He is now back in South Africa – where his brother, Silvino, another fine snooker player, is serving a lengthy sentence for dealing in drugs. Snooker has that effect on some players; it can drag you down – or it can lift you up. The path you ultimately take is up to you.

THIRTEEN

THE DEVIL WENT DOWN TO BOURNEMOUTH

Peewee and I were heading down to Bournemouth on the train. Peewee had sold his car for peanuts because he needed the dough and hadn't saved enough to get another one. With us was a good friend from Manchester, Joe Brittain, who had attached himself to us somewhere along the way. The train rocked through the wild and lovely New Forest where, through the trees, we spotted the occasional shaggy pony or deer.

I had been invited to play John Spencer in an exhibition, where each separate frame was sponsored by local firms, one of which was a casino. We were to be given a nice cheque each for expenses and I was to be supplied with a chauffeured car to take us back to London; but the actual money put on each game, through sponsorship or whatever, was to go to charity. In those days, John Spencer and I would sometimes play each other for a couple of bob, the best of nine, have a good night out and hopefully, some charities would benefit, while we spent the couple of bob on Alka Seltzer and breakfast.

I always liked Bournemouth, with its pier and long, curving coastline, and it was on the pier that the exhibition was being held. Spenny and I didn't play great, just above average, with the crowd yelling each time we missed a pot, giving us plenty of verbal all night. At the end, two of the blokes in the crowd who had been haranguing us the loudest came up to me. One of them, who was – well, if I said he was dressed like a tramp, I'd be paying him a compliment – said, 'I'll play you two and donate £200 to charity if we win. If we lose, we'll give £400.'

'Done,' I said.

The game was chaotic. At one stage I had to go and break up a fight in the crowd while the tramp lined up a shot. Spenny made a handsome 130 break and the tramp didn't get another shot. That was the £400 won; and the place erupted. I was also awarded a silver tankard by the sponsors at the end of the evening. A nice tankard that I thought I might even keep to drink beer out of at home, instead of adding it to the growing collection of cups and crystal trophies that were my mum's pride and joy.

We went backstage to the cubicles which were right over the sea to change. I could hear the roar of the waves and through a hole, the odd spray curled upwards, the entire structure felt very shaky. As I was changing out of my penguin suit back into jeans and shirt, the tramp came shambling in.

'Do you want to come back to my casino?' he asked.

'Casino?' I looked at him doubtfully. His collar was ragged, his jacket torn and missing several buttons, the bottoms of his trousers were frayed and his shoes were down at heel. Now, I've never been one for dressing up like a dog's dinner – but this chap looked like the dinner the dog didn't fancy.

'You'll like it. It's a real nice place, my casino. You'll have a good time.'

I was tempted. I had a cheque for £1200 for expenses, and no other cash on me. Sometimes, cheques are very useful because that way, you can inadvertently arrive home with something to put in the bank. At other times, as now, when you have no cash at all and want even a swift game of kaluki, it can be a bit hard getting credit from total strangers.

Now here was the devil himself dressed as a tramp, trying to tempt me. I should have said, 'Get thee behind me, Satan' – and had Peewee throw him into the sea to clean him up, but I didn't. I whipped out my £1200 cheque and asked those fatal words, 'Can you change this?'

'No problem,' says the tramp.

So we go to the casino, which was real enough; and discovered that the tramp did indeed own the gaff – domes, curlicues, velvet swags, thick plush carpet, and all. I was a bit astonished, but they say that John Paul Getty shuffled around like a down-at-heel bum in the same suit for fifty-five years, which just goes to show. And what about Howard Hughes? Dressed like a bum and washed his hands every five minutes for forty years because of the germs.

I changed the cheque and, before I knew it, was sitting at a table with some top notches, playing Omaha. Joe and Peewee were playing kaluki with Spenny and a couple of other friends who had turned up. The stakes started at £2, rising upwards as the night progressed through £5, £10, and then £20 a game, which is a big game money-wise, although it doesn't sound so much when you say it quickly.

When the game of Omaha started, everyone was speaking English; but, after an hour or so, they started talking Greek – and I don't mean Greek as in 'it's all Greek to me' – I mean the real thing, as spoken in Greece. These were all Greeks and I couldn't understand a word they said. That didn't worry me too much – except that some of them stood behind me having deep conversations about the state of the Hungarian fishing fleet for all I know – only, I knew in my heart that they weren't. What they were actually doing, all in Greek, was of course discussing the contents of my hand.

The old tramp took my money remorselessly, folding it up in half like old geezers do. At four o'clock in the morning, I was cleaned out.

I went outside to where I knew the cab driver was sleeping in his taxi and woke him up. 'How much are you being paid to take us back to London,' I asked.

'One-twenty,' he said.

'Well, give us £80 and you can go home to kip,' I said.

Incredibly, he agreed, I think he was bored to tears with waiting. It took about twenty minutes to do the eighty, and then I rounded up my troops for a retreat down to the beach. It was five past six in the morning, the sun was coming up somewhere over my shoulder, making the waves dance with gold. I didn't have a pot to piss in – except that poxy silver tankard. I raised my arm and threw it in a nice, high curving arc into the sea. Joe shouted, 'Oy, don't sling that – I'll give it to my boy, if you don't want it, Jimmy.'

'It's yours,' I said.

Joe waded out and retrieved the tankard that was bobbing on the briny – maybe it wasn't silver after all, because wouldn't it have sunk? – and brought it back in. It was all bent, but he said he would straighten it up and his kid would be thrilled to bits to have it.

'Right,' I said, 'let's have a whip-round.'

We all emptied out pockets, and in coppers and small silver came up with the princely sum of £3 between us. 'Looks like the milk train home again,' Peewee said, looking towards the town centre.

At Victoria, the ticket inspector looked at us

suspiciously, as well he might. 'Where did you get on?' he asked when we confessed that we had no tickets.'

'Clapham Junction, mate,' I said.

'Right, that'll be £2,' and he held out his hand for the money. We counted it out in shrapnel. That left just enough for a cup of tea to sustain us on our long walk the rest of the way home. It was magic to breathe in the London fumes instead of healthy sea air. Sometimes in my dreams I see myself hurling that silver pot far out to sea, where it should have stayed for ever on the sea bed, like in a Greek legend, inscribed with the message: 'Beware of tramps bearing casinos'.

FOURTEEN

LOVE HURTS

After Maureen and I were married, we moved closer to home, to Bellamy House, a larger council flat in Garratt Lane, Tooting. The flat was on the ground floor, convenient for all my friends to drop by at any time of the day or night, to Maureen's annoyance. She hung net curtains up, but when the light was on, you could still see in.

Peewee often dropped in, literally. It was on his way home, so he always had a look to see if the light was on, and if it was, he'd jump over the garden wall, give a tap on the window like an early warning and go round to the door. One Saturday night he came by very late, very drunk, spotted that the light was on, jumped over the garden wall and crept up to the open window. Peeping in through the net curtains, he saw me in my dressing gown enjoying a Chinese with Maureen, Tony Meo and Denise.

In playful mood, gently, oh so gently, Peewee climbed on to the window sill, pushed the nets to one side and silently as a burglar, unlatched the window wide. I had just opened a bottle of wine, and was pouring some out, when this body suddenly exploded headlong through the window, crashing on the floor at our feet.

I yelled, the wine went up in the air, the Chinese went flying, fried rice and butterfly shrimp – I love butterfly shrimp – decorating the furniture and our hair like confetti. Denise screamed and hid her head under a cushion, Tony, whose immaculate clothes were now dripping with chow mein, was not best pleased; but Maureen just said, 'Hello, Peewee, do you want a beer?'

I felt sorry for our neighbours, though, because Maureen and I argued a lot. I was well known in the district and they all seemed happy enough when we moved in, popping around to meet me, welcoming Maureen, offering to baby-sit Lauren. But gradually, they all moved away; all except one. She was worse than us, a real harridan. To the others, the genteel ones, the quieter, more restrained ones, I apologise. It must have been horrendous listening to us arguing about anything and nothing. People don't always see the other side. It used to get physical, no question. Obviously, I was stronger, but even when I tried to break away, Maureen would never give up. She'd come after me like a tiger. It was hardly surprising that everyone fled, looking for more peaceful pastures.

Although Maureen would be annoyed when I didn't show up, she also worried. She would sit up all night, thinking, 'You'd better be in an accident, or you're in big trouble, Jimmy White.'

Sometimes she would excuse me to herself or to her friends, by saying we met when I was young. She'd had a fairly normal teenage life with school, many interests and friends of both sexes – but I'd had just snooker. All the growing up I had done had been with her and perhaps I was just rebelling – I don't know what against, because I liked being with her. The trouble was, I also liked being with my mates, playing snooker, playing cards and going to the races. I liked it all – and it seemed that almost everything I liked was bad for me, bad for our relationship or caused rows.

Maureen has said that she never knew our kind of life would be her fate. There'd be girls, for instance, who saw me on television, or who gathered around me at the snooker matches. Phone numbers would mysteriously appear in my jeans' pockets which Maureen would find when she was turning them out to launder them. Then there were the numbers in my little black book that I left lying around. Armed with a large tin of white paint and a brush, Maureen would scrawl the phone numbers all over the walls of the house – I joke not. When I came in or woke up, it would be like a bad dream.

'I know you love me,' she would say, furious and paint-spattered. 'And yes, I know your whole life revolves around me – but explain *this* away—' and it would be a new phone number or a fan letter I'd forgotten to crumple up and throw away. Sometimes, she would lock me out. I would bang and kick the door and yell, and she would turn the lights out and go to bed – while all the neighbours' lights sprang on. I'd call and call from the telephone box down the road until I wore her out and she'd let me back in. Things would simmer down until the next episode. There was always a next episode.

Like most women, Maureen has good radar. If I won a lot of money and didn't make it back home with something to show, she knew, oh boy, she knew. For instance, a few years later – 23 April 1992 to be precise, a date which will always be engraved on my soul – I potted 147 at the Crucible in the thirteenth frame against Tony Drago, winning a total of £114,000 for scoring 147 on television plus £14,000 for the tournament's highest break. Tony, bless his heart, was so moved, he wept. I was so moved I soon gambled it away, on cards and on the horses. Then I was running around trying to borrow money against future matches because Maureen had seen me win on TV and was busy 'making plans for Nigel'. That was a bad one, that was, and impossible to articulate 'what made me do it?' Where Maureen is concerned, you'd better run away and hide until it blows over.

I'd creep in sometimes as quiet as a rhino on a gallon of Jack Daniels, just like Inspector Clouseau – who of course, would be expecting Cato, his general factotum, to leap on him and smash him into the middle of next week with a kendo stick. For Clouseau, it was pre-arranged, to keep him on his toes. With me and Maureen, it might just as well have been. For Clouseau muttering, 'Cato, where are you, my little yellow friend?' substitute me on many a dawn hiccoughing endearingly, 'Maureen, where are you, my little flower?' – and substitute the kendo stick for a pool cue, or worse.

We've all see the *Pink Panther* films. Cato leaps out, there's a brief scuffle and then it escalates. In a movie, everything gets smashed, blown up, wrecked and ruined. Well, it was not too different with me and Maureen. A sample invitation for those days of our life would read: 'A snooker exhibition, and after, a quiet candlelit Chinese with butterfly shrimp. Carriages at midnight to St Thomas's Hospital. State blood group on RSVP.'

There was one night when Maureen and I had a right little ding-dong in the flat that accelerated so fast and furiously, it scared me. I kept thinking, is this actually us – can we really be doing this to each other? It was like the final scene in the film *The Wars of the Roses* – where Michael Douglas and Kathleen Turner play a couple who really love each other, desperately and passionately; but neither one will give in and quite literally fight to the death. Maureen and I didn't have a gallery to fall from, nor a chandelier to fall into, but we certainly did our best to wreck what we did have – including each other.

The harridan next door thought murder was being committed and called the police.

Maureen and I were both equally bruised and battered, while I was actually spurting blood. A concerned policewoman pleaded with Maureen to charge me, to have me arrested. Maureen was so angry over what we had fought about in the first place, that she agreed to prosecute. We were both taken separately to the local hospital to be treated. Yes, I know, it sounds unbelievable. No excuses, we did it to each other.

The policewoman actually went to Maureen in the cubicle where she was being attended to, with papers for her to sign so I'd be arrested. What neither one of us knew was that I was lying in the adjoining cubicle having my thumb stitched up. Suddenly, as anger drained away and gave way to pain, I woke up to what was going on right next to me. Through the thin curtains I heard the entire conversation, the policewoman calling all men bastards, Maureen endorsing it and saying she was going to have me locked up and serve me right.

Appalled by this turn of events, I shuffled off the trolley and popped my head through the dividing curtain. 'Hello, Maureen,' I said, and holding out my split thumb, I whimpered, 'look, I'm hurt too.'

She looked at my bloody hand, then at me and said sadly, 'Why do we do this to each other?'

I had no answer. Sometimes the fire burned too wildly. Passion and love, anger and hurt are all so closely entwined, unless you've been touched by that kind of agony and ecstasy you cannot possibly explain it. We held each other close, and vowed never to hurt the other again. But we did – again and again.

It was events like this one that persuaded me to buy Maureen a brand new, red TR7 sports car with some of my winnings, for passing her driving test and also an apology for all my sins, past, present and future. She loved the present and immediately went the whole hog and had a personalised numberplate put on it. Shortly after that, we were burgled. It was Mum's opinion that it was because people now knew where we lived.

'Had it been me,' Mum said, 'I'd have kept my head down.' Then she put it into mum-type perspective by saying, 'But you can't blame them for enjoying it, can you? I mean, they're just kids.'

And quite simply, we *hadn't* moved out of the playground. I think it was because we were just kids who hadn't grown up that we argued so much. Not just arguments, but wild, passionate hand-to-hand rows, no holds barred, that left us breathless with horror at the damage we could inflict. During one argument, I jumped all over Maureen's car, up and down, up and down like a trampoline, kicking, banging and battering it with a dustbin lid. Instantly full of regret, I rushed out to buy her another TR7, this time a gold convertible, which I quite fancied myself, only I didn't drive at the time.

Often, rather than go home to face the music when I had been out too long, I would escape to Victor Yo's house, or Mum's – a sort of pre-emptive damage limitation exercise – creeping in quietly and lying low until Maureen's understandable rage had blown itself out. I had so many bolt-holes all over London, I often forgot where I was – or indeed who I was.

Maureen is the first to say that she hates the hard done by 'little woman' image sometimes projected about her. She would always live her own life and 'do her own thing', refusing to stay at home, constantly worrying and wondering what I was up to. She and Denise would be dressed up, waiting for me and Tony to phone and say goodnight, dear, sleep tight – and they'd be away up the

West End. They had too much respect for themselves to hold us back, or stay in the background, wringing their hands, sobbing and saying 'poor little us'.

And I always knew that she was off and out, although it was unsaid. Knowing that she wasn't sitting at home, moping, did lend an edge of excitement and intrigue to our relationship. After twenty years, it still does.

FIFTEEN

THE CRACK II

The Irish Masters, held in May, often turned out to be more than a little Irish. In 1983, for example, the *Daily Mirror* carried the report that I had beaten Dennis Taylor 5-5 in the semi-final, while Alex Higgins, who had beaten me 5-2 in the quarter-final, gave an interview afterwards which could only be described as a 'Monty Python/Peter Cook' type of monologue – on snooker tables of all things, which is about as boring as you can get.

'I am not trying to flaunt for business,' said Alex, 'but I know another firm in Dublin that could put a better table in. The balls roll two or three inches, which was not fair on Jimmy or me.' After ten minutes of that, he then went on to declare that he lived on twenty-three Shackley vitamin pills a day and babbled about vitamins for another long while – before returning to the topic which grieved him the most, the poor quality of the tables. Everyone was stunned and nobody could get a word in edgeways. When the plug was pulled by a frantic producer, Alex was still in full flood, in a darkened studio, still talking. It was surrealistic snooker and vitamin time. An all-night 'sleepless in Kildare' event. Alex was like an

all-night DJ, where the people called up and said, 'Play
"Misty" for me,' and Alex would say, 'No, let me tell you
about snooker tables with dodgy deviation, which can be
fixed with alfalfa lethicin and a B-12 shot in the baulk
end of Dublin.'

In 1984, when I went to Ireland with a few chums, to
play a little snooker and have a little fun, Maureen
elected to fill her time while I was away, house-hunting.
It was mainly Harvey Lisberg's suggestion that we move
upmarket, in line with the new sharp image of me that he
was trying to promote – suited up by Tommy Nutter and
snapped by Lichfield. Wimbledon definitely fitted into
that category, a place I had never in my wildest dreams
imagined living in.

Alex's babbling brook monologue was in marked
contrast to my interview style at the time, when I was
quite genuinely tongue-tied. It baffled me that anyone
wanted to hear my opinion about anything. It wasn't that
I was rude, the press said, but I didn't know how to com-
municate. Reporter Graham Nickless said, 'All Jimmy
was interested in was potting balls – not potting words in
the direction of a pack of hungry reporters. However, he
is noted for his sense of humour.'

The scene of the Irish Masters was at Goff's in Kill,
County Kildare. Goff's was a purpose built show ring for
horse sales – in fact, although Kill is small, practically a
hamlet on the edge of the rolling Wicklow Mountains,
Goff's is known as the bloodstock nursery of Europe. It
is the fourth-biggest horse sale arena in the world,
annually turning over upwards of ten million pounds in
yearling sales alone. The atmosphere, both of the sales
ring, and of the snooker arena into which it is converted
from time to time, is pure magic. When you are playing,
you can smell that sweet pungent smell of horses and
manure, and you can almost hear the whinny of ghost
horses galloping around.

I had won nothing in Ireland since the Northern Ireland Classic in 1981; and I was not to win the Masters until 1985; but, nevertheless, 1984 was a memorable year for the crack, and in Ireland that is of paramount importance and pleasure.

The World Amateurs was held in Dublin every four years. As a previous winner, I usually came to support everyone and to wish them all luck. On one of these visits I bumped into Con Dunne at Dublin Airport, in the toilet as a matter of fact. Con was at the next stall. 'Jimmy!' he said. 'What are you doing here?' – and that was how it started – again. We got very drunk one night, when young Stephen Hendry asked Con to introduce us. He was such a slight little thing and he looked at me with awe as he took the hand I held out for him to shake. Then he blushed and looked quickly down at his hand. 'You're never going to wash that hand again, are you, Stephen?' teased Con, and poor Stephen went as red as a fire engine.

Of course, it wasn't long before his game caught fire and it was me who needed a fire service.

Shortly before decamping to New York, Con and his brother, Richie, had moved into the transport business, ferrying passengers from Dublin Airport to their various hotels in a courtesy bus. They had also won the franchise from the Irish Pool Billiards and Snooker Association, as their official transport executive – which meant making sure people got from the airport to Goff's. Now, the passengers were either supposed to be transported free of charge, or, in the case of the IPBSA, they were sold round-trip tickets. But Con had worked out that, after a few days in Ireland most tourists, particularly Americans, would be too drunk to notice that he was charging them twice by making them pay for the return trip.

As for Con, he himself was so drunk that people were just grateful to be delivered to their destination in one piece. The bus rides were wild and exhilarating, with Con racketing from one side of the road to the other, and everyone singing lustily away as if they were on an Irish 'beano'. The first time I was with him, we hit the central reservation at eighty, scraping a long panel off the side of the bus. Con screamed to a tyre-burning halt when he saw the metal strip unpeeling in his rear-view mirror. Urgent action was called for, but first, with his bladder bursting, he needed some relief. The bus shuddered to a halt on a bridge over the Liffey so we could join him in a good pee into the bog-brown water. Back in the distance we saw the flashing lights of a police car.

'Let's make for the border!' Con yelled and we piled back into the bus so he could make a run for the neighbouring county of Kildare where, apparently, the police of County Dublin were unable to touch him. Some of the other more delicate passengers were aghast, but, like us, they hung on tight as we careered down the road, loose bits of metal flapping, bus bouncing over humps in the road, clear to the border marker. It was like something out of the *Keystone Cops*.

After Goff's, our own pace accelerated, too. Con had put some gaming tables in a big bar not far away, where the owner asked me to play an exhibition, which went down well. The bar-owner was delighted and, as a treat, organised a grand dinner for me in a big old castle in the Wicklow Mountains. He did not of course know how tense I get when faced with almost any degree of pomp and ceremony. When I walked in and saw the massive stone walls hung with banners, the armoury all around, the dark corners and the flagstoned floor, the high carved chairs on each side of a table that was a twenty-foot slab of polished elm gleaming with silver and pewter and crystal under round iron chandeliers, I felt my spirits sink into my boots and my neck grew rigid. That too-familiar feeling of 'I gotta get outa here' surfaced and I could feel the headache coming on – it's that bad. Rapidly I gabbled some excuse and shot out of there like a scalded cat with Con galloping in my wake, wondering what the hell was up.

'You look like you've just seen a ghost, Jimmy,' Con said outside in the courtyard, where I leaned against his car, struggling for breath and sanity.

'Take me away, Con,' I moaned pitifully. 'Let's find some old bar with sawdust on the floor and have a pint and a game or two.'

We drove around and found a few shabby places were we sat at the bars and talked to some old geezers. 'Don't fence me in or mess me up making me sit at a dinner table,' I said to Con as I sank another strong pint. I had escaped from a mental Colditz.

The rest of the players also liked to hang on after Goff's, often unable to tear themselves away from the magic of Ireland, wanting to relax and unwind before they flew off in their various directions. One of the biggest distractions were the races, where, with the lost days, go lost fortunes. Alex, of course, could lose seven to eight grand a day. The worst example I can remember was at Wolverhampton in 1976, when he lost £13,000 in an afternoon. He would think nothing of spending £100 on a taxi to get there. Grinning like a leprechaun, Alex told me that he got a couple of hot tips the next day, and won every penny of the £13,000 back. Willie Thorne, the demon gambler, has been known to lose the price of a semi-detached in a single bet. Then there was me, who could never turn a bet down. Once I went to Sandown Races because it was one of the last appearances of Desert Orchid and, after he had won on ridiculously short odds, I put £2000 on a horse called Vodkatina in the next race but it got stuck in the stalls. Two grand down, I thought, 'What the hell,' and decided to put £2000 on yet another horse. That lost too, as did the next one. I ended up eight grand down. Trouble is, I can't be a bystander. It's always wanting a bit of the action that loses me small fortunes.

But to return to Goff's, Cliff Thorburn had been beaten early on in the Masters and didn't have that much money to throw around, so, reluctantly, that final Saturday he was checking out of the hotel, when we were asked to the races by a trainer who was an absolute gentleman. A multi-millionaire, he owned half of Kildare but never flaunted it. He had a brother in Canada who also trained horses, so he gave Cliff an Irish £50 note with his brother's name and address on it. 'You guys should get together,' the trainer told us, 'and buy a couple of racehorses. I'd point you in the right direction. It's a grand sport.'

'Actually,' said Cliff, looking his usual elegant self, like an Edwardian gentleman, or maybe a Mississippi riverboat gambler, 'I was thinking of buying a couple of golf courses.'

I thought that was hilarious, considering Cliff really didn't have the proverbial two bob to his name at the time.

The trainer laughed, and said, 'Well, maybe you could train your horses on the golf course.'

That day he gave us plenty of tips and they all came in. He gave us the first and second race winners; then, for the third, he told us to bet on a certain horse not to win, but to be placed. 'Put everything you've got on it,' he emphasised, 'but don't back it to win.'

Now Con might have had wall-to-wall gaming machines in practically every establishment in Ireland but oddly enough he's not a gambler. Puzzled, he said, 'What's the point of backing a horse if it won't win?'

The trainer thought that was a grand joke. 'Look, Con,' he said, 'it won't win, but it will come second,' he said. Sure enough, it did, and we were all celebrating.

Tony Meo and Cliff Thorburn won well over a thousand pounds. Tony bought more dancing shoes, a nice pair of brogues, and Cliff stayed on a week or so longer to squander his share.

I never saw the trainer again and I didn't know until later that, at the time when he was being so warm and friendly he was suffering from terminal cancer. That was his last fine day out, the day he chose to remember this world by. The following day he blew his head off.

It's strange when you think of it. But it's almost tempting the Fates to take tomorrow for granted or make big plans. When you've got a family you've got to take responsibility for their tomorrows – but as for your own? Well, that's in the lap of the Gods. The famous Irish comedian Dave Allen always used to sign off with 'May your God go with you.' That's right – and it's also about as much as you can expect.

Our day at the races turned into several more nights on the run, a drink here, a card game there as, once again, I disappeared. This time, though, Maureen was determined to find me. She had come across a house in Wimbledon that she liked (the second house – we'd lost the first because she couldn't find *me*) and, persuaded by the estate agent that it also would be snapped up by somebody else if we didn't clinch the deal at once, Maureen got him to prepare all the paperwork for me to sign. Having exhausted all avenues in her search for me, and going off her head with frustration, Maureen tucked Lauren under her arm and flew to Ireland where she got a taxi from Dublin Airport and descended on the Fairmile Hotel in high fury.

Reception rang up to say that my wife was downstairs – and, boy, was she angry. The last time that had happened, the staff of the Gresham Hotel in Dublin had been lying, put up to it by the police. Maureen hadn't been there at all, and I had been arrested and clapped in a police cell over that little matter of some moody money. This time, as far as I knew, there were no dodgy notes in circulation – but one never knew. Instead of going downstairs into the lion's jaws, I sent Peewee down to waylay Maureen, if indeed she was there, to spin her a yarn or offer her coffee or a sandwich – while I hastily hid all evidence of a trashed hotel room and the card school that had been in progress for days. I managed to jam the legs of a broken vanity stool into its padded seat, and I climbed into the wardrobe, as Peewee cringed into my room, followed by Maureen and Lauren. He tried not to let his eyes flicker towards the closet where I cowered, and invited Maureen to sit down. To his horror, she chose the vanity stool.

The legs went in one direction and Maureen went in the other. The rats, who had been hovering not very inconspicuously in the background, fled. From the carpet, Maureen muttered through clenched teeth, 'Jimmy! Come out of that cupboard now, or you're dead meat.'

I'll never know how she knew.

I crawled out, saying, 'Hello, love, top o' the morning to you – never expected to see you here. I was just playing cards as it happens – I was coming home today—'

'I bet you were,' said Maureen, climbing to her feet. But little Lauren was delighted to see her father – that broke the ice. After I signed the papers for the house and Maureen had them safely despatched back to London, she decided that, since she had come that far, she would look up her Irish nan, her father's mother, who lived somewhere in the back of beyond in the Wicklow Mountains. This was a lucky break for me. Con got out his powerful old Mercedes and we roared through back lanes full of fern and willow, a family united and happy again. We actually had a lovely time and I found myself wondering why we didn't do this more often.

*

A year or so later, after we moved into the Wimbledon house I got to meet Ronnie Wood (see next chapter). I spent time with him later at his estate in Ireland which conveniently happens to be just outside Kildare, not far from Goff's. I'd got him a snooker table for his home in Richmond, then on his Kildare estate he built a pub to house three more tables for me to practise on. He also converted a massive studio, which he called the Ark, which was his dad's nickname, and filled it with hi-tech gear for his own recording work. There's also a heated sunken swimming pool with steam rising and palm trees like an oasis, a spectacular sight on the rare occasions when it snows. Ronnie goes to all the horse sales and there are racehorses galloping over his two thousand acres. The entire place is a village in its own right, almost like a feudal community, with some two or three dozen people permanently employed to ensure it all runs smoothly.

I've had some unbelievable times there. Ronnie likes to get me to play snooker after I've had five pints of Guinness – and his is the best-kept Guinness in Ireland. I tell him I can't see the ball properly and he pulls another pint for me with that cynical grin on his face.

When I go there I stay in the pub – which is fitted out like a comfortable inn. Ronnie telephones down from the main house to wake me up and I'll rouse whoever else is there. One noon-time, I walked into the bar, to find two policemen pulling themselves a pint of Guinness. I asked them what they were up to and with a jovial laugh, they said, 'Oh, Ron always lets us drop by on Thursdays for a drink, a lovely man he is. Cheers!'

I don't always stay at Ronnie's place, since I don't like taking advantage. One time I was booked into the Fairmile, a handsome hotel, where most of the players stay. The hotel was full, so Peewee booked into a bed and breakfast in Newbridge, a place where he'd often stayed before. On arrival, Peewee gave the old boy who ran the place his suit to be taken to the cleaners, only it was Peewee who was taken to the cleaners – entirely his own fault of course, as it usually is. The first night, he stayed up all night in the Fairmile with me, playing a few hands of cards. The second night, we found a pro gambler's house and stayed there. By now, fading fast, with snooker matches to play during the day, we ended up back at Ronnie Wood's pub, holding our eyelids open with matchsticks and playing snooker day and night. On the fifth day, Peewee returned to his b. & b., and in the morning, ready to play a game of snooker, he asked the owner, 'Didja get my suit done?' He was suited and out before you could say Bob's your uncle.

That night, we were back at the Fairmile after my match, playing cards again. On the final morning, planning to return to England, Peewee nipped over to the b. & b. to get his suitcase – and was astonished to be presented with a bill for £120. He said, 'You can't charge me full whack, I only stayed one night and I didn't even have any breakfast!'

'We were booked right up,' insisted the landlady. 'We could have let your room three times over if the truth were known.'

Of course, there wasn't a sign of any other residents, and, when Peewee sneaked a look at the guest book, it was blank. When he pointed this out, the couple just shrugged.

Just when we were supposed to be heading back home to England, we turned around and stumbled into the Burns Hotel into the middle of the Irish music awards. We sat for a while at the bar, dusting a few while chaos erupted around us. After a while, I went out and decided to borrow one of the limousines parked there. Strolling up to the driver, I said, 'Hello, mate – can you drop us back at our hotel?' I didn't really know what I was talking about since we had checked out, or where we would end up, but it seemed a good idea at the time.

'Well, I've got half an hour spare,' said the driver, a pleasant young man, who looked bored silly just hanging around in his peaked cap doing nothing.

'Right, thanks, mate,' I said as me, Peewee and some other chums clambered aboard. 'Whose car is this, anyway?'

'A-HA,' said the driver. Well, I thought that's what he meant – as in, 'Aha, guess who.' But he was talking about the band of the same name. I jumped in the front with the driver, with my mates in the back. The stretch was a mile long with tinted windows, immaculate inside and out, and off we drove, slowly towards some big gates. Suddenly we were surrounded by thousands of screaming kids. They didn't know who we were – but thought we had to be somebody famous, so screamed anyway.

On a tide of celebrity, we were swept back inside to the awards. I spotted Chris de Burgh and a few other recognisable faces. But most of the time I was muttering to the others, 'Who's he? Who's she? Who's that?' as flashlights popped and the fans screamed.

It was fun; but I much preferred the time the following year, when, after I had won 9-5 against Willie Thorne, to retain my title and win £20,000, I found myself in a small pub, with my dad, Tom, regaling the locals with more stories than they told us. Hour after hour passed in this wonderful way. Sure and there were people passed out on the floor, someone was asleep in the fireplace, along with the family's pet pig; but still the drink and the stories flowed.

Dad was still telling tales all the way back to Fishguard on the boat, a wonderful storyteller. Now, that's what I call the crack.

SIXTEEN

THE WHITES OF WIMBLEDON COMMON WERE WE

For some reason it always took us a long time to move. We had the mortgage, we had the keys to the door, but still we lingered in Tooting. We didn't even linger together all of the time. Maureen and Lauren stayed at her mum's; I stayed at my mum and dad's. Although we had our own flat, we were always returning to our respective mums. I think we were scared of growing up, of being totally responsible for everything. It was easier at home. For Maureen, there was always somebody to talk to; for me it was just being with Mum and Dad and the budgie – familiar territory, no rows, no stress. A large house meant rates and bills, and that meant responsibility. Suddenly I missed the old days, when it was just me and Meo against the world, happy, dangerous times, not knowing what was going to happen next.

'Nowadays you can win and know nobody's going to run off with the cheque,' I said in an interview with more than a tinge of nostalgia. 'It's safe, but it's not the same.

My mum, Lil, showing off the trophies.

My dad, Tom, is as proud as punch.

Facing page: Me and Maureen in love.

Previous page: My first ranking tournament. The party went on for seven days.

Facing page:
Me at work.

Me in the
World
Matchplay
with my old
rival, The
Nugget.

Me, Tony Meo and Steve Bailey outside the Pot Black Snooker Hall
one day, laughing because we got all the money.

One of my better times with Higgins. The only time you have a good time with Higgins is when it's flying for him!

Me and Barry Hearn. He's obviously talking about money – that's why we're smiling.

Facing page: This is me happy. I have to practise because I have a match that evening and I've been on a bender for two days and I've just realised where I am.

Me having a holiday with the family in Majorca.

Dad, Peewee, Me, Dionne my neice and Con Dunne, one of my best friends from New York. I've just got beat in the Benson & Hedges in London, but I still manage to smile.

My princesses.

John Nielsen and a friend, Ron, at the wrestler, Steve Viedor's birthday party.

Left: 1984. Me and Lauren when she won the picture of the month in the *Mirror*. She got £1000 that we put in a Trust Fund in William Hill's.

Me with a fellow genius.

1998. First round of the World Title at Sheffield. Me and Hendry during a break.

Steve congratulates me. I knew it was genuine because he's a good lad.

Overleaf: Me, looking 'different league'.

Winners can laugh. Losers make their own arrangements.'

The temptation of having that big cheque in my hand was what I missed. Now, when tramps sidled up, offering to cash cheques and take me to their casinos, I was protected from myself, hedged about by accountants, managers, lawyers, a whole army of people looking after little Jimmy White. But I didn't want that protection. I preferred to live closer to the edge, but the wild side that made life so unpredictable and exciting looked to be slipping away in bricks, mortar and respectability.

Eventually, we ran out of excuses not to move. The snooker season was over, I had won a great deal of money – and even managed to keep a lot of it. We could afford to move, we could afford to buy some nice things. After a great deal of nagging from Mum, who couldn't see the point of having a lovely new home unless we enjoyed it, we bought some furniture and a giant fridge-freezer, and in October 1984 reluctantly moved into our tall town house just a lob away from the Centre Court. Next summer, we said, we could stroll across to enjoy the tennis and strawberries.

Our house was in a smart terrace, set back a little from a quiet street. You went past the garages and forecourt and down a few steps to a concealed path that ran along all the front doors. The kitchen was at the front of the house, the living room was open plan to French doors that opened on to a small patio. Above were two more floors. It seemed as big as a battleship.

Even with all the furniture in place and the new curtains hung, Maureen and I wandered around the echoing rooms that didn't really feel like ours, homesick already for the familiar sights and sounds of Tooting. I could go off whenever I wanted, but Maureen had to regulate her day around Lauren, whom we had decided to send to a small private school. Having a daughter who had a routine – who indeed was suddenly school age – was another rite of passage for us. Maureen could no longer drop everything and go with me around the country as she had done in the carefree early days after I had bailed out of the Dodgy Bob situation.

With Lauren having to go to school, we couldn't both sit up all night with our friends because somebody – and at first it was always Maureen until she organised some help – had to give a small, undemanding child her breakfast, make sure her uniform was clean and ready, and get her to school on time. The chaos in the mornings, the scramble to find everything, meant that Maureen was often as tired as I was after a late night. Even when she went to bed early, I might come home late and disturb her, or return with a group of friends and disturb her even more. While she was off early driving Lauren to school, I could sleep in.

With the overseas tours, I was away for two months at a time, so when I was home, Maureen didn't see why I couldn't do my bit. Part of the problem was that I came from a background where my mum had always done that kind of thing, as had Maureen's mum for her family; but Maureen was a different kind of woman. She was more independent. The little wife ironing the tea-towels was not the role she saw for herself then, or in the future. Domesticity was a sharp learning curve that the Artful Dodger had to get to grips with. I fought it hard. In the end, all I could do was promise to try.

It was while I was attending a function at Lauren's school, trying to come to grips with my responsibility as a dad, that I met someone who was to become a very good friend. I was videotaping Lauren and her little classmates, doing a play, when I noticed someone else doing exactly the same thing. We laughed sheepishly at our proud father image and got talking. It turned out to be Ronnie Wood, who had a house at Merton. Ronnie told me he loved snooker and was building a private pub on his estate in Ireland just so he could install a table. Apart from that, I thought we came from different worlds, and would have nothing in common. Although, oddly enough, Harvey Lisberg had said to me once when we were discussing my image, 'I always think of you being like the Rolling Stones. Davis is more like the Beatles.'

Wood had grown up in a knockabout way rather like me, except he's 'artistic'. Still, being artistic is not going to help you very much when your fellow axeman in the Stones, Keith Richards, gets extremely pissed off and comes at you with a broken bottle. No, 'artistic' in those situations is suddenly surplus to requirements. No time for quiet introspection then. Ronnie can think fast on his feet, like me. We had that much in common.

Ronnie Wood is easy-going, but he reads books like *The Silence of the Lambs*. I saw the film. He likes evil books, he says. Sometimes, like me, he gets on with what Keith Richards calls the permanent night shift, too. Him and Keith, they play snooker or pool for hours; but when I hang out with the Stones, I always end up making the tea. When they're working, they drink tea. Much good may it do 'em.

You can imagine it, can't you, me saying to Maureen after three days away from home, that I was hanging out with the Stones, drinking tea. Oh sure, Jimmy, she'd say, *very* sarcastically. Though Ronnie does prefer Guinness.

He had a band in the old days, before my time, called the Birds. Not the American Byrds, the British Birds. They never got anywhere. Then he joined up with Ronnie 'Plonk' Lane and the others and they got Rod Stewart to front this new version of The Faces, which used to be The Small Faces. What actually happened was that Steve Marriot, the guitarist and singer in The Small Faces, went off to form a new band with Peter

Frampton, called Humble Pie. That left Ronnie Lane and the drummer, Kenney Jones, and Ian McLagen, the keyboard player, without a guitarist or a front man. So they got Ronnie Wood on a guitar and Rod Stewart in as the singer. Humble Pie were a sort of blues band, really. The Faces were more fun, more rock 'n' roll. Ronnie Lane's dead now. He got multiple sclerosis; and Steve Marriot died when his house caught fire. Someone once said The Faces with Ronnie Wood and Rod Stewart had more 'swagger' than any rock and roll band in history.

Nobody, when I've been tanked up and spraying snooker balls all over the gaff except down the pockets, has said that I had 'swagger'. They always say, 'Hang about, Jimmy's pissed again.' On the other hand, people used to say Rod and Ronnie and his new chums were not always playing 'in concert pitch' on-stage. However, having inquired about this with Mr Wood, I'm told that concert pitch is of a secondary importance compared with natural feel. If they're having fun and sounding like they're having a good time, then their audience will also have a good time. The Faces were certainly a good-time band.

Ronnie did what he refers to as a seventeen-year apprenticeship with the Stones before he got into the big money. Not that it matters, he could support himself with his paintings if he had to. Ronnie, I have discovered, has a great sense of humour. His missus used to go out with Dodi Fayed. In fact, she dumped him for Ronnie, which he says, was a good move on her part. My wife Maureen never went out with Dodi Fayed, so she never had a chance to dump him for me. But if she had gone out with him, she would have dumped him for me and it would have been a good move on her part too.

You learn things about your friends slowly. Through Ronnie I met people whose company I enjoyed enormously, but whom I would probably never have met in the ordinary way. One of the funniest nights of my life was spent with Ronnie, Rod Stewart and Peter Cook. We were driving along in Ronnie's Rolls, Ronnie, Rod and me in the back, the chauffeur up front, when Ronnie got on his mobile.

'Hello, Peter, we're not far away from your place, going to watch Chelsea – want to come?' said Ronnie. 'We'll pick you up.'

'Dear boy!' drawled Peter. 'Don't trouble to come to the house. I'll be the distinguished-looking gentleman in the pink suit next to the red pillar-box on the corner.'

After the match, we went to a pub that was packed with Chelsea supporters making an incredible din – Chelsea must have won. Suddenly, Peter turned around to the crowd and they became his audience. It was effortlessly done, the way he got them to listen, to stop drinking and shouting. He mesmerised them into silence. In no time he had them in fits. He was a natural raconteur, the stories just went on and on, dazzling, outrageous and very funny. To see that noisy crowd change was incredible. Peter was one of those characters who needed an audience to play to – first of all he had us around the table, then, as his stories expanded dramatically, they grew into a performance.

Alex Higgins said he always felt an affinity with Peter because they both travelled everywhere with a clutch of newspapers. Peter was a voracious reader. When he wasn't talking, he was reading – and Alex with all the long journeys he made by train, was the same. They were also both heavy drinkers – and while Peter mellowed, Alex would reveal his mean and dangerous streak, though I often wonder how much of it was put on. One year, for example, Alex was banned as a professional from the Open at Prestatyn for something he'd done. Like a freelance, he turned up anyway, ready to fight his way through the lists. Con Dunne was there for the tournament, so Alex moved in with him. In the chalet, Alex would throw food out on the veranda for the birds, then he'd get a big carving knife and hide behind the curtains like Sylvester the cat, ready to pounce as soon as the birds flew down.

'What on earth are you doing?' Con asked him, baffled. After all, they weren't short of food and didn't need roast pigeon to supplement their diet.

Alex held up his finger to quieten Con, and whispered, 'I'm trying to acquire the killer instinct.' All in his mind, of course.

The other professionals were seeded, but Alex was not invited and was made to enter with the rank and file that year, against the whole pack of 988 other entrants, He whittled them down with some brilliant snooker, getting all the way through game after game – a brilliant, marathon performance, until he was up against Terry Griffiths in the final. Everyone knew how poorly Alex had been treated and respected him for it. It was Terry's home ground, Wales, but in the final, they were stamping the floor down, roaring out *'Higgins! Higgins! Higgins!'* When Alex won the best of 35 the roof lifted off. In those days the games were far longer. It was television that ruined all that – snooker, like so much else made for TV, has to be delivered up in bite-sized pieces. Many players believe that it's the length of the game that separates the men from the boys – many can sprint, but it's the stayers who count.

Alex was always out to outrage and after a few drinks he came alive like Dracula plugged into the mains. That week, Con would be saying all the time, 'Alex, why do you have to say that?' and Alex would say it again, only worse, offending everyone. Con ended up going back to Manchester with him, to stay at Alex's future-mother-in-law's house – this was before Lynn became his wife.

Nobly, Alex gave Con his bed and slept on the couch. The next morning, Lynn's mother took Con a big breakfast of bacon and eggs and a pot of tea before he was properly awake. As Con was rousing himself and fluffing up the pillows so he could sit up to take the tray, Alex slid around the door, holding out a bottle of brandy. Winking at Con, he said, 'He doesn't want breakfast – I know what he wants.'

This was a bottle that he and Con had played for at an exhibition the night before, after a solid week of drinking. It was a classic case of hair of the dog. Con gratefully took the drink, but for years afterwards, wherever they were, whenever Alex wanted Con to do him a favour, he'd start off by saying slyly, 'Oh, Con, do you remember how I saved your life when I gave you that bottle of brandy in the morning?'

Con always says that Alex has a memory like a steel trap, storing information up, to abuse you later with it – but we all laugh fondly when we recount stories like that, because Alex is Alex, very Jekyll and Hyde – and probably the most complex character in a game full of great characters.

The night after the bottle of brandy incident, Con and Alex went to play at Manchester's Potters Club, where Alex scored 147 against Con in four minutes forty-seven seconds. It was a new world record. He should have had two 147s the same night but he just missed the black. It was an exceptional near-miss – and another example of how some of the most thrilling games, games that go down as all-time greats, are rarely captured on camera. You have to be there. (Early in 1995, when playing in an exhibition match against John Virgo, I hammered in two 147s. It was a memorable evening.)

Journalists are fond of saying that the two worst things that ever came out of Northern Ireland were George Best and Alex Higgins; but to my mind, they are sheer geniuses, who have entertained millions and changed the face of their sport for ever. Nobody knows what troughs of despair and private hell Alex goes through. We're all the same, tormented creatures of the night. We're like gunslingers – a cue, a bottle of booze, a packet of cigarettes and a game. Those are the tools of our trade, and with them we can win or lose thousands.

When Alex married Lynn they had a couple of children, Jordan, the younger and Lauren, whose name he always said *we* had borrowed, despite the fact that our daughter Lauren is some months older. I remember once when Alex was staying with us, he said, 'Oh, Maureen, do you think you could change Lauren's name?' Maureen had a fit and gave Alex a piece of her mind. Afterwards, we thought it was hilarious and it has become one of our daughter Lauren's 'dining out' stories.

I got a phone call late one night from Alex. 'Jimmy, please come and save my life,' he said.

I dropped everything, told Maureen I'd see her later and got on the phone to Dad, who was in his social club. 'Dad, we're flying up to Manchester.'

Alex's first home, an enormous bungalow, like something out of *Dallas* in its own spacious grounds on the edge of a village, was blockaded by the press when we arrived in a taxi from Manchester airport at about eight o'clock in the evening. Alex was supposed to have dragged Lynn down the path by her hair, she'd fled, and the press were having a field day. The house looked deserted, but the reporters told us Alex was in there. We walked up the now famous garden path to the front door, and I knocked hard. Nothing. We walked back to the gate, hovered a bit, not wanting to leave but seeing no point in staying while the press corps bombarded us with questions and cracked dirty jokes to keep their spirits up. It had been a long day for them, but I had little sympathy.

Every now and then, I would looked back at the house and bawl, *'Alex! It's Jimmy!'*

After about twenty minutes I was on the point of giving up. Dad and I had decided we'd go to the pub, when the curtains were suddenly pulled and Alex peered out. He flashed the curtains shut quickly before the press could get a picture and we ran for the front door, which was opened and closed quickly behind us. Alex looked terrible, unshaven, with black rings under his eyes.

'Well, Alex, we came,' said Dad. 'We'll sort you out in no time, boy. Now, how about a nice cup of tea?'

Dad went into the kitchen to make the tea, reeling back briefly at the sight of piles of washing up on every surface and heaps of dirty laundry all over the floor. To be honest, until then I've never known Dad to wash up in his life, but these weren't normal conditions. Rolling up his sleeves, in next to no time he had that place shipshape while Alex and I talked things over.

Alex was incredibly depressed. He'd been holed up in his house for days. Even though the place was crawling with reporters, I thought it would do him good to go down the road to the pub, have a couple of drinks with some life around him, then we'd come back and knock a few balls about.

It took a little persuasion before Alex showered, shaved and changed – clean shirts were in short supply as I remember – and we braved the bastinado and the mob. It wasn't that bad – the press may write some pretty tacky things, but face to face, they're not a bad bunch. They crowded in the pub with us and didn't ask too many questions – those they did ask, Alex ignored. In the end, everyone just had a good time. Within an hour of returning to Alex's house, we were both on the table in the basement.

'Good boys,' Dad said, sipping a large Scotch. 'That's the way to forget your worries, a few games and a good laugh. Any old how, we're inside in the warm and that lot are outside there, freezing their bollocks off.' Dad has always looked on Alex and me as the Student and the Gov'nor since the days when I was just a kid and Alex taught me so much.

All of a sudden, the phone rang. It was Lynn. As soon as Alex picked up the telephone, I saw the tension return.

This wasn't surprising really. Lynn had just obtained a court order which banned him from 'assaulting or molesting' her and from seeing his children. After the hearing, Alex had wept copiously as his solicitor explained to him exactly what this meant. Emotionally Alex sobbed and said, 'Oh, not that. Anything but that.'

He told me that the situation had devastated and depressed him unbearably and that he hadn't realised how bad things actually were until he had read about Lynn's divorce application in the papers.

Now on the phone, Alex said, 'I can't earn a living because you're blabbing to the press. Every time you open your mouth the WPBSA bang another nail in my coffin. Why did you tell them I'd dragged you down the path by your hair?'

Lynn said she'd done it because Alex wouldn't let her take the new car he'd bought her. Alex said, 'I should think not, when you sent your heavies down to get it. And who slung the flowerpot through the car window? One of your heavies.'

'Well, he was in a temper because you wouldn't let him take the car.'

'It wasn't his to take,' Alex said. 'We'll put it all right, you can have the car, if you bring Lauren and Jordan home. Until then, forget it.' And he hung up.

Earlier Alex had told me that despite everything he was desperately looking for ways to patch things up, but as he turned away from the phone, I could see that once again it was ending in ultimatum and threats.

During this exchange, Dad was wandering about looking at the piles of expensive toys in the basement, which was part snooker room, part nursery. He turned to Alex, 'I can see how much you care for your kids,' he said. 'There's everything here – it's like a bloomin' toy shop. See, there's two sides to every story and from where I'm standing, I can see this side.'

When Alex and Lynn eventually got back together, his career once more flourished and he sold the bungalow to buy Delveron House, a rather large Georgian style home in Cheshire, with spacious grounds where he could keep a couple of horses, in the hopes that the children would learn to ride. Alex has always loved horses. When he had left Belfast at the age of fifteen to strike out on his own, he become a stable lad and then a jockey. His children, though, were too timid to go near the horses and Lynn wouldn't muck out the stables when Alex was away, so he had to sell them.

But there were to be no roses around the door for Alex and Lynn – their relationship, always stormy, soon ran into deep water again. The press returned in droves to camp out at the wrought iron gates of Desperation Row. At the time, I was in Manchester on business, but off I went once more, to give Alex the benefit of my support, this time taking a couple of good friends, Lenny Cain and Joe Brittain with me. I had met Joe in Geoff Lomas's snooker hall in Manchester and we hit it off from the start.

When we arrived Alex was like a pressure cooker about to explode. He stood at the windows screaming at the press to go away and leave him alone. Since the windows were closed tight, they couldn't hear his violent language. He was in a Paddy McGinty's goat mood. For starters, he kicked the TV all over the place, then picked it up and hurled it at the windows, which were made of little leaded panes. Instead of breaking, the lead strips bent.

The television bounced back and knocked his legs from under him.

We all fell over laughing – it was funny to see a massive television set rebound like that. That released the tension and Alex was forced to laugh with us. Then he picked himself up, grabbed the television again and slung it even harder, but this time with humour instead of anger. Outside, the press gang raised a cheer when the windows smashed and a television came hurtling out.

I was to stay with Alex for four days, basically just drinking and playing snooker in his splendid, panelled billiard room, which was as big as a barn. We used to sneak out the back way and climb over a couple of fences to his local, which was not that far away. It was also full of the press corps, who used to take it in turns to stake out Alex's house, in-between huddling together in the pub. So there we were, hiding out from the reporters at the opposite end of the same bar while others did the stake-out chore.

Alex did get his token of revenge on the press, who really were terrorising him. At the top of the stairs in Delveron House was a kind of porthole window. Through this Alex would take occasional pot-shots at the reporters with an air gun he had. He was too far away to do any harm, but occasionally one of them would feel a wasp-like sting on the bum or the back of his neck. And in the dark of Delveron House there would be a long dark cackle followed by the pop of another cork.

SEVENTEEN

NEVER BRING AN OVERCOAT WHEN YOU'RE OUT WITH JAMES

Con Dunne always says that he never knows what will happen when he goes out with me. This is not deliberate – it's just the way the cards fall. We were discussing it only recently.

'There's always colour and atmosphere when you're around,' Con said reflectively. 'But the trouble with telling a yarn is it's like repeating a joke you've heard; at a distance it somehow never sounds the same at the second telling. Like with Alex Higgins, you're on the edge all the time – who wants to kill him, who does he want to kill? And when you're out with him, are you his minder or what? Because you can see this thug or that bruiser thinking dark thoughts and I'm thinking, "Oh no, not me, I try to mind my own business. I just know the chap – I hardly know him at all, in fact." But with you, Jimmy, it's different. I always feel safe. However, I have learned one thing.'

'What's that?'

'Never bring an overcoat when you're out with James,' Con laughed uproariously.

It all came about one cold winter's evening in the days before Con stopped drinking, when he had just bought an expensive sheepskin coat in London. We met up with Peewee and set off on a tour of all the nightclubs. But some nights I just can't settle, nothing feels right. The first place we went was the Inn On The Park, where Howard Hughes used to take the entire top floor so he could stop the germs coming in and grow his fingernails in peace and quiet like a holy man, and, so legend goes, there was a Spruce Goose cooped up somewhere on the roof.

While Peewee and I went to the bar and ordered a double vodka and orange each, Con had checked in the sheepskin.

Two vodkas and orange, straight down, and it was 'Let's go,' as I said to Peewee, the atmosphere not being what I was looking for that night. We were on our way out just as Con was saying to the check-in girl, 'Now, you'll be taking good care of it for me, won't you?' Very proud of his new coat, was Con.

'Where are you going?' Con said.

'Out,' I said.

We lingered on the pavement in the frost while Con got his coat back. He came running, as I flagged down a taxi and it was on to Stringfellows.

Con checked in his coat while Peewee and I ordered at the bar. We had just downed our second vodka and orange, when Con came hurrying up. 'There, that's me coat stowed away,' he said cheerily. 'Now, I'll be having another one of those, Jimmy.'

'We're leaving,' I said.

Ten minutes later, drinkless and irritated, Con joined us on the pavement. 'What kept you?' I asked. And it was on to the next place, where Con checked in his coat while Peewee and I once more headed for the bar. Con made the girl hurry but, still, our glasses were hitting the counter by the time he arrived.

'Let's go,' I said.

'Jimmy,' said Con, 'I want a drink. Me tongue's hanging out with all this coming and going.'

'Catch us up, then,' I said. 'We'll be at the Hilton.'

Now the bar at the Hilton is somewhere near the top. I lingered there a little, to see if I could recognise any of Victor Yo's old chums from the days when I used to crash out in his nan's house. By the time we were on our second vodka and orange, Con had arrived, his coat neatly stowed somewhere on the lower floors.

'Ah, so you've decided to stay here,' said Con.

'Actually, no, we were just about to leave,' I said, pocketing my credit cards and tipping the waiter.

Con's face fell. 'But, Jimmy, I haven't had a bloody drink yet.'

At Tramp, Con decided to take his coat in to the bar. But the coat was large and the bar was small and, as we ordered, he decided he looked silly standing there with it upright between us as if it were the Invisible Man. He decided to check it in after all.

'Now, Jimmy,' Con asked, 'are you staying or are you leaving?'

'Give me a chance,' I said, 'we've only just arrived.'

Con was just picking up his ticket as Peewee and I headed past him. 'We'll wait for you outside,' I said. 'Don't be too long.'

In the taxi to the next spot Con grumbled, 'The trouble with you, Jimmy, is you're hyperactive. I don't know what you're looking for, but all I want is a bloody drink. I haven't had one yet and we've been in six establishments.'

'All right,' I said, 'next pit-stop, I promise, you can have a drink – if you promise not to check in your coat.'

'Done,' he said.

But at La Valbonne, the manager prevented Con from taking his coat through in case someone mistook it for a sheep and tried to dip it against foot-rot in one of the three-foot square swimming pools they had in the centre of the dance-floor. Maybe they thought he was concealing some kind of hardware. He does have an Irish brogue. So, no sheepskins in the bar.

'Jimmy, Jimmy,' Con said as we left, 'let's stay somewhere, please. I've checked my coat in twelve times – and not one drink have I had.'

'Bootleggers,' I said. 'I'll stay there, Con, I promise you.'

But, Bootleggers didn't work out either.

We ended up in some backstreet pub in Battersea, called The Invitation. As soon as I walked through the door, I felt this was it – the place I had been looking for all evening. We had been flying in and out of expensive hotels and clubs, and finally, we were content in this spit and sawdust bar till all hours of the morning, playing pool, drinking large Bacardis and coke – with the famous sheepskin coat in the sawdust under the table like a large, contented cat.

At some stage, someone decided to wind Con up. They had a word with the publican who, after a suitable interval, wandered across to Con and asked him if he wouldn't mind checking his cat in at the cat room. 'Out back, sir,' he said. Then, pointing under the table, 'You know, sir, someone might mistake it for a coat and pick it up and try to wear it. You can't be too careful.'

'What?' cried Con. 'Jimmy!'

But the publican lost it and he reeled off laughing to pour us another round, while Con looked at me sideways and wagged his finger.

EIGHTEEN

AND TAKE YOUR FRIEND
WITH YOU

It was Alex Higgins's opinion that because Con had given up drinking for the tournament, he was vulnerable.

Con was over in London from Dublin, playing for the Irish Amateur team in the World Series at the Connaught Rooms in the Tottenham Court Road. I was there as a professional, officially to represent England, though I wasn't playing. I think they called me a celebrity guest. On the second day of the tournament, Con managed to get run over by a taxi; but foolishly, and in a great deal of pain, he played on before being carted back to his hotel, where he collapsed.

I heard about it the next day and, because I was required at the tournament, I sent a car around immediately, with instructions to my driver to assess the situation and accept no nonsense from Con about 'He'll be all right after a bottle of brandy and a couple of aspirin.' The driver found Con delirious, his leg as big as a tree-trunk and, mindful of my warning, insisted on taking Con to University College Hospital, where the X-ray confirmed that it was broken. By then, I was able to leave the Connaught Rooms and collected Con from the plaster-room at the hospital.

'He can't stand on it for some weeks,' said the doctor.

'What about playing snooker?' asked Con.

'Absolutely no way,' said the doctor.

I put Con in the car, went round to the hotel to collect his case and drove him home to Wimbledon.

Carefully we negotiated the steps leading down to the front door and I called out, 'I'm home, my little flower—' or words to that effect. 'Con Dunne's broken his leg, so I've brought him to stay until he can travel home.'

Maureen is very fond of Con, so she was pleased to welcome him and make up a bed close to a bathroom.

Con was doped up to his eyeballs with painkillers and the first day passed with no problems. It was the second day that Maureen began to get a glimmering of what was to be the pattern of our days, when I insisted that Con joined me on a quick spin to see some buddies in Tooting.

'For goodness' sake, Jimmy,' said Maureen, 'Con can't come downstairs, they're far too steep. He'll fall and break the other leg or worse.'

Con didn't want to be a nuisance and was anxious to show Maureen that he could bump his way down the stairs on his bottom, and up again on his hands and knees with the minimum of fuss. A week later, with Con going bumpety-bump up and down the steep stairs, carrying on with me and returning at all hours of the morning, Maureen had had enough.

'He goes, or I go,' she said when she came home, worn out and heavy-eyed after dropping Lauren off at school. 'Jimmy, I can't stand it any more. I haven't had any sleep in a week.'

Con and I went out, giving Maureen a chance to simmer down; although in Con's opinion all I needed was an excuse to go on the piss. When we returned that night, our suitcases had been left outside in the street.

'Go and talk to her,' Con urged. 'She'll be all right.'

I shook my head. 'No, you don't know Maureen. She's as stubborn as me. Come on, Con, let's go.'

My driver put our cases in the car, and off we went.

We were missing in London for seven weeks, a record even for me. We woke up to a different ceiling every day, we did every nightclub in town, from Stringfellows and Xenon to the Hippodrome, where the doorman used to carry Con up and down the stairs. Some places wouldn't allow Con in, so we would leave him with the doorman, sending drinks out to him and collecting him on the way out. Con could write a book on doormen, he's spent hours talking to them all.

We'd meet all the footballers, who always wanted to know what had happened to his foot – 'Oh, I broke it playing snooker!'

Eventually, Con went home to Ireland – I'm not sure, but I have an idea I flew with him to play in the Benson & Hedges Irish Masters, which I won, then I telephoned Maureen and told her I wanted to come home.

'I won the Irish cup,' I said, like a small boy bringing an apple for teacher.

Maureen said later that she didn't have the heart to bring me down. 'Come home, Jimmy,' she said, 'Lauren misses you.'

In the midst of all these gallivantings, I was still showing up for the snooker and all the other PR events. Harvey, bless his heart, went to great lengths to protect my reputation, only to be rocked almost off his feet when a little scandal surfaced.

Harvey heard on the grapevine that the *News of the World* was about to print a double spread about some alleged misdemeanour of mine. Hundreds of thousands of pounds' worth of merchandising and sponsorship deals were at stake.

Harvey called me. 'Jimmy, I simply don't want two pages of scandal all over the place. It will destroy the image we are trying to project. What on earth have you been up to?'

'Nothing,' I assured him. 'It's all lies, isn't it?'

'What's all lies, Jimmy?' A slightly alarmed tone crept into Harvey's voice. 'Tell me – I need to know.'

'Whatever it is, it's all lies,' I said. 'I've been as quiet as a mouse.'

Harvey could see that he wasn't going to get very far with this line of questioning and decided it was time to call in some favours. He knew the *Sun* was considering a large 'puff' piece on me, and they weren't very pleased that the *News of the World* had an apparent scoop. Harvey also knew Leslie Perrin very well, who had been the Beatles' PR and had plenty of clout. (Leslie died young; this was shortly before his death.) Anyway, Leslie was good friends with the editor of the *News of the World*, and he called him now, to ask what the story was.

Apparently, it was something to do with me living with somebody else (absolutely untrue), having moved out of our Wimbledon home (partly true). For a large sum of money a model who was a bit hard up swore blind I had moved in with her. In those days this was big news; today someone not sleeping at home wouldn't even make the letters page. The thing is I had never moved in with anyone.

As soon as Harvey found out what the story was, he called the editor and said, 'No, this is absolutely not true. Jimmy has not left home.' The editor apparently replied that they sent someone around to the house early in the morning and my wife had said I wasn't there.

'Well, of course, Jimmy does go away very frequently to tournaments and exhibitions and so on,' Harvey said. The editor said that was funny – I had been seen at

Stringfellows the night before and they had photos to prove it.

Harvey got on the phone to me and said he didn't care what my differences with Maureen were, he didn't care what she said to me later, but the papers would be stacking up all the reporters outside my front door at six o'clock in the morning, and I'd better be inside to answer it when they rang the bell. Leslie Perrin had also heard that some reporters were to be strategically parked outside the house all night to prevent my surreptitious arrival.

The houses in my street were quite densely packed, with back gardens backing on to other back gardens. I had to climb over fences in the dark, stumble through bushes, I was even bitten on the ankle by a little dog let out for a midnight pee. But I did make it through my own back door.

Maureen was furious – but she entered into the spirit of the conspiracy and next morning, when the doorbell rang, we were like a honeymoon couple, swearing eternal love. The reporters slunk off and the story never appeared.

I was now confronted with two very irritated people. Harvey said, 'These pantomimes have to stop, Jimmy. We're talking about some serious sponsorship deals, involving serious money.'

As for Maureen, she waited until I went out before throwing my cue in the dustbin. The bins were kept at the front of the house in a kind of little forecourt. As soon as she heard the dustmen arrive, Maureen ran out, waving my cue at them. They looked a bit taken aback, and she said, 'Go on, take it, he doesn't want it any more, so you might as well keep it.'

When I found out two days later what she had done, I had to laugh, even though there was a tournament coming up. It was my mum who got on the phone, trying to track down which dustmen emptied in our street that day. I assumed it was probably on some rubbish dump, or on a barge going out to sea by now, but Mum had the tenacity of an Indian scout in the Wild West and of course she got it back. Maureen said if anyone could do such a thing it was my mum – next time, she would put *me* out for the dustmen – only when Mum found me, she could keep me.

NINETEEN

JUST PICK UP THE PHONE AND CALL

Harvey Lisberg was in his office in Manchester, when the telephone rang. It was Maureen, looking for me.

'Hello, Harvey – I've not heard from Jimmy for a few days, not since Pontins last week,' Maureen said. 'There's something I've got to talk to him about.'

Maureen would never call over anything frivolous, and, ever the diplomat, Harvey said he would look in the diary to see where, if anywhere, I should be.

'So he doesn't have a fixture?' Maureen asked, very quick on the uptake. She knew if anything had been in the diary, Harvey would have been aware of it.

'Geoff might have fixed up something, or the PR people,' Harvey said. 'I'll track him down and get him to call you.'

Harvey started the process of looking for me, which was not always as easy as it sounds. He always said that one of the functions of a manager was to keep bad news out of the headlines; and while he was around, he was determined that there would be minimum bad press. A show-biz impresario, he was used to sweeping up the crumbs of chaos, having managed top rock bands and musicians for some years from the time when he discovered Herman's Hermits in the early 'sixties, going on to manage Sad Café and 10CC – whom, after thirty years, he still represents, which says a lot about his integrity. He has also promoted in concert the likes of Meatloaf, Abba, Queen, Elton John – the list goes on.

Harvey said, 'Snooker just had a magic at the time I came into it, around '81. I got more publicity in six weeks representing Jimmy White than in twenty years representing world superstars. Snooker was like the pop music of the 'sixties and the players were stars in their own right.'

Drugs were always a problem in any high-profile business, especially when dealing with highly strung pop stars. When he got into snooker, the one thing that horrified Harvey was seeing the same dealers who used to be around backstage at pop concerts turning up at the big tournaments. They homed in like sharks looking for fresh blood. Harvey had always looked on all sports as being basically 'clean'. But, as crazy sums of money started exchanging hands from soccer to snooker, the rot set in.

However, Harvey would always say, hand on heart, that while I might be wild and uncontrollable, my problem was never drugs. He said, 'When Jimmy had lots to drink, he really didn't know what he was doing. He would end up in situations that he shouldn't have been in. But he would always surface as if butter wouldn't melt in his mouth, always charming and mischievous.'

Harvey really hadn't a clue where I was but it didn't take him long to locate me, starting with my last known address – a tournament at Pontins Holiday Camp at Prestatyn, where my office had booked a chalet for me. It was quite a change from the hit-and-miss early days when we always arrived broke and in some disarray, hoping to find a still-warm bed abandoned by some departing player.

Pontins reported that someone had spotted me at the bar late the previous night. No, the chalets didn't have telephones, and yes, they'd leave a message. In the days before mobiles, when there was only a pay phone in the social club, it was almost impossible to get hold of anyone. Harvey would leave endless messages, that sooner or later I would get, and some time after that, I would maybe get around to responding – maybe. It depended.

'Jimmy, would you call Maureen, please?' Harvey would say; and I would say, 'Yeah, okay, soon as I hang up, Harvey.' Then Maureen would call and give Harvey some stick, saying she still hadn't heard from me. Harvey would sigh resignedly and say, 'I can't believe he's not phoned you.' Once again, he'd get on the blower to me.

After some days of this, Maureen blew a fuse. She telephoned Harvey and yelled down the phone at him. 'I don't believe you've even talked to Jimmy! I've still not heard from him.'

'Maureen, I've spoken to him, I really have,' Harvey pleaded. 'He promised me faithfully that he was going to call you at once – when he hung up on me, in fact.'

In the end, Harvey called his chauffeur – a driver who'd been with him for about twenty years – and got into his stretch limousine with the tinted windows, having stopped off at the bank to pick up a large bag of 10p pieces.

Harvey – who was an important and influential figure in his world – was partly amused, partly furious at having to go to Pontins in person. He had better things to do than 'delve his way through all the little huts and god knows what'. When eventually he located the chalet where I was holed up, he knocked politely on the door, but there was no response. So he roamed around a bit, looking in the bars, the bookie's, the snooker rooms, in search of me. Then he had several cups of tea to calm his nerves, where he bumped into someone who claimed I was in the chalet, sleeping off another late night. Having driven all that way and not wanting to admit to Maureen that he had been within a hair's breadth of his prey, Harvey managed to find somebody who had a master key to all the chalets and got them to open the door.

It was not our code of practice, in fact it was totally out of order. And if he was shocked by what he saw (he was), it was his own fault.

In the fetid gloom, about fifteen male bodies were sprawled around the room, all fully clothed, all snoring drunkenly away. Harvey reeled back, waving his chauffeur on, as if saying, 'You go in first. If it's safe, I'll follow.'

The chauffeur shook his head.

Taking a deep breath, Harvey dived in, tripping over bodies, bottles, lager cans, spilled packs of cards, drifts of bank notes, stepping on faces and hands, crawling on hands and knees to look under the bed and the table, inspecting three bodies in the bathroom and one in the tub, trying to identify me. For all he knew, some of us could have been dead.

'Jimmy!' he said, shaking the shoulder of a man who was sprawled half in the wardrobe, half on the carpet. A bleary, bloodshot eye opened and Harvey stepped back. 'Sorry, thought you were Jimmy.'

Eventually Harvey found me, buried under grubby pillows on the bed with a couple of other bodies passed out at right angles across my legs. He lifted me by my shoulders and dragged me out. But I couldn't stand and crashed to the floor with the most terrible pins and needles.

'Jimmy! Wake up! Find the bloody phone! You've got to call Maureen!' Harvey shouted in my ear.

'Why, is somebody dead?' I croaked.

'No – but you will be if you keep on like this, Jimmy,'

Harvey said. He jangled the bag of 10p pieces in my face. 'CALL MAUREEN! GOTTIT?'

'Yeah.' Shuffling across bodies to the bathroom, I had a drink of tepid tapwater and splashed my face. 'Can't you come back later, Harve? I got a bit of a hangover. I can't talk to Maureen like this. I got to get my head together.'

'Call her now!' Harvey snapped and stalked out to the veranda where he could breath in some fresh air from the North Sea.

Like a deathly pale vampire, I followed him outside, staggering back as the rays of the sun hit me full in the face. Harvey jangled the bag of coins in my face again.

'I'll see you after I've called Maureen,' I croaked.

'I'll be waiting in my car. And don't put it all in the fruit machine!' Harvey walked off to the sanctuary of his immaculate limousine, where he could see his freshly shaved face reflected in the polished walnut panels and could remind himself that his life didn't have to be like this. I was going to tell him that I never *put* money *in* fruit machines, but he was already looking too stunned to take in any more – and besides, my head hurt.

I called Maureen. I never found out exactly why she wanted me in the first place; because now all she wanted was a divorce.

'I'm sorry, honest, I'll make it up to you, I promise,' I said, fishing around in my repertoire for a 22-carat excuse. I didn't get the chance to try it on for size, because, after telling me that I would be hearing from her solicitor, she slammed the phone down.

'I dunno why she wanted me,' I reported back to Harvey. 'She hung up.'

'Can you blame her?' was Harvey's only response. Then he drove me into Rhyl for some dinner and a fatherly chat.

'Jimmy, why didn't you just call home?' Harvey

wanted to know. 'It would have been so easy.'

'I dunno,' I confessed. 'I was on a bender and was just keeping out of the way. I feel really bad about not getting in touch with home and all, honest, Harve. I wish I knew what came over me.'

'That's the trouble with you, Jimmy,' Harvey said. 'You must have a terrible conscience, but you won't do anything about it. You really aren't all that sensible. A simple little phone call, and you could have carried on and done what you wanted. You just can't keep on ignoring the girl. It's not right.'

I sat and listened, feeling as sick as a parrot. 'Yeah, you're right,' I said. 'But right now, I couldn't half do with a drink. Something to clear me 'ead.'

Maureen didn't divorce me, but after the incident at Prestatyn, Harvey and I drifted apart. I know he thought the scene in the chalet was the limit as far as he was concerned and I couldn't blame him. My five-year contract was nearing its end, and, when an old friend, Noel Miller-Cheevers, a businessman I had known since I was a kid, offered to manage me, I accepted.

Noel had acted as a friendly coach and mentor to the UK junior amateur players. In 1976, when I was fourteen, he had invited me, Willie Thorne, Tony Meo and Patsy Fagan to a specially staged pro-am tournament to mark the opening of his new club, the Pot Black snooker centre. Oddly enough the two amateurs – Tony and me – beat the two pros, Willie and Patsy and I beat Tony, to win overall. I also knocked in the club's first century in my match against Willie. At the time that Noel, a self-made property millionaire, approached me with management in mind, he had recently bought the Golden Leisure complex, putting his 21-year-old son, Gary, in to manage the fastest growing chain of snooker clubs in England.

I think Noel was looking at the model of the highly successful Matchroom setup with Barry Hearn and Steve Davis, and, like Barry, he obviously intended to get into snooker in a big way. Barry's acquisition of the Luciana chain of twenty billiard halls had coincided with the legalisation of fruit machines. It was a gold mine. Retaining just the hall above his Romford HQ as well as the gaming machines end of the business, at the end of the 1970s Barry sold the rest of the halls to Riley Leisure, makers of snooker tables, personally making £2,500,000 profit. He also negotiated a hefty slice of Riley for himself and Steve Davis. It was a very sweet setup with lots of endorsement possibilities and I could see the attraction of a rival chain for Noel, with me as the figurehead, like Steve was with Matchroom and Riley.

Unfortunately, Harvey Lisberg didn't see it quite like that. In February 1985 he took out an injunction in Manchester High Court to prevent me changing management. It was a very unhappy period because I liked and respected Harvey. He was a nice, quiet sort of fellow, and while there were some of my friends I wouldn't want him to meet, we had a great laugh together and I really enjoyed his company.

'You were what you might call difficult to handle,' Harvey said later. 'But I suppose if you were like everybody else, you wouldn't be able to play snooker the way you do, would you?' He felt that I didn't have the right kind of vision and application to make the most of my profession – because money really didn't mean that much to me. But, said Harvey, in deeply philosophical mode, it wasn't a matter of me not seeing the rabbits for the trees – most of the time I couldn't even see the bloody trees.

Harvey lost the injunction application because, even as his own barrister pointed out, you can't hold anybody under contract for service. All you can do is get damages.

Over a decade on Harvey and I are still friends. Of our legal problems he said, 'I thought it was pathetic that a manager could work himself into the grave for years and if somebody wants to leave, all you can get is damages – well, that wasn't what I wanted. I wanted the opportunity to help make you the best in the world.'

Harvey said it wasn't just his experience with me that convinced him to get out of snooker. True, he was disappointed when I left, but he had already half made up his mind to focus on his music companies. There had also been the problem with Alex Higgins when he was managed by Sportsworld. Alex could be so abusive when he telephoned, that the receptionist refused to take his calls.

Today, Harvey splits his time between Palm Springs, California, where he is involved with movies, and Manchester, where he still operates his music publishing and pop management business.

As it turned out, Noel found he didn't have enough time, with his property business, to get personally involved with me. Instead, he brought a bloke called Howard Kruger, whose father, Jeffrey, was a big promoter of country-music festivals and owner of a well-known Soho jazz club, the Flamingo. Howard – or 'H' as he liked to be called – had become involved in snooker only recently after bumping into Tony Knowles on a beach in Marbella in 1985. They got talking and Tony confided that he had a problem: a former girlfriend had blown the whistle on him by selling the 'Tony wears ladies' undies for sex romps' story to the newspapers. Tony was lying low – but the press pack was hunting for him high and low and he couldn't dodge them for ever. Howard offered to sort out the problem by preparing a carefully worded press statement. This worked, although Tony couldn't have been that bothered by the furore. It wasn't long before he got paid a reputed £25,000 by the

Sun to let them photograph him and a girl spread-eagled topless in her suspenders across a snooker table. The WPBSA were livid and fined him a pony for bringing the game into disrepute.

Howard's style was very flamboyant, and all this press activity piqued his interest in snooker. It was only a matter of weeks before he set up a company called Framework Management to handle what was soon to become a stable of snooker players. Later, Alex Higgins, Joe Johnson, Dean Reynolds, Peter Francisco and also John Parrott signed up.

Howard was like a rich kid who's been given a lot of money by his dad to go away and play. He would turn up in his Roller with a couple of blondes, sign up snooker players – ruin them – and get into something else. For the snooker, he opened luxury offices in Belgravia and hired no end of staff. He had a penthouse in Brighton, and a yacht moored in the marina, a red Rolls-Royce, photographers and a full-time PR man. At a snooker tournament, when another manager was paged to contact his driver, Howard at once arranged to be paged to 'contact his pilot'. What none of us knew at the time was that we were all paying for the yacht, the Roller and the helicopter. Alex, who doesn't drive, blew the lid off the setup when he discovered that, while he was travelling everywhere by train like a peasant, he was paying for Howard to descend like a demi-god from his chopper at the various venues. Eventually, Alex, who never stands any nonsense, made Framework bankrupt, but he, as well as the rest of us, is still waiting for his money.

Howard and I finally parted over an exhibition that he had set up in Brighton between me and Alex for a fee of two grand apiece. I forgot about it and while I should have been down there having my picture taken by the press, getting into my dinner jacket, doing all the publicity, I disappeared. Howard went potty. He careered around London in his Roller, looking in all my regular hiding places, eventually tracking me down in some really scruffy dive where I'd fallen asleep on a filthy floor under the table. He dragged me out, stuffed me in the front seat of the car and off we roared down the A3 to Brighton.

The car was a beautiful carmine red with an all-white interior, from the thick wool carpet, to the leather upholstery and even the facia, which was made of some kind of bleached white wood. And there I was in all this splendour, fast asleep, and filthy as a chimney-sweep. When I scuffed my grimy sneakers over the white facia Howard went mad, but there wasn't much he could do.

By the time we got to Brighton I was awake enough to play, though I can't remember a thing about it. When it was time to settle up, Howard insisted, 'I owe you nothing. Your filthy shoes have ruined the inside of the Rolls.'

'C'mon, H,' I protested, 'it doesn't cost two grand for a little valetting.'

'My car will never be the same again,' he grumbled. 'You're lucky I'm not charging you more.'

Howard's ways weren't Noel's fault, but it sealed the end of our management arrangement; although he still advises me at times on a strictly friendly basis. We got in touch with Harvey Lisberg, who under the terms of our settlement after my switch to Noel, was entitled to a percentage of my earnings for five years, and he very kindly negotiated a management contract for me with Barry Hearn. Life gets complicated, don't it?

I never thought the day would come when I would go mainstream; but finally there I was, joining the same stable as Steve Davis and all the others. Everyone wondered whether the snooker world would ever be the same again.

TWENTY

THE NINETEENTH HOLE

According to Maureen, I am an enthusiast whose enthusiasms don't last very long. She is fond of quoting the jogging saga. Shortly after we moved to leafy Wimbledon ('On a clear day,' joked the estate agent, 'you can see Oliver Reed,' who lived across the common) and all fired up by the sight of those green acres of parkland, I rushed out and bought hundreds of pounds worth of the best running gear, from designer-label headbands to state-of-the-art Nikes.

Having done a few limbering-up exercises, I started off for the park, while Maureen got out the vacuum cleaner to do a little housework in peace. Only a few minutes later, Maureen heard a footfall behind her. She screamed and the Hoover went up in the air.

'I've done enough for one day,' I said. 'You've got to ease into this running lark slowly. I caught a cab back, don't want to sprain the old hamstrings, do I?' It was like that cereal advertisement, where the well-kitted jogger, fuelled on fruit and bran and high ideals, runs down the driveway, where he gets in his car to go down the newsagent's to buy a copy of the *Sun* and *Total Sport*.

My experience with golf is not dissimilar. Alex Higgins had invited me to play a round with him on a course called the National, I think, shortly after I had signed up with Barry Hearn. It had been raining for days, and, when we got to the club, it was mud, mud, mud, everywhere. So we swapped clubs for snooker cues. Apparently, our bar bill amounted to something like £1600. I thought we had drunk maybe eight or nine beers each during the course of our game. The truth is, I was new to golf and short of equipment, so at some stage I must have wandered into the pro shop and stocked up. When the bills came in, the press got hold of the story, and claimed that Alex and I had drunk the golf club bar dry and I even believed it myself, until some time later when I discovered all this new golfing gear, still wrapped up in the boot of my car.

Alex and I actually did play a game of golf just outside Blackpool on a course with a nice little clubhouse and a couple of snooker tables. We had a young Northern Irish kid, Seamus Cassidy, along with us (that's not his real name but he tells me he is embarrassed by this story). Now Seamus didn't know anything about golf, the rules or anything, so Alex and I played each other while Seamus communed with nature in his brown leather greatcoat, looking like Boris from the KGB.

Alex is good at golf – I know this to be true because he told me – and I, while not very experienced, have a natural affinity with white balls, so the game was going swimmingly on this lovely sunny day. We got to the sixth hole, not far from the clubhouse, and Seamus dived inside.

About to tee off, Alex looked up in amazement as Seamus swooped down on us, leather coat flapping in the breeze, and a huge plate of sandwiches held aloft. 'Bloody hell, what's Boris up to?' Alex asked, waving his iron for him to get off the fairway.

'Here, have a sandwich,' Seamus offered. 'There's cheese and pickle, egg, ham and mustard—'

'Get off the fairway, you bloody fool!' Alex howled.

Seamus's face fell. 'I thought you might be hungry,' he said, proffering the plate again. 'The cheese sandwiches are really delicious.'

To humour Seamus, Alex took a handful of sandwiches, wrapped them up in a spare sweater, stuffed them in his golfing bag, and turned to get on with the game. Things were quite close, with Alex just nudging ahead. Then I drew level.

Alex had a longish chip to make a five and narrowed his eyes, wondering if he could make it. It was several yards to the green. Seamus was buzzing around the flag like a big brown bumblebee, looking for a place to settle.

'Leave the flag alone,' Alex yelled, waving his iron. 'Get away! Leave the bloody post alone, you big idiot!'

Seamus backed off, then, at the very last moment, just as Alex hit the ball, Seamus leaped forward and snatched the flag, waving it over his head. Alex's ball rolled right over the top of the hole, trickling to a sneaky little stop after a few inches.

'If it had hit the pole it would have gone down the hole!' Alex yelled, setting off after Seamus, who took to his heels, still waving the flag, sandwiches falling out of his pockets. Alex and I had had a bet on whether that particular ball would go down that particular hole. Thanks to Boris, the mad Russian saboteur, I won.

It was on the same course on another occasion that Alex arranged to play two rounds of golf with Doug Parry, his manager, and Colin McGuire, while waiting for his match in the Mercantile Credit Classic (which used to be held in Blackpool). Neither of them had any golf clubs, but Alex was assured when he telephoned the club and spoke to the secretary that it would be 'no problem, no problem whatsoever, Mr Higgins.'

When they arrived in the afternoon, it was to discover that there was only one set of clubs for hire. Alex had no intention of returning to Blackpool when he'd set his heart on some fresh air and a round of golf, so he accepted the one bag and off they went to the first hole. It was a little awkward, three men sharing the same bag, hitting three balls with just one set of irons, but not impossible. There were several minor fistfights and a lot of very bad language, but all in all a nice day out was had by all.

After about ten or twelve holes, they were in the process of switching irons when a fellow shouted 'Hey! – Hey! You!' as he galloped along the fairway.

'It must be an autograph hunter,' Alex muttered, but he waited courteously enough and even hunted for a pencil.

Up puffed this fellow, all red in the face. 'Never in my born days have I seen anything like this – three men playing out of the one set!' he bawled. 'Absolutely disgraceful!'

'I don't think he wants an autograph,' Doug muttered.

'I bloody well don't! I am the captain of this club and you're banned!' the man yelled.

'Well then, you can stick your golf clubs up your jacksie!' Alex said. He shoved the bag into the man's arms and strode off with massive dignity towards the bar.

This golfing story involves myself, the broadcaster Ray Edmunds, snooker legend John Spencer, and the chairman of the Royal Liver Insurance company. Ray and I were partners against John and the chairman, but only sharing a buggy this time. To start off, John and Ray both hit drives, John a fairly conventional one and Ray a fairly low one. When we got down the fairway, 220 yards down the row, they found their balls were snuggling up together on the grass like a pair of lovebirds. 'Spenny, come over here – what's the rule on a touching ball?' I asked. This, of course is the snooker question and to my knowledge has never been used in golf.

'Absolutely forbidden!' Spenny replied.

It made us all laugh; but it was an incredible thing, two people hitting balls over 220 yards to end up in that position. It must be a million to one.

TWENTY-ONE

GIMME THE MONEY

I had known Johnny Nielsen since I was a boy skiving off from school at Zan's, the local snooker hall in Tooting, and he would lend me his cue. John was a big fellow, with Viking blood in his veins. You could imagine him striding up the beach from his longship, ready for action, looking for the enemy with one eye and the hospitality tent with the other. He was a gentle giant really, but he didn't stand for any nonsense. After I had turned professional, John once received a call from someone he'd never met before. 'Ron's given me your number,' the man said. 'He said you can get Jimmy to do an exhibition for me.'

'Jimmy who?' John asked.

'Jimmy White,' came the reply.

John said, 'I don't think so. I don't think Ron would have told you that.' John was thinking of a pal of his called Ron, but it soon became obvious that this other fellow wasn't talking about John's friend. It turned out he was talking about a Mr Kray. 'Ron told me that Jimmy would help out.'

Then, it transpired that it wasn't Ronnie Kray, it was his twin brother, Reg, the man was talking about. John, who happened to know all the Krays, said, 'Look, Reg can't just tell you I can get Jimmy to do an exhibition just like that. It's out of order. Like anyone else you've got to pay. If he agrees to do it, he'll want his exes at least.'

'What?'

'His expenses.'

'Oh yeah, right. Sure.'

'You with me now?'

'Well, yeah, of course,' said this fellow, 'that's okay.' And went on to explain that he'd got this young kid he was trying to launch on the circuit and he wanted to start him off with an exhibition against Jimmy White. He was going to donate some of the proceeds to this charity, that good cause, that concern . . .

John rang me and we talked it through. I agreed that I would do it for expenses. But, unknown to me, naturally John added on a few quid for himself – I never did find out how much. So John rang the other fellow – I'll call him Bill – and made arrangements for us to go somewhere up North on the train. When we got to the station he was waiting for us. He was a brash young fellow, dressed up like Al Capone. He had a big motor, with a smart driver in a suit and tie. As we walked out, I whispered to John, 'The money! Sort out the money!'

'Right,' said John. He asked Bill for the cash. And so it started.

'Look,' Bill said, 'there's only half an hour to get to the hotel and get changed. We'll sort it out later, if you don't mind.'

On the way to the hotel he told us he was a bit of a boxing promoter, too. He was involved with people like Frank Warren and Don King. Bill was coming across like Mr Big in that part of the world, using terms like 'my man', which we found a bit sad. If he had come to London with that attitude he would have been mimicked first, taken for a ride, set up and then eaten alive.

When we got to the hotel, I nudged John.

'What about the money?' he said.

'We haven't got a lot of time right now – we'll sort it out when we get to the venue,' Bill replied.

The exhibition had been set up at very short notice but Bill had managed to advertise it and people were queuing around the block, so it looked kosher. But I was experiencing that sinking feeling.

Before I was taken to the dressing room, John asked again, 'Just a minute. Now look, we need the money!'

'My brother's bringing it over,' Bill said, shiftily.

'Your brother?'

'Yes, he's got a nightclub—'

'A nightclub?'

'And he's got it in the safe but he has to take care of this that and the other.'

'Right,' John said with remarkable patience. 'And when will your brother be here?'

'He shouldn't be long. Half an hour.'

'OK,' said John, 'half an hour, okay?'

'No problem,' Bill assured him, before vanishing into the crowd.

Well, this palaver went on all evening. Each time there was an interval, I muttered to John, 'Money here yet?' – and each time, poor old John had to tell me that no, as a matter of fact, it wasn't. The game was almost through when John went up to the promoter, who saw the question coming. 'Look, what we're doing is, we're taking you for a meal. Then afterwards we're going to take you on to the nightclub—'

'Perhaps you're taking us for a ride,' John suggested.

'No, no. Look, my brother's just about to leave his club and bring it down to the restaurant – trust me, he'll be there.'

So, we're in the restaurant having dinner, when John said to Bill, rather obviously I thought, 'Forgive me if I'm wrong, but your brother hasn't turned up yet, has he? You know, the one with the nightclub.'

'No,' said Bill. 'He's probably counting the takings. What we'll do is we'll get it off him when we get to the club.'

'I'm not going to any club,' I said, 'I'm going back to the hotel.'

John got up and said, 'So am I—' and to Bill he said, 'and so are you, my son. Let's go—' helping Bill up out of his seat with one hand.

Back at the hotel, I went up to my room and they waited together in the bar. John told Bill to get on the phone and get his brother over pronto. It was like a big breakfast room really, with the bar at one end and tables at the other. Scattered around were a few of Bill's men, examining their fingernails, studying the labels on sauce bottles and tomorrow's selection of breakfasts. John sat on his own and watched the clock. Still no brother. It's one o'clock; two. He asked Bill again what was going on.

Bill said, 'He'll be here, no sweat.'

At three o'clock, John calls the man over and says in that quiet voice of his, 'You – sit down here, Bill,' pointing to the seat on the opposite side of the table. 'Now, I'm coming to the conclusion you've been taking the piss.'

'No,' says Bill, beginning to shake just a little. 'No, I haven't, I swear.'

John says, 'Well, what does that clock say up there on the wall? And bear in mind that if you say tick-tock I won't be too pleased.'

'Three o'clock.'

'That's right. Three o'clock and you say you're not taking the piss?' Suddenly he stands up, grabs Bill by his Mafia suit and pins him up against the wall. This would have been the correct moment for Bill's cronies to have made their move; but none of them even twitch a muscle.

They suddenly get extra busy with the menus, drinks coasters and other assorted reading matter. One of them even puts on his glasses.

John says, 'I'm telling you one thing – if I don't get my money I'm going to rip your throat out.'

Bill gets about £10 worth of ten pence pieces out of the till and he's telephoning, waking people up, saying stuff like, 'How much have you got in your safe?' and, 'I'm in a lot of trouble' – and 'Don't tell me that. You haven't seen the size of this guy.' It's obvious they're all saying stuff like, 'I can't help you. I haven't got anything', or 'Go away 'cos I'm not getting out of bed' and soon he's done the whole tenner on the phone.

By now, John can hardly keep his eyes open – but he can't let Bill know that. He can't risk giving him the chance of doing a runner, even though at the back of his mind he knows Bill's girlfriend is asleep upstairs in the room across from me. So he says, 'I'll do you a favour – I'll give you a couple of hours' kip. But then you're up at seven and you're back on that phone – because now I'm getting really upset.'

Bill nods, and John goes to bed.

The next morning, John hears the maid calling me. He looks at his watch and leaps out of bed swearing. When he bangs on the promoter's door, Bill answers it fully dressed. 'Good morning,' he says. 'I've rung my bank manager and he's calling me back in ten minutes.'

John said, 'You've rung your bank manager at eight o'clock in the bloody morning? Where is he? Chicago?'

'He's opening the bank up special. It's only five minutes down the road – I'll go down now and he'll give me the money.'

'Fine,' says John. 'We'll come with you.'

We get into the motor, and John says very quietly, 'If you don't give me my money in the next fifteen minutes, I'm going to have to rip your throat out like I promised.

You do understand my position?'

We arrive at the bank. 'I'll be right back,' says Bill.

'Aren't you going with him?' I ask John, a bit concerned.

John shrugged his huge shoulders, 'So where's he going to go? If he runs we'll take the car and run him over, right?'

We watch Bill ring the bell. Unbelievably, the door opens – and he's inside.

We never found out how he managed it. Maybe he had something on that bank manager to get him to open up at that hour.

'Here you are,' he said finally, handing over a wad of bills. 'Your money!'

'Thank you,' said John, dividing the money quickly.

'Personally, I never doubted the man,' I said. 'He had an honest face.'

TWENTY-TWO

ALRIGHT, SQUIRE?

'No way am I going to move down here,' she said, 'and I'm not going to swim in that water.'

Maureen was staring at the edge of a blue-tiled swimming pool set in the middle of a large expanse of green lawn, outside a rambling, Tudor-style house.

'You're having me on, aren't you?' I said.

She tossed her blonde hair. 'No, I'm not. If you get me down here, I'm stuck, aren't I? Suppose you upset me, or something, I couldn't just get up and go, could I? It's not like my mum's around the corner, is it?'

'I wouldn't upset you, Maureen – I'd be happy here, with my own snooker room and everything, wouldn't I?' I coaxed.

'And I'd miss all my girlfriends,' she added – and there was no answer to that.

Wimbledon had seemed green enough, and the house enormous when we'd first bought it, but with three more little girls – Ashleigh, Georgia and Breeze – and Lauren, who was now ten, and a nanny, our tall town house was bursting at the seams. The small back garden was so full of tricycles, prams, swings, sandpits and slides, there was nowhere to sit on the patio in peace and quiet. More important, there was nowhere to put the snooker table I needed to practise at home without disappearing into what Maureen termed 'those seedy little dives'. In truth, although I like simple things – like seedy little dives – the idea of my very own snooker room was very seductive.

Harvey also wanted me to keep out of mischief and improve my image. There had been so many narrow escapes from bad, or negative publicity as he called it, that he was more convinced than Maureen that keeping me at home would keep me out of the snakepits. If he could have locked me in, only letting me out to play, he would have done just that. Failing that, he wanted me to be so content at home I'd stay in. 'All the other players have a snooker room at home, Jimmy,' Harvey urged. 'You're going up in the world. You *need* your very own snooker table.'

'Going up in the world' has never been an ambition of mine. I was quite happy with my situation, but I could see the value of being able to practise whenever I wanted. And I could definitely see the point, as I tripped over yet another doll or teddy-bear on the steep stairs, of having more space. The solution seemed to be a large, rambling home in a few acres, where there would be room for us all. Large and rambling in London costs millions of pounds; while you can get the same, and more, in the country at a discount.

When I saw the swimming pool and the miles of forest to walk through, I felt we had to have it, this was what we had been looking for.

'Can we afford it, Jimmy?' Maureen asked.

I was making loads of money and the mortgage offers were there, so the answer was yes. But Maureen was having second thoughts.

'No way am I going to move down here,' she said, 'and I'm not going to swim in that water.'

*

When Maureen's sister Helen, who lived with us as a
kind of nanny in Wimbledon, announced that she
wanted to get married, Maureen didn't fancy getting a
stranger in to help out. That was when she started to
weigh her options and, for the very first time, gave
serious thought to the move. I had thought it would be
an awfully big adventure and it made sense, moving
into a larger house, even for me, a London boy. I'd
thought that Maureen, who was born in Peckham,
before moving to Tooting when she was four, would be
delirious with happiness. But she wasn't. She even
refused to move after we'd bought the house. She didn't
know anybody down there, and where would we eat?
That question might sound strange to the average
housewife – but Maureen wasn't the average housewife.
To start with, she had never wanted to be a housewife.
She had never needed to cook and had never learned. I
was very easy-going and, although my mother was a
good cook, I was quite happy with takeaways, a habit
born of years of life on the road. Even when the girls
came along, we'd eat out as a family every night like
they do in Europe, or we would have something sent in.
The children were used to it. Maureen complained that
out in the country she would have to get an estate car
and go to the supermarket once a month. My God,
she'd have to learn to cook! She'd be isolated and lonely
– *and cooking*; so she kept putting it off. She put it off for
eighteen months.

But suddenly, Maureen made up her mind and off we
went.

All the newspapers sent reporters and photographers
out to take pictures and write up our new lifestyle.
Anyone would have thought we'd gone to the moon,
instead of twenty-five miles down the road. Maureen
told the interviewers how delirious with joy she was; but

the truth was she hated it. For months she drove back to Wimbledon to get the shopping in all the familiar places. Then, one day, she ran out of bread or Opium perfume or something simple like that and it seemed ridiculous driving all the way to London, so she popped into a local store and was amazed to discover that they sold the same kind of stuff she was used to buying at home – and the people were every bit as friendly. It was a revelation. She still misses the market with all the stalls and the friendly banter, but you can't have everything.

Things got better gradually. Maureen started to learn to cook simple things for the children. Sandwiches and fish-fingers were a staple, then she got to grips with the Sunday lunch, which became a regular fixture: two o'clock on Sunday afternoons, often with our families coming down from London.

When Jackie, my sister, and her husband, Clive, came one weekend while I was away, they returned from an evening at the local pub, bringing a load of Thai food back with them.

'Where did you get that?' Maureen asked excitedly.

'The Vic,' Jackie said. 'They've got a Thai cook, it's all authentic.'

Maureen was amazed to think that one of our favourite kinds of food was available just up the road at the pub, and she hadn't known. Tired after a day with the children, she filled a plate and took it to bed to have a midnight feast by herself.

Out of the blue, some leaflets were delivered, offering takeaway Chinese and Indian meals locally. Now she'd got everything, Maureen said, picking up the phone to order that night's dinner.

No, I said, we hadn't quite got everything. We had a cat; but what we hadn't got was a dog. I decided we needed something between a slavering Hound of the Baskervilles who'd guard the homestead when I was away and a puppyish playmate for the girls to grow up with and take on long walks.

Maureen reckoned that a dog was worse than a child, because at least you can get someone to look after a child – but how many people offer to have a dog for the day? I kept on, but Maureen was adamant. 'Who's going to look after it and feed it?' she asked. 'Not you, because you're never here.'

Maureen thought that was the end of the matter, but it was just the beginning. One day, Maureen and Lauren returned from shopping to find a note from our next-door neighbour, whom Maureen had never even seen, let alone spoken to, pushed under the door. The note stated: 'I've got your puppy.'

Lauren was despatched to the neighbour's house, while Maureen tried to reach me on the phone. A few minutes later, Lauren came up the drive with a tiny little puppy in her arms. It had the sweetest face. Already Lauren was in love with it, and was kissing and cooing over it; Ashleigh and Georgia toddled across and started poking it and Breeze, the baby, swam over the carpet like a tadpole, chuckling with delight. But Maureen was furious.

'I'm going out to a party tonight,' she raged. 'Your dad's done this on purpose. I'll kill him!'

As it happens, all I had done was to mention my desire to have a puppy to Alan Stockton, my Manchester snooker agent. Alan happened to know somebody whose dog had just produced a litter and, as a surprise, he arranged for a friend to drive all the way from Liverpool to deliver to my house a six-week old Staffordshire bull-terrier puppy. And there it was, snuffling and squeaking and peeing on the carpet.

'Poor little thing, it's hungry, Mum,' said Lauren.

'I don't know what you feed puppies on, we've only got catfood,' Maureen said, her fingers jabbing at every numerical combination in the universe, but she was unable to locate me. Eventually, Maureen got hold of a friend of mine at a social club closer to home. 'I can't believe what Jimmy's done to me,' she stormed. 'I've got this puppy here and I don't want it.'

'Well, if you don't want it, I'll have it,' said the bloke at the club.

'Lovely,' said Maureen, 'it's yours.' She got out the cat-box. The puppy was tucked inside and sent over by cab. When I returned, two or three days later, Maureen, who had simmered down a lot – in fact, she had even made friends with the neighbour – told me what she had done.

'I'll go and get it,' I said. 'You can't just give it away.'

Maureen shook her head. 'I don't want it,' she insisted. 'I've never wanted a dog. I've got four children, three of whom are babies and into everything. And there's the cat. That's a full-time job on its own. I'm telling you, Jimmy, I can't look after a dog as well . . .'

Splinter grew up to be a rotund, overfed dog who is rarely taken on enough walks, who barks at all the wrong things, who craves constant attention, particularly from strangers, whom he licks to death – but he's all ours and we love him. This was brought home to us one evening when he disappeared. No one could remember when they had least seen him. The girls had been running in and out, Splinter had been running in and out – then they'd come back for their tea, and Splinter was nowhere in sight. Maureen and I scoured the woods, calling and shouting, eventually having to return home empty-handed. The girls were in tears, so upset that I offered a reward of £300.

Within hours, someone calling himself Malcolm of Tunbridge Wells span me a yarn about being offered a Staffordshire bull-terrier that exactly fitted Splinter's description in exchange for his lurcher by some pikeys he'd bumped into casually.

'So I took the Staff 'cos he looked a good 'un,' said Malcolm, 'and give 'em me lurcher.'

'That's great, mate,' I said. 'I'll be over.'

'The dog's worth money to me,' said Malcolm, a cunning whine creeping into his voice. 'And I'll need compensation 'cos I ain't got me lurcher no more.'

I was all for calling the police. By then we had discovered that a couple of Labradors had gone missing at the same time from our neighbours' homes; and there was talk of dogs being stolen for badger-baiting or illegal dog fights. Maureen was horrified. 'Pay the bastard what he wants, Jimmy,' she said. 'Poor little Splint.'

Having arranged a rendezvous with Malcolm, I waited on a lonely stretch of road on Epsom Downs with my driver. A scruffy white van pulled up and a big pikey with ear-rings and tattoos got out, while the van drove a short distance away.

'I got your dog, mate,' said the pikey. ''Ow about the reward?'

'Three hundred quid's on the table,' I said, showing him the notes.

'Nah, that's a valuable dog you've got there,' he smirked. 'I'll take two grand.'

'I don't have that kind of money on me, I'll have to go to the bank,' I said, while my driver made a point of noting the number-plate of the van.

The pikey made up his mind. 'A grand, then,' he said, sticking his hand out. As soon as I paid up, he ran to the van, opened the back door, and Splinter jumped out.

'Good old Splinter, here, boy!' I called. Splinter started to run towards me, his pink tongue lolling out, then he turned his head and looked at the white van, where Mr Tattoo was closing the doors. There was the slightest moment of irresolution, then Splinter ran back as fast as his short little legs would carry him. He jumped up into the van, grinning at me from the rear as if saying,

'Only a grand? You skinflint, I'm worth more than that!'

The pikey dragged him out and the van drove off while Splinter sat on his fat little behind staring mournfully as his new chums disappeared into the distance.

'You ungrateful little rat,' I said as I stuffed him in the back seat. 'Next time, I'll let them turn you into sausage meat.'

A couple of days later, the two Labradors wandered back on their own, no harm done apparently. We guessed the pikeys must have been scared off when we'd clocked the van number. I should have set the police on them.

After that little episode, the locals got very friendly and people would often stop for a chat in the supermarket when we did our big shop for the week. Maureen's brother Michael was living with us at the time, and he had installed a couple of lights at the end of our drive for us. I had spotted these two big globe lights from a pub that was being renovated, and bought them because they were like giant white snooker balls. The lights had proved a nightmare to fix in place, partly because of the length of the drive.

While Maureen and I were out shopping, Michael called Kiss Radio to arrange a wind-up. Right in the middle of the supermarket, my mobile rang. It was someone pretending to be a local resident, saying they'd had nothing but complaints about my lights.

'I know you're a famous snooker player and all that, and I suppose you think they represent snooker balls,' he ranted. 'Well, we all think they're bringing the tone down.'

'Who's we?' I asked, rattled, but trying to keep my voice low.

'We are your neighbours,' he said, 'and we're fed up! We're getting up a petition – those lights have got to go!'

I told him they were not coming down – I had too much trouble getting them up – we had to dig a 200-yard long ditch in the drive for the cable – etcetera etcetera – ending with, 'and anyway I can't find the switch to turn them off.'

The person I assumed was the neighbourhood vigilante was in an exceptionally argumentative mood, while I was rising to the bait. Maureen was giving me strange looks, people were staring and the supermarket backroom staff, who were tuned into Kiss Radio, came out into the store for a good giggle. Luckily, I kept my language down. Just as well, because this was a live broadcast, and half the district had tuned in.

There was even a skit on the radio – ' "Home is the snooker player, home from the hills . . ." I'm sorry, I'll start that again. "Home is the *famous* snooker player, home from the halls . . . He's got lights in his driveway like white snooker balls." '

TWENTY-THREE

THE AMAZING WINDSHIELD FACTOR

This all happened well before Alex was banned from my local pub and the bookie's next door. The ban occurred when Alex was visiting me for a day or two. I had a little bit of business to attend to, so first I dropped Alex off at the Queen Vic, telling him I would only be an hour or so. When I returned, Alex wasn't anywhere in sight. Before I could open my mouth the publican, a kindly man, noted for his patience and tact said, 'He's gone, Jimmy, he's walking home.' He shook his head. 'I'm sorry to tell you that we had to ask him to leave.'

I didn't even need to enquire why. Alex has been banned from more hostelries up and down and sideways across the United Kingdom than the entire Millwall supporters' club. It's not so much that he drinks and gets out of control, as much as the acid way he has with words that can soon have people roaring with indignation.

But the events I am about to relate took place before Alex was banned, and shortly after Maureen and I moved to the country, where we hoped to get on well with our neighbours, not to bother the police too often and to bring our girls up in quiet and harmonious surroundings.

On the night in question, Peewee, Alex and I popped out to dust a few. In due course, when the publican indicated that he wanted to close up, I asked him to order a taxi. He looked at me with a pained expression. 'This isn't London, you know, Jimmy,' he said. 'This isn't just south of the water. This is *deep* in the country. Injun territory. Round here, there's no such thing as a taxi after nine o'clock at night.'

'What about chucking-out time? Like when you've had too much to drink? How are you supposed to get home, then?'

'You walk, Jimmy. In the country, people think nothing of walking five or six miles. You'll soon get used to it,' the publican chuckled, wiping down the counter.

Peewee and I had gone into a state of shock, but Alex is used to walking everywhere, loves it, he says, which no doubt he does, sober. But we'd had a few and, besides, it was raining.

When we went out my car was the only one still parked there. 'The other buggers haven't walked any deeper into the heart of the country, then,' said Peewee, pulling up the collar of his denim jacket. 'Come on, Jimmy, I ain't walking in this, it's chucking it down.'

We all piled into the car and started off for home. I know I was acting irresponsibly, but there wasn't another car on the road, and the rain-slicked black tarmac stretched ahead for mile after empty mile. We would take it easy. It was just us cruising gently through the night to the hiss of the tyres and the swishing of the windscreen wipers until I took a wide bend too fast and lost it. I braked hard, and the car went out of control, rearing up a grassy bank, to sideswipe a long low wall at the top. I shot forward and wrapped my chest around the steering wheel. In the back, Peewee, who was the only one to have strapped himself in, which is typical of him, shot forward, banged me on the back of the head, before recoiling back, where he stayed against the back seat, the belt having ridden up under his chin to half-strangle him. But Alex just sailed through the air with the greatest of ease, hitting the windscreen with his head on his way out. Fortunately, the windscreen was the kind that springs out on impact. Alex followed it, gracefully taking a horizontal flight path through the gaping hole and disappeared.

I sat in the driving seat, stunned and fighting for breath, convinced that all my ribs were broken. (The large, circular bruise made by the steering wheel was there for weeks, a painful reminder whenever I had to lean over the edge of a snooker table.) Peewee gurgled in the back as he fought to untangle his neck from the seat belt. And as for Alex – well, there could be little hope for him, but I shouted into the darkness, 'Alex! Alex! Are you all right, mate?'

Nothing. Total silence. I struggled to open the car door, but it was bent inwards and jammed. 'Alex!' I shouted again, before putting the car into reverse to ease off the wall so I could climb out through the other door. The wheels spun on the wet grass, then the car backed away with half the wall coming with it. Faintly, I heard someone calling from somewhere in the darkness, 'I'm all right, James. Do not upset yourself.' Then there he was, crawling through the gap in the wall, up over the bonnet and in through the empty space where the windscreen had been, and through the crazy back and forth swipe of the windscreen wipers.

He was radiant in the glow. Paradise by the dashboard light, as Meatloaf once sang. 'I'm born again!' he cried, settling himself into the front seat. And, as he picked off twigs and leaves, he kept up an ecstatic mantra: 'I am alive! I have relived! I am not lost anymore! I am . . .'

The wheels spun again, we shot backwards off the bank and landed on the road with a chassis-crunching '*whump*'.

'. . . reborn!' Alex warbled in my ear. 'I've a new lease on life, James! I've been saved!'

'Good,' I said. The wipers, which I couldn't turn off, were now flailing about madly inside the car. Peewee was screaming, 'Shut the eff up, Alex!' But Alex was unstoppable. 'Saved! I'm saved! I'm saved – I'm saved – I'm saved – I'm s-a-v-e-d . . .' to the rhythm of the wipers. I was still a mile from home, concerned with nothing but getting the car off the road and out of sight as quickly as possible.

Pulling into the drive, I pressed the button to open the garage doors, and shot what was left of the car inside. As I did so, the engine fell out. The entire car rose up from the rear, like a whale in its death throes, before settling back down, steam and petrol vapour rising in clouds, oil puddling on to the garage floor like dark blood.

'Hallelujah!' cried Lazarus O'Higgins.

I just sat there, visualising what would almost certainly have happened if the engine had fallen out as we careered along the road that last mile away from the scene of the crime. The car would have tipped over and we would have been very dead.

Inside the house, I got on the telephone to an all-night taxi service in London, insisting that someone had to come out at once. I didn't tell them it was to drive me back to find the windscreen, which had the road-tax disc attached with my car number on it. A couple of hours later, I walked back into my house, having shoved the incriminating windscreen into the garage, along with the dead car, to find that Alex had set the balls up. His miraculous escape – without as much as a cut or a bruise – had turned his head and he wanted to play me for £300. An odd sum, but that was what Alex in his deluded state had hit upon, and he was ready.

'I have a new lease of life,' he said. 'Luck is on my side.'

Furious that he wanted to gamble with me after such a traumatic accident, I snapped and slung him out of the house. Apparently quite unperturbed, Alex wandered off into the night, to assault the front door of the only neighbour that I don't speak to.

'Wake up! It's Alex Higgins seeking sanctuary! Bless all here!' he shouted as he banged on the door and rang the bell. From the lawn, he could see lights come on upstairs, and then the front door opened.

'I've just escaped with my life!' Alex said melodramatically. 'Jimmy White's just attacked me! Now hitch up the horses and take me to Reading.'

This was Alex at four o'clock in the morning, asking a total stranger to drive him a hundred miles, to Reading of all places, to descend on another friend. Astonishingly, my neighbour got dressed, got out his car, and took Alex where he asked. He was either too stunned to argue, or he wanted to get this raving madman away from his family – or perhaps Alex had indeed been born again, and his already legendary powers of persuasion had been magically heightened. Maybe luck *was* on his side.

The next day, Alex telephoned from Reading as though nothing had happened. 'Hello, James, how are you?'

That is always the story with Alex. Whenever we argue, I take no notice because the next day it will be forgotten. Seven years on, when Alex is reminded of that strange night, he says, 'Don't be ridiculous now, James. There was no stone wall. I did not fly out of the car, as you are well aware. I used to be a jockey, so I braced myself with my knees, feet and both hands, exactly like riding a horse, it's the training you know. You did not throw me out of your house and it was my manager,

Dougie, we telephoned to come over from Barnet and fetch the broken plastic numberplate, not a taxi. Reading was on an entirely different occasion. I was due to play at the Hexagon there and you had promised to take me, but you were hanging out with some racketeers and never came back. As you know, I have never missed a match yet. At six a.m. I went for a walk, looking for the railway station because I had to play in a tournament the next day. A mile or two down the road, there was a woman who happened to be in her garden, doing a little early gardening, so I went up and introduced myself, though she recognised me, of course. I asked if I could come in and telephone for a taxi to take me to Reading. You've got it all wrong, James. *Again!*'

He's a master. I shake my head and laugh because I will never forget the sight of Alex crawling back in through that windscreen. Seven years later, the stone wall is still down – and, for the first time, my neighbour will know where to send the bill. And what's more – Peewee remembers the story exactly as I do. That's two against one, Alex, old mate! But I know he hears only what he wants to hear.

TWENTY-FOUR

RUNNING ON EMPTY

I was running out of control. Something had to stop my reckless downward spiral. Maureen didn't know how to help me. Anything she said ended in another big argument. And rather than let the kids see the state I was in, or let them hear the dreadful arguments, when I was on a bender I would go to earth for days on end. That made things worse, because Maureen never knew where I was. There's nothing worse than being furious with someone and not be able to confront them. As for me, I always excused my disappearing acts by saying that when you've got a massive hangover, you don't need the flak. Better to hide away, switch off your mobile phone until you feel yourself again and are able to deal with the situation.

On one particular occasion, when I'd been on the missing list for four days, I returned to find all the locks had been changed. There was nothing strange about that – during those lost years Maureen changed them every two months. That's how often we split up. Looking back, it was unbelievable the way we were living. This time, I came back very much the worse for wear. I could hear

Splinter barking inside, but otherwise the house was deserted and Maureen's car was not in the drive. My keys didn't fit. Fed up, shattered and very emotional, I broke one of the windows in the kitchen, climbed in and went to bed.

What I didn't know was that Maureen's girlfriend, Debra, had come over to help her with the housework. Running out of polish or window-cleaner, they had driven to the village to do some quick shopping. On their return, they saw the broken window at once.

'My God!' said Maureen, 'we've been burgled!'

'I can't believe it,' Maureen whispered. 'Us down here on our own – and a burglar hiding in a cupboard or something.'

They decided not to go in for heroics, but to call the police and stay put in the kitchen near the phone.

It took the police half an hour to come; but a lot less time for them to do a search and find me asleep in bed, looking like some old tramp. The police thought it was hysterical, but Maureen was livid at being made to look silly. As soon as the police had left, everything got out of hand again and somehow Maureen ended up with a black eye, which I'm not proud of, but it's a fact. I don't even know how it happened. Someone spotted the bruise at its multi-hued best when she took the children to school, and tipped off the newspapers, which just goes to show that even in the heart of rural Surrey, there's eyes and ears behind every bush. You can't get away with a thing.

By then we had made up again, so naturally, when reporters started calling, we denied there was anything amiss. 'Everything's sweet,' I said. Then GMTV telephoned, asking if I was prepared to confirm that all was well between Maureen and myself by being interviewed by Eamonn Holmes and Anthea Turner on their breakfast show. I had no intention of getting up at some unearthly hour to air my dirty washing on television, and refused. However, very foolishly calling their bluff, I said, 'There's nothing to confirm or deny. Maureen and I are just fine. What black eye? Come and see for yourselves if you want.'

'So we've got your permission to come to your house?' they said.

'Sure,' I said, convinced they wouldn't bother. I was woken at eight o'clock the next morning with a knock on the front door. Maureen and the girls were already up for school, having breakfast in the kitchen and she called me to sort it out. I stumbled downstairs, unshaven and unkempt to answer the door and was astounded to be confronted by a GMTV reporter linked up to Eamonn Holmes, bright as a button, thrusting a microphone in my face. Behind him in the drive was a satellite truck as big as a double-decker bus with the moon on top and technicians buzzing about all over the place.

It was a bit of a shock.

'Good morning, Jimmy,' Eamonn chirruped brightly through the earpiece, while I gave a ghastly grin, wondering if I was on air or not. Judging by the enormous lens of the camera hovering over the reporter's shoulder, I would say I was.

'How is Maureen?'

'She's fine, lovely,' I managed to say.

'Can we talk to her?' Eamonn asked.

'I dunno where she is,' I said.

'So you're not prepared to let the viewers see her?' Eamonn pressed.

Maureen, who had her wits about her, had rushed upstairs to rapidly apply a healthy dollop of make-up over the rainbow hues of her shiner. By the time she emerged, hair freshly brushed and wearing a pretty outfit, she looked radiant. 'I'm fine,' she smiled for the benefit of four million viewers, 'I don't know what the fuss is about. Of course I love Jimmy and he loves me, don't you darling?'

We acted our hearts out and sent them on their way. As soon as they had gone, Maureen looked at me, and said, 'Right, if you ever do that to me again we're finished for good.'

I assured her I would never stay out overnight again unless I was working – and I promised she would certainly never find me breaking into the house like that again. I lied, of course – or, at least, I ensured that she wouldn't find any bits of broken glass lying around by getting Peewee to fix my own special window with a blend of soft putty. I continued to sneak in, go and get changed and creep out again, and Maureen never knew I'd come and gone.

During that period they should have hung a placard around my neck saying 'Man Behaving Badly'. One morning, at three-thirty or four o'clock, I was on my way home with Peewee, both of us very drunk, with me doing the driving. The police were somewhere behind us, but by doing eighty-five miles an hour I had shaken them off – or so I thought. They radioed ahead to ask a mate up ahead in another police car to waylay us. By then, I had screeched to a halt outside Ronnie Wood's house on Richmond Green, pulling up between two trees – quite hidden I thought – while we scrabbled around, pressing the buzzer, trying to open Ronnie's big iron gates.

Once we got in, we would have been safe. We could say that someone had dropped us off because the car was parked. Ronnie often had musicians there until all hours and my deranged plan was to get one of them to say he was driving my car – or, if they had been drinking, I'd go through his garden and be gone. You can't breathalyse a phantom.

The gates remained firmly shut. I didn't know that

Ronnie had been burgled the day before and that very
same day had fitted remote-controlled gates. Just my
luck. Meanwhile, there's a blue light flashing directly
behind and cops surrounding us. What a sickener.

With all the hullabaloo on his doorstep, Ronnie ran
down and tried to help, but it was too late. Ludicrously,
since he was even more drunk than I was, I turned to
Peewee and tried to grass him up. I said, 'You were
driving the car, weren't you, John?'

But my good mate, Peewee John Malloy, said, 'What
car?'

That did it. They took us off to the nick. Now, when
Peewee's had a few, he's one of those people who won't
shut up. He runs on like a babbling brook until you either
kill him, gag him, or you run away. Well, the cops
couldn't gag him and I couldn't leave, at least not
immediately, so they nicked him for being drunk and
disorderly – really for being a pest.

Now it was my turn. Grinning nastily, the police said
an old man had had to jump out of the way on a zebra
crossing as I hurtled straight across doing a ton. I was
lucky not to have killed him.

'Go on,' I said, astounded. 'An old man on a zebra
crossing on Richmond Green at four o'clock in the
morning? What colour was the zebra? – Pink?'

That didn't go down very well, but, by signing my life
away, I was allowed to leave a couple of hours later. I
returned to Ronnie's house where I'd left my car. As for
Peewee, he was kept in all night because he wouldn't
shut up. *Rabbit rabbit rabbit* he went, like the Chas and
Dave song. They said, if you don't keep quiet we're going
to put you away, and he went *rabbit rabbit rabbit* again. In
desperation they hauled him off to a proper cell and
slammed the door shut. Then he refused to take his
earring off, so they kept him standing a couple of hours
until he condescended to put it through the hole. When

he joined us later in Ronnie's house, Peewee was still very drunk, so drunk that he dropped a whole bottle of red wine all over the carpet at the foot of one of Ronnie's remarkable works, a ten-foot long oil painting of the Beggar's Banquet, taken from one of the Stones's albums.

Over the years Ronnie, who could easily make a living as an artist, has given me some stylish drawings of various rock stars – people like Eric Clapton and other members of the Stones. He does mainly portraits. A few years ago, I invited him to the World Championship to watch me play. He got somebody to make a guitar out of a snooker cue with a few strings attached, adding a little bit of something for the bridge and the neck. During a televised interview, he picked this up and started picking the TV theme tune for the Championships. It was a magic moment.

But there were no magic moments when I returned home. Maureen wouldn't accept that being banged up in a police station was a reason to stay out all night. To her, it was just another pathetic excuse.

'I've had enough,' she said. 'I want a divorce.'

So I rented a large, unfurnished house in Esher a few miles down the road and carried on behaving badly. The trouble with having no furniture, nothing except a bed, is you want to be home even less. It wasn't home – it was just somewhere I could crash out, somewhere close to the girls so I could spend time with them. Maureen told someone that I was always round, and now she couldn't get rid of me. 'Well, it's not over till it's over,' she said. 'There's always hope we can get back together unless I meet someone else, or until Jimmy meets someone else. But he's got to grow up.'

'It's like being in a black hole and not being able to crawl out,' I tried to explain. Being in a black hole was waking up in a flat, unable to telephone anybody to come and get me because I didn't know where I was; it was walking out of there in a daze, not knowing if I should turn left or right. (It took me three weeks to discover whose place I'd been in on one particular night.) My trouble was I had such a good time when I was out drinking, playing a little snooker, the odd game of cards, that I didn't want to stop.

But Maureen didn't sit at home being the poor little wifey, oh no. She got on with things, looked after the girls, went on holiday to Spain or the Caribbean, went out with her girlfriends. She was doing all the things that a single woman did, 'So I might just as well be single,' she said. 'Then I wouldn't lie awake worrying about car crashes and accidents, and whether you were in Dublin, Bangkok or the nick, would I?'

The press were hounding Maureen trying to get a story out of her – and what she didn't say, they made up. I half-believed she'd dished the dirt and that made matters worse between us. Meanwhile, letters from the court summoning me to appear went to our home, not to where I was living on my own like a hermit. Maureen would religiously re-address them and still they never reached me. Now it's quite possible they did get lost in the post – but it's more likely that I didn't bother to open them. I told my barrister I hadn't responded because I hadn't received the summons, and the case kept getting adjourned until the court finally ran out of patience – and I ran out of excuses. I ended up breaking bail, which didn't go down very well, and a warrant was issued for my arrest.

At the hearing, I didn't endear myself to the magistrate because I kept interrupting with a bad case of the Peewees. I always knew it was contagious. My barrister tried to shut me up, but I wasn't having any. When I heard the policeman who was giving evidence say there was this old geezer who'd had to leap for his life when I almost ran him over on the zebra crossing, I leaped up and said, 'That's not true! It was four o'clock in the bleedin' morning! There was nobody there – the streets were deserted.'

The magistrate told me to sit down and keep quiet. I sat down, but I wouldn't shut up. Loudly I said to my barrister, 'Old men don't go roaming around in the early hours of the morning. There's just drunks and burglars out that time of night.' Yes, *drunks* and *burglars*, I said – very clever, that.

I was given 120 hours' community service and a three-year driving ban, a lot for my first offence. I believe that they threw the book at me because four teenagers were killed in the Richmond area the weekend before my case came up.

I didn't appeal because I had been drunk and had driven a car more times than I like to think about and never got caught. I deserved my sentence. Drinking and driving is bloody stupid. I'm very lucky that I didn't hurt anybody, and these days I never get in a car with anybody who's had a drink, including myself.

Recently, Salad, my driver, said he needed a little help. Not guessing what was coming next, I said, 'Whatever I can do.'

'I've got to go to court,' he said. 'I've had it adjourned twice already and now I've got to be there.'

I knew that any problem Salad had couldn't possibly have anything to do with drink-driving, because he never touched a drop.

'Never mind, mate,' I said sympathetically, 'I've been there meself. I'll get you a barrister.'

'Thanks, Jimmy,' Salad said. Then he asked a little hesitantly, 'Could you come along to the court, to speak for me?'

'Sure,' I agreed.

Salad was one of those kids who won't face up to things. He thinks it will go away if he just ignores it. (I can think of at least one other person like that.) On the way to court he suddenly confessed that actually, he was being done for not having any car insurance – not on my car, I hasten to add, which was insured to the hilt – but on his own.

I reckoned he should throw himself on the court's mercy and pay up. But there was worse to come. We were nearly there when Salad suddenly confessed that he'd been banned for having no insurance a year ago. Added to that he had also been nicked for having a bald tyre, no MOT – plus he'd got about £400 worth of unpaid fines.

'Sorry, Jimmy,' he said meekly. 'But you'll still say something to the beak, won't you?'

'Oh sure. This is my new driver, your honour. His name is Salad. He doesn't drink or smoke or gamble and he's useless at snooker. In fact, what can I say? Ten years would be doing us all a favour, I can't say fairer than that.'

But, you've got to help a mate in trouble, haven't you? And I needed him. So in court I spoke for him, telling the judge that he's got a job with me, he's a safe driver and he'll never do it again.

The judge nodded solemnly. 'Thank you, Mr White. Six points on his licence, £75 fine for no insurance and £50 for the bald tyre. Next case!'

That judge was obviously a snooker fan.

TWENTY-FIVE

THE OLDEST SWINGERS IN TOWN

It was the community service that helped get me and Maureen back together, although not before she made me sweat a little. I couldn't go out on the tiles when I had almost a proper job to do every day. In the afternoons or weekends when I went round to play with the girls, Maureen saw how hard I was trying, and how difficult I found it, and gradually, we got talking and she thawed. I didn't exactly become a saint overnight, but I was trying to be more considerate, especially when I got to see what it was like to be old and not wanted by your family.

I had wanted to coach kids, like Eric Cantona, or do exhibitions for local charities. I would have made a lot of money that could have been put to good use, but the authorities wouldn't have it. They knew I'd have too much fun. Instead, they sent me to an old folks' home in Ashford, Middlesex, where I swapped my cue for a mop and bucket six hours a day, scrubbing and cleaning.

For the first time in months, I saw daylight, having to be at work by nine o'clock in the morning. I got a cup of tea, and then was told to make beds, serve lunch, do dusting, clean windows, mop out the loos, clean the kitchens. I didn't realise there was so much to housework. I also had to feed some of the fifty pensioners there who couldn't feed themselves. Some of the old gals used to smother themselves in thick layers of Nivea cream and face powder and cover me with kisses. I have a soft spot for old ducks, but that powder was a bit overwhelming at nine o'clock in the morning.

I got close to a couple of old men, Harold and George. George had a daughter, but she lived miles away and was able to come only every two or three weeks. Harold had been an author in his younger days; he'd met royalty, travelled. Now, with his sons not wanting to know, he sat all day in a chair, looking very down in the dumps.

'I gave them a good schooling, Jimmy,' he said sadly. 'But when they got older, they didn't want to know. They shunted me off here as fast as they could.'

I felt sorry for him, and for the many old people who can't be looked after by their busy families, although the home was a good and caring place. After I had done my six hours one day, I told Harold and George that I was taking them to the races tomorrow.

'What, do you mean we're actually going out somewhere?' said George.

'Kempton Park,' I said. 'We'll have a little flutter, shall we?'

The next day, they were ready and waiting. We went to Kempton Park, had a drink and a little bet – George backed four winners – and I returned them safe and sound to the nursing home. 'We'll do it again, boys, shall we?' I asked.

'You bet, Jimmy, I really can't remember the last time we had so much fun,' Harold said.

George was half asleep, clutching his winnings, a big grin on his face. 'I'll buy my daughter some flowers, that'll please her,' he decided. 'Thanks, Jimmy. If I die tonight, I'll die happy.'

'Oh go on,' I said, 'we've only just started. Sandown tomorrow, eh, boys?'

The next day, I stopped off at the Services Club in Tooting to pick up my dad, Tommy. Of course, we had to go in first, to introduce the old boys to everyone. Then it was drinks all round, a little snooker and off to the races. Tommy would take them on his own sometimes. It would be a case of the oldest swingers club in town hitting every pub between London and Sandown. When they were delivered back to the nursing home, Harold, who had Parkinson's disease, was so wobbly he could hardly stand.

'Night, Jimmy,' he'd say, grabbing my hand and squeezing it tightly. 'Thanks for another grand day out.'

Eventually I was tumbled. Matron came up to me. 'Jimmy,' she said severely, 'have you been taking them out drinking?'

'Just a little one, Matron, for medicinal purposes.'

'Well, Harold can't take his medication. In future, please ensure he sticks to orange juice,' she said. 'There is nothing medicinal about six large Scotches.'

Harold's face was a picture. 'I'm eighty-five years old – what difference will my medicine make to me, one way or another? I want a bit of fun before I go,' he said. 'Screw the orange juice.'

Three or four years later, George had a stroke and is confined now to a wheelchair, not aware of too much, and poor old Harold died.

But the other members of the oldest swingers club, Dad and Ron Gross, continued to do their stuff. I was playing Steven Hendry at the Bournemouth Grand Prix, held in the International Centre there. Dad, Ron and I were sleeping in the same hotel room when Rod Stewart, who I had met through Ronnie Wood, telephoned to wish me luck. No sooner had we got back to sleep, than it was Ronnie Wood calling from America.

'With all that luck, you should play a blinder,' Dad said.

The next day, Ron Gross went to bed fairly late – but not as late as Dad, who was still up, having a couple of drinks in the Bournemouth Labour Club. At about one or two o'clock in the morning, the phone rang. It was Dad. 'Do you know how Jimmy's doing?' he said.

'No, I'm asleep,' Ron replied.

'He's winning eight-nil against Stephen Hendry. Come on up to the club, Ron. We're watching it on the telly. When you get here, we'll go on down to the auditorium.'

'Well, I'm bloody well awake now,' Ron said, 'so I might as well. I'll never get back to sleep.'

At the club, they started playing a few hands of cards, watching the game on the television at the same time. 'What about going to the auditorium?' Ron would say, then another frame started and they were glued to the screen. It was a long game, to nineteen, and I was winning frame after frame. 'Cor, that's my son,' said Dad, sinking another pint. 'Lovely boy, never given me any trouble. A mite unpredictable at times, but there you go.'

Or, as Mum might have said, 'May God look sideways on you.'

'What about the auditorium? The match will be over before we get there,' said Ron.

'When young Stephen starts to win a frame, then we'll pop across,' said Dad.

Stephen did win a few frames – the match went to 10-4 – but the old swingers never did make it to the auditorium. They stayed where they were all night, playing cards and sinking beer.

At Bournemouth in 1997, I was beaten in the semi-final by a relative newcomer, Dominic Dale. After the match, I telephoned Maureen to say I was having a bit of dinner to unwind, but would be leaving soon for home. With Dad, John Virgo and a few more friends I went to the Royal Bath Hotel. Before I knew what was happening, a small card school started and I moved into that twilight zone that has no night, and no day, no sense and no wives or children at home.

TWENTY-SIX

AROUND THE WORLD IN EIGHTY FRAMES

The snooker scene was opening up in Canada, and I was invited to play in one of the early tournaments. I took Dad with me that first time. We were waiting in the VIP lounge at Heathrow when there was a bit of a stir up ahead.

'Blimey, look over there,' said Dad, 'that's Vera Lynn. I'll just nip over and say hello.'

'Hang on, Dad,' I said. 'No need to be making a fool of yourself.'

But he was gone.

'Hello, Vera, fancy meeting you here,' Dad called out cheerfully, and to Harry, Dame Vera's husband of nearly fifty years, he said, 'Hello, H – so you stuck with her, then?'

To my surprise, I heard the unmistakable tones of the Forces' Sweetheart saying, 'Tommy White, what a surprise! What are you doing here, darling?'

And there was my dad giving Dame Vera a great smacker on her forehead, and she was flinging her arms about him, her husband Harry shaking his hand and slapping him on the back, saying 'Nice to see you, Tommy, old son, how's it going?'

'I'm going to Canada, with my son – we're going to Toronto,' said Dad. 'Come and meet him, lovely boy he is.'

'Your son?' said Dame Vera.

'Yes, Jimmy White, you know.'

'Not the snooker player!' Dame Vera exclaimed. 'Well, fancy that, Tommy, I never put the names together. Well, let's meet him then.'

I felt really embarrassed. I was just a scruffy youth of nineteen who could pot a few balls a bit sharpish.

Dame Vera was going to Toronto to sing in the Armistice celebrations on 11 November, which took Dad right back. They chatted about the war, and about the time they had first met, during the terrible winter of 1947. Everything was frozen so solid that in the building trade many people were practically starving. Vera Lynn came to do panto at the Tooting Granada. Because Mum worked there as an usherette, she was able to get Dad and some of his mates some work shifting scenery; it was a job lot, eight men for a pound, half a crown an hour each, but believe you me, as Dad would say, with the Welfare State just lurching into being and so many back from the war looking for work, they were grateful to get anything. Dad used to get Vera her bottles of Guinness, which she'd drink between shows with a sandwich to keep her strength up and he'd run round to the bookie's and put bets on for Harry.

'If Harry had a win, I had a win, know what I mean?' said Dad, and they all had a good laugh. Then Vera tucked her arm in mine one side and Dad's the other and we walked her through the lounge, with all the press clamouring around and photographers snapping away.

'There she goes,' said Dad when we parted. 'Auf wiedersehen, Sweetheart! What a grand gal she is,' he sighed. 'It's people like her what won the war, you know, salt of the earth.'

The first thing we noticed about Canada was the police wore guns. The second was how clean Toronto was. 'Blimey, if you want to sling an apple core into the curb round here,' said Dad, in the cab on the way to the hotel, 'you'll be arrested.'

I thought the venue for the snooker would be like that, held in a cool, clean place with the hush of a cathedral; but I was wrong. It was like walking into a massive circus tent with a rodeo in one corner, a fairground in another, a battle of the bands mixed up with a wrestling match and a frontier dance-hall – with somewhere in the middle, a spit and sawdust area cleared for the snooker knock-outs. There were cannons going off, fireworks, noise, dirt and chaos.

As a sign said in the tournament office: 'Conditions are as is.'

The clanking, clanging air conditioning swirled the already sweltering air in exhausted spirals and up to where we were trying to play. It was so hot we all sweated like hogs. Normal dress suits were discarded in favour of open-neck shirts and a whole host of garish outfits were to be seen. Alex Higgins was in his element. He had always had a problem with the penguin suits we were expected to wear in Britain. He had even been fined once for wearing an amazing elf-green suit – but his biggest problem was the constriction of the bow tie, which he said gave him a rash. In India, complaining about the unbearable heat and humidity, he had caused an outroar (and earned himself another fine) by taking off first his tie, then his waistcoat – then his shirt – in a tournament. But he had vindicated himself by producing a doctor's letter to say that he was allergic to ties – something nobody else but Alex could have thought of, or got away with.

We had to learn a whole new lingo, too. Hook = snooker; rail = cushion; scratch = go in off; draw = screw; english = side; run = break.

There were many strange characters, like Danny, who would bet on anything, including whether or not a particular player would wear socks that day; there was Tony le May, a player so huge that when he took afternoon naps on the park bench behind the players' screen, he looked like a giant jellyfish stranded on a rock; there was Automatic Eddie Agha, a wizened old midget with a speech defect, who was one of the best I've ever seen at trick shots.

One day, one of the locals came up to me in the hotel and challenged me to a game or two at his place in downtown Toronto. Well, that was right up my street, so Tony Meo, Kirk Stevens and I got our money together and rolled along. We took him to the cleaners all night – but he was in front of his own crowd. Suddenly, he smashed his cue and came charging towards us, growling like a grizzly, with his gang behind him, baying for our blood. We ran for our lives. It was like the old days.

In Calgary the tournaments were wilder than almost anywhere else. They never iron their tables there. In November 1982, the entire tournament was delayed, at the referee's insistence, while a special iron was flown from England. When it finally arrived (by which time we were all practically under the tables from too much partying) the voltage was wrong – different system. Some burly brute, looking like Desperate Dan, found a blow-lamp and fired it up under the iron to get it to the right temperature. It was like being in a frontier town at the turn of the century, where men are men, riding tall in cars big enough to accommodate their high Stetsons, and disputes are settled in the old-fashioned way. Guns, fists, tomahawks and the turn of a card.

★

I have been to Thailand many times. The first trip was organised by Barry Hearn. Steve Davis and I received a Beatles-style welcome. Tens of thousands of people greeted our plane with garlands of flowers and music, and lined the streets. The crowds were massive – I have never seen anything like it. There were swarms of people in the hotel. Every time you went down to reception, twenty or more would be waiting patiently for autographs. It's all a bit more commercial now, with nearly a quarter of the 46 million population hooked by the game; but then – just fifteen short years ago – it was unbelievable.

Sports writer Steve Acteson once wrote an amusing piece about the state of snooker in Fiji, where there is an enthusiastic following in the United Sports and Social Club in Suva – but they could do with some decent chalk, he said.

All I can remember about Japan is how expensive it was. There was just one snooker hall – on the fourth floor above a furniture store, where players were charged the astronomical fee of £9 an hour – compared with about 50p in the UK.

In China, which we referred to as the Bamboo Curtain, the entrance charge was 10p – but even that proved too much and the maximum crowd was 1500 in the 51,800-capacity huge bamboo arena they set up. It was seen on nationwide TV, but, since it was state owned, there was no fee for broadcast rights. And yes, I went up the Great Wall on a donkey, one of Barry Hearn's great ideas. Willie Thorne – because he likes to bet – was making a book all the way up the Wall on who would actually get to the next segment without falling off. It felt a long way from Tooting.

In downtown Colombo you squeezed through a black, tattered curtain to get to the table, which was surrounded by two tiers of hard seating. The atmosphere was steamy and exotic. You could hear jungle animals roaring and screeching in the night out there beyond the palm trees and the night-scented lilies.

A lazy fan turned slowly above the table, and little boys hung about the corners of the army indoor stadium, ready with palmetto fans to give the players personal attention when pores began to open and the sweat dripped off the end of our cues in that sauna-like atmosphere. There were two pedestal floor fans intended for the players, but only one worked – but not all the time. There were manual scoreboards – but the chalk was too damp to chalk.

Deauville, in Normandy, was an exhibition in more ways than one. All the top players were invited for the opening of a new casino which adjoined the famous racetrack. It was such a tempting invitation that not even Alex Higgins, with a broken leg and about forty other assorted broken bones, could resist. Somehow – don't ask – Alex had fallen backwards out of a third floor window. Where? – at home. He was drunk, he admits it. If he had been less drunk he would have died. And now, there he was in bandages and plaster from ankle to neck being loaded aboard the private plane that was to take us there.

A brisk storm had broken when we arrived. Blown off course and unable to see the golf course where he was expected to land, the pilot put us down on the racetrack, although it could have been a ploughed field, judging by the way we bounced along rainswept turf.

Dinner the first night was spectacular. We were seated amongst the cream of French society, with star guests like Roger Moore, Dustin Hoffman and Christopher Lee. They had laid on a female vocalist who sang in such a high falsetto that most of the guests – including me – fled to the casino, where Roger, who was playing James

Bond at the time, did a great impersonation of 007, strolling amongst the tables with us poor snooker louts shambling along in his wake, trying to pick up a few good tips on how to appear sophisticated – i.e. how to sip a vodka martini instead of slurp – and win every time.

The weather had cleared a little by the time they herded us all down to the beach for a fireworks display. It was like the Normandy landings out there, rockets screaming down and the great Atlantic waves booming down on to the long stretch of sand. The weather was so bad that the next day, when they wanted Steve Mizerak and me to go out in a boat for a publicity shoot, they found that not only had somebody misjudged the tides and the sea was half a mile out, but those few boats that hadn't been washed away in the storms of the previous day were dangling like dead kippers from the sea-wall. After a little thought, some inspired person brought us a rod and line, but no hook or bait, and told us to sit on the quay and pretend we were fishing.

The actual snooker exhibition was not quite so well organised. There was a crowd of one – an enthusiastic young woman – not a snooker player, but clearly a keen fan – who had travelled from the Shetland Islands via three planes and a train in the fond hope of seeing me win. Because the match was going to be televised, it was delayed for 45 minutes while they rounded up some spectators, mostly fishermen who weren't busy because they'd lost their boats and a bunch of road-sweepers, judging by the look of them – all to watch Alex, who refused to defer to his war wounds, and somehow managed to pot a few balls, hobbling round the table on his crutches. There were a couple of players along for the ride who were so stonkers with free champagne they could hardly see the balls let alone pot them. I made it to the semi-final – not difficult under the circumstances – to be beaten by Steve Mizerak, a demon pool player from

New Jersey, who not only thought all Europeans were crazy, but proved it by winning the Fiat trophy and £35,000.

As for me, I won £21,000 but lost it all in the casino and the race-track the next day, thus bearing out Steve Mizerak's claim that we are indeed all potty. *Que serà serà* – a good time was had by all. Just don't tell Maureen. Don't tell my manager. Don't tell the press – and especially, don't tell me. I've heard it all before.

One time I played pool properly was in Hong Kong – an eight-ball competition in which you put in $200 each for a friendly before the opening ceremony. I happened to win it, against Steve Davis, Oliver 'The Machine' Ortmann and another German. At the tournament, which was a round-robin that included some Americans, we beat the best players in the world, who in my opinion, *en masse*, are the Filipinos.

Not too many people – and certainly not the general public in the States – are aware of their skill in the pool world because Filipinos can't get visas to go to America. Over the years, since the Vietnam war, when the game was first introduced to Asia, young Filipino men have taken to it big time. On the whole, they come from the streets. The sharks know this and they will hustle a talented young boy to play pool against Americans. One thing will lead to another, ending up with the boys being shipped into America illegally. Once there, at the underground matches, a Mob-type manager will offer to take care of them, and take 5-1 of their winnings (that is, the player is left with one-fifth of his money). They have no choice, and that's how they're there, on this underground circuit, playing with the best players in the world with no credit, never winning any titles, just happy they're off the streets of Manila and in the USA.

But this particular night in Hong Kong, Bobby Moore

(not the great captain of England's football team which won the World Championship in 1966) had managed to get visas for the Philippines to play us. But I think they must have been overawed by the dress suits and the cameras. So we beat them – and won the world team 9-ball competition.

In 1988, I romped through the Canadian Masters to win. For the John Labatt Classic, leg three of the World Series, it was a narrow squeak. I nearly didn't make the tournament at all. Someone wrote, 'Jimmy White's dazzling play and generous heart makes him deservedly one of the most popular players – but the Whirlwind is also one of the least punctual people in the entire world. So it was no surprise when the Toronto-bound Wardair DC10 carrying the cream of the world snooker and three snooker scribes and WPBSA tournament director, Paul Hatherell, zoomed into the skies above Gatwick, Jimbo was still at home in Wimbledon and not in his allotted first-class seat.'

Everyone thought it was terribly funny but not Barry Hearn. He told me that if ever he was going to have a heart attack, it would be over me. However, I wasn't the only one who was late – if you can call a trophy 'one'. Barry Hearn had inadvertently left the trophy – a silver and gold maple-leaf – in Matchroom's Romford offices. But, like me, it reached Canada just in time to be put on display at ringside.

Ten minutes before the start of CBC's four-hour live transmission – I went missing again. 'Where's Jimmy?' the cry went up. And where was I? Having my hair cut, of course. I had to sprint to the venue, and turned up with my waistcoat buttoned all wrong.

Steve Davis had won the trophy the previous year, 1987. This was the same year he had sung his single, 'Snooker Loopy', in the Japanese restaurant and karaoke bar owned by top Canadian female player Grace Nakamara's parents. It quite a night.

The year I was late, 1988, Dennis Taylor was to win the trophy, beating Steve and then me in what was described as an electrifying final.

I was also late for the flight back, which was then diverted to Stansted because of fog and my luggage was still apparently stuck in Toronto. You play around the world in eighty frames and end up waiting by the carousel at Stansted for nothing to come around. You stand there watching the rubber flaps on a little door that leads to yesterday; and from where nothing appears. You can't go back, you see, you can only go forward. Then someone asks you for your autograph and you're still on autopilot. You stare at them. They know lots of things that you don't – like, where you are and who you are.

Gary Lineker said on the *Michael Parkinson Show* that he was so used to signing his autograph on autopilot that once, when he sent his missus a birthday card, he wrote, 'Happy Birthday, Gary Lineker'. She was not best pleased. I know how they both felt.

TWENTY-SEVEN

HONG KONG 9-BALL
BOOGIE

Bobby Moore was one of the strangest characters I've ever known. He came from New Zealand (where he had started his career as a golfing caddie to Curtis Strange), but by the time I met him he had established a multi-million dollar gambling business in Hong Kong. He operated out of a huge flat overlooking the winning post of the Happy Valley racetrack, as an international better for all the big shipping tycoons who didn't want anybody to know when they laid a lot of money off on races where they had inside information. His passion for 9-ball pool led him to organise a 4-day tournament in Hong Kong with me, Steve Davis and six of the world's best. I had already been to Hong Kong for a small exhibition between me and Steve Davis, when both the fee and the hospitality provided by Bobby had been lavish, even though we didn't get to meet the man himself. This time, when I got the invitation for the 9-ball tournament, I was only too happy to go, arranging to fly directly to Honkers from Bangkok at the end of the Thai Open.

Steve Davis, who had also played at the Thai Open,

gave me a wake-up call at the crack of dawn in my hotel room. Eyes tight shut, I muttered, 'Go away, there's a good boy, Steve. I've only just got to bed. We're not playing until tomorrow. What's the rush?'

'Jimmy, we've got to be on that plane, we're expected today,' Saint Steve insisted. 'They'll be waiting for us.'

'I'm not going anywhere right now. I'll speak to you later.' I rolled over and promptly fell fast asleep again until a more civilised hour. After a leisurely late-afternoon sherbet or two, I caught the night flight.

As I came through the customs, I saw three enormous bodyguards, holding up a placard with a picture of me and the words 'Jimmy White' in big letters over the top. 'Hi, fellers, you must be looking for me,' I said. Ignoring my outstretched hand, they grabbed my cases and walked me out, firmly wedged between their beefy shoulders, to a massive black Mercedes with dark tinted windows.

The car slid away, with me in the back seat between a pair of silent gorillas, feeling distinctly uneasy. Suddenly, the phone rang. The hatchet-faced gorilla in the front answered it. 'Yeah, we've got him, guv!' He laughed dark and dirty, looking at me in the rear-view mirror. Then he handed me the phone over his shoulder without a word.

'So you finally made it then?' Bobby said into my left ear.

'What's this all about?,' I said. 'You trying to give me some grief or something? 'Cos your gorillas don't scare me.'

'They're ex-SAS, actually,' Bobby said. 'Northern Ireland and assorted dirty desert wars, the lot. They're in the disposal business, know what I mean?'

'Really? Yeah, well,' I said. 'What's going on here? I'm not getting a lot of feedback from your boys.'

'You've already broken your contract, Jimmy.' And the line went dead.

It was two in the morning when we arrived at a plush apartment block. A fast, private lift shot us silently up to the penthouse suite. Doors slid open, and I was shown into about half an acre of polished blond floors and marble with banks of computers along a far wall showing bets going down and the odds all over the world. Beyond, the lights of Hong Kong twinkled and danced. The next thing I saw was the Nugget, as I like to call Steve Davis, especially when we're playing pool. He was laughing and joking, and something the worse for wear. It was the first time ever that I'd seen him legless – and I suspect I'm the only person in the entire world who can claim that. When Steve spotted me, his eyes went up and around like a one-armed bandit, then he toppled, arms whirling, into a drinks cabinet. There was smashed glass and rivers of alcohol everywhere. Looking up at me from the floor, he smiled and said, 'All right, Jimmy?'

A dark-haired man in a light suit strode over to me, very fit, tall, with a wide grin, and held out his hand. 'Bobby Moore,' he said. 'Nice to meet you at last.' Turning towards the Nugget, he clapped his hands, and a team of helpers arrived to help Steve to his feet and clear up the mess.

'Sorry about the strong-arm tactics at the airport,' he said. 'I reckoned it was the only thing that would get you here. You've got quite a reputation.'

'Not me,' I said, 'you've got the wrong man.'

'You know what I mean – going on the lam – having it off on your toes,' he said. He went on to explain that he had a great friend in Hong Kong, who knew my form, and who had warned that nobody would see me until the very last moment, when I was due to play. After which I would disappear again. 'Anyway,' Bobby said. 'Now you're here, and we can get to know each other. No harm done, I hope . . .'

'Nah, it's all right,' I said, 'I knew it was just a joke.' I didn't tell him that I'd been as nervous as hell. The East can be a funny spot with some very dodgy characters.

The tournament venue was the best restaurant in Hong Kong, but the play went on a lot longer than planned. The TV people came up to Bobby. 'Your money's running out,' they said. He'd booked the place and a camera crew for seven or eight hours, and it was now almost 2 a.m. Bobby said, 'Don't worry about it. Just double your fee and send me the bill.'

The restaurateur came up, wringing his hands, and went into a spiel about how he had to pay his staff overtime, and again Bobby said, 'Don't worry about it. Double your fee.'

It was double your fee all over the place, money no object. Halfway through the match, Bobby suddenly stopped play. 'I'd like to make a presentation,' he said. And flashing an 18-carat smile into the cameras, he whipped out a case containing at least half a million pounds' worth of diamond necklace, set in about six pounds (and I'm talking weight here) of gold. His girlfriend shimmied into a pre-arranged X marks the spot for the camera, dressed in a tight-fitting sequinned outfit, while Bobby proudly hung the necklace about her neck, like the Lord Mayor of London's ceremonial chain of office. She loved it. He looked as though he liked it too. She had quite a figure.

After the game, back at Bobby's flat, he showed me his latest bank statement – £9 million it read – while he puffed on a cigar. 'Lot of money, huh?' he chuckled. 'And plenty more where that came from.' He showed me how his business operated, with his four secretaries, ten computers and big TV screens showing the races, the times of the races and the odds.

Going to restaurants with Bobby was a voyage into the unknown. The Nugget and I went to one place, a bar-cum-restaurant, when halfway through the aperitif

Bobby decided to sign up the band as their manager. He sent one of his gorillas, who went everywhere with him, to find a lawyer to draw up a contract. The band had signed before we'd got to the dessert trolley.

On another occasion, he took us to a place where he insisted on having a table that was already full. The manager lost that famous Oriental reserve and wept in despair, but Bobby ignored this display of emotion and reached into his pocket for a great wad of cash. Halfway through their salad, the knives and forks were taken out of the diners' hands, the cloth was whipped off and they found themselves moved to some poky little corner, while we trooped across the room to take their table, by now relaid for us.

I was seriously embarrassed by this and said, 'Bobby, you're not doing anything for me. You're just making yourself look stupid. No offence, but you are.'

He took not the slightest notice, ordering champagne and oysters, convinced that money would buy anything. Inevitably, his behaviour made him a lot of enemies, including, so rumour has it, some of the Triads whose families were the ones shoved into the corner that evening.

Bobby's intelligence network was incredible. Once, he even got the better of our manager, the amazing Barry Hearn. Barry had seen the potential to get us into Macao and, without informing Bobby, had flown over to the island to do the deal. When Bobby confronted him, Barry shrugged his shoulders. Bobby then produced a fax which proved his case and stuck it under Barry's nose. It was the first time I have actually seen Barry Hearn throw up his hands and submit.

Bobby used to phone me all the time and came to London only last year to watch me play snooker. We ended up in my garage – the place where nobody thinks to look when I go missing – and did the old 9-ball boogie.

Two months later, he was dead. It was terrible news to hear that this larger than life, happy-go-lucky character had committed suicide in his flat. People said he'd lost a lot of money and his bank accounts had been frozen. I wasn't entirely convinced. He lived dangerously in a very dangerous world.

TWENTY-EIGHT

A TIME FOR TEARS

1995 to 1997 will always be remembered by me as a bad dream. The Queen might have had an *annus horribilis* – well, I had not one, but three horrible years.

When my brother Martin was diagnosed in 1995 as having cancer at the age of fifty-two, I thought things couldn't get worse. But they did. In April of the same year while Martin was so ill, I discovered I also had cancer. I had been to my doctor for the regular check-up for insurance purposes, and, just as I was leaving his office, with my hand on the doorknob, almost as an afterthought I mumbled something about a little lump in my left testicle. 'I felt it when I was drying myself,' I volunteered, thinking I was just wasting his time.

The doctor had a look and said, 'Hmm, I don't like it.' Which made the hairs prickle on the back of my neck, because nobody outside the immediate family knew what Martin was going through. I was some eighteen years younger – how could I also be affected? The next morning, I saw a specialist at the Royal Marsden Hospital for a second opinion. 'We would like to operate at once,' they told me, but I said I had an exhibition on the

Wednesday, so I was booked into the operating theatre for the Thursday.

When they told me, I must admit my bottle went completely. I felt suddenly very frightened I might not see my kids grow up. I wanted to run away – but this was one thing I couldn't escape. So I switched off my mobile and went off to have a drink and a long think.

I had two choices – I could give in, or I could fight. I decided to fight, to try to use the power of mind over matter to will myself well.

When the doctors came to operate they found two malignant growths and whipped the left testicle away. The right one was fine, thank God, and I've still got it.

A week later I played the British Open. I was in agony from the stitches when I stretched across the table, but I still managed to pot a break of 141 during a 5-1 first round victory over Mark Flowerdew. I didn't want anyone to know the state I was in because it would look like I was making excuses up if I didn't win. Groggy on painkillers and still walking gingerly, I was knocked out by what everyone termed a 'surprise 5-2 defeat' by Mick Price in the third round. I was late for another tournament because I felt so rough and was about to be hauled up before the WPBSA. But when they learned the truth they actually apologised to me. When I had to face Peter Francisco in the World Championships at Sheffield I had been given the all-clear by my doctors, so I felt I could go public.

As if that wasn't bad enough, I had some cosmetic surgery on my scalp to fix a bald spot. Personally I wasn't concerned that I was thinning a bit – honest. It had been happening gradually since I was twenty-six years old. But it was noticeable when I bent down over the table, and I felt it would look better on television if it wasn't there. I had so little ego over the whole operation, that I even let the photographers in. Basically, what happened was the doctors made a horseshoe-shaped incision in my scalp with a laser – in the photos you can actually see steam rising – and they inserted a kind of elastic spring that would gradually draw the edges where there was hair together. To my horror – and pain – within days I had two black eyes, like a panda, my face went black and blue and I bloated up as fluid filled my neck and face. I was so stiff I could hardly move or talk.

I joked that I had to wear sunglasses so I wouldn't scare the kids. But Maureen was not very happy that I had put myself through so much. 'Okay if you've got a brain tumour, Jimmy,' she said, 'but why would you want your head cut open for no good reason?' She added that she didn't give a toss whether I had hair or not – and looking into the mirror, I felt she had a point.

But none of that seemed important when Martin died in October of that year. Martin was the big brother who had once offered to buy me my first snooker cue. It just didn't seem possible that he was dead. The whole family gathered around to comfort Mum – who'd lost her first-born – and each other, especially Martin's wife, Della and his son, Mitchell. The night before the funeral, a couple of us boys sat around with some of Martin's best mates, having a bit of a party, remembering and celebrating Martin's life.

Someone said, 'If Martin was here he wouldn't want us to be miserable – he'd have a laugh, and say, "Cheers! Here's looking at you."'

I don't know who it was suggested that we went and got him to join the party - after all, the party was for him. It was like the guest of honour wasn't there. The idea, which at any other time might have seemed outrageous, sounded like the most natural thing in the world. It wasn't as if it was illegal – plenty of people spent their last night in their own homes, for family and friends to pay their last respects.

We caught a taxi, an old-fashioned black cab, and asked it to wait while we popped into the Co-op chapel. The atmosphere inside was hushed and peaceful. It smelled faintly of lilies and aromatic oils.

I could imagine Martin saying, 'And about time! Let's go!' He wouldn't have tolerated any airs and graces. Gently, we lifted him out of the coffin, where he was lying in his best suit and his lucky hat, and walked him out of the door between us.

Back at the party we sat Martin in the seat of honour, put a drink in front of him and dealt him a hand of cards. 'Here's to you, brother,' I said, 'we'll all miss you.'

We drank a few more toasts, played cards and told a few more family stories. There was one that Dad always told about Martin's name. When Mum was expecting him, as was customary, Dad told her if it was a girl she could call it what she liked, but if it was a boy, she should call it Tom. Mum wasn't too keen on Tom at that time, although it was Dad's name – not because she didn't like it but because some of her friends had told her it was too common – everybody was called Tom, Dick or Harry. Dad had a man called Martin working for him who he liked, Mum had no problems with his name, so Martin it was.

Thirty-eight years later, when Dad accompanied me to the Irish Open he discovered that Martin was the common name out there – it wasn't Tom, Dick and Harry – it was Martin, Liam and Sean. When he got home, he said to Mum, 'Do you know what Martin's name means in Ireland?'

'What?' she said.

'Tom!' said Dad and laughed fit to bust. Well, Mum went around all her Irish friends in Tooting and found out for herself that it was true. They both thought that it was a great joke, especially since my second oldest brother got the name Tom after Dad anyway.

So, here was Martin enjoying the crack. It was a good party and we all felt better for it. Afterwards, we called another cab and reversed the process. In the morning the undertaker called to say that everything was in order – except that our brother's hat was missing. He apologised profusely, saying that nothing like that had ever happened in all their years in the business – and they couldn't imagine where it had gone.

I know that Martin, more than anyone, would have appreciated the joke. The next day, on the way to the cemetery, we asked if the cortege could take a detour past Wimbledon dog track – it was Martin's last little look at a place that had given him such pleasure over the years.

Just over a year later, Mum died. She hadn't been well for a long time, but nothing prepares you. Again, as a family we gathered around, glad only that she was going to join Martin.

We decided that we would scatter Mum's and Martin's ashes on Sandown racecourse. Martin loved any kind of gambling and Mum liked a little flutter as well. We chose an evening meeting and sponsored the 8.20 race over a mile and a quarter, naming it the Lillian and Martin White Maiden Stakes. One of the top jockeys, L. 'Frankie' Dettori, rode the winner, which was horse number 9, Bold Demand, for a prize of £4900. Oddly enough, John Nielsen and his girlfriend, Nina, backed Bold Demand. Their ticket had snooker's magic number on it – 147. When Johnny saw the number he nudged Nina, 'Looks like we're on to the winner,' he said.

Everything was laid on very nicely for us. All our family and friends were shown in to the members' enclosure, to a room where a buffet supper was ready. It was cold and damp when we walked on to the track after the last race. The atmosphere, with the last light of the sun going down behind the clouds, was quiet and peaceful. We felt this was a more personal and fitting ceremony for Mum and Martin than scattering the ashes in the rose garden of the crematorium.

You could cry, but you shouldn't really. I come from South of the River – where Shakespeare hung out at the old George Tavern in Southwark just a stone's throw away from the Thames. Shakespeare was a man of the people. Most of his plays were performed in The Globe Theatre which is just around the corner from The George, down a couple of cobbled back alleys. The Globe looks remarkably like snooker's very own theatre – the Crucible at Sheffield – so in a way I understand what life in the round means.

Shakespeare and Elvis once said something like, 'All the world's a stage and each must play a part.' We play our parts best we can and then we have to get off. Well, some of us just have to get off a bit sooner, that's all.

TWENTY-NINE

FIELD OF DREAMS

In the death it's all down to one shot. In fact, it's always down to one shot. Everything is down to one shot, if I'm being philosophical for a minute. Luckily it's one shot at a time. In sport in particular, because there is no script, we never know when these shots are going to turn up. I'm happy with that. Some people ask, 'Who's calling the shots?' Let me pass on some advice. There are two sides to calling the shots. The benefit and the burden. The benefit is that you're in charge. It's your baby. The burden is that with being in charge comes responsibility.

Now, in snooker we have the cue ball. The white ball. Before anything can happen you have to actually hit the cue ball. Like golf, like tennis, like Gareth Southgate, like getting up in the morning and competing. Because if you don't get up and join the rest of the competing world, you may as well stay in bed.

Poor old Gareth had an England shirt on his back on the day when he stepped up to take his disastrous shot. I only had a Jimmy White shirt on. All snooker players wear their own 'colours', so to speak. Except Kirk

Stevens, who once stole my trousers and had the nerve to wear them in a match against me.

Gareth Southgate had the whole team's fortunes riding on his penalty, whereas I play for my own fortune. I'm using the word fortune here in the widest sense, of course, meaning *life* and all life's attendant benefits and burdens. My personal burden is the weight, the extra baggage you carry around when you lose a big one. Benefits? Mum, Dad, brothers, sisters, Maureen, kids, friends, fans – and let's not forget the guy who wrote to me and said when I lost that big game he kicked his telly in.

No, I mean 'fortune' like someone coming to London to 'seek their fortune'. As in the wheel of. Because it's all theatre. Sport is theatre.

Somebody once said that there were only two stories in the whole of life's rich, sodding pageant: Dick Whittington, and Cinderella – but if Cinderella had gone to the ball earlier, she would not have met the shoe fetishist, Prince Charming. If Mr Whittington had not 'turned again' when he'd obviously had a gutful, he would never have become Lord Mayor of London and governor of Newgate prison – the world's first private prison. So it goes, and when people talk about a black you missed, or a blue, or a simple red (none of 'em are simple on a stage, or in an arena, or on TV) or a polka-dot or a peppermint candy-striped one, it's all relative. More to the point, it's all a bit misleading, because, if you hit the white ball straight and true, the shot you are going for will work. This, praying aside, is an inescapable fact. If you hit it wrong, gut-wrenchingly wrong, or give just the tiniest too much side, bend, spin or dip, from the moment it leaves the tip of your cue, it's a round rolling bomb. But it doesn't explode near the target you just missed. It explodes inside you.

However, when a shot does miss the target, you might

just as well ride with the recoil, go back to your seat and wait to see if you get another chance at the table. Kind of like life, eh? Any other thought you might have is pointless. There are no ants moving bloody rubber tree plants.

Life – like snooker – is not like, 'I'm sorry I'll read that again', and it never will be when you miss a shot. You can't just wave your opponent away like he was a waiter when it's his turn, and say, 'How about if I give that one another whirl, eh?' If your opponent is Ronnie O'Sullivan and you say that, he'll either laugh and say, 'Go ahead,' or he'll wrap his favourite cue round your head.

No, the last shot you played is consigned to history. Go and sit down. It's yesterday's shot, is the only sane way to deal with it. I don't see anyone handing out money for the player who scores the maximum anguish after a poxy shot. Could you imagine the ref intoning sonorously, 'Jimmy White, 200 for his most excellent wringing of the hands and 500 for breaking down and blubbing and making a complete and utter prat of himself. Plus, 1000 for his positional play, vis-à-vis lying on the floor kicking his legs up in the air and groaning.'

No, I'll take my bad luck straight up. Otherwise it's like watching instant replays of your bad shots in a hall of mirrors.

The past belongs to the pundits and the statistics boys. There is only 'tomorrow' to deal with, which is as it should be. Look to the next shot. It might rain tomorrow, and it might not. But that's why people who live by duckin' an' divin' always say, 'Be lucky.' There is no greater farewell or toast in my book.

According to my mum, losing saved my life. She didn't tell me how she felt at the time. She said it to my friend Lenny, as they drove away from the Crucible once. She said that she thought I was so wild that she feared for my survival. She wanted badly for me to win the World Championship, more than me I think, but she had decided, as mums do, that later would be better. It would keep, she thought, until I was more equipped mentally and had slowed down a bit. She feared for my life had I won. This, of course, I will always have to deal with in private now that Mum's gone.

The World Championship final of 1994, between me and Stephen Hendry, went right down to the wire. Going into the last frame, it was, famously, 17 frames apiece, but thirty-seven points to twenty-four in my favour. Looking back, as I 'got up' out of my seat, I saw the cup in my mind like it was the 'Holy Grail'. And it was mine.

When Stephen missed his shot and vacated the table, I don't think I 'got up' and approached the table so much as *flew out of my chair*, and started to pot balls. A couple of reds and colours. Then suddenly, there was the black. Referred to now as *'That Black'*. Everyone gets tense and under pressure at a moment like that. The adrenalin's pumping. I just rushed the shot.

A referee who was watching, name of Len Ganley, said later, 'Jimmy actually just threw his arm at the black. It wasn't a cool calculated black.'

And in the back of the car, my mother cried.

THIRTY

MIDNIGHT AT THE
MOSCONI CUP

I suppose it's something of a compliment to be given a nickname like 'The Whirlwind', but when you play pool you gotta have a nickname. Otherwise I don't think you're even allowed to play. You've got to have a *'nom de pool'*. Of course, it's the influence of what is basically a full-tilt American version of snooker, in which, for the sake of fun and atmosphere, it's decreed that veddy veddy British stiff upper cues like Mr Steven Davis become 'The Nugget', and Mr Ronald O'Sullivan is 'The Rocket', which of course he is anyway. You can hear it even now at The Grand Hotel in Brighton, or wherever he lands on the rear end of a long night's revelry, as the Maitre d' announces formally, 'Mr Rocket will be taking his breakfast at the bar,' and Ronnie becomes part of a fraternal pool-playing 'Rack Pack', like in Hollywood the young guns and roaring boys are part of the Brat Pack.

However, pool also allows the wilder side of fan clubs, like Ronnie's, the chance to let off some steam. It's the roar of the crowd, which is, quite rightly, a capital offence during a frame of snooker, but actually *encouraged* where pool is concerned.

You don't find many snooker tables in pubs these days. It's all pool. The game has really caught on. We could have a lot of fun inventing *noms de pool* for the grand old guard like Joe Davis, and his brother Fred; Ray Reardon, Dennis Taylor, John Virgo and Terry Griffiths, but we'll save that game to amuse ourselves on the next long flight to the Antipodes, or Thailand, or some far-flung outpost of the ball, baize and cue.

I read recently that snooker had caught on in California. Apparently it's also big in Chinatown in Los Angeles and in San Francisco. I remember watching an old episode of *The Beverly Hillbillies*. When the family moved from Tennessee to this big mansion in Beverly Hills, they found a room devoted to pool with a marvellous table in the centre, which they immediately thought was a 'fancy eatin' table', complete with a lip so's the food wouldn't fall off. So they sharpened up the cues with a Bowie knife and used them to spear great chunks of meat to roast over a fire. I've been all over the world, and believe me, sharpening cues to stab meat is not that far-fetched.

Neither is giving nicknames to pool players a recent promotional invention. It's a part of American folklore that renegades and what society calls the 'one-percenters' – like Bikers, Hillbillies, drifters and pool sharks – are all labelled up good and proper, like Vincent 'The Chin' Gigante. Or with the Jewish mob, where it was 'Bugsy' Siegel. A great driver in the days of Prohibition was called 'Feets' Edson, after his ability to perform drag turns and assorted two-footed magic whilst escaping from Eliot Ness. So there's something of a sporting tradition here. Like 'Babe' Ruth, or the great long distance runner who was called the 'Flying Finn'.

Back in the world of the green baize and pocket, Paul

Newman was 'Fast Eddie' Felson in the film of *The Hustler*, and his famous adversary was named 'Minnesota Fats'. In the long-awaited follow-up *The Color of Money*, one of Tom Cruise's pool coaches was a guy called Louis Roberts. Now Louis's nickname, was 'St. Louis Louis', with Louis pronounced Looey, by the way. I say was – past tense – because Louis has handed in his pool cue along with his dinner plate. He died after an apparently self-inflicted gunshot wound. Which goes to show that hustling and drinking and gambling and all that good stuff don't really mix. Except in the movies.

St Louis Louis was Budweiser World champion *twice* in Las Vegas, which is a big deal, big money tournament over there. He managed to leave Las Vegas, having lifted cheque and trophy on both the mornings after, without even keeping enough for the cab fare to the airport. Which is only slightly ahead of Nicholas Cage's movie character in *Leaving Las Vegas*, who really cracked the nut, and managed not to leave the city at all. Louis had done his bollocks at the tables, like a lunatic bricklayer in the bookie's shop of a Friday afternoon. He spent a fair bit on the toot both times as well, I hear. I tell this story second-hand to put some of my own tabloid exploits into perspective. I've heard, because unfortunately I never saw him play, that St Louis Louis could break a rack with so much speed, strength and precision that the 9-ball would shoot up in the air, curve, and land in a pocket. A 9-ball genius! Wizardry.

However, on the down and seamy side, I have an acquaintance who told me that when Louis was teaching him to play pool during many long southern fried nights, he would sometimes have to walk him around and around the pool table, trying to keep him awake and alive. Like any potential die-hard, Louis had a real problem habit. A two-fold problem really, because he would shoot up coke and then boil his works in a saucepan on the wood-stove to sterilise them. Unfortunately he would forget whether he had already shot up, or was about to shoot up. Obviously this is a very tricky decision, somewhat akin to playing Russian Roulette.

Now, my old buddy, Mike 'Tennessee Tarzan' Massey, also has many stories like that. When I was a lad at Zan's and trying to hustle a crust, Mike was often hanging around. Later on, when we moved to the country and had a large house with a pool, he came and visited with me and Maureen a couple of times and marvelled at my good fortune – like, who'd have thought it of a snooker-hall urchin? Of course, Mike was a different old 'Tennessee Tarzan' back then. He drank. With a vengeance! He's a big feller, and, my word, he could beat his chest. Drinking, smoking, gambling, chasing the ladies.

But after a good run, Mike took a nasty turn. The accidental ingestion of a rather large dose of psychedelic drugs when someone spiked his drink, together with a slight altercation with the American Bill, followed by longish cure in a psychiatric ward to 'straighten his ass right out', as he told me later when he was better. Absolutely. Mike has been 'saved' too, and good luck to him, I say – but next time I go missing in the badlands of Pontins Holiday Camp in Prestatyn with a bandolero of vodka bottles and one in the chamber, whilst clutching a sweaty can of Guinness as backup, I shall feel sorely constrained to point out that this is *mild* horseplay compared with what some of the guys get up to.

But everybody has to grow up sometime. When Mike Massey appeared last year on Jim Davidson's *Big Break* television programme, he was on super form. Straightening up suits some people. Mike is a trick-shot champion. He's great entertainment. He has a string of world-class titles, from pool to billiards. He also plays guitar and sings and drives his well-appointed Winnebago around the States, spends a lot of time in Nashville – and his European agent is based in Switzerland. So he must be doing something right. There is a balance for everyone, and Mike has found his.

Talking of Mike Massey brings me to The Mosconi Cup. This tournament is played every year between a team of the finest pool players in America and the best team we can muster from Europe.

I like to play pool. Now, I can play fast, we know that, and the atmosphere for pool is, as we've said, more relaxing and a lot less serious than snooker, but – and this is a big but – *winning* is still of paramount importance. This is Europe in the guise of Fast Eddie, the contender, the new kid in town; while America is Minnesota Fats, the professional representative of Pool-town America, who says, 'Put your money where your mouth is, boy!'

They dress up. I dress down. Out they come in their red, white and blue, stars and stripes waistcoats. I traditionally wear my full-length leather and a cigarette; and Alex wears a little something by Gucci, and a bottle of Bailey's. A couple of years ago I reached a personal zenith in this tournament. It's held over four days, and the way it was shaping up, it looked like I was scheduled to play last, the reason for which temporarily escapes me. Anyway, here's the set-up: Outside, somewhere in Essex, it's misty and cold. Inside it's smoky, noisy, there are fake fog and dry ice machines, lasers and lights. The pool tables are either blue, pink, or orange, instead of the usual green. The MC wears a purple jacket as he emerges from the haze. Barry 'The Organiser' Hearn is in charge. Sid 'Louder than Bombs' Waddell is the commentator for Sky TV. On the American team are: Mike 'Tennessee Tarzan' Massey; Bob 'Sundance' Hunter; John 'The Bull' DiToro; Mark 'The Shooter' Wilson; 'Machine Gun' Lou Buttera; Dallas 'Big D' West. There's a 'Baby Face' this or that, too. It is all to Mr Hearn's credit that it is indeed well organised in typical Matchroom style, and he's a happy man. We know this because he has told everybody he is a happy man. He even went so far as to say that he could 'smell the greenbacks'. So there you are.

By Saturday though, Europe is losing. The score is 8-10. Suddenly Alex and me are called to the table, from the bar. It's a doubles match against Sundance and Tarzan. The scene is right up Alex's street. He is the man of the moment. The crowd is baying. It's like one of those Ralph Steadman drawings from Hunter Thompson's books. Chaos, cheers, and clicking balls. Alex plays two- and three-cushion shots, and doubles, cannons, and plants. He's like a manic semi-classical Celtic Jug Band. Everything is in tune and on song and harmonious when there's no doubt it shouldn't really be working at all. But who cares? The more unstraightforwardly Alex plays a shot, the better it seems to comes off. Today, when Alex flukes one, he nods his head to show you that he meant it. The cue-ball was obviously supposed to go around the table three times, swerve past a couple of spectators, drop its shoulder and go past the ref – feint right and go left, nip out to the coffee for pancakes and maple syrup with a side order of toasted soda bread, call for the check, belch and disappear down a pocket. I'm surprised that Alex has not got up on the table with the balls and showed us Riverdancing without tears in his tasselled Gucci loafers.

Out of the corner of my eye, I see the Tennessee Tarzan shaking his head in amazement and utter disbelief. He looks like Blackbeard the Pirate, who just received a broadside of cannonballs and 'two-headed angels' from the Irish navy – which he didn't know existed until they drew up alongside and threw him a V sign. Mike, this bear-like showman trick shotster, is open-mouthed in fuzzy wonder; but I know that he's enjoying it. That's the point. The buzz is important – that and winning.

Luke Riches, part of the Matchroom team, shouts, 'It's bloody carnage!'

'Europe, Europe, Europe, Europe!' chants the crowd.

'Bailey's, Bailey's, Bailey's!' chants Alex, holding up his cue like a bloody sword. He starts to dance. The Bull joins in. The dance moves from the bar to the tables, the matador with the finesse of Nureyev and the bull, pawing the floor and snorting out fire. The crowd goes wild; the Sky floor manager tears out his hair.

First set of this doubles match goes to Europe. In the second set, Sundance and Tarzan play some truly spirited, fighting pool – and it's evens. Here comes the decider, and I'm ready now. I'm up for it. It's my turn.

All through the game, Alex, they tell me later, has been frantically whispering in my ear. It makes no difference. I dish up, as they say, and Alex and I take the third set three-to-nothing. The crowd goes absolutely bananas! People crowd around and ask me what Alex was whispering to me. I say, 'What are you talking about?'

'Was it divine inspiration, Jimmy? – What were Alex's words of wisdom? For the benefit of the people watching at home as well as us, will you please tell us what he said to you?'

'Honestly,' I say, 'your guess is as good as mine!'

On Sunday morning the hangovers are everywhere. Our man, Daryl 'Razzle Dazzle' Peach, is playing Mike 'Tennessee Tarzan' Massey. Daryl is an ex-snooker pro who took to pool like a duck to water and never looked back to shore. He's as thin as a rake and, when you see him and Mike together at the table, it's comical. He's also winning. He's on wonderful form and completely routs the big guy, giving Europe an 11-10 lead. Next up is Steve 'The Nugget' Davis playing against The Bull.

In snooker, you toss a coin to see who breaks first; but with pool you have what's known as *the lug*. What happens with the lug is that both players step up and play the ball down the table. The ball hits the far cushion, rebounds up the baize and the player whose ball ends up closest to the baulk cushion as it comes to rest gets to go first. Breaking first is a big advantage in pool, as against in snooker. Steve wins and it's 12-10 now.

The great German pool player, Oliver 'The Machine' Ortmann, steps up to take on Mark 'The Shooter' Wilson, and takes him straight to the cleaners. On the Breakometer, Olly is registering 24.2 miles per hour. Very fast. It's 13-10 to us, and the crowd's back on the case, really giving it some wellie. Lee 'The Fox' Kendall and Tom 'The Storm' Storm (that's his name, although he comes from Abba-land) take on 'Tarzan' and Mike 'Baby Face' Gulyassy. Sid 'Louder than Bombs' Waddell is shouting things like 'From zero to hero!' and 'The States are looking shaky!' in his broad Geordie accent, but the crowd in true cockney style is giving it 'Beat the septics! Beat the septics! Beat the septics! Beat the septics!'

All the Londoners have tears streaming down their faces, but no one else has a clue what a septic is. 'Who are zese Goddam zeptics that ze peasants keep shouting about?' says Oliver Ortmann of all people, with a huge grin – and when he's told it's cockney rhyming slang ('Septic tanks = Yanks') he cracks up, nods his head and says, 'Oh *ja*, I like that very much!'

After Lee Kendall and the Swede mop up the Yanks, the score moves on to 14-10. The crowd begins to sing and dance. Now they're a cross between a darts' crowd and a football crowd. Olly 'The Machine', who has finished telling people about 'ze zeptics', is once more the unemotional German. His face is a study in clinical precision as he smacks ze Zeptic Zundance all over the table. It's 15-10.

'We are the champions!' sing the crowd. Of course, it all has to start going wrong sometime and now, needing just one more game to win the whole tournament, with the fanfares and the fog machine going full blast, here comes Alex, to play again, against Lou 'Machine Gun' Buttera. For two racks Alex can do no wrong. He is once again at the top of his game, and then some. However, the Machine Gun starts to fire rapidly. He begins to move very fast around the table, chalking his cue and smacking the balls down one after the other, as if something has really upset him. He is just determined to do or die and get the hell out of Dodge.

After just over thirty minutes of pool, Alex, after taking the first two racks, is on his way back to the Bailey's. It's 15-11. Dallas West starts knocking six bells out of the Swede. 15-12.

Don't panic, boys, it'll come good. No sweat. In a minute we will win another game and that will be that. It's only a matter of time, we all say, like when you're playing the best of, say nine, and you're 5-1 up, the other guy has then got to win all the remaining games without one lapse. Having been in almost that very situation against Stephen 'The Alien' Hendry, and having sat in my corner dying as I watched while he won ten straight games, I should know better. Oh-oh! – Daryl Peach loses his game. 15-13. Then Tom the Swede and Oliver Ortmann get whacked in the longest match of the tournament so far, against Sundance and 'Shooter' Wilson, and it's 15-14.

'Could the Europeans be on the end of the most amazing comeback since Lazarus?' asks Sid, excitedly.

Oh no! Surely the Septics can't steal the Mosconi Cup now? It would be too much. It would rank with the Battle of New Orleans.

Now it's getting on for midnight, but the crowd are getting noisier than ever. I tell you, some of the language is disgraceful. Ah, here comes The Nugget and Lee Kendall to take on Big D and Baby Face, and they literally get swept away. The Septics are delirious. They're jumping all over the place. They're drinking beer. They're doing their group hug shit, as it comes down to the wire. 15-15.

The tournament is tied. It's all down to a decider. Sudden death in Essex. I haven't even been near the practice table. However, as the Americans themselves always say, 'It ain't over 'til it's over'. A journalist summed up the atmosphere when he described the rabble of nutters that was once a crowd. But this is not to say that they have lost their voice. Far from it. The chorus begins. It is like opera: *'You can do it, Jimmy . . . You can do it, Jimmy . . . You can do it, Jimmy . . .'.*

For once in my life, as the song goes, I never doubted it. I went to the table. The crowd was roaring. I shook hands with my opponent and dished up four racks to the two that Lou 'Machine Gun' Buttera scored – and repaired to the bar, as they say, a happy man.

THIRTY-ONE

TUXEDO JUNCTION

Yes, there were many high points in my life – but overall my game was on a downward spiral. For over four years I had been on a losing curve. Journalists tried to rationalise it by making excuses for me, mentioning the personal problems and tragedies in my life, and perhaps these things were a big part of it. But I felt it must go deeper than that. Why had I been in six world finals at the Crucible in Sheffield – the game's Holy Grail – and yet never won once?

Dad had not taken his tuxedo to the last four tournaments, a sure sign – him subtly telling me that he wouldn't be needing it for the final since *I* wouldn't be playing. But to me, it was about as subtle as a flying mallet.

I had to face the fact that I was at a junction in my life and, for once, I had no real answers. Early in February 1998, the *Sunday Times* (yes, I do glance at it now and then) ran an article, headed 'The Wild Card Shuffles Back', which basically said I had a few good years left in me and I knew I could get back to the top. The question I couldn't answer was – how?

A couple of days later, a letter arrived in the post from Advance Training and Development Ltd, a company in Preston I had never heard of, saying they believed they could help me. Someone in their office had read that *Sunday Times* article and shown it to one of their directors, Andrew O'Donoghue, who immediately decided to write to me offering their services. Although it was late in the evening – about eight o'clock or so – when I read the letter, I decided to telephone them at once. Andrew answered the phone. I could tell he was very surprised by such a rapid response; in fact, he said he almost leapt off his seat.

'Hello, it's Jimmy White – how soon can we meet?'

Andrew and his partner, Michael Finnegan, drove down the following day. We met in a coffee shop in Esher, where they filled me in on their background, which, essentially, was to 'pump up' blue chip companies, working with managing directors and chairmen to help them focus and achieve their aims, or, more to the point, to stop them under-achieving, like me. Mike had started off in life wanting to be a professional footballer and failed, even though he was signed up to Blackburn Rovers' youth team and later played in the reserves. Unable to make that big breakthrough into the team proper, he went into banking and eventually got promoted to where he was calling on successful customers of the bank to arrange financing for their expansion programmes. Curious to learn how they had achieved their success, he asked questions and started making notes. Someone gave him a book, *Think and Grow Rich* by Napoleon 'Somebody', which led him into the field of training. For Mike it was a quest. Learning about what made for success taught him a lot about himself, about why he hadn't been successful in the one thing he had really wanted to achieve.

'A lot of that was a bit of a cleansing for me really, –

how come when I was such a talented footballer I couldn't make it? How come someone else, half as talented as me, got offered a pro contract and I didn't? I understood then it wasn't about a gift. Certainly, it was a bit of that – but it was also a lot of something else – dedication. My problem was inconsistency. It's like you, Jimmy,' Mike said. 'You're magic in the semi-final, and then you go to pieces, you self-destruct in the final. *Why?* Now, with me,' said Mike, 'it was fear; fear of success, fear of flying, you could say. We have to find out what's happening in your case. You send out all these mixed messages, conflicting signals. We have to figure out what they mean.'

Mike went on to explain that he had the chance of putting his research into the psychology of motivation and the psychology of success into forming his own company in 1996. He asked a couple of sound people with a good background to join him – Andrew for example, was a solicitor, useful since, apart from the big international companies, they also worked on a more intimate scale with professionals, such as doctors, solicitors and accountants, and, in the sports area, some golfers.

My ears pricked up at the golfers. 'So you do work with sports people?' I asked.

Mike nodded. 'A few. We have eight golfers, who shot over par. Now they shoot under par. We always see them the night before a tournament, to make sure they're focused.'

After chatting for an hour and a half, I felt reassured that they weren't con merchants, nutters, Moonies, or cranks. When you get into these concepts of motivation, people are never sure what it is – they think it's mumbo jumbo. But these were business people, working with businesses to produce business results; an upgrade in performance, if you like. We agreed we would go away and think about it. They needed to think whether they really did want to diversify by working in the field of snooker – about which they knew nothing – while I wanted to consider whether I could trust them to make a difference for me.

'You have to say you *choose* to work with us,' Mike said, 'otherwise you'll just be wasting your time and your money. Remember, we're not saying we can make you a better sportsman, but we can help you improve your *business* – which in your case is snooker – and get a tangible result that pays for the training effectively.'

I must admit, although I was liking what I was hearing, a part of me was also saying, what's with this 'I choose to work with you' lark? It was a bit like the 'one day at a time' policy of Alcoholics and Gamblers Anonymous, both of which I had joined recently after a life-time of drinking too much and losing – so I understood from my accountant – something in the region of £3 million. There was no doubt I needed all the help I could get, but, on the other hand, was I going to overdose on the personal improvement front? I could just see the tabloid banner headlines – 'White finally cracks, not *it*, but *up*!'

My mind wandered further – to a vision of me rising at four a.m. to kneel in front of my green baize shrine, at the balk end of course, to bang a few bells and light a couple of aromatherapy sticks while chanting, 'Every day I'm getting richer and richer and gooder and gooder'.

There was no danger of that. I couldn't imagine changing beyond all recognition. Anyway, rising at four a.m., I would pass myself on the stairs on my way to bed.

A few days later, we decided to go for it. I had nothing to lose, and perhaps much to gain. They said they were not actually going to teach me to play snooker – they were going to teach me how to get my head straight and better snooker would come as a result. For the first time, I had lost so many ranking points, I had to qualify to play in the World tournament. It was an unthinkable position. I simply couldn't afford to lose, otherwise I wouldn't be at the Crucible for the first time in seventeen years. The qualifier was being held in two or three weeks at Telford, so, if I was to make any changes in myself, time really was of the essence.

Mike gave up his weekend to come down. he checked into the local Hilton, from which I picked him up to take him to my home. He met Maureen and the girls, and then we went into my snooker room and settled down for the first three-hour session. The concepts Mike was teaching me were scientific as well as psychological. He provided me with work books and talked very slowly to give me a chance to write it all down. When he saw that I was just listening, he kept asking if I was sure I didn't want to make notes?

Finally I said, 'I'm not into writing things down. You keep talking, don't worry – I'm right with you.' What he hadn't yet realised was that because I don't enjoy writing I have compensated by really focusing my memory on things I need to remember.

After two hours I'd had enough. I said, 'That's enough. My head's hurting.'

Mike looked surprised, then apprehensive. 'We've got another four hours to fit in today,' he noted.

'I know,' I said, 'we'll get to it. Let's have some lunch.'

Afterwards, we did another hour before I said, 'I've got it. I've got it now. I know where you're coming from. We're done for today.'

Later, Mike was to say that was when his first real doubts crept in. He was used to working with chairmen of public companies who gave him their time, men in suits, all very professional, with him taking the lead. Now, he said, here I was taking control of the situation. he wasn't used to it, wasn't sure if we had 'connected'.

He was thinking to himself he'd come all the way down from Lancashire, 250 miles, we'd done three hours of work, and then I say *we're finished*. He wasn't sure if I had realised how deep this programme was.

'Right,' I said, 'go back to the hotel, have a shower, have something to eat, I'll pick you up later on. I'm playing a practice match; you can come and watch.'

What Mike didn't know was that I had absorbed and remembered it all. I was fired up, my head buzzing with so many new ideas and concepts, seeing how I could apply them in my life. When I picked him up from his hotel, I talked a mile a minute, going over it all. It had really made me think, made me start to reposition things that had happened to me – and, above all, refocus.

'Honestly, I thought you hadn't taken any of it in!' Mike exclaimed.

As we drove, he explained that they wanted the whole lives of the people they worked with to be dedicated to excellence. 'We can't show you how to go onto a snooker table and suddenly be brilliant,' Mike said. 'But we'll talk to you about every single thought you ever think; the whole aspect of life. People who work with us have to commit to being an excellent mum, an excellent dad, wife, businessman – a healthy person, a contributor to society. They can sit down at the end of the day with a cup of tea in front of the telly and think – I've put in a good day today. I've been good. I have added value to whoever I've met.'

I nearly swerved off the road. Was this Jimmy White he was talking about? The boy who once went to Ireland for three days and stayed for six weeks – the lad who used to vanish and surface days later, unwashed, unkempt, hung over? Now, this was me, twenty years on, looking for direction. Some things just have to change – why not for the better? From sinner to saint in five easy lessons. Was

I ready? Probably not. Knowing me, I would probably begin to fight it.

Mike seemed to sense what I was thinking. 'It won't happen all at once,' he soothed. 'We'll take it slowly. However, Jimmy, in view of the time scale, with the qualifier coming up so soon and the World Cup right on its heels, we are talking about minutes and snatched hours – snatched seconds almost.'

I had arranged for an organised practice session that evening back at the house with Alfie Burdett. Now, young Alfie is interesting. Rather like Mike Finnegan and Blackburn Rovers, Alfie was an up and coming star at Arsenal until a bad leg injury virtually forced him out of the game. He came with his driver and a friend who acted as referee. I didn't introduce Mike, who sat out of the way behind the bar with a pad of paper and a pen, watching and making notes. And they were very thorough notes, as I was to find out later. How does that song go – *Every move you make . . .* ? Well, he was watching everything I did, every shot, every stride, every sigh. I won the best of 15: 8–2. After the match, Alfie, who was dressed in jeans and a T-shirt, wandered over to Mike and started chatting. I don't think Mike was used to how casual snooker players could be and was astonished to discover Alfie wasn't just some kid – he was a top snooker player, ranked in the world's top 100, and was also qualifying next week at Telford.

'You absolutely murdered him,' Mike said to me when I came back in. 'There's not much wrong with you, Jimmy, if you can do that to a player of this calibre.'

We played another ten frames and this time, Alfie slaughtered me, winning all ten. So overall, I'd actually lost, 12-8. Meanwhile, I saw Mike scribbling furiously, and I wondered what he had found so interesting.

He went back to his hotel room, holding his head in his hands, thinking: 'It's ten o'clock at night, you've played solidly for five hours. We've had nothing to eat – I've had one drink of water – and you've been answering the phone, Maureen's been calling, the kids have been shouting, the dog's been wandering in and out and I'm thinking, this guy's supposed to be world championship material – what's going on here? This is not world championship practice.'

Was he right?

The next day – 16 March – was Mike's daughter, Rose's birthday. He had elected to forego it in order to fit in another session with me. When I picked him up that morning, I said, 'Last night I had the first night's solid deep sleep that I can remember. I slept like a log. I don't know what you've done to me.'

'Jimmy, we've only done three hours,' Mike said.

'Maybe – but all that stuff you were talking about yesterday, it makes sense,' I said.

As we drove along, I said, 'You know how people have always told me I've been unlucky – in not winning the world trophy?'

Mike said, 'Well, yes, that's what they say.'

I said, 'It's nothing to do with luck, is it? It's design. In some way I decided to lose those finals.'

Mike nodded. 'I think you did, I really do.'

I said, 'And I feel better, because I know. It's not luck, it's what I deserved. I deserved to come second – I haven't deserved to be world champion.'

Mike was very encouraged by that. He told me that in his experience most company managing directors or chairmen he worked with weren't as far along as this after ten hours. 'What are we going to do when we've done thirty hours?' he enthused.

'So I'm not too old to learn?' I said, half in jest.

Mike treated the question seriously. 'You're never too old to achieve your potential. People in life who have self-destructed can come back at age 55, 60, 65, and they can turn it around. With time, they find out the secret and understand that they've done it to themselves and therefore if that was the choice, then they can change that choice, and they can change that performance. It doesn't matter how old they are. Now you, Jimmy, you can do it, you can be world champion. If you think you can, you will.'

Back in the snooker room, the first thing we did was to go through the seventy-five points Mike had listed from the match the night before. For example, he wasn't saying to me obvious things like limit your practice sessions to three hours. He didn't need to because I had worked it out.

I said, 'You know, I think I'm practising too long.'

Mike said, 'Are you? Well, Jimmy, when was the last time you played a match that lasted for eight hours?'

I said, 'Never!' It was like a light bulb going on. We moved on to flip charts and more concepts until I felt my head beginning to go. 'Stop,' I said, 'I've had enough. It's your little girl's birthday. I want you to go home and have tea with her.' It was nice because Maureen had been shopping for a present, and came in with a stack of goodies from the Body Shop and a birthday card from the family.

On the way back to the hotel, I got Dad on the mobile. 'Dad, get your tux to the cleaners! We're going all the way at Sheffield next month!' Then I put Dad on to Mike.

'What have you done to my boy?' Dad asked. 'He's been telling me all about you.'

A few days before I was due at Telford, Mike telephoned to say he and Andrew had prepared a short video and an audio cassette to help me focus because I had made no notes. They had also summarised the main points on little plastic cards, based on the seventy-odd things he'd noticed from the practice session and from talking to me, plus little hints about the way I was playing and the way I was feeling. Things I needed to say to myself when I was at the table. He said they would get them to me a couple of days beforehand.

I was alarmed, and said, 'That's too late, I need more time.'

Mike and Andrew arrived at Telford the night before I was due to play and spent an hour with me in my hotel room while I watched the video and listened to the cassette, which I said I would play again the following morning as a boost to my confidence. I felt very good, particularly since, for some unknown reason, I had not missed a night's sleep since that first night. I'm known for being hyperactive, so this was a big improvement. I noticed though, that the behind-the-scenes atmosphere was quite a shock to Mike and Andrew, who'd never seen anything like it. Players eating meat pies, smoking and drinking beer when they were about to go out. To say they were taken aback would be an understatement, and when one player tossed back a double brandy, picked up his cue and proceeded to play, Mike actually looked shocked. It would never happen in football! I thought back to the early years of my career, skating unconcerned through acres of cigarette ash and debris around the tables in those sleazy snooker halls. I wondered what Andrew and Mike would have made of that.

The next day I played against Bradley Jones, who the previous year at Sheffield had come inches from beating John Parrott, and won a comfortable 10–5. I was just relieved that I would be going to Sheffield. I even felt good about having my name pulled out of the hat with Stephen Hendry's in the draw. I hadn't won a match against him since 1991, but now I felt I had a good chance.

Someone reminded me later that in a phone call just after the draw, they said, 'Jimmy, is it true you've drawn

Hendry in the first round?' – and, apparently, very matter of fact, I said, 'Yeah, and after I put him away, it'll be plain sailing. That's the way I look at it.'

They thought I was having a laugh until they sussed this was a different Jimmy speaking. 'So it'll be all White on the night?' they said.

'Absolutely,' I said.

Mike said, 'You don't win a world title, you pot a snooker ball, then another one. It's important not to get carried away.'

He and Andrew had come to Sheffield, basically to hold my hand since we'd had so few sessions. They saw all the lads – Hendry, Davis, Higgins, Doherty, O'Sullivan – and as they pointed out to me, these particular 'star' players weren't there swilling pints, they weren't involved with a million hangers-on who were smoking and drinking and playing cards – they weren't doing these things. They walked in, had an orange juice, practised for an hour and then went away to get some rest. They carried themselves properly. 'With the deportment of champions,' Andrew said, highly impressed.

I think it was then that I started to understand about my past conditioning, about coming from an area which isn't conducive to what is called peak performance. The people who are successful seem to be the ones who step to one side from the baggage of confusion and chaos that I'd carried around for years. They seemed to be saying, it's OK for you lot to carry on like that – we're just going to sit over here at a slight distance and focus on the job we're here to do, because we're at work now. We're not sat in a bar drinking pint after pint with the lads – we're working now and we're going to behave as if we're working.

I was coming to understand why human beings do the things they do, how behaviour is influenced by the way they feel at the time, by their attitude. By the belief systems that we have, by the environmental conditioning we're getting all the time and the feedback we're getting from our own environment which tells us what kind of a person we are. I had always chosen to view it in a buccaneering, que serà serà way – and that was why I was getting negative results. I needed to view myself in a positive way and reinforce the positive aspects. We've all heard those words and phrases before, and you can laugh. But, believe me, losing is not a laugh. In fact, losing is not like it used to be – when it *was* a laugh – because excellence isn't about something you put on for a day when you're playing snooker. It's a way of life.

For some, it must be a radical change of personality. But I knew that I didn't need to change – I just needed to *think* differently. What goes on in your head is important. In a pragmatic, practical way, if you think you're going to lose then you're going to lose. Basically if you think you're going to win, you have a much better chance of winning.

Talk about a crash course in self-esteem and learning how not to self-destruct! Oddly enough, even though my head was exploding with all these new thoughts and ideas, I felt very calm. The force was really with me now.

They say that I looked very assured and calm in that first-round match against Hendry. Andrew and Mike sat in the audience so I could gain support from them. We had worked out various signals – not how to play – but how to think. For example, when Hendry missed a shot, I got up from my seat, having just lit a cigarette. I put the still-burning cigarette down in the ashtray and started to walk to the table. Then I stopped. That burning cigarette was a signal, both to Hendry – and, more importantly, to myself – that I *expected* to miss the shot, that I would be back in my seat very quickly. Deliberately, I turned back, stubbed out the cigarette, straightened my shoulders and went on to win the frame.

Mike had asked me what I was thinking when the other player was on the table and I was sitting out. 'I'm enjoying watching the guy playing,' I said.

'Well, you can stop that straight away!' Mike said.

'But I like snooker,' I protested. 'You've got to admire the other guy if he's good.'

'Yes, I understand that,' Mike said. 'But can I just tell you what I would do if it were me? I would be sitting there thinking you'd better not miss – 'cos if you miss you're in big trouble.'

Mike asked how long it took me to suss out the position of the balls. 'Three nano-seconds,' I replied.

'So what are you looking at the balls for? If it was me I wouldn't be watching, enjoying, thinking to myself he's good, he's cueing well, he's playing beautifully. You're sitting there, watching Hendry potting all those balls – what is it doing to your confidence?' Mike said.

'You're right,' I said. 'OK, I won't watch him play any more.' Which is why I sat with my head in my hands, or my face in my towel. People thought I was in despair or even hung over, but I was focusing on making time stand still. I was working from the inside, concentrating nearly harder than when I was actually playing. Playing is easy for me, concentrating is not.

In the past, when I have missed an easy shot, the missing of that shot gets to me. I start to think about why and how I missed, and thinking, 'if I was that stupid, I don't deserve to win', so I blow the rest of the game – as in that calamitous penultimate game against Hendry in the 1992 final. The score was 14–8 in my favour. I missed a black, and Stephen went on to clean up, winning ten straight games, finally lifting the trophy with a score of 18–14.

But I now knew that instead of thinking 'it's all over'

in that epic match, I should have said: 'No, what's happening here is the battle has just begun. Now! How can I regain the high ground?' (There was another gut-wrenching missed ball in 1994, when I was just one pot away from winning the title, and Stephen went on to an 18–17 victory. So near, and yet so far – that still takes a lot of getting over.)

One of the things I had agreed with Mike and Andrew was that they would be anonymous unless I won. They were at all the sessions, totally discreet in business dress, passes hidden inside their jackets. We thought it was vital that no one knew who they were. But somehow, after the match against Hendry, I let it slip, first to John Virgo, who was in my dressing room when they came in to congratulate me.

'These are the boys who helped me win,' I said. That was it – it was as if I had produced a pair of magicians or a brace of white rabbits out of a hat. Their cover was blown and all the papers wrote about our winning formula. It was quite a dazzling time, because, after the first day against Hendry, when I was doing well, there was a definite buzz, first at Sheffield, then across the nation. There was even a record seven pages on the BBC teletext. The second day's play drew nearly eleven million viewers. By the time I shook hands with Darren Morgan at the start of the second-round match, I was told that half the country was switched on – people were even taking time off work to watch. And I did feel that there was something magic going on as I pulled off shots I hadn't seen myself produce for years. I expected to pull them off, too.

In the *Sunday Times*, Ian Chadband reported: '*The Rolls Royce smoothness . . . told of a man who is clearly convinced the fairytale has just started. . . . He may not have topped that Wednesday session where he played Hendry off the table with almost flawless brilliance, but there were moments when he could have touched the moon. Morgan was forced to break into a rueful smile as White, homing in on the highest break prize in the penultimate frame, produced one extraordinary shot after another. . . . It was wonderful stuff and one had to ponder if this really was the same man who just a few weeks ago was beaten in Plymouth by an unknown Mark Gray, ranked 150 in the world.'*

I beat Darren 13–3 and prepared to face Ronnie O'Sullivan in the quarter-final. I know the country was holding its breath, but I can't explain exactly what happened. I only know I didn't feel right when I stepped into the arena. When Steve Davis was reported as saying: 'In a way perhaps beating Hendry was Jimmy's final', he wasn't that far off the mark. It's impossible to explain exactly what you think, or why you do certain things. Later, Mike and Andrew said, 'Maybe Jimmy's dream was not to win it this year – maybe his dream was to beat Hendry and get back his self-respect and win some money. It is a classic example of how people achieve their own goals. You can't set a goal for other people, they set it themselves.'

It was enough to show the world that I was back. I went into that last game thinking it's the Rocket against the Whirlwind – and a bit of the old showman came back. I knew that was probably the wrong attitude, but I couldn't help myself. There were moments, like the crucial time on the first day when Ronnie was 7–2. If I had gone 6–3 at the end of that session, I might have felt different, but it went to 7–2. I recovered a little the next day, but Ronnie outplayed me. Simple as that.

There were other moments I still cherish. Forgetting Maureen's birthday was one of them. I didn't exactly forget it, I just forgot to buy a card. Well, that could have been grounds for divorce. Maureen has threatened to divorce me so many times that in the end she just left our marriage licence with her solicitor. Ten o'clock on the morning of 27 April saw me practically running into the press room.

'Help me out, boys,' I croaked. 'Can you get a message to Maureen on the teletext?'

Absolutely not – *verboten*, they said. 'Oh, go on,' I wheedled. 'Do you want to be responsible for breaking up a family?'

Put like that, how could they refuse? They're a nice bunch of lads. I believe it was the first and only time a personal message has been delivered on the teletext. As soon as I knew it was going to happen, I telephoned Maureen and told her to switch on the teletext. She was over the moon – especially since she couldn't be with me as she was shortly expecting our fifth child. Later, I was humbled when, in an interview, Maureen said, 'I've never been happier – I've got my husband back.'

No one knows what the future holds. Like the song says, what will be, will be. What I do know is I feel better about myself. I know that it doesn't matter where you were yesterday, it doesn't matter what happened five years ago; you can't change any of that. That was then. That was the person that was – and this is the person who is. The past is in the past, the present is now.

ACKNOWLEDGEMENTS

Many people have helped with this book, giving their time and reminding me of a few of my past exploits – whether funny or sad or mad, bad and dangerous. I would like to thank them all, particularly the following (in alphabetical order, so they won't get upset that they're not first):

Lenny Cain; Michael Conetta; John Dee; Sue Doyle; Conleth Dunne; Ray Edmunds; Paul Ennis; Clive Everton; Patsy Fagin; Michael Finnegan; Dermot Gillece; Ron Gross; Pat and Shane Halls; Barry Hearn; Alex Higgins; Jim Langham; Harvey Lisberg; Geoff Lomas; Colin McGuire; John Peewee Malloy; John Martin; Liz Metcalfe; Noel Miller-Cheevers; John Nielsen; Joe O'Boye; Andrew O'Donoghue; Salad; Ann Yates; Phil Yates; Victor Yo; and many others, too numerous to mention.

Born Fighter

Reg Kray

Reg Kray was one of Britain's most notorious criminals. Together with his brother Ron, he rose through the ranks of London's East End gangland to run an evil empire of vice and villainy. Here, in his own words, is the true story of his life with Ron, the chilling career of two-streetwise kids who became standard-bearers of violence – from fire-bombings, to shootings and cold-blooded murder.

But here too is the inner voice of a one-time mobster who learned compassion through his own struggle to come to terms with a life sentence. As Reg says, 'we were better at violence than the others ... but I believe that our lives were better for the saving'.

Candid, compelling and often shocking, *Born Fighter* is the definitive book on the life and times of the Krays.

arrow books

The Life and Death of Peter Sellers

Roger Lewis

Sellers has long been acknowledged as one of the screen's greatest comic actors. In this definitive biography, now made into a major film starring Geoffrey Rush, Roger Lewis shows how Sellers succeeded, and why it was at such terrible cost to himself and to those whom he professed to love.

'An absolute revelation, the book grips from the first page to the last and is packed with the kind of facts and anecdotes that make one drool. Brilliant'
Howard Maxford, *Film Review*

'It is a mad book – but then the subject is a madman ... I love Lewis's passion – he is nutty about Sellers, the intensity of his engagement makes you feel like a voyeur ... I recommend it'
Lynn Barber, *Sunday Times*

'Lewis is a great critic of great performances ... this book represents perhaps the most searching life of a non-classical actor ever written'
Boyd Tonkin, *New Statesman & Society*

'Lewis brings to the showbiz biography a comprehensiveness of research and an intensity of attention more frequently found in the best literary biographies... Reinventing its genre as well as reassessing its subject with formidable intelligence, this book is a remarkable achievement'
John Dugdale, *Literary Review*

arrow books

**Order further Arrow titles
from your local bookshop, or have them delivered
direct to your door by Bookpost**

☐ **The Life and Death of Peter Sellers**
Roger Lewis   0 09 974700 6   £9.99

☐ **Born Fighter** Reg Kray   0 09 987810 0   £5.99

Free post and packing
Overseas customers allow £2 per paperback

Phone: 01624 677237

Post: Random House Books
c/o Bookpost, PO Box 29, Douglas, Isle of Man IM99 1BQ

Fax: 01624 670923

email: bookshop@enterprise.net

Cheques (payable to Bookpost) and credit cards accepted

Prices and availability subject to change without notice.
Allow 28 days for delivery.
When placing your order, please state if you do not wish to receive any
additional information.

www.randomhouse.co.uk/arrowbooks

arrow books